You, Me
& other People

FIONNUALA KEARNEY

HARPER

Harper
An imprint of HarperCollins*Publishers*
1 London Bridge Street,
London SE1 9GF

www.harpercollins.co.uk

A Paperback Original 2015
1

A catalogue record for this book
is available from the British Library

ISBN: 9780007593972

Typeset by Palimpsest Book Production Ltd, Falkirk, Stirlingshire

Printed and bound in Great Britain by
Clays Ltd, St Ives plc

PART ONE

They say best men are moulded out of faults,
And, for the most, become much more the better
For being a little bad . . .

William Shakespeare, *Measure for Measure*

Prologue

I should not be here. As sure as I know my name, my NHS number by heart and my daughter's date and time of birth, I know I shouldn't be here. Adam Hall . . . NC 100Z9T . . . The third of March 1994, 8.04 a.m., Meg Sarah-Louise Hall, born by caesarean delivery, firstborn child to my wife Beth and me. My head shakes of its own accord, my conscience nudging me, reminding me that I shouldn't be here.

I drive by the house. There's no parking, so I'm forced to keep going. On the passenger seat of my car, a gift sits boxed, wrapped. Today is someone else's birthday. I spent time choosing this gift, wanting to get it right. It's important to me, important that they know how I feel. I do a U-turn at the top of the narrow street, try again to get a nearby parking spot. About ten houses away, someone has pulled out, and I slip my car in their space.

Up ahead, there's a party going on, the house marked by the telltale bunch of balloons on the pillar. I glance at the box. When I wrapped it earlier, I doubled over the

Sellotape so that it's unseen on the outside of the paper. Beth showed me how to do it one Christmas. 'You have to hide it. Makes it so much neater,' she'd said. She's right. Hidden things are so much neater.

I open the window. Loud voices come from the house with the balloons. A woman passes by, a heavy-looking handbag slung high on her shoulder, a small package and a bottle of wine in her hands. I have no idea who she is, but she's walking quickly, as if she's late. Less than three feet from my car, just the width of a narrow footpath away, is a blooming jasmine plant. I inhale the heady scent, close my eyes, immediately cast back in time to my mother's floral perfume. My left hand grips the handbrake as a childhood nursery rhyme she used to sing about Dick Whittington sounds in my head. *Turn around*. I glance at the gift. My bottom teeth chew my top lip. I shouldn't be here.

I start the engine. I'll get rid of the box and I won't come back here. I promise myself I won't return. I say it out loud, address myself in the rear-view mirror and speak the words slowly, like my life depends on it . . .

And, on the drive back, I look forward to the Sunday evening meal that awaits me. I'll enter our home, kiss my wife. I'll choose to have a shower to wash away my morning of madness. I'll immerse myself in the life I love. I imagine it gift-wrapped, the outside wrapping seamless, double-sided sticky tape, or whatever it takes, to keep some of the inner content neat and tidy – hidden from the people I love.

Chapter One

'My husband is a philanderer,' I reply. She sits, her legs crossed, taking notes in her feint-lined legal pad. 'That's a four-syllable word for a cheating dickwit. How am I supposed to feel? He's screwing a waitress . . . ' The last word tastes like Marmite on my tongue. In my head, I apologize to all the nice waitresses in the world. Aloud, I reveal how I really feel as my right hand clutches my upper left side. 'I feel betrayed.' I lower my voice. 'And it hurts.'

Dr Caroline Gothenburg offers a sympathetic nodding motion. She has olive-coloured eyes, set in a wide face, flanked by titian curls; long, shapely legs encased in glossy tights – and I can't help wondering if she has ever been betrayed in her shiny life. Lots of qualifications set in pencil-thin chrome frames adorn her wall. Bright as well as beautiful . . . I find myself focusing on her rather than me.

'I'd like you to do me a timeline for the next session,' she interrupts my thoughts. I feel crevices begin to stack one above the other on my forehead. I'm an intelligent woman. What the hell am I doing here? Glancing across her coffee table towards her neat, ordered frame, I swallow the panic creeping up my throat.

'It will help me get to know you,' she says. 'Who is Beth? What makes Beth be Beth? I'd like to understand who you are, where you come from.'

A siren sounds in the distance, as if to warn me of an impending emergency.

'Me too,' I whisper.

In the car, my smart phone tells me I have three missed calls. One from Josh, my agent, and two from Adam. If my phone was really smart, it would delete Adam's number. I've thought about it – but erasing him from my phone will not remove him from my brain. I switch on the Bluetooth, return Josh's call and head to the nearest super-market.

Twenty minutes later, I unload the contents of my wire basket and watch them move along a conveyor belt. Navel oranges, tuna, sweetcorn, trashy mags, a dodgy chicken wrap and two bottles of chilled sauvignon blanc.

'Is Your Man a Love Cheat?' screams a headline from one of the moving magazines. There are four, all with similar revelations, to reassure myself that I'm not alone, that there is in fact mass treachery in the world.

'Points?' a young girl with coffee skin and almond eyes asks from behind the till.

'Points?' I reply.

'You got a points card?' she says, stifling a yawn. I notice a tiny yin and yang tattoo on the back of her wrist.

I find I want to shout at Miss Points Yin-yang. I want to scream at her, tell her not to ask such a stupid question; ask her whether or not she noticed the vital subject matter of the magazines in my basket; tell her, if she didn't, that she receives nil points for customer service today. I want to hurl a stream of nasty words at her – they're already formed in my head. Then I remind myself she's no older than Meg, my nineteen-year-old daughter, and as such, she should not yet know what betrayal tastes like. I breathe deeply – it really isn't Miss Yin-yang's fault that my husband is a shit . . .

So instead, I shake my head at her. No, I am all out of points. I am trembling all over by the time I'm back in the car. Silently, I count to a hundred, and push the facts that he has really left me and that I have just spent an hour in a therapist's office to the back folds of my mind. I still my hands by sitting on them for a moment, then shake them out, start the ignition and point the car towards home.

Our home is a beautiful, three-floor, semi-detached Edwardian house in a sycamore-lined avenue in Surrey's commuter belt. We bought it as a wreck fourteen years ago. Red-bricked, with original bay windows, inside we knocked walls down, built new ones – a bit like our marriage really, except today the house looks like something from *Homes & Gardens* and I, one half of our marriage, look like a 'before' picture in a plastic surgeon's office.

As the gravel crunches under my wheels, I stare at the building I love, wonder if it will have to be sold, if I'll end up in a tiny cottage-ette somewhere called nowhere. My hand massages my churning stomach and, not for the first time, the waitress flashes across my mind. She's an incomplete image, blurred around the edges. I'm unaware if she has long or short hair, blonde or dark, curly or straight. Is she thirties or forties? Not twenties, please. I'd find that hard to take, not to mention how Meg would cope. The idea of her beloved father screwing someone who buys her clothes in Topshop would be too much.

A sudden image of them having sex ambushes me. Does she cry out like me? Does he hold her hair at the nape of her neck the same way he does mine? Silent tears fall. I have to stop this . . . I wipe them with my sleeve, staying a while to stare at Adam's garden. Quite quickly, I come to one conclusion. He is not selling my home. He'll have to take me out of here in a pine box.

Inside, I dump the shopping and head upstairs to my workspace in the loft. Flooded with natural light from three angled Velux windows, it is where, opposite my two large screens displaying notes and melodies, I sit to handwrite the requested timeline. Within a minute, six hastily written lines and I'm already a convent-educated, only surviving child of an eccentric mother and a drinking father. I continue, silently praying that Dr Gothenburg is good at her job, my hand scrawling my past onto the page. Very soon, I'm a child who loses her father to his love of alcohol, a wife whose husband has already notched up a previous one-night stand and a mother who feels guilty about wanting more than motherhood alone.

Staring at it, spaced over two sheets of paper, it's not a spectacular life. Nor is it the stuff that keeps the Samaritans busy, but will it help Dr Gothenburg get to know me? Will the existence of a baby brother who died when he was three and I was six divulge something I'm not aware of?

Does my ambition to succeed as a songwriter help frame me as a person? Josh assures me regularly I'm the next best thing to hit country pop. It's me who's not so sure. What I *am* sure about – what screams at me from the second page – is that my husband is a cheat. Considering he's been offside at least twice, that makes him a serial cheat. It's there in black and white for Dr Gothenburg to read. The words, confirming his failure, might as well be sticking out on stalks.

The mobile sounds and this time I laugh aloud at the sight of his number. He genuinely thinks that if he keeps calling, one day I'll just stop being angry. Another part of me hopes he's right, because this anger is eating me up from the inside out. I can feel it coil itself around my very being, munching away; as if a sound effect is required, my stomach grumbles loudly. I head back downstairs, passing the photo-lined walls on the way.

Rogues' gallery . . . The fingers of my right hand hover above them, yearning to touch the baby shots of Meg, to tap into those younger grinning images of Adam and me. An old wedding shot, so full of hope and love. One of him taken at a barbecue next door – Adam posing like a catalogue model, his face looking at the camera, his chin tilted upwards; his long legs, tanned in Bermuda shorts, his dirty blond, close-cropped hair flashing in the summer sun. I take the stairs slowly, lost in years of memories. By the last step, I try to comprehend that if someone had asked me only weeks ago if we were happy, I'd have given them a rather smug, 'Yes, of course.' That's how good a liar my husband is.

In the kitchen, I grab a wine glass and fill it to the rim with cold sauvignon. Rummaging through one of the shopping bags, I remove the chicken wrap and chew it slowly, obediently listening to the voice in my head that tells me I have to eat. I don't want to eat. I just want to drink. Taking a large swallow of wine, I feel the alcohol slide down, immediately hitting the spot it needs to.

Late-afternoon September sun slices through the bi-fold doors that back onto the rear garden. I walk in and out of its shadows, chicken wrap in one hand and glass in the other. One mouthful of food for each gulp of wine . . . In between, I hum the words of a song I wrote yesterday and feel the faint curve of a smile on my face. Thesaurus had obliged with a rhyme for bastard. 'Dastard' – a sneaky malicious coward. Adam the 'dastard'. The grin on my face makes it even harder to chew.

Needing to immerse myself in work, I start back upstairs, only to turn around and sit, motionless, on the fourth step. I stare into the living room opposite, unable to move. The cognitive part of my brain has switched off. My legs refuse to stand, my hands seem glued to my knees. Assailed by snapshot memories of places we've been, songs we've sung, moments we've shared, I'm numb with the fear of starting again. Where do I begin? If I just breathe in and out, will time just pass? I nod. Yes, that's what will happen. I just have to wait this out and suddenly it will be next month and this new beginning will already have happened without me even having to register it.

I only stir when darkness surrounds me. I step downstairs, switch on a light and carry the bottle of wine from the fridge to the living room. Thirty minutes later, I'm watching Adam's oversized, penile-extension plasma screen when the landline rings.

'You're fired!' Lord Alan Sugar fills the screen as he points an index finger at some underperforming female.

'Yeah, mate, I know how you feel,' I sympathize. 'Beth, you're fired!' I point my glass at Lord Sugar's evictee and pick up the phone, sure that it will be Meg at this hour.

'Meg?'

'Beth, it's me . . . '

It's not Meg, my precious girl. It's him, the bastard that provided half of her DNA, the dastard who, as soon as I hear his voice, I miss with every fibre of my being. My heart pulses loudly behind my ribcage.

'How are you?' he asks. 'Beth, don't hang up. Please, we need to talk?'

'I don't want to talk to you.'

He is silent.

'Are you with her?' I ask.

He remains guiltily silent.

'Do you know you're a dastard?' The wine speaks.

He sighs. 'Yes, you've told me many times.'

'No, I've told you many times you're a "bastard", now I'm telling you you're a "dastard" too.' No reply.

I can hear kitchen sounds in the background, like a dishwasher being unloaded. I picture the scene. How domestic. How very Jamie and Nigella. He speaks in a hushed voice, as if he doesn't want to be heard on the phone.

'Oh just fuck off, Adam.' I slam the phone down. I look at the bottle and my father's genes beckon.

Chapter Two

I stare at the small screen. Call ended. She hung up on me. Again . . . And she swore at me. Beth knows how much I hate her potty mouth. Two weeks since I left and she still won't talk without swearing.

Through the open door to the kitchen, I see Emma bend down to reach the lower shelf of the dishwasher. Clad in a figure-hugging black dress, the sight makes my head reel; images of Emma naked, Beth naked, cloud my fuzzy brain. I breathe deeply, filling my anxious lungs as quietly as I can.

'I know you're staring.' Emma looks over her left shoulder and catches my eye. In one swift movement, she crosses her hands, grabs the hem of her dress and pulls it over her head. She's wearing stockings. No knickers, just hold-ups, a tiny bra, and I feel immediate stirrings as she walks towards me. Some instinct tells me to back away from her, raise my palms in the air, say, 'No, Emma, no,' but it's way too late for that. If I'd been a better man, I'd have said that months ago. So, I let my more primal instincts rule, the ones that make me want to take her here on her white Amtico kitchen floor. Before I know it, she's on her knees, unzipping me. I squeeze my eyes shut. With one hand, I steady myself on the doorway, with the other I hold her head, just at the nape of her neck, my fingers lacing her long blonde hair.

I knew I was in trouble the moment I met her. It had started out a simple evening with a group from work in the restaurant where she works. She flirted with me. Private winks, smiles. At first I thought I was imagining it, until Matt, my business partner, cornered me outside the loo.

'Don't do it, mate,' he said.

'What?'

'Don't go there. You're so flattered some blonde totty fancies you, you've been twirling your wedding ring under the table all night.'

'I have not.'

'Don't be such a tosser, Adam. You and Beth have a good thing.'

But by the time I shared a taxi home with Emma, my ring was in my pocket, my choice made. I thought of Beth, my gorgeous, loyal, talented wife; the woman who made me laugh at least once a day; the woman I loved, the woman I would have died for, still would. I *did* think of her, but only briefly.

Emma was the most forward woman I'd ever met, launching herself on me in the back of the taxi, cupping my balls with long manicured fingers. I was weak, power-less. And months later, I'm still a weak forty-three-year-old man who has hurt his wife so much he doesn't know how to fix it, so chooses to ignore it and indulge in copious amounts of fantastic, life-affirming sex with a new and younger woman.

I leave the office early, exit the underground car park to a beautiful September evening, the sun still quite high in the sky. Just across the river to my right, I see the shape of the London Eye, its capsules laden with carefree tourists. It's Friday and normally I'd be heading across the river and down the A3 towards home, after staying the week in town. Eight months ago, Beth and I decided to 'borrow' my brother Ben's flat while he's abroad for a year. Both parties have a good deal. We pay a lot less than market rent, covering his mortgage, and he knows his tenants. The plan was we'd stay there during the week, cut out the commute for me, and Beth could enjoy London and write her songs. A new environment, new inspirations – that was the plan.

I turn the car east towards the highway, heading to Docklands, to the one-bedroom flat near the river, intent on staying in this evening. Tonight's plan is for an Emma-free zone; give myself some head-space with a takeaway and Sky Plus footie on the telly. Why then do I keep driving east along the A13, towards the M25, taking a long route towards the house I used to call home?

I call ahead on the hands-free. She'll kill me if I just turn up. I can imagine dying on the spot in the power of her penetrating stare. But I feel the need to see her, to try and explain. I have no words, just the will to try, because I can't bear her hating me. The phone rings out and I hear her voice.

'You have reached Adam and Beth Hall. Sorry we can't

get to the phone – leave a message. We'll get back to you.'

Only she hasn't got back to me yet. I dial another number, hoping the other person I've hurt is still talking to me.

'Hey, Dad,' she says, picking up on the third ring.

'Hey, Meg.' I resist using my pet name of Pumpkin for her. 'You all right?' I can hear my heartbeat.

'As all right as I possibly can be with an arsehole for a father . . . '

I sigh – an audible, slow sigh. 'I deserve that. I'm sorry.'

'You do and somehow sorry doesn't quite cut it. Are you still with her?'

Straight for the jugular – she may have my eyes, my long legs and the hair colour that Beth calls conker, directly from my gene pool, but when it comes down to it, Meg is Beth's daughter. She doesn't believe in wasting words.

So I respond in the same vein. 'Yes.'

'Right . . . Why did you call?'

'You're my daughter, Meg. I'd like to see you. Please?'

'And what? Introduce me to your bitch totty so we can play dysfunctional families?'

I flinch at her words. And blame Beth. My daughter has a potty mouth too.

'I—'

'Look, Dad. It's too soon. Too raw. You're not the man I thought you were. The man I respected.' I can imagine her shaking her head as she continues. 'You're just not that man.'

I bite my lower lip, feel it tremble. She's right. I'm not that man, but then, I never have been. 'I'm sorry,' I offer lamely.

'Blah, blah, blah.' She hangs up.

I pull over to the hard shoulder. The contents of my

15

stomach heave onto the edge of the A13. I have managed to pebble-dash the door of my beloved Lexus. Words of my long-dead mother echo in my ears: '*I hope you're proud of yourself, Adam.*' I wipe my mouth with my shirtsleeve, stare across three lanes of fast-flowing traffic and look up to the sky. Meg hates me. I have screwed up. I have really screwed up large.

The house looks just the same. I'm not sure why I thought it wouldn't. The time I've been away has been no longer than an average holiday, yet so much has changed. Beth's car is not in the driveway and I wonder if she's using the garage, now that mine isn't here. I pop a mint into my mouth and without thinking too much about what I'm about to do, step out of the car.

The bell trills under my fingertip. No answer. I try the phone. Answerphone. I have keys but I dare not . . . I walk towards the garage, peer in the side window. No car, so she's definitely out. I clean the glass with the back of my hand and stare inside. Tidy shelves line the sides, everything organized. The empty space in the middle reserved for the car I loved, the one that now has puke on the passenger door.

I decide to use the keys and try the lower Chubb. No luck. The Banham refuses to move too. Then it dawns – she's changed the locks. Suddenly, I have a feeling that she's in there. She's been there all the time. I prise open the letterbox.

'Beth! Open the door!' I am greeted by silence. Now I'm on my knees peering through the letterbox, my head tilted sideways.

'Hello, Adam.'

I leap to my feet. Sylvia, our next-door neighbour, the one we're attached to, is standing at a gap in the laurel hedge.

'Sylvia,' I say, wiping the dust from my trousers. 'I er—'

'The locks have been changed,' she confirms, staring at the driveway.

'I see.' I aim for eye contact; after all, we have been dinner-party mates for more than ten years. 'I don't suppose . . . ' Sylvia is also key-holder for the alarm company.

'Don't ask me that, Adam, please.'

'No.' I nod. 'Sorry. Do you know where she is?'

Sylvia shrugs. I see it then. Sadness, pity, in her expression. I'm not sure what to call it, but I am sure I'm not ready to be judged on my own doorstep.

'Okay, not to worry. I'll call her later.' With that, I nod to my erstwhile dinner-party mate and head to the safety of my pukey Lexus. Jesus . . . I lean back into the soft leather of the driver's seat and wonder where my wife is. She could be out with her mate, Karen. I start the engine, do a three-point turn out of the driveway. In the rear-view mirror, I see the house sign, 'The Lodge', shrink as I move away. I'm feeling a slow reality check develop in the pit of my stomach. Beth can do as she likes. I no longer have the right to wonder where she is on a Friday night – or any night, for that matter. An image of her with another man flashes briefly in my brain. And I don't like it. I don't like it one bit. By the time I reach the motorway, I can only conclude that I like myself even less.

Chapter Three

'I'd like you to write about yourself,' she says, just as the hour is up. 'I want you to only write about *you* – not Adam, not Meg, nor your mum, your alcoholic father, your dead baby brother or anyone else – just you. Don't think about it too much. Just let it flow.'

I write every day, but the idea of me, and only me, being my subject matter makes me want to grab my knees and rock back and forth in my chair.

'Use the Russian doll idea,' she suggests, picking up a small barrel-shaped doll from the coffee table. Last time I was here, I noticed a whole shelf of them nearby. Opening it up, she reveals five layers, with the final one being the size and shape of a monkey nut.

'That's where you need to get to,' she says, pointing a filed French nail to the monkey nut centre. 'Peel back the outer layers, get to yourself. Your core.' She is smiling, as though she's rather pleased with herself.

'I'm not sure . . . ' The anxiety in my voice is audible. 'I can't get that small, I don't think I'd know my inner bits if they walked up and introduced themselves.'

'Maybe you could start with, "Who am I?",' she says, leaning back.

I imagine this in my head using word association, and panic as I only have enough words to cover the two outer dolls at most. She tells me to breathe, breathe, slowly in and out.

I close my eyes.

'Then go on to "How do I feel?",' she continues.

Oh God, I feel a little sick. Please don't let that be vomit at the back of my throat.

'And then maybe what do I like and dislike?'

'Okay, stop!' I get it. I look at her and her coffee-table toy. 'You're going to need a bigger doll.'

Caroline, as she has insisted on me calling her, has suggested that I borrow some books and CDs on relaxation techniques. She showed me a reflexology pressure point on the fleshy part of my hand, between my thumb and index finger, advising me to press it gently whenever I feel panicky. I think Abba songs work well too, so I'm singing 'Fernando' aloud when I reach Weybridge High Street. It's the afternoon school run and the traffic has formed a long, snaking queue.

'Fernando' over, I tackle 'The Winner Takes It All', only to decide, midway, that it's a bad song choice. I push one of Caroline's CDs into the player. The sound of the sea crashing against rocks and some dolphin-like 'clicks' fill the car. I breathe in deeply through my nose and exhale through my mouth, just like she showed me. Three minutes later, I haven't moved an inch and I leap at the Bluetooth trill of the mobile.

'Hey, darling,' I say.

'Hi, Mum. You okay?'

'Great.' I never lie to Meg, but now is not the moment to confirm that neither Abba nor dolphins are resolving my anxiety. I glance at the clock. 'Didn't you say you had lectures all afternoon?'

'I did. I do. I didn't go in.'

'I see . . . '

'He called me.'

'Okay . . . ' The traffic still at a standstill, I prod the fleshy part on my left hand with my right thumb.

'I mean, I'm not sure what he wants me to say? He leaves you – I mean us – for another woman, phones me up and just wants to have a chat! I asked him. I mean, I asked him if he was still with her. He didn't even have the balls to just admit it.'

Meg takes a moment to breathe and I remove my foot from the brake, inch the car forward, jab the flesh again. I'm sure I'll have a bruise tomorrow.

I'm determined to say the right thing. 'Meg, love, don't cut him off. This is about me and him. It's our marriage that's the problem, not you and him. He's still your father and he loves you with all his heart.' Even as I'm saying this, I can imagine her twisted grimace. She and I have wondered lately if he even has a heart.

'He's a liar,' is her angry reply.

'Yes, yes he is, but it's me he's lied to, not you.'

'His lies still affect me! Can't you see that, Mum?'

'I'm sorry.' My head is nodding. Of course I can see it. I've always been able to see it, but something tells me that, while she hates him now, it's a temporary thing. Soon, she'll love him again, and I don't want her to feel she needs my permission. They are, and will always be, thick as thieves. 'Just talk to him if he calls. Don't cut him off for my sake. You need each other.'

She makes a 'hmph'-like sound and I change the subject, urge her back to classes, insist she keep carrying on as normal. She hangs up with a promise to visit next week.

The entire exchange with my daughter lasts a few minutes and I'm still stuck in the High Street. There is nothing else for it. I press play on the CD player and surround myself with more 'Flipper' noises.

By the time I get home, I feel quite serene, if a little seasick. I park the car a few metres back from the double garage. It's separate from the house, set back on the unattached side, and it's another of Adam's anally tidy spaces.

I enter through the up-and-over door. Inside, there is floor-to-ceiling shelving on one side, with various selections of paint, paint brushes, rollers, cleaning fluids – all filed beautifully in shades and can sizes. I find a tin of gold spray paint, which I used last Christmas to colour pine cones. I can't quite comprehend that I ever considered pine-cone colour important. Opposite the paint shelves is the 'car section', with a selection of chamois leathers, T-Cut, car shampoo, mini-vacuum, wax, rolls of soft cloth.

I move a few things around. I put some paint in the car section, throw the chamois leathers on the floor and dance like a dervish on them. I remove the bag from his mini-vacuum and empty it over the chamois, then tear the bag up and replace it in the vacuum. I mix big cans with little cans of paint and, whilst I'm busy generally messing with

Adam's space, I find the can of paint I bought for the hall last year. I remember Adam being adamant.

'No way,' he'd said, 'it's awful.'

And I remember just accepting that.

It's much later, after my tuna sandwich dinner, when I return to the garage. I retrieve the can of paint, a wonderful shade of 'Tiffany' blue, some brushes and a roller, and begin to redecorate the hall. I've never liked the cold stone shade that Adam chose. The preparation – taking all the pictures down, washing the walls – takes ages, and I'm just about to give up when I pick up the tiniest brush and dip it in the paint. It seems to have a life of its own, writing in Tiffany blue over cold stone:

I am Beth. I am strong. I am middle aged. I like champagne, chocolate, the ocean, lacy stockings, Ikea meatballs, flip-flops, Touche Éclat, music and lyrics. I don't like politicians, call centres, size zero women, snobs, punk rock, horseradish, dastards and women who sleep with dastards

I stand back and admire my work. Without realizing it, I've created a sort of text box on the hallway wall. Drawing a square around it, I underline 'dastards and women who sleep with dastards'. I'm not sure it's exactly what Caroline had in mind when she said 'write about yourself', but it works for me. Before going to bed, I take another peek. Marvellous.

Sleep, however, has become another problem for me. An hour later, I'm still wide awake, with the television on mute and the laptop perched next to me. A small whirring noise lets me know it's still turned on. Lucky laptop. I leap out of bed, not wanting to think about sex.

In our en-suite bathroom, I am assaulted by images of myself. The French oval wall mirror above the walnut unit housing double sinks confirms that though my green eyes remain my best feature, they have been particularly challenged by Adam leaving. Even my fabulous Touche Éclat struggles to keep up with the dark shadowy veins of a broken marriage.

The full-length mirror to the right of the bath reveals legs that are far too short for my torso. A couple of grey pubic hairs prove beyond any Dead Sea Scrolls that God is a man. The loose bit of my skin overhanging the top of my knickers reminds me I'm a mother, as if I need reminding . . . My hair which – when I was twenty-two – used to be long, dark brown and shiny, is – now I am forty-two – short, dark brown and matt, compliments of L'Oréal, because I'm worth it. I cleanse my face with a wipe one more time and start to sing. I sing 'Missing', the last song of mine that Josh sold, which has earned me the princely sum of £10,500 so far.

'The mirror doesn't lie, but who is she and where am I?' I blast out the lyric with gusto as I head downstairs and take the vacuum from the hall cupboard. I sing louder in my best voice above the drone.

I vacuum the living room, then the dining room and finally the hall. I pass my artwork and smile. When I put the vacuum away and liberate the limescale loo cleaner from the cupboard under the sink, I realize I'm having what Adam used to call an OCD moment, an episode that my therapist would probably have a proper Latin word for. Yellow gloves are snapped into place before I scrub the loos, still singing, with a scourer in one hand and a newly poured glass of wine in the other. If someone could see me, they'd think me quite mad. If there are any aliens watching, they'll kidnap Sylvia next door instead. They could never take the risk.

Chapter Four

I'm sitting in my office, my head in my hands, my elbows rested on the scarred walnut antique desk that Beth sourced somewhere in rural Brittany. My wristwatch claims its ten thirty, which means I've been here two hours. Despite the two large screens on the wall opposite, with Bloomberg blinking red downward arrows at me, all I've done since I got in is paper-shuffle. Outside my door, the plaque six feet away in the reception area says HALL & FRY. The name is well known in the City. It tells people that we are a respected wealth-management firm, a highly regarded family office. If your family has money, come to us; we'll look after it, help it grow. You want art? You want to invest in property? The markets? We are specialist consultants. Offering advice. I wish to hell someone would offer me some.

As if on cue, Matt – my business partner for almost twenty years – enters without knocking.

'You look like shit,' is his opening line.

I rub my two-day-old facial hair. 'We're not seeing clients,' is my only offer of defence.

'I still have to look at you.' He throws a couple of files on my desk. 'Can you have these back by four and we *do* have to see clients tomorrow, the Granger brothers? So a shave might be in order?'

I ignore the client reference, ignore Matt's worried face looking at the screens, lean back and put my feet up on my desk. 'You pissed off at me for some reason?'

'Now what would make you think that?' Matt turns back to me, peers at me above his glasses, then reconsiders and removes them completely. It gives him something to wave at me. 'Why in the world would anyone be pissed off at the wonderful Adam Hall?'

'Yeah well, join the queue,' I mutter, removing my feet.

Matt sits in the chair opposite, runs a hand through his scant hair.

'What is it you're doing, Adam? Do you even know? I mean, do you love this girl?'

I stand and look out of the window, try to lose myself in the urban sounds below. The loud hum of traffic, the odd siren, riverboat horns . . . My office overlooks Tower Bridge and there isn't a day goes by where I don't look down from my sixth-floor room and pinch myself. I'm a lucky guy. At least I was a lucky guy. Now I'm a lucky bastard. Lucky dastard. A lucky dastardly bastard. I feel Matt's eyes bore holes in my back.

'Adam?'

'That's three questions. Which one would you like me to answer first?'

'Whichever.'

I turn to face him. 'The truth is, I don't know what I'm doing. I don't think I'm in love, but I'm drawn to this woman—'

Matt makes a 'haruuumph'-type sound. 'It's called lust,' he says, matter-of-factly.

I feel my head shake in defence.

'If it's not lust and it's not love, what is it? Do you have anything in common with her?'

'*Her* name is Emma.'

'Emma then.' Matt shrugs as he stands, replaces his glasses. 'What is it you have in common with Emma?'

'She's . . . ' I hesitate for just a moment too long.

'She *is* gorgeous,' he offers. I think in a strange way, he's trying to help.

She's ten years younger than me. She comes from money, while my DNA originated in Bethnal Green. She doesn't even know who The Eagles are and I've been to every concert they've played in the UK. She couldn't sing along to Bruce Springsteen with me. She lives in a clutter-free, white, sterile house, whereas I'm – I mean Beth's – a hoarder.

'She is gorgeous,' I agree. 'And, frankly, the sex is phenomenal.'

I stare at his suited back as he exits the room.

'Lust.' He looks back over his shoulder. 'Told you so . . . Speaking of which,' he says grinning, 'you have a lunch appointment with the subject of my dreams.'

My eyes squeeze shut as the door closes.

Bloody hell. Karen. I have a lunch appointment with the woman Matt has been lusting after for years. Karen, our outsourced IT specialist and Beth's best friend in the world.

* * *

As she approaches, I notice men staring. Karen is stunning: a tall, willowy redhead with a slim figure. Straight, short, spiky hair; wide brown eyes flanked by long lashes; a pert nose and full lips. She's wearing a fitted jacket and loose flared trousers. Karen refuses my air kiss, turns her head away and slowly begins to fold her long legs into the booth I've reserved for lunch. I hand her an envelope.

'I'm sorry,' I say. 'I could've just sent it by BACS, but I wanted to apologize in person. That brings us all up to date.'

She nods, doesn't look at me and immediately begins to remove her limbs from the booth again.

'What? That's it?' I hear my voice sound as if I'm fourteen and it's about to break.

She looks me up and down. 'Adam, I agreed to meet you when you guys owed me six grand. I thought I'd have to butter you up to be paid. I thought I'd get quoted the fact that times are bad, that we're all still feeling the pain of recession. That your clients haven't paid you, so you're a little slow in paying contractors, but hey . . . ' She waves an arm dramatically as she swings her designer handbag over her other shoulder. 'Here we are and you've already paid me!'

'Stay for lunch . . . '

'I'd rather starve.'

'Please.' I meet her narrowed eyes. 'I need to talk to you, to someone.'

'Try Yell.com. Look under "Counselling for fucktards".' She is still standing.

'Please? Beth won't talk to me.'

She relents a little and sits down, no legs under the table,

28

just seated on the edge, ready for a speedy exit. It's good enough for me.

'Drink?'

She shakes her head.

'Do you mind if I have one?'

More head-shaking. I motion to the waiter by pointing to my empty G&T glass, mouthing 'another' to him. Karen is looking at her feet.

'Where do I start?' I place both my palms on the table, clutching the edge with my thumbs.

'Well, you could explain why you're playing hunt the sausage with some blonde waitress?'

'She's not a waitress,' I begin, 'she part-owns the restaurant.' I've recently learned this fact and feel eager to share it with Karen.

'Bully for her. Explain then why you're playing hunt the sausage with a blonde part-restaurant owner. *Again* . . . '

She spits the last word out. For a moment I'm confused. Then I realize. This is Karen; Beth tells her everything. Of course she would know about the last time, but that was different. And it was such a long time ago.

'That was a long time ago,' I whisper.

'What? I can't hear you,' she says, raising a palm to her ear. 'I'm assuming it was an apology for breaking Beth's heart. *Again.*'

I almost snatch the G&T from the waiter's tray as he walks by.

'I am sorry. Of course, I'm sorry. Every day I'm sorry—'

'Words, Adam, just words . . . Thank you for the cheque.' She stands up, straightens out her tailored trousers and eyeballs me. 'I do hope that we can continue a working relationship, but when it comes to your behaviour and Beth, don't ever expect me to take your side.'

'I don't, Karen.' I reach out and grab her arm. 'Look, I only want to talk to her. Just talk to her, try and explain.'

'Don't you get it?' She pulls away. 'You've hurt her too badly this time. There is no explanation you could possibly offer.'

'But we've been married for—'

Karen tuts loudly, shakes me off her and walks away. Men stare in her wake, then look back at me. It looks like a lovers' tiff and I'm the baddie. Well. They're half right.

'Twenty years,' I finish my sentence, addressing my G&T. I swallow back the remains of the drink in one gulp, realizing for the first time that this is it, the possible end of my marriage, and I wonder how the hell I ended up being so arrogant. What had I thought? That she'd just take me back again. Yes. That's exactly what I'd thought. That I could have a bit of fun, admit my mistake and that Beth would take me back. Fuck. Shit. Fuck. The words roll around my head and I hear myself speaking just like her. I'm trying 'Beth-speak', potty-mouth stuff. I leave the restaurant, thinking I'm due at Emma's in five hours for dinner. Fuck. Double plus fuck.

I'm a little drunk. Home-cooked, slow-braised lamb shank is staring up at me from a white plate – on a white table. I'm sitting on a white chair on a white rug. I have a white linen napkin on my lap. I'm in the White House.

'You're not perfect, you know.' I point a fork at the figure sitting opposite me. 'Not all that . . . ' I look at my surroundings, searching for the right word. 'White,' I add.

'More wine?' she offers.

'You're not innocent. No way, not at all. You knew I was married. Yes, you knew.'

She sips her wine. 'I did,' she agrees.

'All this white.' I wave my cutlery around the room, splashing gravy on the white rug below. 'Oops,' I place a slightly drunken hand to my mouth, 'a stain. Emma, you have a stain.'

She stands up, walks to the kitchen and returns with a spray cleaner and a cloth. She lowers herself and tries to rub the blemish away.

'I have a stain too – on my soul,' I whisper. 'No, two actually . . . two big ugly black marks on my soul.'

She looks up at me, nods and returns to the rug below.

'But hey, while you're down there,' I say, and laugh out loud. I'm fucking hilarious, I am.

Chapter Five

'Don't be so hard on yourself,' she says. I'd been talking about my work. How I feel that I'm not good enough, that I may never be 'successful'.

'What would it be like if you achieved everything you wanted, rather than feeling you have to sabotage it?' Caroline asks.

I am momentarily horrified. 'Sabotage?' I exhale loudly. Is that what I do? I let her question linger and my shoulders unlock and lift.

'I've been listening to you.' She leans forward. 'And you're really hard on yourself. If anyone else treated you like that, you could sue for harassment.'

I scan the copy of the crumpled timeline in my hand for a hint. What went wrong? I want to scream out loud and blame Adam, but I can't. I suspect I also played a part in getting to this place today.

'He did it once before you know.' I begin to cry. 'Years ago . . . but I forgave him.'

She makes a face, an acknowledging grimace. 'What happened?'

'Some client . . . ' I rub some white lint from my navy blazer. 'A woman he was working on some deal with. I never found out who. Meg was only nine at the time. I didn't want to know, I just wanted it fixed – so we worked on it.' The lint is gone but I'm still rubbing my arm. 'Though what really happened is: *I* worked on it and *he* just nodded, played along.' I shake my head. 'To hell with him. Let's concentrate on me . . . '

'Okay. Some homework.' Caroline claps her hands lightly. 'I want you to try and reinstate upbeat thoughts into your life. Try reciting some positive affirmations, almost mantra-like.'

I can do that. I offer a rare smile. No problem.

'Try to be spontaneous. Imagine what it might be like to do something unplanned.'

My immediate instinct is to tell her not to be stupid. I don't do unplanned, and I invented control-freakery. 'I'm not sure,' I say.

'What is it you're afraid of?' she challenges.

Everything, I realize, I am afraid of everything.

When I arrive home, there's a familiar car in the driveway and Karen is sitting on my doorstep with a large bunch of yolk-yellow gerbera daisies, my favourite flowers, and a bottle of orange label bubbles. Her face is raised to the morning sun.

I hug her. 'It's ten a.m. Why aren't you in work?'

'I work for myself; took a few hours off, figured you might

need this?' She waves the bottle as I unlock the front door.

'It's ten a.m.,' I repeat, smiling.

'So what? It's a half-bottle and I brought orange juice too if you want to spoil the taste.' Her nose wrinkles, a pout that says she couldn't imagine anything worse. I reach out and hug her again, whisper a quiet 'thank you' into her ear. In that moment, I'm so grateful to have her. Her antennae twitch whenever I need her. As if to prove the point, when we reach the kitchen, she whips out some fresh bagels filled with salmon and cream cheese from a tiny cool bag in her titan handbag.

'You need to eat something healthy,' she says as she pours champagne. The irony is lost and we munch, talk and drink, or at least she munches and I talk and drink. Occasionally, she just shakes her head. I tell her about this morning's session with Dr Gothenburg.

'Well?' she says, creasing her brow, 'What *are* you afraid of?'

I hesitate, but just for a moment, before the tears fall. 'I'm constantly afraid.'

She pushes the already empty glasses aside and reaches for my hand. 'Go on.'

'Being alone . . . taking him back and not trusting him; something happening to Meg; being with someone else . . . I'm not sure I could.'

'Pah,' she splutters, as she stands up and heads towards the sink. 'If it comes to that,' she shakes the kettle then flicks the switch, 'believe me – a cock is a cock is a cock.'

I shudder and she laughs.

'The devil, witches and aliens,' I continue, counting out my fears on my fingers.

'Be serious.'

'I am, Karen, I really am.'

Her bottom lip protrudes. 'I see.'

'Losing it someday.' I raise my eyebrows.

'Losing what?'

'My temper . . . control . . . I feel if I show the world how angry I actually am, that I'd be locked up and the key thrown away.'

'I'll buy you a punchbag. Next?'

'I worry about Meg, what this is going to do to her. She worships her father.'

'Meg will be fine. She's young and strong and she's got too much of you in her to let this defeat her.'

'It won't defeat her, but it might shape how she views men.'

'Rubbish.'

'Getting cancer,' I add. 'What if pentapeptides are found to be carcinogenic? What if I like my alcohol too much? What if my father's genes take over?'

'And what if you're overreacting?'

I ignore her. 'Oh, and the dark and deep water and air travel and wait . . . I've apparently got an inner saboteur.'

Karen's quiet. She hovers by the boiled kettle, deep in thought, so I get up, usher her back to her stool and make two mugs of steaming Earl Grey.

Her hands straddle her cup. 'I saw him last week.'

'You did?' The mood in the room shifts.

'He owed me money and I went to collect a cheque. He looks like shit.'

'Yeah well, he's screwing some waitress. He deserves to look like shit.' I take a seat opposite her.

'She's not a waitress. He told me that she part-owns the restaurant.'

'She does? Well, I couldn't give a shit if she whole-owns the restaurant. I don't give a rat's arse if she whole-owns a chain of restaurants. She's a husband-stealing bitch.'

Karen laughs.

'Did he ask about me?' I'm not sure why I want to know. I just do.

'Of course. He wants to know if I'll speak to you on his behalf. I told him to go screw himself. Smug bastard . . . Enough about him!' She suddenly slaps a hand on the breakfast bar and I flinch. 'What about if I come down next weekend?' she says. 'We could have a takeaway and sleepover, maybe go out to a wine bar. I'm not sure you're ready yet, but maybe if you pulled someone, you know, just a snog—'

I groan out loud and lay my head in my hands.

'I was talking a quick snog, not a frigging wedding.'

'You know what? I'm bored. Let's talk about *your* love life.'

'Hmmm . . . ' Karen replies. 'Nothing new to report except a decision.'

I raise my head and my eyebrows.

'I've decided,' she continues, 'that I need an older man. A solvent, older, mature, loving man.'

I smile. 'Good decision. You do know that means a man in his forties.'

Karen sticks her tongue out, ignoring my jibe about the fact that she's forty this year.

'Anyhow, now you and I can go on the pull together.'

'That's not going to happen.' I cannot imagine anything worse in the world right now.

'Never say never.'

'I'm saying never.'

'Really?' She pours me another glass, ignores her own. 'C'mon, Beth, feel the fear and do it anyway! Never is an awfully long time. Take it from me. You'll need a snog. And soon.' She adds the last two words as if my very life will depend on me swapping saliva. Soon.

I shudder visibly, catch her eye and we both hoot.

Painful belly laughs later, somehow we're back to discussing more of my inner fears when she glances at her watch and makes a face. 'Sorry, I've really got to go.' She comes to hug me.

'Relying on my "rampant rabbit" for sex?' I offer as a parting shot.

She puts her coat on in the hall. 'Sounds like my life. Be afraid,' she says gravely, 'be very afraid . . . ' And just as I think she's out of the door, she stops, narrows her eyes and points to the wall with a questioning tilt of her head.

'Oh, yeah.' I raise my eyebrows. 'That. I'm redecorating. What do you think of the colour?'

She reads the words, a hint of a smile appearing on her full lips.

'The colour's bloody awful,' she says finally. 'And is "dastard" a real word?'

Later that day, when I'm upstairs working in the loft, my stomach flips when I check my emails.

-----Original Message-----
From: ahall@hall&fryuk.net
Sent: 23 September 2014 15:37 PM

To: bhall@intranethalluk.net
Subject: You (and me)

Hi,
I'm sure I'm the last person you want to hear from
now but I really feel the need to talk to you. I hope
you're okay. I'm okay. I'm thinking of you. I miss
you. A x

Stomach still playing leapfrog, I type my reply.

-----Original Message-----
From: bhall@intranethalluk.net
Sent: 23 September 2014 15:45 PM
To: ahall@hall&fryuk.net
Subject: Your mail

I am SO fed up with your needs. You needed to leave
me to shag another woman. Now you need to talk to
me. Miss me – you left me! What bloody planet are
you on? And shove your 'x' directly up your ass. Beth.

Just as I press send, I hear the front door slam and my
heart clenches. Shit. I creep to the door and listen. I'm not
ready to see him. All sorts of thoughts skip through my
head. Heart thumping, I remember I've changed the locks,
but it's only when I hear the footsteps on the stairs being
taken two at a time and a telltale 'Mum?' that I realize
I've been holding my breath. I'm sitting down, pressing
that spot between my thumb and forefinger, when Meg
peers around the door.

'There you are! Should have known! God, Mum, open a window!' She comes across the room and embraces me, then walks back to the first Velux, pushing it open.

'How can you work? It's like a coffin in here! Any food in? C'mon,' she pulls my hand. 'I'm famished.'

'You'll be lucky,' I say, following her downstairs. 'I was going to food-shop tonight.' The lie slips easily off my tongue. 'Why are you home anyway? I wasn't expecting you until tomorrow.'

Meg turns on the stairway and stares at me with Adam's eyes.

'Look at you. I guess I just knew,' is her explanation.

'What?' I'm a bit miffed because, midnight OCD episodes aside, I feel I'm doing pretty well. I tug self-consciously at my worn-out tracksuit, run a hand through my limp hair.

'Tell you what.' She nods towards my art text box. 'Give me time to have a shower and freshen up, then take me to Guido's for supper and I won't mention how you're generally behaving weirdly.'

'Deal,' I say, suddenly very grateful that she's there.

'I miss him,' she confesses later over her gnocchi.

'Sweetheart, it's me he's stopped loving, not you.'

The eyes look at me again. 'Mum, Dad will never stop loving you. It's just that he loves himself more.'

Oh, the words of the wise.

'But he loves you the most,' I add. 'Never forget that.'

I can tell she's trying not to cry, tearing a little piece of garlic bread off every few seconds. It's like, if she keeps chewing, the tears won't come.

'I still can't quite believe it,' she confesses. 'Every morning

I wake up and think of how he's behaved and I just shake my head.'

I nod mine.

'It's so bloody clichéd. I thought he was better than that.'

'Didn't we all?' I sigh, a deep sigh. 'Eat your food, it'll get cold.'

She takes her fork and stabs some gnocchi, raises it to her mouth.

And, in that moment, watching her, I'm cast back in time to a three-year-old Meg. Her lower lip would tremble, just like it's starting to now; she'd take a deep breath and she would either howl like a feral vixen or keep the lip-tremble going, stubbornly refusing to cry. Tonight there is no wild sound but the floodgates open anyway. Silent tears slide down her face. She looks away, searching for an escape route to the Ladies and I reach for her hand, clutch it tightly.

'Stay,' I plead. 'You're okay . . . ' The restaurant only has four other diners and we're seated far enough away from them. I can feel the taste of my own cries in the back of my jaw. Controlling them, I hand her tissues and whisper, 'It's going to be okay.' The words seem empty and hollow to me. I hope they sound different to her.

'Will you,' she sniffs, wipes her eyes, 'will you take him back?'

The hope in those eyes makes me want to gasp, grab at some extra air to help me come to terms with what her expression means. Despite her strength, despite her obvious anger at her father, all she wants is for this to be over and her family back together again. I want to kill Adam. I want to kill him for doing this to her and to me. I shake my head slowly. 'I don't know, Meg, I just don't know yet.'

She nods, looks away, places the cooling gnocchi in her mouth and chews slowly. I watch her pierce another piece and repeat. Letting go of her hand, I take my own fork and swirl some spaghetti around its end. The bolognese is garlic heavy and I think about how Adam always shied away from garlic kisses. It feels something like spite when I clear my plate slowly.

We chat about anything that is nothing to do with Adam and me, or Adam and me and her. Her coursework, her flatmates, her tutors and her shower, which has mould in the tiling grout. Soon her tears have turned to laughter and I smile and she does too. She stands, comes over to my side of the table and hugs me. Tight. No more words are needed. She's strong. She will be all right and, as long as she's all right, I will be too.

Later, after late-night cocoa at home, Meg apologizes again for not staying the night and pulls a jumper on over her T-shirt. 'I'm sorry, Mum. I've got an important tutorial first thing. You okay?' I take her in my arms, not an easy feat as she's a lot taller than me. I stroke her beautiful chestnut curls.

'I'm fine if you are,' I whisper into their softness.

'The "f" word, Mum. That bad, eh?'

'Fine' is a swearword in our house, usually meaning, 'fed-up, insecure, neurotic and emotional'.

She kisses me, a slight touch of lips. 'Take care, Mum.' I want to keep hold of her as we hug, wrap her up in my clothes or shrink her, put her in my pocket for safekeeping. As soon as she leaves, I run to my handbag, remove my notebook and my Dictaphone. As I write the words, I record the melody I'm humming. I call it 'The F Word'.

I'm not fine,
No, I'm not fine this time,
I can't even say that word in this hell of mine.

I close my eyes and positively visualize it performed on a worldwide stage.

Maybe given time,
Fine might mean fine,
But right now it's early days,
I hurt in a hundred ways,
And I'm not fine.

Climbing the stairs to bed, I yawn – a long, gaping, sleepy yawn, and am so relieved that I crawl fully clothed under the bed covers. In my dreams, Gordon Ramsay is in my bed.

'You can't call it "The F Word",' he says.

'How did you get here?' I say.

He doesn't answer but I have to admit that he looks quite dishy there, his head resting on Adam's pillow.

'But since you're here, does the "F" stand for fuck or for fine?' I lean up on my left elbow. 'See, around here when you say "fine", it's called "The F Word",' I explain.

'No,' he says, raising his head to meet mine. 'It definitely stands for *fuck* in our house.'

'But this is my house,' I pout. In my dreams, my pout is suggestive, my lips dressed in scarlet gloss.

'Who the fuck cares,' he says, and kisses me. Gordon, it seems, is not averse to my garlic kisses.

Chapter Six

Emma has a fourteen-year-old son called Harold. Not Harry – Harold. I imagine him to be complete with spots and a pathological hatred of both his name and his divorced parents.

So far, because I generally visit the White House at weekends, when Harold is with his father, Alan, I have avoided meeting him. Last night was an exception to this rule. A Wednesday and dinner at the White House was on, because Alan had taken Harold to the cinema straight after his school tennis match. They would not be back until ten, by which time, having eaten dinner, I would be gone. That was the plan. Like all best-laid plans in my life, it didn't quite pan out – which is why I'm sitting in St Thomas's A&E department, nursing a minor head wound. I don't blame Harold. He and Alan had argued, so he'd come back early. Any child of fourteen who'd walked in to find a stranger mounted on his mother on the white rug would do the same thing. I think his tennis racket came off worse.

'How are you feeling?' Meg asks. I haven't yet explained what happened since calling her on a payphone.

'Fine, it looks worse than it is.' I tug on the bandage.

'Leave it,' she says, 'I don't think the bleeding's stopped yet.'

I look around. No sign of a doctor with the X-ray results yet.

'Did she bring you here?'

I nod, slightly.

'So, where is she? Why did you call me?'

'She had to go, be with her boy.'

'She has a son?'

I nod again.

'How old?'

'Fourteen. With a hell of a right swing . . . '

Meg's face scrunches. She looks me up and down, and frowns in a way that makes her look like her mother. 'Please tell me he didn't catch you,' she whispers.

I remain silent. I feel nauseous, and the antiseptic scent of the surroundings doesn't help; that clawing taste that lingers at the back of my throat.

'You already have Mum in therapy and now some poor child will probably need counselling for the rest of his life. You're disgusting,' she says, looking far into the distance, 'absolutely disgusting.'

I would nod again, agree with her, but I'm afraid the motion would make me puke.

'Mr Hall?'

We both turn to see the doctor who'd spoken to me earlier. I raise my hand, acknowledging my name.

'Ahh, there you are. Well, the good news is there's nothing

broken, no fractures. You have a mild concussion. You may feel nauseous, even vomit, but if it lasts longer than twenty-four hours, come straight back to us.' He smiles at Meg. 'You are?'

'His daughter,' she says, her lips curling in distaste.

'He shouldn't be alone, just in case he's sick?'

She nods, pulls me upright and pushes me towards the exit.

'His clothes?' The doctor, noting my state of undress, looks back towards the A&E department. I have no shoes or socks on, no shirt; just a large, blood-splattered white bath sheet, presumably Emma's.

'Doctor, he doesn't deserve clothes,' is her response, as I'm pushed through the swinging door to the car park and the bite of the midnight air.

I awake to the sound of birdsong. Meg is standing above me with a glass of water in her hands.

'Drink,' she orders.

I do as I'm told, the cold, limey tap water a relief on my furry tongue. I'm in her room, in the house she shares with two other girls in Clapham. From here, it's not far to where she studies at Westminster.

'Why am I here?' I sit up in her narrow bed. 'Where did you sleep?'

She points to a couple of duvets on the floor. 'You fell asleep in the car and we were nearer here than Ben's. Don't you remember getting here?'

'No. Look, I'm sorry, Meg.' I move to get up, the pain in my head sudden and sharp, like a machete has pierced my skull. I fight the urge to vomit.

'Stay put. Let's make sure you keep the water down.'

'I need to call the office.' I look for my jacket, my phone.

Meg shrugs. 'I assume your stuff is still at *hers*. Besides. I've already called Matt and told him you're not coming in today.'

'You did?' I close my eyes and lean back on her thin pillow, the throbbing in my head mirroring the beating of my heart. 'How?'

'I called Mum for his number.'

My eyes shoot open and I groan aloud. 'No, Meg, please tell me you didn't—'

She raises a palm to silence me. 'Enough, Dad. I didn't tell her the truth. See?' She swings her long hair around at me, looks like an ad image for shampoo, except for the anger flashing in her eyes. 'See, now you even have me lying to her. Christ, you're a piece of work.'

'What did you tell her?'

'Well, I had to tell her you were hurt. I just lied about the circumstances – told her you'd been mugged.'

A soft smile shapes my lips. 'Well I was, sort of.'

She tries not to grin, but I can see her fight it. 'By a jealous fourteen-year-old boy . . . no, I didn't tell her that bit.'

'Thank you, Pumpkin.' I reach for her hand, hanging loose by her side just inches away from me in the tiny room. She snatches it back.

'I didn't do it for you. I did it for her,' she says simply.

'I know that. Thank you anyway?'

She nods. 'Right, if you haven't barfed in the next few hours, I'm going to try and get to my three o'clock lecture. Do you think you can stay alive for an hour without me?'

'Sure.' I straighten up in the bed. The clock on the wall says eleven thirty, which reminds me I should be in work. 'What did Matt say, by the way?'

Meg smiles. 'I didn't lie to Matt, Dad. I told him you'd been bashed over the head by your mistress's sprog.'

I feel the limited contents of my stomach churn. 'Oh shit . . . '

'Funnily enough,' Meg laughs as she pulls up a chair to sit at her desk, 'that's exactly what he said. Now, sleep. Talk to yourself in your head, whatever, but I have to study.'

'I'm going.' I move to get out of the bed.

'Lie the hell down,' she shouts at me, and there's that flash in the eyes again. 'You have to stay here until tonight. Then I have to drive you home since you have *no* clothes.'

'I'm fine.' I sit stubbornly on the side of the bed, ignoring the hammering in my head.

'Dad, you've used the "f" word. You're anything but fine, so be a good boy and lie down.' Her voice softens. 'Please?'

I do what she says. My head is fuzzy, crowded with imaginary scenes. Beth getting the call from Meg; Emma, unable to call me since my phone was still at hers. Harold, would he be damaged, having attacked his mother's lover? Did Meg say something last night about Beth being in therapy?

I watch my daughter at her desk, surrounded by books on her chosen subject, criminology. Faces of famous serial killers stare up at her from large hardback tomes. Her room is a weird space – a pink draped bed with fairy lights on the headboard and every free gap crammed full of books on vicious minds. I notice she holds herself so upright, years of her mother teaching her not to slouch. She's only pretending to read a particularly thick book with small writing, but I can tell she's not concentrating.

'Have you seen your mum lately?'

'Last night, earlier, I was on my way back here when you called,' she replies, without lifting her eyes from the page.

'I sent her an email.' I don't tell Meg about the return one telling me where to shove my kisses. 'How is she?'

'Better than the last time I saw her. She's getting there.'

I wonder where 'there' is. 'Do you think she'll ever forgive me?'

Meg seems to ignore the question.

'Meg?'

She lifts her eyes to mine. 'Would you?' she says.

'What do you mean?'

'Well, it's not the first time, is it, Dad?'

I flinch. My past is obviously now out there for debate by all and sundry, but I find myself unable to answer the question. I try to imagine how I'd feel if the roles had been reversed. Not nice, more stomach-churning, and I wonder why I do what I do. Why I can hurt the people I love, why I assume forgiveness should be their first port of call. My brain nudges images of my parents forward, and I'm reminded how their tutoring meant I was always expected to do the forgiving. I close my eyes . . .

'I didn't think so.' Meg returns to Ted Bundy, preferring the antics of a serial killer to occupy the space in her head.

Just as I think I couldn't possibly sink lower in my daughter's eyes, the expression on her face when she opens the door to my brother Ben's flat with her spare key tells me otherwise. Emma has got there before us.

'Darling! I've been so worried.' Emma leaps from the sofa, which is visible from the front door. She sees Meg immediately and I watch her face process the facts, putting two and two together. 'Your keys . . . ' She points to my jacket and the rest of the clothes she's returned, my CK jocks taking pride of place on top of the pile. 'They were in your pocket. I hope you don't mind.'

'Well, it seems you'll be okay from here.' Meg turns to leave.

'Don't go.' I grab her jumper.

'Don't touch me,' she hisses.

My fingers immediately release her.

'It's good to meet you, Meg.' Emma tries. 'I'm sorry it's under such strange circumstances.' She raises both her shoulders upwards.

Meg nods in her direction, then bolts.

'Darling,' Emma repeats as the door closes. She nuzzles into my neck. 'I'm so sorry, so very sorry. I don't know what came over Harold. I left him with Alan, told him to think about his behaviour, told him I expect him to apologize to you.'

I can see both our reflections in the tall windows of the living room. The sliding door to the tiny balcony is open and I can hear the sounds of the busy road below. In the glass, Emma's tall body almost dwarfs mine as she holds me. I see myself, a forty-three-year-old idiot with a gash in his head.

Chapter Seven

'I am just so *angry* all the time.' I try to explain. 'Angry and frightened and confused . . . ' I tell her that Karen came around with her builder brother, Brian, and they fitted a punchbag in the garage.

She grins. 'Have you used it yet?'

'Oh yes.' I hold my hand out to show her the tiny bruise on the second knuckle of my right hand. 'I convinced myself I was working out, but actually I have a picture of Adam on it.'

'So, why exactly are you angry, Beth?' She puts it so simply that I find myself getting annoyed at her too.

'I'm angry because my dickwit of a husband cheated on me. I'm angry because I bet he's stupid enough to think he's in love. I'm angry because his fragile forty-three-year-old male ego needs to be massaged by another woman. I am angry because he's greedy, immature and selfish. I'm angry at myself because I forgave him once before when he was greedy, immature and selfish, and I'm angry because he's made us just another statistic.'

Tears pool in my eyes and I reach for the tissue she hands me.

'Before, you know, it took ages . . . It was only a one-night stand, at least that's what he swore to me, but it took a long time to rebuild that trust again.'

Caroline is still handing me tissues. 'Research shows,' she says, 'that it takes between one and three years to recover from a breach of loyalty within a marriage, so why do *you* think he did it again?'

'Because he could? Because he's a bastard? I don't know, are you trying to say that this could be my fault; something I didn't see?'

'No, no, of course not, but if you raise the point, is it valid?'

Now, I'm furious. I resist the urge to march out through the door and never come back. But something keeps me here, rooted to the chair, and she at least has the grace to avoid my eyes. Silence.

The fact is, she's right. There were signs. We weren't as physically close as usual and he seemed uncommunicative, emotionally detached for months before the night I found out. I ignored it. I can feel my neck colour, feel my part in this whole mess crawl up my face. My defences are now on red alert. Since when has it become my burden to stop my husband dropping his pants?

'Apparently,' I break the silence, 'somewhere between fifty and seventy per cent of married men have an affair at some time, as opposed to between twenty and forty per cent for women? A lot of marriages survive and, of those that don't, up to eighty per cent of those who divorce over an affair regret their decision.' I am armed with my own research, compliments of a survey in a trashy magazine.

Caroline nods sagely.

'So, without going all Mars and Venus on me, why is it, Dr Gothenburg, that men are bigger fuckers, literally?'

A hint of a smile. 'Well, evolutionary psychology says that men are predisposed to spread their seed but, if we bring evolution into it, historically women would have feared sex more because of the possibility of pregnancy, so maybe they just didn't indulge as willingly, who knows?' she finishes, shaking her head.

'Or maybe they're just greedy, immature and selfish?' I say, and we laugh together.

My agent Josh has an office just off Soho Square. He rents first-floor space in a dilapidated old building and insists the building's more 'shabby' and less 'chic' appearance is a must for 'creatives'. He's asked me in for coffee, which will accompany a good portion of the 'Now, this is what we're going to do about your career' chat. I'm sitting opposite him in his favourite old leather Conran chair. I only know Terence Conran designed it because Josh tells me he did. On the low-slung coffee table in between us is the predictable array of tiny pastries. In my hand is a hot mug of Arabica roast with lashings of frothy milk. In the thirteen years I have known Josh, we have never consumed anything together other than cake and coffee.

He starts the 'chat' by bringing me up to speed on the sales of 'Missing', which are better than I'd expected. He confirms that two Nashville publishers have options on three other songs. My eyebrows rise: this is all good news, really good news, so I reach for a Danish. Then he tells me about the fact that he's been approached for me to write a song for a movie. I put the Danish down and listen.

'It's all hush-hush for now.' He taps the end of his nose with his forefinger. 'But they're looking at three UK writers and you're one of them.'

I nod, feeling excited, so I pick up the cake again, allowing myself a small swirly bit. It tastes like sugary paste. I've been here before, supposedly shortlisted, presented newly written material, only to be told: maybe next time; not quite what we were looking for.

'Think "Twilight",' Josh adds. He wanders around the office, searching in various different piles of paper for something. Upstairs the sound of a lunchtime soap's theme music vibrates through the floorboards. 'Which movie was it? You know, the one with Bella's wedding to the Dracula guy?'

I smile. 'Not Dracula, Edward.'

'Edward, whoever. Anyway that song, the one about him loving her for a thousand years? Or her loving him for a thousand years, whatever.'

I nod my head.

'Think that!' He points at me, wagging his finger. 'Only not that, obviously. We have to be different. And better,' he adds, handing me a red folder. 'The script. Page 312 is where the song appears. Make it work?'

I ignore the slight pleading inflection. 'Right. Love song. Wedding. Make it work.'

He scratches his head. 'Read the script. It's not a wedding. It's a love song. It's a sort of "I've loved you forever, will always love you" love song. But the storyline is a couple who split up, get back together and er . . . ' He eyeballs me. 'Well, they get back together and—'

'Live happily ever after?' I snort loudly, then sip my cooling coffee. 'Movies,' I say. 'Only in the movies.'

'Write the song.' He's back opposite me, wide-eyed. 'Please?'

'I'll write the song.'

'Beth, have you talked to Adam yet?' He refills his own mug from a shiny red machine in the corner.

I don't look at him. Instead I think about his American accent and the way he says Beth. Coming from Nashville, he's the only living person I know who can add a twang to a one-syllable word.

'Beth?' He's suddenly standing beside me.

There it is again. I look up. 'Josh, I really have nothing to say to Adam.'

'You never did tell me exactly what happened. I mean, how did you know? I mean, I know he had an affair and left and that it's not the first time, but what actually *happened*?'

He says all of this without taking a breath. And I realize I'm holding mine as the memory of the night plays in sepia in my head:

'Where have you been till now, Adam?'

'Matt and I worked late on a new pitch, then went for a curry.'

'You didn't think to call?'

'I just didn't notice the time, Beth, sorry.'

He then undresses in the bathroom. And scrubs his teeth. Not brushes them, scrubs them. Then, he takes a shower.

'You tired?' I ask when he gets into bed.

'*Mmmm. Beat.*' *He plants a brief kiss on my cheek then turns over. I get up and go to the bathroom. He has pushed his clothes into the end of the linen basket, covered them with other items. I sit on the loo and pull it towards me. His shirt is in my hands. I smell it. Lemons. Citrus perfume. From the doorway, I rub my right hand slowly left to right over the place I know my heart lies beneath my skin. It's like I'm massaging it, willing it to keep beating. I look at his body, already curled away from my side of the bed.*

'*Adam. Who is she?*'

I shake my head. 'Nothing much "happened". I smelt perfume on his clothes, tackled him, he folded and I asked him to leave. End of story.' I give a gentle shrug.

Josh reaches over, takes my hand, and stares for a long time at my ring-less finger. 'You're a songwriter,' he says, shaking his head. 'That is never the end of the story.'

Home by three, I check the answerphone to find a message from my mother. Hearing her voice makes me sigh. Hearing what she says makes me scrunch my face painfully. 'Elizabeth! If you do not call me back, I shall be forced to get in my car and drive to see you. I'd prefer not to have to get in my car to drive to see you, but I will.'

I call her back, knowing that if I think about it too much, I'll never call her. I have no idea what I'm going to say, but I do know it will be laced with lies. I cannot tell her that Adam left me. As it happens, I only have to lie to her answerphone. Giddy fibs trip easily from my tongue as I tell her machine that I'm sorry for not being in touch, that I've been busy with an amazing project. I guess I have, really. I've been surviving. Ending it with a 'Let's meet for lunch?' comment seems like a good idea.

I put a recorded episode of *CSI* on the telly and start surfing the net on my iPad. I Google everything that has anything to do with infidelity. I find all sorts of stories and heart-wrenching tales that make me feel quite lucky. At least my dastardly husband is a crap liar. At least the smug bastard confessed when confronted. According to the Internet, I'm lucky that he hasn't been running three wives at a time and that he doesn't wear my knickers while shagging them. I've found a website full of questionnaires that are supposed to tell you how you're dealing with betrayal and I'm completing my third one. I think that it's helping:

Question One: Did you know something was wrong before you found out?

Answer: No. (There is only a 'yes' or 'no' response box. There is none that says 'well, maybe, maybe just a little'.)

Question Two: Has your partner ever been unfaithful before in your or in previous relationships?

Answer: Yes. (The bastard.)

Question Three: Do you find yourself consumed with the physical betrayal?

Answer: Yes. (I can't stop thinking about Adam being inside another woman.)

Question Four: Are you finding it difficult to cope with your anger?

Answer: Yes.

Question Five: Do you believe your marriage can be saved?

Shit . . . I surf again and find lots and lots of positive mantras, the sort that Caroline wants me to embrace. I send them to my printer upstairs. Tomorrow, I will place them randomly all over the house, making sure to use Sellotape rather than Blu-tack, just because I can and because I know it would piss him off. I then discover an Internet forum site that has live web-chats for women who have been cheated on.

Amy from Hull is online.

'Sometimes I just want to call him up and say, "Okay, point proved. Come on home now." Then, other times I want to smash his face in,' she says.

Patsy from Seattle replies.

'Oh, I get that one! My best friend was so angry with her ex that she posted frozen prawns to him every day for a week when she knew he was away. Even though my ex is awful, I don't think I'd have the nerve.'

I laugh out loud. 'Hi,' I type. 'My name is Beth and I'm almost an alcoholic.' I hope they get the irony and don't really think I'm an alcoholic. I touch my wine glass, which is almost empty, and put it to one side. In reality, I think I *am* drinking too much, beginning to rely on that glass of wine, self-medicating.

'Hi Beth, LOL and welcome! What's your story?' Sally from Manchester . . . Shit. Where do I begin?

'My husband cheated on me with a younger woman. He is immature and selfish and I am so angry with him that although I don't want to smash his face in, I think I quite like the prawn idea.' I hit the return button.

'Is she beautiful?' Sally asks. 'My husband is currently shagging an ex-Miss Great Britain,' she says. 'As I'm twenty pounds overweight from giving birth to his one son-and-heir six months ago, I find this fact harder to take than the fact that he has cheated. He cheated on me with a younger, solvent, skinny woman with a flat, scar-free stomach and pert tits.'

'Chin up Sally.' Briana from Queens . . . 'Mine left me for a man. Sorry for appearing to downgrade your pain, but I think I'd prefer an ex-beauty queen to another man.'

Christ. It's overwhelming. I take a break and make a cup of tea before resuming my position on the sofa, where I read a few more tales of woe before finally deciding to be more proactive. Having spent an entire episode of *CSI* on the worldwide web of betrayal, I am armed and dangerous. I email Adam.

-----Original Message-----
From: bhall@intranethalluk.net
30 September 2014 21:42 PM
To: ahall@hall&fryuk.net
Subject: You

I don't want to talk to you, but I do want to let you know how I feel. The dictionary says that monogamy is 'a state of being paired with a single mate'. So, Adam, a question: What do you have in common with gibbon apes, grey wolves, swans, barn owls, beavers, black vultures, whales and termites?

Answer: Absolutely nothing. They all mate for life. You, on the other hand, are a specimen beneath the level of a termite. How does that make you feel? Proud of yourself?

Now that I've got that off my chest, I'd like you to stay away from me.

Beth

PS Meg said you were mugged. I'm trying to be sympathetic but sort of feel it may be some karmic force at work. Meg assures me you're well and completely unaffected by what happened and knowing this has allowed me to send this email. I mean what I say Adam, I want nothing to do with you any more.

After I press the send button, I make my way to the garage to do some left-handed damage to the punchbag.

Chapter Eight

I'm sipping my first coffee of the day, sitting at the tiny wrought-iron bistro table on Ben's balcony. Though the noise of the street below is sometimes intrusive, today I find it a positive distraction from the noise in my head. I have to go to work, but I want to crawl back into bed.

Though, if I do, the nightmares will be back. Dreams of my parents when they were alive, dreams of Beth and I when we were young . . . It seems my brain simply doesn't want to sleep. It seems my brain is in frightening overdrive as soon as my head nears a pillow. Last night, my mother was shouting at me about Ben's broken guitar, telling me that I was responsible. Then she burst into song. It was like something from *The Sound of Music*. Then Beth called her a termite. I asked her if she meant me. Isn't it me who's the termite? Just before I woke, Beth morphed into an enormous insect and bit my mother's head off. Completely screwed. My head is completely screwed.

In the kitchen, I munch on a week-old croissant that I find in the bread bin. It tastes stale but the cupboards are bare. I've never really had to consider food shopping before. Beth always took care of it and the cooking. Briefly I wonder how she is, if she's ready to talk.

The email from her telling me she wants nothing to do with me, the one that is probably the root cause of my nightmares, is now a week old. I was tempted, so tempted to tell her to sod off and pay for everything if she's so goddamned independent, but I didn't. I slam the plate and coffee cup into the sink, head to the bathroom to brush my teeth. My head is banging. I touch the back of it, run my fingers over the scar Harold gave me. It still feels bruised and sore. I root through the tiny medicine box that Beth brought up from the house; there are plasters, antiseptic lotion, some loose gauze but no paracetamol. In need of some form of analgesic, I stare at my mirror image and am horrified to see it start to cry.

Sitting on the edge of the bath, my tears fall. I'm painfully aware that the last time I cried was twenty-two years earlier when my parents died together. I held onto Ben at the graveside and knew our lives would never be the same.

'*Big boys don't cry, Adam.*'

My head hurts more when I shake the memory of one of my mother's favourite mantras from my head. I don't know what Beth would do now – possibly magic up some pain relief from a pocket somewhere – but I do know she'd fix this, just like she fixed me then, when she walked into my life a year later. And I can't ask her because she's not talking to me, has told me to stay away from her and would probably rather I curled up and died. A fate I possibly deserve.

*   *   *

I peer around the door of the office opposite mine and smile my brightest smile.

'Jen!'

Jen, who has been both Matt and my shared PA for many years, looks up from the floor where she is sitting amongst three archive boxes full of files.

'Ooh,' she says, scrunching her face on seeing me. 'Still not sleeping?'

'Not great. As the authorized first-aider on site, please tell me you have a bucketfull of paracetamol. The Grangers are due in and my head's lifting.'

She stands up, stretches her back out. 'You should see your doctor, get something to help you sleep.'

I watch her open the meds cabinet; my eyes are wide like a junkie waiting for a fix.

'Did you hear me?'

'I did. It'll pass. I've got a lot on my mind.'

'You look exhausted.'

'I am exhausted.' I manage a smile. 'I'll be fine. Matt in yet?'

'Already on his second coffee. Can I get you one?' She hands me six paracetamol.

I smile again. 'Thanks, Jen. I'll be down with him doing prep.'

She grabs my hand as she passes the tablets. 'We've known each other a while, yeah?'

Smile disappeared, I'm immediately concerned. An image of her resigning and somehow Matt blaming me pops up.

'Well, you need to look after yourself. Ever since you and Beth split, you've been heading straight down the shitter.'

My eyebrows rise. 'Succinctly put, Moneypenny. I'll take that under advisement.'

She laughs.

And I head down to Matt's office to prepare for a meeting with our biggest client.

For the second time in a month, my car is headed towards Weybridge, apparently driving of its own accord. Somehow, I got through the working day, but now, I need to try and sort this mess with Beth out; plus, I desperately need some fresh clothes. I haven't called ahead. If she's in, she's in. If not, I have a cunning plan.

It was during the Granger meeting I noticed. It was a difficult meeting, with the clients more antsy than usual, the markets having given us a thrashing these last months. I made the right noises but, as I moved my keys around in my pocket, I felt it. The back door key . . . She can't lock me out of the house! My cunning plan – talk to her if she's in, but enter my own home if she's not. Get some clothes, have a wander around, just because I can . . . Maybe wait for her to come home, lounging on the over-sized sofa in the living room, a glass of rioja in my hand. I hold my breath for most of the A3. When I reach Weybridge, I see that Beth's car isn't there and I park around the corner from the house.

From the car, I phone the house. Answerphone . . . I approach slowly, quietly, ring the doorbell. She's definitely out. I'm careful not to make too much noise. I don't want snoopy Sylvia peering over the hedge again. I head around the side entrance and place the key in the backdoor lock, turning it quickly. Smiling, I enter, feeling like a thief in the night. I lean on the back door, praying that as usual she won't have set the alarm. Beth forgetting to set the alarm when she leaves the house was a constant battle for us. Not looking forward to the telltale siren and mad dash to the box by the front door, my heart is racing in my chest. Nothing, she has left it off. I'm thrilled yet irritated.

Slowly, my heartbeat returns to something close to normal and I move around the house. It's October and really I could do with the lights on, but I dare not; instead I use my phone light to navigate my way. In the kitchen I run my hand along the granite worktop. Everything looks just the same as it did all those weeks ago. If anything it's tidier because I'm not here.

I climb the stairs slowly towards our bedroom. In the en-suite, I open the wall cabinet. My things are still there: aftershave, moisturizer, razor, toenail clippers. On the back of the door, my navy striped robe hangs on the hook next to Beth's. I walk towards the bed, feeling a Goldilocks moment. I sit down on her side, then lie down, inhaling her scent. I stare at the ceiling. This was my home. This was the home we made and shared together. It still feels like home. The only thing that's different is I'm not in it any more. I sit up, overwhelmed by a feeling of guilt.

As I exit the bedroom and walk downstairs, I look at my watch and can't believe I've already been here for over an hour. And it's at that moment that I hear the front door opening.

I dart into the living room, towards the back door. It's locked. Shit! Did I lock it again when I came in? Where are my keys? I hear Beth humming to herself, pottering about in the kitchen. I can tell by the opening of the fridge and the slamming of a cupboard door, she's getting a glass of wine. Shit. She'll come in here to drink it. I hear the glug sound of the wine pouring, search my jeans pockets. *Shit!* As I hear Beth's steps pace across the marble hallway, I do the only thing possible and hide behind the curtains. When Beth ordered them about five years ago, I was horrified by their sheer floor-to-ceiling size and the cost. Cost aside, I'm now grateful for their mass. Racking my brain, I come across an image. My keys. I left them by the bathroom sink while I was handling my toiletries. *Shit!*

From behind the curtain, after an entire episode of *The Apprentice*, I pray she'll get another drink. C'mon, Beth, you always have two, why not tonight? Or have a pee? Your bladder is like a sieve, surely you need a pee? As if on cue, she heads to the kitchen. I listen for the swish of the fridge door opening but hear the sound of the kettle being filled instead. It is quickly followed by the closing click of the cloakroom door.

I race out of the living room and up the stairs. I grab the keys, listen from the top of the stairs and take my chance. I'm in the hallway, just short of the front door, when she emerges. Leaning against the door to the coats cupboard, I catch my breath. She can't see me from inside. She'd need to actually come out into the hall. Once she settles down to the TV again, I can open the door and slip out quietly. Passing by, she stops and turns the lamps in the hallway on, from a switch just inside. The room is now bright; if she moves just a half metre to her right I am screwed with a capital 'S'.

She doesn't. Instead she takes her place on the sofa by the laptop again and drinks her cup of tea. I can tell all of this by sound alone. The irony is, I haven't seen her. I can't tell if she looks well, or drawn. I take a deep breath and then I see it, a floodlit message written on the hallway wall in paint:

> *I am Beth. I am strong. I am middle aged. I like*
> *champagne, chocolate, the ocean, lacy stockings,*
> *Ikea meatballs, flip-flops, Touche Éclat, music and*
> *lyrics. I don't like politicians, call centres, size zero*
> *women, snobs, punk rock, horseradish, dastards and*
> *women who sleep with dastards*

I can't help but smile as, without even one item of fresh clothing, I slip silently out through the front door. Horseradish . . . Who knew?

Chapter Nine

Her office is cold today. I shiver visibly as soon as I take my seat, rub my hands together. Without moving from her chair, Caroline leans back and tweaks a thermostat on the wall behind her.

We chat a bit about the minutiae of my life and then it's as if she goes straight for my solar plexus. 'Tell me about Simon?' she says. 'How he died, if you remember how you felt at the time?'

I'm suddenly mute, assaulted by memories of the little boy who was my brother. His dark curly hair, his tiny, ticklish feet, his laugh . . . I realize I haven't thought about Simon for a very long time.

'He was,' I finally speak, 'the sweetest child, a cherub, always laughing. He chatted all the time, such a little chatterbox and . . . he loved me. It was meningitis . . . ' I hesitate a moment. 'Meningitis killed him.'

Caroline is listening, not a poised pen in sight. Briefly, I wonder if this is some new tactic of hers.

'What do you remember of the time around his death?'

I nibble along the width of my top lip. 'I just remember him being gone. The house emptied. That's how it felt, like a vacuum. Hollow . . . '

'What did your parents tell you?'

'That he'd been sick, that he'd gone to heaven. My dad described it and it sounded such a beautiful place that I just didn't understand why we couldn't all go there. Together . . . '

I clamp my teeth together, take a deep breath through my nose, and release it slowly through my mouth. 'I haven't thought about this for years,' I confess.

'It's painful, obviously; an incredible loss for you at such a young age. For someone you loved, someone who was there for half of your life up to that point, for them just not to be there ever again. It leaves a big hole.'

My eyebrows stretch upwards.

'And, of course, your parents would have been different afterwards.'

It's a question without it sounding like one. I nod in silent agreement. I'm not ready to talk about my parents and the almost disintegration of their marriage after Simon died. I didn't understand it then and don't really understand it now. Besides, I'm here to discuss the disintegration of my own.

Caroline senses she has almost lost me. 'Let's park that for now if you'd prefer?'

'I'd prefer,' I tell her, 'but I'd also rather get it over with. The truth is my parents were in trouble for years afterwards. A couple living together, but mentally apart . . . I became their everything and I became their nothing.'

Oh shit, her pen is up. It's like it's appeared from nowhere and she's writing. 'That's a powerful statement. "Their every-thing and their nothing",' she repeats. 'Can you elaborate?'

'I was quiet, thoughtful, pensive – their only surviving child, yet I was nothing like him, a constant reminder of their loss. Simon had filled the house with laughter and joy, and suddenly it was gone. All of it.'

'Did you feel guilty?'

I sigh. 'I think, even as a child, I knew how useless that would be, so no . . . "guilty" isn't the right word. But I did feel like they'd been short-changed and that I had too. I'd lost my brother and I knew I could never fill that hole.'

'You had . . . ' Caroline taps her pad with the nib of her pen. 'You had been short-changed, all of you . . . '

We're both quiet for a minute, then she is first to speak. 'Do you see any parallels between your own and your parents' marriage?'

'Other than the fact that they both hit the skids at some time, no . . . '

'Who was it that mentally left your parents' marriage, if you had to say? After Simon's death – your mother or your father?'

Really? Sometimes this woman has a talent for making me wince with her jabbing questions. I don't reply, not out loud at least, now that I can see where she's going with this particular train of thought. Yes, my father was the bastard. Yes, Adam is the bastard.

I lean forward. 'How is any of this relevant, Caroline?'

'Maybe it's not.' She shrugs. 'But it's probably worth exploring.'

'Can we park it for another time?' I use her expression for ignoring it at the moment.

'Of course,' she says, making sure that, as she says that, our eyes lock; making sure she lets me know that she knows I'm merely hiding.

Caroline assured me before I left today that most learned behaviours can be unlearned, most bad habits broken. It's six p.m. and I've just drunk a half-litre bottle of sparkling water, brushed my teeth, popped a chewing gum into my mouth – anything to try and convince myself I don't want crisps. I can unlearn my salt-and-vinegar crisp habit. I do not need crisps. They are wasted calories. My image looks back at me from the mirror in the hallway, the one that's wall-mounted above the console table. I tilt my head left and right slowly, releasing the creaking tension. 'What you looking at, bitch?' I ask my inner saboteur.

'Not much,' she replies in my head.

'You're horrible, you know that, don't you?'

'You want crisps, you know that, don't you?'

I run my fingers through my hair like a comb.

'You want crisps, you want salt-and-vinegar crisps,' she taunts me again.

The phone rings and I grab the receiver. It's Mum. She's brief, since she's dashing out; just wants to make sure I'm still all right for tomorrow.

I'm not all right for tomorrow. I feel like I lost a layer of skin with Caroline today, like somehow I'll be painfully susceptible to a mother's probing. Much as I want to cancel, I confirm our plans.

The next day, as suspected, my mother is no pushover. Having worried myself sick that she will be able to read me like a book when I see her, I insisted we meet for lunch halfway, purely to keep her away from the house. Allowed into the house, she would, like an anteater, sniff out the absence of Adam. Instead, we are lunching and shopping at John Lewis in High Wycombe.

Unusually, Mum is full of chat about herself. Her latest course at the local adult education centre, where she is learning how to manicure nails; her friend Trish who cheats at bridge; the vicar's wife who's seeing the guy who runs the off-licence. I listen for ages, smile, and laugh appropriately. I love my mother deeply. Sybil Moir has polar-white hair, having refused to succumb to hair dye like the rest of us. It is styled in flicked curls that curve away from her face. A few facial lines reveal she's in her sixties, but it's her grey eyes that light her face. If eyes can make a face smile, my mother's, fringed with thick silver lashes, do – without ever needing the curve of her lips.

Her staple clothes choice of jeans, a polo-neck sweater and Barbour jacket hasn't changed in years. Today, a bottle-green sweater hugs her neck. Black jeans ride above black leather ankle boots, Chelsea style – Mum doesn't do heels – and her black padded jacket hangs on the back of the café chair.

I'm quite tickled at the fact that my phone lies have worked so far and all is going swimmingly until, grey eyes looking down into her latte, she asks me how Adam is. Really is. She just detects that maybe all's not well. Then she looks up and stares right at me.

I dig deep. Right down into that monkey-nut inner core, match her gaze and tell her that Adam's fine. Really. He's really fine. This isn't even a lie. He is allegedly very fine.

He's having lots of sex with another, younger woman. What man wouldn't be?

'And you?' she asks. 'I suppose you're fine too?'

'I am. And Meg, she's—'

'Yes, she's fine. I know. Meg returns my calls.'

I take the dig.

'Well, as long as everyone's fine.' She smacks her hands lightly on the edge of the table. 'Let's see what John Lewis has to offer?'

A few hours of shopping later, she seems satisfied, heading back to the Cotswolds as I wave her off. I climb into the car and chew my cheek. I know I've only dodged the ball. She's like Arnie, my mum. She'll be back.

After a fairly sleepless night, I wake to the sound of staccato showers and someone singing in my head. I always wake to some random track playing in my brain. Adam used to ask me every morning who was featuring and what they were singing. He believed it used to dictate my mood. Today, it's someone whose name I can't remember, but she's telling me I've got to live my life and do what I want to do.

I head to the shower clutching my stomach. Whenever I think of him, of what he's doing with his day, I feel my insides churn, then coil around themselves so tightly that it physically hurts. I close my eyes, hold my head up to the scalding, pulsing water as I soap my body. I dismiss him from my head, deciding that I will have a proactive work day today and I will start by reading the movie script Josh gave me. Again . . . I've tried and failed before, finding anything love-related too sweet to endure.

Three hours and four cups of coffee later, I'm sitting at the dual computer screens in the loft. The left one shows my petty attempt at a lyric while the right one displays the musical effort. My head is buzzing as I open YouTube and I watch the Twilight song Josh had spoken about. Again, I'm immediately consumed with song-writing envy. How does that woman Christina Whatsit do it? I watch the clip a few more times and then get back to the script. I can do this, I tell myself, my head in my hands. They asked for me. I'm one of three they asked for – I can do this. On the wall, all around my writing area, are the inspirational mantras I'd found weeks ago, printed in purple gothic font. Some I'd copied and some are all my own work. I stare up at 'I AM A SONGWRITING PHENOMENON!!!' And I almost believe it, as I set to work.

I work through lunchtime and only move away from the screen when my stomach is doing a hunger dance. Downstairs, I eat a bag of crisps. A voice inside my head tells me that I have to do a food shop, as I tear open today's mail.

My bank statement shows me that, early last week, Adam paid the same amount that he has paid into my bank account for years, a monthly sum, to run the house, pay for food and bills, etc. I lick the crisps from the end of my fingers as a new fear blindsides me. What if he stops doing that? What if he just decides not to pay it? We have no dependent children any more and it's all very well me telling him to fuck right off, but what happens practically? We both own the house, it's not mortgaged, but I want to stay living here. Panic seeps from my brain through my entire system.

The hard fact is that I do not make nearly enough money to run this house alone. Even with my latest increase in royalties, I would have to get a job as well . . . The thought of getting a job, a real job that pays me a regular wage, terrifies me. I'm forty-two. The country has been in a double-dip recession; thousands of graduates and highly qualified people are out of work. My eyelids droop momentarily. Maybe that termite email was a bit much. Maybe I need to calm down a bit and maybe we do need to talk.

I don't want to have time to change my mind, so I send Adam a text, asking him to come by the house. I keep it simple and it is only minutes before my phone pings a reply.

'R u in tonite?'

I feel immediately irritated, angry even. I hate text language, and anyone who knows me respects that and uses proper English words when texting me. I've told them for years not to be so bloody lazy.

'No. I'm not in tonight,' I lie. 'I'm out.'

'Wen then?' chimes back.

'You idle bastard. Since when have you forgotten I hate lazy texting? I'm not your stupid bimbo whore. Yes, whore is spelt with a "w".'

The landline rings and I ignore it. He has such an ability to rile me.

'Idle?' The mobile responds instead. 'You call ME idle! Some of us are WORKING 24/7 for a living!'

My hand goes automatically to my mouth. Shit. My eyes flash to the bank statement and I text him back.

'Sorry. Come by Friday?'

'C U Fri at 8.'

I inhale a deep sigh and toss my mobile across the worktop.

I've abandoned the idea of writing an Oscar-nominated song for film this afternoon and instead I'm riffling through random papers in Adam's desk. It struck me, seeing my bank balance, that I haven't seen a statement in months from Adam's bank account. He has a habit of leaving paper around, but there's nothing – no statements anywhere.

I open up the bank's web page saved on his computer. Keying in what I know to be his default password, 'BeautifulMeg', the account opens before me. I make a note of the common standing orders and direct debits on a blank page, just so I'm fully up to speed with what goes out on normal expenses – insurances, cars, etc., etc. On another blank page, I note all the other sundry spends, including the restaurants he's been visiting with his bimbo whore. Nearly five hundred pounds last month. Then I see it. A transaction for two hundred and ninety pounds in Agent Provocateur . . . I set my pen down on his desk and stare at it until the letters become jumbled.

Images of Adam shagging a faceless but scantily clad woman swim in my brain like scenes from some Swedish porn movie. I hear the soundtrack in my head. Something shifts in that moment and I'm past angry. Now, I just want to know how long my husband has been lying to me and about what. Scanning the account for the last six months, I send the information to the printer.

Leaning on his desk with both hands, I contemplate how the hell I'm supposed to write about love right now, when all I feel is a furious sense of having been taken for a complete idiot. I head out to the hall table, grab my car keys and walk to the shop at the nearby garage. I need crisps and lots of them.

Sylvia is outside her house with Ted, her Yorkshire terrier, on a lead. 'Hey,' she says as I exit the gate.

'Hi.' I automatically hug her. 'I'm sorry it's been a while, I've been busy licking my wounds.'

'You're entitled. Where you headed?'

'The garage, I need crisps.'

She giggles. 'I'll walk with you. Just taking Ted out for a stretch.'

'How're Nigel and the kids?'

'They're great. Now . . . That's enough small talk. How are you?'

'All the better for all the food you bring me.' I link her arm for a moment. 'Seriously, I'd probably have fallen down a grate without you.'

'You look like you probably will anyway. How much weight have you lost? No, don't tell me. Maybe I can persuade Nige to leave me, just for a while.' She yanks on Ted's lead, pulling him closer. 'Sorry, too soon?'

I shake my head, attempt a smile. We walk for a few minutes; when we reach the main road, the smell of traffic fumes almost overcomes me.

'Come over for dinner tonight when the kids are in bed,' she says. 'Just you, me and Nige. You don't have to talk about anything to do with Adam. Just eat homemade chicken.'

'Tempting.' I can feel myself salivate at the thought. 'But

no, I really have to work and I'm not ready to socialize yet. Soon, I promise. Please don't stop asking.'

'I won't.' She steers me into the garage shop and again, I breathe deep to combat the smell of fuel outside. 'Salt-and-vinegar crisps,' she tells the guy at the till. 'A big bag. A big bag with lots of little bags, you know the type?'

Seb, as his badge reveals he's been named, looks at Sylvia like she's a lunatic. 'You need a supermarket for multi-bags,' he says, already bored.

'Well, just fill a plastic bag with as many little bags as you can.' She rolls her eyes at me.

I'm not even sure I want crisps any more. I shiver, pray I'm not coming down with something.

'Have you noticed?' Sylvia asks.

'What?' I remove my purse from my pocket, get it ready for Seb as he's done exactly what Sylvia asked.

She tugs on my cotton jacket. 'It's mid-October. The trees will soon be bare. Evenings will be dark, the sun shielded by dense layers of cloud, not to be seen again until spring-time. It's cold out there.' She speaks as if she's in a Shakespearean play; makes the word 'cold' sound very long and very loud.

I shudder on cue and nod. 'Note to self. Summer jackets to be put away.'

'Warm jackets to be worn on late-afternoon jaunts for crisps . . .'

Walking back, she makes me laugh with stories of the kids and Nigel; when we stop outside the house, Ted does an enormous circular crap right in the centre of my driveway. Sylvia scoops it up into a plastic bag and asks me if I want her to let it harden a little and send it to Adam. 'Shit for a shit.' She shrugs. 'Seems reasonable . . . '

I don't disagree. After hugging her goodbye, I'm soon back in the kitchen, tearing open a bag of crisps. And there, on my own, the dark night drawing in, I turn the thermostat up, throw a cardigan from a pile of washing around me. I flick the tiny kitchen television into life with the remote and scroll through channels until I find a rerun of *Game of Thrones*. Leaning on the worktop, I lick my salty fingertips, as Catelyn Stark tells me, her face grave, that 'Winter is Coming.'

Chapter Ten

'Why are you still wearing your ring?'

I stop twirling it around my finger and look at Matt. 'I'm a married man until Beth tells me otherwise,' I say.

'Do you think she will?' Matt keeps glancing at the clock on the meeting room wall. I'm sure he's trying diversionary tactics, rather than discussing the more immediate elephant in the room.

'Forget my wedding ring, Matt. We need to figure out our response. They'll be here in forty minutes.'

He's nodding, biting his bottom lip, and I can tell he's worried. Matt and I go way back to university days and I first saw him chew his lip when Shelly Lewis dumped him. I stare at him, can practically hear his brain whirring, and Shelly Lewis pales into insignificance as the reality of the Granger brothers, our largest single family account, potentially sacking us, dawns.

'Look,' he offers, 'we directly advised them, yes. They've lost a shitload of money, yes. Of course they're not happy. Shit, I'm not happy.' He runs a hand over his head of thinning hair. 'We did our due diligence. The fund seemed right. But, there is something else.' Matt is now standing and staring out of my office window.

I hear laughter in the corridor outside but, for some reason, I can feel my stomach sink.

He turns slowly. 'I need you here for the meeting today, obviously, we've got to face them together about this latest dip, but they've asked for you to be removed from the account. There, I've said it – there's no easy way.'

I know my face is scrunching as I process what he's just said. The Granger brothers want me off the account. That can't be right. I brought the Granger brothers to the firm. I discovered the family business, nurtured them and have looked after them for the last God-knows-how-many years. 'I don't understand—'

He interrupts. 'Yes, you do. You've had your eye off the ball for months now. I've made allowances, everyone has, but this – ' he raises his hands to the heavens – 'this midlife crisis, or whatever it is, has made you lose your edge. You just don't seem to care?'

'I care.' I feel my neck redden under my shirt collar and loosen my tie automatically. 'Of course I care. I can't believe you're saying this and saying it now.' I jab a finger at my watch, indicating we have even less time to figure out what to do about the Grangers. I ignore what he's said for a minute. 'Will they sack us?' I ask.

'I think so, I don't know . . . '

I'm baffled. 'They're almost thirty per cent of our business.' My voice is almost a whisper.

'I know that.' Matt removes his glasses, rubs both his eyes with a forefinger and thumb.

'And what? You blame me? They blame me? The markets aren't *my* fault.'

'I know that too.' He raises a calming hand. 'They know that, but they also know you've been away with the fairies during meetings, and now with this . . . They need a scapegoat.'

'And I'm it. Adam and his midlife crisis, eh? How convenient.' I stand up and take my jacket from the back of my chair.

'Where are you going?' His voice raises a notch when he sees me head for the door.

'You don't need me. They want me off the account. I'm sure you'll handle it from here.'

'Do *not* walk out, Adam.'

I slam the door for added effect and Jen, who's sitting in reception, averts her eyes. I ignore Matt calling my name and press the button for the lift. Taking deep breaths, I process the facts. We've probably lost thirty per cent of our business. I've played a part in that. I lean a hand on the mirrored wall of the lift, breathe slowly, in and out. Everything is falling apart. Exiting the lift, I do what any man in that position would. I call Emma.

As I drive to Weybridge for what will probably be the second row of the day, I'm calm. After a steak sandwich in the White House, followed by a soothing massage to 'release the stress knots' in my shoulders, followed by sex – yes, I'm calm. The wrestling session has left me exhausted but I'm calm. And shallow. Shallow enough to need sexual release when everything is going to rat-shit. Shallow enough to keep going back to Emma since she's the only one who seems to think I'm incredible.

My phone pings a text from Matt. 'Call me. Urgent.'

I dial the number via the Bluetooth connection.

'About time,' he says almost instantly. 'Where have you been?'

I decline to answer on the grounds that I would definitely incriminate myself.

'It doesn't matter,' he says. 'I need to bring you up to speed. Adam?'

'I'm here.'

'Well, they didn't fire us.' He sighs. 'But it was a tough meeting. As suspected, you're off the account.'

I remain silent.

'Where are you? Can we meet?'

'No. I'm a few minutes from Weybridge. Meeting Beth tonight to see what happens from here. I won't get back until late.'

'Early breakfast meeting? Starbucks? We need to talk.'

'I think you've probably said enough.'

'Adam, not everything is about you? We need to discuss this mess we've been left with and you need to get your arse in gear, get your finger back on the pulse.'

I can't even speak. Matt telling me off like a child makes my blood boil, even if he's right – probably *because* he's right.

'Starbucks at seven thirty,' he continues. 'Oh, and by the way – it's not me, it's you.'

I hear the phone disconnect and can't help a short-lived smile at his attempt at break-up humour. Moments later, the smile fades as I steer into the driveway of what was my beautiful home and now appears to be Beth's beautiful home.

She answers the door so quickly, I don't really have time to gather my thoughts.

'Hi.' She stands back and ushers me in. She looks well. She's wearing a little makeup, eyeliner, lip gloss, blusher. She has on what I know to be jeans from her 'skinny' clothes, kept on the left-hand side of the walk-in wardrobe we shared. The blouse, too, I recognize from the same rack of clothes that Beth now fits easily.

'I never knew,' I say, as she takes my jacket.

'Knew what?'

'That you don't like horseradish.' My head nudges to the wall art and she shrugs.

'I guess you know now,' she replies. We head to the kitchen. 'Wine?'

'No thanks, I'll just have a coffee.' I pass a photo of Beth and me taken years ago on a ski trip. We're smiling and there is such love in our eyes that it rattles me. She flicks the kettle on, takes out two cups and the scene seems so normal. I realize I miss this. This afternoon's sex, the last few months, all seem to disappear when I see a photo of Beth and me the way we were and she's making me a cup of coffee in our kitchen.

'How've you been?' she asks.

'I'm okay. A tough day at the coalface . . . You?'

She shrugs, doesn't reply. She hands me my mug, takes her cup of green tea and sits opposite me at the island in the kitchen. I try to catch her eye. 'Beth, I . . . ' I reach across and touch her free hand. She snatches it away.

'Please, I need to explain.'

'I forgot you take sugar,' she says, heading back to the larder, removing the bowl and handing it to me with a teaspoon. 'Have you heard from Meg this week?'

'No. I . . . Look, there's not much point in saying it just happened, but it did, really. She came on to me. No, I didn't stop her. I should have stopped her. I wish I'd stopped her, I wish I'd stopped myself. I wish none of it had happened and I was home here with you.' I banish any thoughts of this afternoon's antics from my mind. I am here to talk to Beth. I'm here to try and get her to listen. I'm not even sure what I want to say, but I do know that here and now, in this moment, I'll tell any lie necessary, because I'm not ready for my marriage to end.

Beth is staring downwards at the oak flooring. 'Meg's got her exams soon, don't forget.'

'Beth? It's sex, just sex. You and I, we . . . '

Beth, her head still pointed downwards, looks as though she's trying to swallow a golf ball. I shrug, helpless. 'Sex, that's all . . . You stopped wanting me.' I bite my tongue; the last thing I want to do is make her feel like I'm blaming her.

She looks up. 'We need to sort out the details. What happens, how we actually separate . . . I don't want to lose the house.'

Jesus Christ. I sip my coffee. 'Is that the only reason I'm here, Beth? My wallet, the house?'

'You left to shack up with your whore,' she murmurs.

'I'm not shacked up with her. I'm living in Ben's place. And you threw me out.' I don't bother defending Emma's honour.

'I don't want to do this.' She's standing suddenly, one hand on her hip.

I don't move. 'What, you don't want to do it now? Or never? We *have* to do this. We can't pretend nothing happened and just talk money!'

'Why not?' She finally looks at me.

Suddenly, I'm weary. 'Don't you want to talk? We're broken, Beth. I know it's all my fault, but please—'

'Adam, are you still with that woman?' Both hands are now on her hips and she seems to be saying that as long as Emma is in the picture, conversation is pointless.

I think of this afternoon, debate lying, and decide against it. 'It depends on what you mean, but I guess the answer is yes, I'm still seeing Emma.'

Beth's beautiful head shakes in slow motion.

'Seeing her . . . How quaint. Don't you mean: shagging her and letting her give you the rampant blow jobs that you think you never got at home? Maybe in some of the underwear you bought for her?'

For the second time today, I feel colour course through my neck and land firmly on my cheeks.

'Transparent, that's what you are. What could you possibly have to say? To "talk" about?' She turns back towards the sink, tosses her green tea into it and heads to the fridge. There, she takes out a wine bottle and pours herself a glass. She takes a large gulp from it and speaks with her back still to me. 'You just don't get it, do you? Back then, way back whenever, *that's* when we should have talked. You could have and should have talked to me then.'

'You're right,' I tell her spine. 'I'm sorry.'

She stares into the kitchen window. With her back still to me, she asks my reflection. 'When did it start?'

'Beth—'

'I need to know, Adam.' She turns around. 'How long have you been lying to me?'

I sit very still. *That* is a very difficult question, and has so many potential answers that I quickly reason she must only mean Emma.

'Not long.'

'How long exactly?'

Though I know the answer to be about five months, I hear my considered reply. 'Three months.'

She focuses on my eyes, blinks twice and then looks away. I know she's trying hard not to cry. I watch her take a wedge of paper from one of the kitchen drawers. Taking another mouthful of wine, she waves them at me. 'Bank account stuff,' she says. 'I just wanted to get up to speed with who pays what every month before we talked tonight.'

I feel a deep-rooted pulse develop behind my eyes.

'There's over five months' worth here,' she continues. 'I'm not even going to ask you when the last time you took me to Langham's was, or the last time you bought me something in Agent Provocateur. But, here's the thing: every lie you tell makes me care less and less.'

My heart hurts looking at her. The pulse is now throbbing behind my eyeballs and I wonder briefly if guilt can present as pure pain.

'Do you know,' she turns to face me, her eyes pools of tears, 'there's hardly a day goes by where I don't cry. Sometimes, I'm angry, so angry, that I hate you, and other days I'm just sad.' She seems to linger over the word 'sad'.

'What do you want me to do?' I hear the resignation in my own voice.

'Stop lying for a start.'

I sigh, a weary, heavy sound.

'Do I need to get myself checked out?' Her voice sounds remote, distant.

I shake my head. 'I've always used something.'

'Maybe I should anyway. I've been sort of ignoring it.' She seems to be talking to no one in particular.

'You don't need to worry, Beth.'

'I need not to worry about money.' Her wet eyes refuse mine. 'I need not to have to worry about losing my home because of your dick. I need time to think about my life without you in it and I need you to think about *my* needs for once.'

I find myself nodding because she's right. I can't think right now about me and where I'll live when Ben gets back and if I can actually afford to run two homes. A brief image of me living in the White House with Emma and Harold clouds my thoughts and I shudder. I imagine my straightjacket would be crispy white.

As I excuse myself to go to the loo, I hear myself reassure Beth that I will continue to take care of things. I sit on the seat in the downstairs cloakroom, wondering what that means. I'm not sure, but Beth needs to hear what I'm telling her right now and it's what I want her to believe. So I sit for a while, with my head in my hands, ignoring the red flag waving in it telling me that I don't really believe it – which can only mean that it's more lies.

Chapter Eleven

'Adam told me I stopped wanting him. It was there in the middle of some long spiel of his, like a barbed accusation.'

'And did you? Stop wanting him?'

I've been asking myself the same question since. Carefully, I clean underneath my left thumbnail with my right one. 'It's just not that simple. We've been married a long time. It was one of those phases where I only wanted to sleep. I don't think I stopped wanting him as much as stopped having sex for a while.'

'Did you talk about it?'

I shake my head. 'I know now that I wanted him to. I wanted him to notice and talk to me, ask me how I felt. Rather than the other way around. It's always me who does the talking. It's exhausting.' I look up. 'It didn't last long, maybe a couple of months. We had sex again as soon as I gave in and made the first move.' I sigh. 'Of course, I'd lost him by then . . . '

'Do you remember a few weeks ago we spoke about your fears?' Caroline blows her coffee as she changes the subject.

I can only nod.

'You say things are clearer, so tell me what your greatest fear is, right now, in this space in time?'

I close my eyes and immediately wonder if I *can* live without Adam, if I actually want to, or is forgiving him again and trying to reboot our marriage an option? The clenching behind my ribs assures me that this is indeed a fear rather than a solution.

'Taking Adam back, nothing really changing, me just carrying on with my head hovered above the sand.' There, I've said it out loud.

'Anything else?' she prods.

'Leading half a life . . . '

She raises a questioning eyebrow.

'What if I can't move from this small world I've created for myself? What if I don't allow another man near me and, worse, if I did, what if I discovered I had "Go ahead – cheat on me" stamped on my forehead?'

She smiles. 'You have nothing stamped on your forehead,' she reassures me, 'just on your brain.'

I lean forward, pick up the Russian doll she used weeks ago with me and I slowly open the five parts. I caress the tiniest figure, and the fear floodgates are well and truly opened.

'Personal failure,' I hear myself say. 'I know I'm good; my agent tells me just to get on with it – success will come if I work hard. It's just that inner saboteur constantly waiting to leap.'

'You're going to have to find a way to gag her.' Caroline shrugs. 'I find that imagery actually helps. Maybe name her too? If you feel negativity creep up on you, visualize her, how she looks, what she's wearing and then gag her with a cloth – really tightly.'

I'm fascinated. 'You have an inner saboteur too?'

'A lot of people do.' She grins, as if it's just the most normal thing in the world to be gagging an imaginary part of your head with a cloth – really tightly.

'So, she's gagged, you're successful in your own right, maybe you're even happy living alone. What do you think you have to put in place to get there?'

My roll grinds to a vicious halt. Me. Happy. Living alone. I like that thought, but still shake my head vigorously. 'I don't know . . . '

Caroline takes a book from her desk, opens it where it's marked with a Post-it note.

'"We gain strength, and courage,"' she quotes aloud from the page, '"and confidence by each experience in which we really stop to look fear in the face . . . we must do that which we think we cannot."' She emphasizes the last few words as she shuts the book. 'Eleanor Roosevelt,' she says.

Swallowing hard, I put the doll together again and place it back on the table, my head still disagreeing. 'Whatever that is,' I tell her, 'I'm not ready.'

'Take the doll with you,' she says, 'for more positive imagery – if it helps? Her name's Babushka.'

I stare at the figure, then reach for her and put her in my handbag. Somehow it makes sense, but I avoid Caroline's eye. Christ Almighty, I'm in therapy with an adult who gags her inner saboteur and names her dolls.

This week, I've written half of a song. There is an air of excitement in the loft as I've probably written half of '*the*' song. My devil-like inner saboteur, whom I have now named 'Lucy Fir', has been well and truly gagged. Eleanor Roosevelt lives on in my head. I've listened to lots of fantastic music, watched some classic movies and somehow tapped into the world of love again. I've forced myself, for work purposes, to wallow in love's glorious potential. I haven't got a title for *the* song yet, but it's about a couple being the right fit. About the fact that they just don't fit anyone else except one another and that they fall apart without each other. It's all still first-draft stuff, but I think I'm onto something. I'm just sending a sound-bite through to Josh, when I hear the doorbell downstairs ringing persistently.

The sound pulses through the house, again and again.

'I'm coming, I'm coming,' I mutter, taking the stairs down two at a time. I peer through the spyhole, wondering who on earth can be so determined. My shoulders droop and I rest my forehead on the white gloss door.

'Stop peering through the thingy, Elizabeth. Open up.'

I pull it towards me.

'Darling,' she says, giving me a kiss on my cheek and moving past me, glancing only briefly at my text wall art. 'It's drizzling a bit out there,' she says, placing a long, neon-pink umbrella in the hallstand next to Adam's cricket bat.

'Mum,' I reply. 'What brings you here?'

'Meg called me.' She holds a small kitbag up. 'I've come to do your nails.'

I'm lost for words as she walks away from me. I can hear her unpack what must be manicure regalia onto the dining table before I've even shut the front door.

'Mum,' I stand in the living room doorway, feeling a prickle of anxiety, wondering what Meg has said. 'My nails are fine, I . . . ' I'm trying to find the words that express what I feel but are not – *Please leave, Mum. I need to write an Oscar-nominated song. I don't want to tell you what's going on in my world. I like to pretend that everything's all right on the phone. Can you please piss off back to the Cotswolds?*

'Open a bottle of wine, Elizabeth, I'm staying the night.' Her stone-grey eyes catch mine and her eyebrows arch as if to say, '*Go on, I dare you. Tell me you're too busy.*' She says nothing, then continues to unpack an array of tiny, multicoloured bottles.

My husband has left me and I've just been up in the loft convincing myself I can earn a proper living song-writing, yet it seems – I glance down at my fingernails – that a manicure is more important. 'I'll get the wine.' I walk towards the fridge, hoping she won't follow me, and discover the lack of food and abundance of crisps. There is, however, a beef stew I'd forgotten about. Sylvia. I offer up a silent thanks to her.

Having filled two glasses, I place them both on the dining table and take a seat. She's standing at the bi-folds, staring out into the garden. The tail end of a rain shower spits on the glazing.

'You'll have to take up gardening,' she says, her arms folded across her chest.

I know then that Meg has revealed enough. 'I was going to tell you.'

'When, exactly?' She hasn't taken her eyes off the lawn.

'When I felt I could.' I shrug. 'It's only just beginning to be real to me.'

The sounds of Sylvia's children, rushing into their garden after the rain, permeate the room. I stare at an ancient ring of a coffee cup on the walnut dining table, as my mother takes a seat next to me. She raises her wine glass to her mouth and I can tell she's fighting tears. She then pulls an antiseptic wipe from a plastic container, leans forward and grabs one of my hands. She uses both of hers to gently clean mine. 'I'm sorry,' she says.

My shoulders move up and down again. 'It is what it is.'

'What happened?' She asks the question as she wipes clean my other hand.

'How much did Meg say?'

'She just told me that he'd gone, implied there was another woman.' Her eyes once again meet mine. 'Was there? Is there?'

I let her words hang in the air a moment before replying. 'Yes and yes.'

'Bastard,' she whispers, picking out a particularly lurid bottle. 'Fuchsia, I think. You need brightening up.'

I don't reply; know there's no point. If my mother has made up her mind that I need fuchsia nails, then that's exactly what I'm going to get. She has already travelled a hundred miles. She picks up the file and gets to work.

Minutes later, she speaks again. 'You're not alone.'

I tap her arm affectionately. 'I know that, Mum. Thank you.'

'We all have crosses to bear. Most of us have faulty husbands and most of us learn to live with them.'

She is, of course, referring to the fact that my father's first love was alcohol, over and above both her and me.

She squeezes my hand in hers. 'I loved your dad,' she says, 'and he loved me.'

I remember lots of tears; my mother weeping into her coffee cup, her bed sheets, her book . . . I can't hide my discomfort, and I shift awkwardly in the chair. 'He had a funny way of showing it,' I say.

Mum frowns. 'Don't judge.' Her voice has a hint of scolding to it. 'I get what you're going through but . . . there's nothing worse in this world than losing a child. When Simon died, a big part of your dad did too. It was after that he changed. He was running away from the hell of it all.'

I start to interrupt but she stops me.

'This was before people talked about their feelings. There was no such thing as counselling. Grief counselling was what he needed but, to be honest, even if it had been around, he wouldn't have gone. Instead he drank bourbon to help face the pain.'

I wait until she draws breath. 'I'm not judging, Mum. I just don't understand why you'd put up with that.'

'You were young. And then, suddenly, you weren't. Why change something that worked in so many ways for us? Besides . . . ' She smiles and cocks her head at me. 'We were happy.'

I bite my lip. And my tongue. She's right. I have never had to deal with the heartache of losing a child. And who am I to judge her when I forgave Adam once before too? I convinced myself we could get past his failings.

'Can you forgive him, maybe forget about this, and put it behind you?' she asks. It's as if she can hear my thoughts, see into my very soul.

'No.' My tone is emphatic. 'I hope someday I won't care, so maybe I can forgive him, but I'll never forget how he's hurt me.' I do not say the word 'again' out loud. My mother doesn't need to know about the last time.

She nods, doesn't push the point.

I hear my last words echo in my head and feel a huge weight lift from my locked shoulders. After many weeks of therapy, it's taken my mum talking to make me say it out loud. I will not be taking Adam back. My marriage is over.

I can almost hear the tiny monkey-nut-size baby Babushka cry. I may finally be back in touch with my core, but it hurts – as if my heart is being squeezed in a vice. The coffee ring on the table blurs as my eyes fill and my mouth begins to tremble. My mother drops my fuchsia hand and pulls me into her arms.

I can't sleep. Today's emotions have just been too much. I feel spent, exhausted, but somehow I'm not sleepy. I'm sitting up in bed, my back against the silver-button-punched, fabric headboard, having a conversation online with Sally from Manchester. We've kept in touch since we found each other on an Internet forum months ago. For someone whose husband has made mine look like the archangel Gabriel, I'm astounded at her capacity for forgiveness. She has taken him back. She makes no apologies for the fact that she loves him; he's still her husband and the father of her child. Part of me admires her and part of me feels for her.

'He'll do it again!' I want to shout at the screen, type the words, but I don't. I wish her well, but secretly believe that 'her Colin', as she calls him, will soon be back in the arms of the skinny, solvent woman he was shagging, or someone else just as accommodating.

I stare into space. Maybe my mother is right. Maybe I judge far too quickly, and just maybe I shouldn't. Then again, I focus on the image of Adam actually shagging his bitch whore girlfriend. I grit my teeth and almost visualize penetration.

Nope. No forgiveness here anytime soon.

Chapter Twelve

I have, since meeting with Matt in Starbucks, wallowed in my own filth for almost a week. All he did then was tell me nicely what a wanker I've been and suggest I try and be less of a wanker. Now, we're back in the same American coffee house, but I have showered, shaved and am dressed in dry-cleaned jeans and a crisp white shirt. I still haven't figured out how to use the washing machine without getting creased clothes that can't possibly be ironed.

'I'm taking a few more days off.' I'm aware I'm telling Matt rather than discussing it as we would normally do. I blow the steam from my second latte and end up with frothy milk on my spotless jeans.

He nods, staring at me over his steepled hands. For the last half-hour, we've redone the whole Granger thing and I've been suitably placed on the naughty step.

'Just the rest of the week,' I add. 'I'll be back on Monday.'

'Are you all right?' he asks.

'Peachy,' I say, 'just have to get my head around the fact that my marriage is falling apart, my brother comes back in four weeks and I'll have nowhere to live. And, oh, you've tossed me off an account I brought to the firm.'

Matt inhales deeply. I can tell he's trying to decide on the right reply. I know there is none, that this isn't his fault, but I need someone to blame for the Grangers' betrayal. I'm knee-deep in my own.

'They'll calm down after a while, Adam. Let it settle for a bit. Why don't you take some time away in the sun?'

I don't reply, but imagine me away sunning myself – on my own. I have never holidayed alone and I don't intend to start now.

'Maybe Emma would like to go?' He seems to read my mind.

She probably would, but the thought of Emma and I playing happily on a sandy beach, her frolicking in a white bikini, does not fill me with the lusty urge I expected it to.

'I'll be back on Monday.' I walk away, leaving him gnawing his lower lip.

I shouldn't be here. I knew it on the drive over. I know it passing her house and still know it when I turn the car around and do another drive-by. It's something I habitually do a couple of times a year but this – this breaks the mould. This is screwed up . . . I have no clue why I'm here now, other than the fact that I feel so alone that I need to glance at their lives; catch a glimpse; maybe even stop the car and knock on her door and ask Kiera Granger why the fuck her brothers have sent me to Coventry.

Her home, in one of Hampstead's narrower roads, nestles between the heath and the High Street. I'm parked a few car-lengths away from the large, double-fronted mews. It's the kind of house that few of us who work for a living could ever afford; the kind of house that comes from trust-fund money. It sits in a small but manicured garden, two tapered bay trees flanking the glossy doorway.

Feeding on the nerves jangling through my body, I close my eyes and imagine myself walking up the slim flagstones leading to the front door. In my mind, I lift the chrome door-knocker and sound it twice. From memory, it's large and shaped like a unicorn's head – sourced, I think I remember her saying, from some antique shop in a nearby cobbled lane. I imagine hearing heels making a clacking sound on what I know to be black-and-white, chequered Victorian tiles. I imagine her opening the door. The years will have been kind to her. Apart from just a few faint lines on the edges of her deep-set blue eyes, she would look the same: straight black hair pinned back in a tight bun framing her face; still beautiful. She's ushering me into a house filled with the sound of childhood laughter. This home is nothing like the one Ben and I came from, but it does look like the one Beth and I created for Meg.

Beth . . . Meg . . . My eyes blink open. From the safety of my driver's seat, I lean forward, my head on the steering wheel, both of my hands on my thighs. I scrape the earlier milk stain on my jeans with my thumbnail. Opening the window a fraction, I lean towards the outside air, feel it nourish my hungry lungs.

With a final glance, I drive past the house, promising myself I won't do this again. Instead, I call Tim Granger for the hundredth time. I'm determined, if he picks up, to find out why, after a particularly vicious run in the markets, they felt the need to blame me. Turning the car down Heath Street, I realize after the fourth ring that he's not going to answer. I hang up, prepare myself to stew in the car in dense London traffic, dwelling on my fragmented life. Neither of the Granger brothers will speak to me; my business partner is humouring me; my wife tolerates me, and my lover seems to want only to sit astride my dick, morning to night – which was fine at first but, at this point, I crave conversation more. I call Meg.

'Dad,' she says.

'How're you fixed at the moment? Fancy a few days away in the sun, all expenses paid?'

'Dad, I've got exams?'

'Oh, I—'

'Of course, I thought you knew that. That you'd care.'

The next sound I hear is a click. I imagine her tossing the phone across the room and I'm suddenly afraid. I seem to be capable of nothing except upsetting people at the moment. The thought of an afternoon sagging under the weight of my own inadequacies makes me bring the car to a stop, do a U-turn and head northeast towards a cemetery in Highgate. I'll go and see the only people in the world who can't judge me.

My parents are buried together, side by side in death as they were in life. Almost oblivious to Ben and me, I always thought they should never really have had children. Nearing their plot, I'm aware of the silence. Not a sound, apart from the distant hum of traffic beyond the cemetery's boundary. It's early afternoon. Most people are in work so, apart from a few scattered staff, hunched over, clearing brittle leaves from under the shedding trees, I'm alone. The low winter sun has ducked behind gathering cloud, instantly chilling the afternoon.

Automatically, I hunker down and tend to the pots, pulling out a plastic bag that I had tucked behind one of them the last time I was here. I lay it out on the damp grass and kneel on it, tug at a few tiny weeds. From the right, my mother's voice seems to carry on the wind, filling the quiet. I can hear her telling us how much she loved Ben and me; I hear her ask why I've never told Beth the truth.

My hands move quickly and soon I've got a small pile of browning plant detritus. My knees squelch through the plastic bag; the latest rainfall, still sitting on top of the mounded earth, trickles over one side of it. I watch as the soiled water seeps through the denim around my knees. Beth would be able to get those stains out, the milk one too. Clothes stains, life stains, Beth always knows what to do.

Again, I hear them questioning me, asking me why, if she always knows what to do, why not trust her way back then? I shudder under my overcoat. It's like they've never left. I feel as I used to, like a chastised child, never able to do the right thing. I smile at the irony – my far-from-perfect dead parents, pointing out *my* lies.

Standing up, I gather the bits into the plastic bag. So much for not being judged. My legs, unwilling to hold my weight, head for a bench close by. Beneath a looming oak, it sits weathered and worn and seems to groan as I slump onto its middle.

I want to flail at the memory of her voice, to lash out at thin air, to have those few staff stand upright to look at the poor sod waving his arms like Don Quixote. I want to yell that she talked utter crap. They never loved me. If they did, they would never have left me. Not like they did. Not like that.

And, as for not telling Beth the truth . . . Why would I have risked telling this beautiful woman – this person who had turned up in my life with her fun and her laugh and her songs and her words . . . She helped me to forget. What words would I have used then, or since, when I still can't say it out loud?

It's starting to rain as I leave the cemetery. After getting rid of the rubbish, I increase my pace towards the shelter of the car. With my back to their burial ground, my mother's standard phrase when she was disappointed in me rings in my ears: '*I hope you're proud of yourself, Adam.*' I laugh out loud. 'No, I'm not, Mum. What about you? You proud of *yourself*?'

It is ten past ten at night. Julie Etchingham has just been confirming from the television that the human race is still killing one another – from the Gaza Strip to a tragic gun-crazed maniac in a school in Dallas. I'm lying prostrate on the sofa, drained by the day and the relentlessly bad news in the world. When my phone trills beside me, the only reason I look at it is in the hope that it might be Tim Granger returning one of my calls.

I jolt upright at the name on the screen. Shit . . . My right palm flattens against my mouth. Was I seen? *Do not answer*. I should pick up. *And she could help. She's a Granger, after all* . . . I slide the answer icon across the screen. 'Kiera,' I say, 'good to hear from you.'

Her voice has the same timbre it always had – a smooth, soothing sound. Her words, however, are not the words I'd expected to hear. Seeing her name flash on the phone, I thought she might tell me she'd spotted my drive-by, ask me what the hell I thought I was doing. Instead, I hear other words, scary words, and my heart beats so wildly it seems to finally give up and clamp itself to my ribcage. My response, after I've listened and before I hang up, is a sloshing jumble of fused phrases where I hope I say the right thing.

As soon as I cut the connection, I rush to the bathroom and throw up. My cheek rests on the ceramic bowl. I wipe my mouth with the back of my hand. Jesus H. Christ . . .

Chapter Thirteen

I've been dreaming about Simon. We're playing in a tree house and he falls out. When I climb down to the bottom, he's dead, his curls damp on his forehead but, somehow, he's still smiling. Back in her office, I tell Caroline this and show her a couple of the photographs I've found at home. There's one of the four of us on holiday, Mum and Dad towering behind Simon and me. I have my arm around him – a protective, proud arm. Touching this sepia image, I can smell the seaweed, I can hear the gulls squawking; taste the whipped ice cream that drips from a cone in his hand.

'There are loads like that.' My shoulders twitch. 'And a lot less like this.' I hand her one of the few that I've found of our family taken after his death. It shows the three of us, and a big empty space where Simon used to be.

'They just stopped taking photographs.' I take it back and put them both in my bag. Caroline, I can tell, is going to make me fill the empty pauses today. I swallow half a glass of water in front of me. 'She turned up out of the blue the other night. Mum. Meg had told her about Adam leaving.'

'Oh . . . '

'Yes, "Oh . . . ", She was great, actually. Arrived with her manicure kit, made me feel like pink nails was all I needed to make me better.'

'Your mother probably understands loss,' Caroline responds.

'She does . . . and she did help me come to the conclusion that my marriage is possibly over.'

Caroline doesn't move – not even a flicker of an eye.

'See,' I lean forward and hunch over my knees, 'I think I've decided it's over. I think I want to live without him and I think I can move on. But can I really? Or am I still just pissed off at him, wanting to make him suffer, maybe giving him time to miss me and beg me to take him back . . . ' I take a break to breathe. I rub the centre of my left palm with my right thumb. 'I do know that this anger's not healthy. If I don't move on, ideally forgive him and move on, it'll eat me up and spit me out.'

My therapist is nodding, a vigorous nod, as though she's pleased at my light-bulb moment. Encouraged, I remove a notebook from my bag. 'I've made a list of some goals like you asked me to.'

Caroline's face breaks into a wide smile. Teacher is thrilled with me today and I find myself smiling too, a rare event in this office. 'Okay, number one is to go to Los Angeles.' I meet her eyes. 'Josh, my agent, is always trying to get me to go. He says I need to actually meet the publishers already interested in my work. Number two. I need to get a local job – just part time.' I hesitate a moment, then look up from my notebook. 'Adam's playing ball now – moneywise – but, honestly, I don't know how long that will last. My royalties are very erratic and I need to earn more regular money, which brings me to number three . . . ' I close the notebook. 'I'm going to get the house valued. I truly love my home and won't give it up without a fight but, that said, I need to know the facts of life. You know, what I'd be left with if the shit really hit the fan.'

I shove the book back in the bag, my fingers grazing the photos. 'I've just thought of a number four.' I remove and wave the holiday one at her. 'I'm going to frame this and hang it up at home, with all my other family shots. I've only got one shot of Simon there. We need more.' I chew my cheek. 'And I'm going to find the hammer and nails and hang it myself.'

'I'd give you three gold stars if you were a toddler,' Caroline smiles.

'Only three?'

'That's the max available. One hundred per cent . . . '

'Okay then.' I grin. 'That'll do. Three gold stars, eh? Babushka *will* be pleased.'

I've just found an old letter from Adam. It's handwritten, dated early 2004. That was during the bad times – well, the last bad times, when Adam dropped his pants for one night with another woman. I was devastated, but never asked him to leave. It had been once only and I had a daughter who loved him nearly as much as I did. The last line of the letter, in his spidery handwriting, seems to have a voice of its own as I read it – 'Thank you, my darling

Beth, for loving me enough to fight for me.' I feel those words today like a punch in the gut.

I did. I really loved him enough. Content in the knowledge that it had been one minor lapse in all our years together, I ignored the whispering doubts in my head. I never asked any questions, believing naively that what we had was bigger and worth fighting for. Now, almost a decade later, I have no fight left. If I did, I'm not sure who I'd be fighting. Emma? I barely know the woman's name . . . I fold the letter back on its crease and slip it into a drawer.

Part of me, though, can't help wondering as I contemplate the demise of my marriage, what would have happened if I hadn't told him to leave this time. Would his affair with Emma have fizzled out? Curious, I open up Google and search the restaurant where I know she works, though not, according to my best friend Karen, as a waitress. I'd tried Facebook ages ago to find out what she looked like, but it told me I had to be her friend. The chances of that happening were as likely as snowballs in hell. But now, thanks to Karen's Intel . . . I open the 'About Us' tab on the Pear Tree restaurant. It reveals the two partners, Abe Colvin and Emma Shine.

'Shine?' I say aloud. 'Her surname's "Shine"?' I stare at her photo. She's pretty, but then, I knew she would be. She's blonde, but so much so I doubt it's real. She looks happy, her arm linked through Abe's. I close the laptop, pondering the nagging question of fighting to save our marriage, and feel a new sadness seep into my very being. Yes, I've probably decided not to fight for him any more, but why the hell is he not fighting for me? The harsh truth is that – with or without Ms Shine in his life – Adam simply doesn't love me enough.

Karen and I are chopping vegetables. It's Friday night and she's come down from London for a sleepover. She's brought champagne and matching Humpty Dumpty pyjamas. After insisting I put them on there and then in the middle of the kitchen, she told me that those king's horses and king's men were crap – and that she will help put me together again.

She now has 'I Will Survive' playing from a specially created playlist of tracks on her iPhone. It's sitting in Adam's docking station next to the kettle and, in between chopping red peppers, Karen is doing some weird dance that seems to have a lot of slamming door action in it. I'm laughing out loud for the first time in ages and it feels so good. I put the knife down and join in her moves until Gloria Gaynor has exhausted herself and us. I hug Karen, tell her I love her. She holds me tight and whispers: 'You more . . . '

We are interrupted by the sudden sound of the front doorbell.

'We could just ignore it,' she says, turning the sound down on the iPhone, as if this alone will make whoever is at the door go away.

'It might be Sylvia.' I glance at the neon numbers on the oven. 'After nine, who else?'

'It's probably Adam.' Karen has made her way to the hall.

'Shit!' I reach across and turn the music up again. If Adam is at the door, we really should have Gloria on

109

repeat. I wait until she's in full flow, then signal to Karen to open the door.

'Shit!' I repeat louder at the sight of the figure in the doorway. The man, carrying a rucksack on his back, breaks into a wide grin and holds his arms out wide.

'Lizzie!' he cries. 'You're in! I was afraid I'd come all this way and you wouldn't be.'

I can't help it. Tears cascade down my face as I walk towards him and am engulfed by his huge hug. It's the unexpected sight of him – all six foot four of him. It's the familiar sound of his voice. It's the way he calls me 'Lizzie', when everyone else abbreviates my name to Beth. He smells musky, in a just-showered musky way. I pull back and stare up at his face. His skin has become tanned and his hair is naturally highlighted by a year spent in the sun. Reaching up, I tug on a lock. 'It's longer.' I sniffle. 'It suits you.'

'You okay?' He blinks at me, seeming a little confused by my apparent overreaction.

I nod, but I'm not sure. Gloria is waxing lyrical about all the strength she needed not to fall apart and, in my head, my inner saboteur Lucy Fir is telling me I'll never be okay again, that I just might fall apart, right here, right now.

Karen coughs, a tiny interrupting sound, letting me know she's there. 'God, sorry . . . ' I reach across for her elbow and pull her to me. 'Karen, remember Ben, Adam's brother?'

Ben takes her offered right hand and shakes it firmly.

Karen smiles. 'Good to meet you again, Ben. It's been years.'

'Too many.' He grins, and slides the rucksack onto the floor. 'I went to the flat first, thought I'd catch Adam, then cadge a lift back here with him to see everyone. Think I missed him, though, so I just threw the bags in, grabbed a shower, got the train and here I am. He not home yet?'

I don't reply and instead link arms with Ben, steering him past the hallway art as we walk into the kitchen. Karen walks ahead, turns the music back down again, then holds two bottles aloft. 'Red or white?'

'White,' I say, 'a large glass.'

'Or beer?' Karen frowns. 'I'm sure you have beer some-where, Beth?'

I know she's talking deliberately, nervously filling in the speaking space before we have to state the obvious.

'Wine's fine.' Ben glances around downstairs. 'I'll have white too. I tried calling Adam, but his phone just goes straight to voicemail.'

He takes a seat at the breakfast bar and smiles as Karen hands him a glass. 'Have I interrupted a girls' night?' He nods to our matching pyjamas.

'No,' I say. 'Well, yes, but it doesn't matter. It's good to see you, really.'

'Ahh,' he takes a sip. 'Sorry for intruding, ladies. Tell you what, just tell me which bar he's in and I'll join him. Surprise him . . . Out with your boyfriend, is he?' Ben is looking at Karen, really looking at Karen, eyeball-to-eyeball looking at Karen. She tucks a stray piece of hair behind her ear and smiles. It is far too shy a smile for Karen, and I notice a tiny flush of red seep into her cheeks. 'No, not my boyfriend, no—' Her voice is unusually coy.

'Karen's single.' I interrupt their moment. 'Adam's not out with her boyfriend, but I guess . . . ' I take a large gulp of wine. 'I guess he could be out with his girlfriend.'

Ben's face seems to freeze-frame and turn towards me in slow motion. 'He . . . what?'

'I'll start the spag bol,' Karen mutters. She turns the gas on, pours some oil in the pan and throws the already chopped onions and peppers in. She turns them slowly with a wooden spoon. We are silent but for the dulcet tones of Adele. Tears threaten again so I glare at Karen for such an apt playlist.

I take the breakfast stool next to Ben's. Adele's lyrics tell an ex how she will never let him get close enough to hurt her again.

'What's going on, Lizzie?' His eyes look down into his glass, afraid to meet mine.

'He's gone. Her name's Emma. Emma Shine, actually. She part-owns a restaurant in town. She's blonde, pretty, young . . . well, younger than me. Meg tells me she has a son. So, yes . . . Adam's gone. Vamoosed. Left. In love with Emma. Left me, yes, no more Adam and Beth . . . '

Ben is chewing his cheek as he listens. He reaches across and pinches a slice of red pepper from Karen's pile of vegetables, nibbles on it instead. 'Do you think that spag bol will stretch to three people?' His eyes, carefully avoiding mine, meet Karen's.

'Sure,' she says.

Then he turns to me and takes my hand in his. 'Adam . . . That explains the tears,' he says and that's it, I'm off again. He puts an arm around my shoulders and rests his forehead on me. 'Idiot,' he murmurs, and Karen and I both nod.

'Yes, but you know, I'm okay. Really,' I squeeze his hand. 'It's taken months. It's taken therapy.' I give a snotty giggle. 'But I'm there. I think I can finally move on.'

'Months?' Ben's face wrinkles in horror. 'Christ, how long ago did this happen? How long? Move on? Beth . . . I—'

'More wine?' Karen reaches across and tops his glass up without waiting for a reply.

'Is it that serious? I mean . . . '

I smile through my distress. 'I don't care any more, Ben. That's the saddest thing. I really don't care if it's serious, if she's the love of his life or just another of his stupid mistakes. I've had to look after me, and now I'm ready to live without him.'

Ben is quiet. I notice a tiny tear form in his left eye. I reach across with my thumb to smudge it away.

'But you're his glue, Lizzie . . . Even though he's always been too stupid to know that. You're his glue. You're his missing part and he was lucky to find you. You're his glue,' he repeats, shaking his head.

'Not any more . . . '

'Idiot.' Ben seems unable to hide the disgust in his voice.

'Totally,' Karen agrees. 'I hope you like it cheesy.' She addresses my brother-in-law, who is now slumped across the breakfast bar, before she tosses several spoons of Parmesan into the pan. '"Shine", by the way?' She makes a face as she stirs the mixture vigorously. 'Stupid name . . . And she has a son? I didn't know that.'

'Apparently so . . . Okay, enough about her. You'll stay the night?' I give Ben's hand another squeeze. 'There's lots of room.'

Ben nods. 'Yes please. I can't go home. If he's there, I'll kill him.'

We don't speak for a moment, until the music changes

113

and, yet again, I glance at Karen. The Hollies – 'He Ain't Heavy'. I know she chose this song since I'd shared with her recently how I've been feeling about Simon, but somehow, right now, it takes on another meaning.

'Stupid song . . . ' Both Ben and Karen speak in total synchronicity, then immediately giggle at each other.

I look from one to the other, notice the sparks of physical attraction as if they were visible fireflies, and I fill my glass, swallowing the lump in my throat. Feeling a pang of loneliness, I wonder briefly where Adam is, who he's with, what he's doing, and if Ben is right. If I really am the glue, will he fall apart without me?

Chapter Fourteen

Lately, I feel as though I'm falling apart, as if somehow I've become detached from whatever used to anchor me. Today, I'm sure of it. I've become a floating thing – floating around the life I used to lead. I want to reach out, grab something to tether me, but I can't. On my way to Clapham, I'm trying not to dwell on Kiera's news – the most likely reason for my separation from life as I knew it.

Meg is still pissed off, despite another grovelling apology. It was only when I begged her to forgive me, told her how sorry I am for forgetting she's got exams looming, reminded her she still needs to eat and said 'hashtagyesdadisanass holebuthe'sasorryasshole' that she laughed and finally relented to have supper with me.

We've come next door but two from her flat. She has given me sixty minutes of her time and I'm hoping Pizza Express is up to the challenge. We order quickly. I apologize again and she glares at me with my own eyes.

'For – what – exact – ly?' Her staccato words jab the air.

'Everything. I'm an idiot.'

'You can never put toothpaste back in the tube.' She removes her phone from her bag, stares at the screen and begins to thumb a message.

My own particular brand of toothpaste has caused one big fat mess that's about to get messier. 'I needed to see you.'

'Well, your needs are all-important.' She stops texting and looks up.

'There are things you couldn't possibly understand.'

'Oh, puh-lease. Don't be so patronizing. I don't need to understand any more than I do. You cheated on Mum. She told you she wouldn't forgive your repeat performance. You left her. What bit am I missing?'

I grab her hand across the table and, though she tries to pull away, I refuse to let it go. 'Listen, Meg. I screwed up. If I could turn back time—'

'Dad,' she yanks her hand from mine. 'Have you any clue what you've done to me? Do you realize what having a parent who thinks of you last does to you?'

Yes, my darling Meg, yes I do . . . My eyes blink rapidly. I lick my lips before speaking. 'I've let you down. Believe it or not, it's the one thing I hate doing, letting people down. Most of the time, Meg, I got it right with you. Right up until this, this thing, I think I got it right with you.'

She looks off to her left, sniffs rhythmically and rolls her tongue over her top lip. Her head in her phone, we don't speak.

As we share a pizza, I'm first to break the silence. 'Things are awful, Meg, and they may get worse before they get better. I wanted to see you tonight to say one thing. I love you. I love you with all my heart.'

116

She chews, stares at me. 'Things may get worse? Are you div-orc-ing Mum?'

I shake my head. 'No, no, I don't mean . . . Of course not . . . Look, I just mean I know you have a hard time forgiving me. That's all.' My phone pings a text. It's Kiera. Not a good moment, but I motion to Meg that I need to read it. She shrugs.

The text is neither good nor bad news, just a status update. Meg is watching me and, as her face breaks into a smile, I wonder if this might, in fact, be the right time.

'You're like a magpie, Dad, attracted by anything that's shiny and new for all of five minutes. I love you too, but right now it's hard to remember the best of you.'

I nod. Grateful for the small lifeline. I wonder if it will be enough to secure me. I want to ask her here and now to rein me in, hold me tight and never let me go. No sooner does the thought cross my mind that I remind myself that this is not my daughter's job. It's my job to reassure her, to hold her, to make her feel safe. So, no, this is not the right time.

'I have nightmares,' she says, 'dreams of you and Mum never speaking, and I'm stuck in the middle, loving you both. I wake up and want to phone you and scream that you just have to get back together, even if it's just for me, for my sake.'

I close my eyes.

'Then I think what I'd do if I were Mum. Would I forgive you, even for my daughter's sake?'

I have a bitter taste in my mouth, like metal, and I realize I've bitten my cheek.

'But she's done that already, hasn't she, that last time?' Meg goes on.

It's a question that doesn't need an answer.

'Then I think: what should you be doing? What are you doing to at least try and persuade her that you want her back? You do want her back, don't you?'

I can't speak so I just nod.

'You say that, but you do nothing. Nothing at all – I don't get that?'

It appears she's on a roll.

'And in the middle of all of this confusion, I've met a guy. He's a nice guy, yet I'm holding back. I tell him it's because of my exams, but the truth is I'm not sure I can trust him. I grew up watching you and Mum love each other. And, since that was a lie, I don't think I'll ever trust again.' Meg pushes her plate away, food practically untouched.

'Your mum and I were never a lie.' My voice is louder than I intend and a couple next to us turn to stare. 'I loved her, love her still . . . '

She hesitates, then nods softly.

'Don't be afraid to love someone, Meg. Don't lose that because of me?' I see her check her watch and I wave for the bill.

Still sitting, she wraps her coat around her. 'Maybe you should just try harder, Dad. Try to fight for her.'

My daughter's face is suddenly filled with hope, a Disney-like hope for a happy ending, like in all the childhood films we watched together. All the saccharine finales that have nothing to do with real life – nothing to do with Beth and me and all the messy toothpaste that won't ever go back in the tube.

'Your nana thinks the same,' I say. 'She left a message on my phone earlier.'

Meg grins for the first time tonight. 'Can I hear it? Did she shout at you?'

'No, it's typical of Sybil. Says what it needs to say.' I find it on my phone, press play and pass it to Meg.

'Adam, this is Sybil. My, my, you've been stupid, haven't you? That said, the time has come for forgiveness, and I can forgive you if Beth can. You need to work harder on that. Fight for my daughter. You know she's worth it.'

Meg chuckles. 'Only Nana . . . Straight to the point.'

The walk back to her flat is forty-five steps. Meg links her arm through mine and I have less than a minute to say something that can make a difference without murdering her hopes. 'I'm not sure she can actually forgive me, Meg.'

She turns to me. 'And I'm quite sure that you haven't even tried. Both Nana and I think you need to fight. C'mon, Dad! A grand gesture or two. Just do something to get her talking.'

'I'll try,' I hear myself telling Meg. And I'm still amazed how lies can breed lies. Even as she's hugging me goodbye, the contact I've yearned for, the shades of forgiveness already forming in her eyes, I can feel myself let go. When she pulls from the embrace, I slip away, feel the tenuous lifeline she'd offered slide from my grip. And I'm floating again. Untethered. Insecure. Isolated . . .

As I unlock the car, a siren sounds in the next street – someone else is in trouble. I balance myself against a lamp-post, remove my buzzing phone from my pocket. A text from Emma, wanting to know where I am, if I'm coming around.

'Not tonite' is my reply.

*   *   *

I am aware of a cold feeling. 'What the—?' I leap upwards in the bed.

'Morning, sunshine.'

Rubbing my damp face, I blink a few times, unable to believe that my brother Ben is standing above me, with what seems like an empty glass of water in his hand.

'Ben?' My brain registers him being there, but that's impossible – he's not due back for another fortnight.

'You total bloody idiot,' he says. His tone is angry and I know then that he's really here and that he's been to Weybridge. I slump backwards, pulling one of the pillows over my head.

'A prize idiot . . . '

I hear his muted voice and beg it to be gone. Pray for it to be a bad dream. Pray for it all to be one bad dream that I can learn from and wake up being a better man. I hear him move to the kitchen, clatter about with the kettle, and I toss the pillow to the floor.

He puts his head around the door. 'Did you hear what I said?'

'I'm glad you're back. I've missed you.'

'You're an idiot, Adam. Beth is what holds you together and what do you do? Screw it up large.'

I use the second pillow to drown him out again. 'I missed you.' I shout again through the cotton, his words reverberating in my head. Beth is what holds me together. And Beth will never forgive me. Kiera skips through my brain. 'Beth will never forgive me Noah.' I realize I must have been speaking aloud when Ben lifts the corner of the pillow upwards, stares at me and says:

'Who the hell is Noah?'

Chapter Fifteen

'Why the urgency, Beth, are you okay?'

'Thanks for squeezing me in. I know I only saw you a few days ago, but something's changed and I needed to let you know. For the next few minutes, I watch Caroline's facial expressions turn from intrigue to something like pride as I explain I've decided – enough with the therapy, the introspection – it's time to move on with life. We chat for just a few minutes and, as I'm about to leave, I tell her I'm having the house valued today. 'Someone called Giles.' I laugh and she makes a face that tells me that she, like me, knows exactly what to expect from an estate agent called Giles. 'I didn't catch his surname but it will be double barrelled and he'll have a pinkie on his little finger.'

She smiles, indulging me for the few moments we have left.

'Do you remember I named my inner saboteur Lucy Fir?'

'Indeed I do.' Caroline laughs out loud – the Lucifer connection had always amused her.

'Anyway, she's been busy this morning. I was clearing out my "fat wardrobe", putting all my old, bigger clothes into charity bags, and she was whispering in my ear telling me to wait a while, that I'd probably grow into them again.'

'What did you do?'

'They're downstairs in the boot, tied tighter than her gag.'

Caroline laughs again and I realize it's a sound I've not really heard before. I'm making my therapist laugh – perhaps it really is time to move on.

'You know, I'm not claiming it doesn't hurt any more, but I used to walk around with a tight knot lodged in my chest and it's gone. Adam and me, it doesn't take up every moment of my day any more.'

'Time . . . ' She shrugs. 'It can heal the most determined, deep feelings.'

'I like my life. I loved my life with Adam but I've got to learn to love it without him. I know I can. It's what I want going forward.' I offer her my right hand.

Her grasp is warm and sincere. 'My door is always open,' she smiles.

Meg is angry with me – furious, actually – for two reasons. Firstly, I've asked for her help in creating a CV and her response was that she'd have to make it all up, because I am a songwriter looking for a real job. I laughed and told her that this is the real world and that I'm going to have to find a *real job*, because her *errant* father may not continue being as compliant as he has been. Bad move. Bad Mummy . . .

The second reason is because I told her that I'm having

the house .valued. When I responded to her angry tirade with, 'I refer you to the answer I gave earlier,' she stormed off in her car and I haven't seen her since. It's probably just as well as, any moment now, Giles, the estate agent, will be on the doorstep.

When I hear the sound of the bell, I am shocked to see Karen. She left here this morning with Ben, telling me she'd drop him off at a Tube station en route.

'Yeah, I know,' she says. 'I got home and then realized that maybe I should have stayed the weekend. So I thought I'd surprise you. Anyway, I'm back. Three tickets for the Odeon, eight o'clock showing of the latest Morgan Freeman movie. You, me, Meg.' She waves three stubs at me, tells me if we're quick we can get a pizza in, that she has vouchers for that too. Behind her, I see a man in a pinstripe suit walk up the drive.

Moving her gently to one side with my left arm, I hold out my right one, extending my hand. 'Giles?'

'Mrs Hall? Good to meet you. Yes, I'm Giles. What a lovely property.'

'Thank you, do come in.' From the corner of my eye, I can see Karen, tickets in her hand, an expression of pure horror on her gaping face. 'Close your mouth, Karen,' I whisper behind Giles's back.

'You're selling the house?' she hisses.

I push her towards the kitchen, aware that Giles has stopped to read my artwork in the hall. 'Yes, about that,' I call back to him, 'I can explain.' I park Karen on a breakfast stool, glare at her to be silent, then rush back to the hall. 'I didn't have time to fix it, I'm afraid. I mean, when I rang and you said you could come around today,

I . . . I mean, obviously I'll paint over it, but just while you're here, valuing, I mean, I thought it's fine.'

Giles is nodding. He's very good-looking, I note, in an older, distinguished-looking man kind of way. Tightly cut, caramel-coloured hair that gives him an ex-army look. I imagine he's mid-forties and, for some inexplicable reason, my eyes dart towards his wedding hand. No ring. Good. No tan lines from a ring. Good.

He catches me looking. 'I love Ikea meatballs and I hate horseradish too. It's great.' He nods towards my wall art. 'I'd leave it.'

In that moment, I decide I'm a little bit in love with Giles.

I can hear Karen putting the kettle on in the kitchen. 'Would you like a tea or a coffee?' I ask.

'No, I won't thanks. I'm sure you guys are busy, so we'll just get on. Do you mind showing me around?'

'No problem, let's start at the top in the loft.'

Giles follows me and I find myself wishing I was wearing something other than my standard 'writing' uniform of jeans and a T-shirt. He glances back at Karen in the kitchen. 'Great movie by the way, I saw it on Monday. Really good thriller, you'll love it.' Karen, despite herself, is immediately charmed and smiles back.

I have been cleaning like a dervish all morning, so am really pissed off at the state of Meg's room when we're there. 'I'm sorry. My daughter's nineteen. She's just arrived back from uni for a few days.' I look at the clothes strewn across the bed and the floor. She probably did it deliberately. I'm surprised she didn't smear Nutella on the wall of her bathroom.

'Please.' Giles doesn't even look up from his clipboard. 'Don't apologize. I've got two teenage daughters, who seem to have inherited some mutant gene that means they can't keep anywhere tidy.'

Married then . . .

'They're only with me weekends, and in three days they manage to make my place look like the storeroom in a charity shop.'

Separated . . . 'How old are they?' I ask.

'Sixteen – twins, Amélie and Brigitte. Their mother's French,' he tells me.

I nod as we navigate our way to my room, what was Adam and my bedroom. 'This is the master,' I tell Giles. I want to tell Giles that this is my bedroom. Mine alone. That I don't share it with anyone. Hey, look, Giles – I'm single! I want to tell him that months of therapy are willing me to say this out loud. I want to ask him if he cheated on his wife, if that's why they're not together any more. I want to ask him if he's a kind man, if he's worth investing a bit of time in, because for the first time in over twenty years, I'm looking at another man. I want to say all these things, but I have a clear vision of him going back to his office talking about the psycho in Laurel Avenue, so I smile sweetly and say nothing.

Back in the kitchen, Giles has his electronic measuring thing held against the wall at the far end of the open-plan room. Karen catches my eye, cocks her head in his direction and licks her lips suggestively.

'You're dis-gust-ing.' I mouth the words to her.

She nods, grins widely, then licks her lips again. I pass her on my way to meet Giles and give her a thump.

'So, all done?'

'Yes.' He holds out his hand again, shakes mine firmly. 'It's a fabulous house, one we'd have no problem selling if you decide to put it on the market. Let me go back to the office and chat with some colleagues for the best valuation. There's one around the corner on—'

Giles's pitch is interrupted by a yelling sound in the hall. Both of us move back a couple of steps and stare at the letterbox.

'Muuuuum. I'm sorrreeeeee. Open up, I forgot my house key. I'll even help you with your CV. I'm sorreeeee. I know you need to get a job and I know it's 'cause Dad's a dickwit.'

I gulp loudly. I can feel a flush – that I suspect is purple rather than a delicate shade of red – crawl along my chest, up my neck and plant itself firmly on my cheeks.

Giles gives an understanding smile. 'Teenagers,' he whispers.

Meg, however, has not finished. 'Is that Karen's car? I thought she'd left? Whatevs. She can help. Between the three of us, we'll have you employed in a week. Please don't sell the house, Mum. You can have one of my kidneys?'

I rush to the front door, open it quickly and pull her kneeling figure upright.

'Mum!' She puts her arms around me and hugs me tight.

'Meg.' I wrestle away from her. 'This is Giles, the estate agent valuing the house.'

Giles nods in her direction and now it's Meg's turn to colour brightly, a shade she has definitely inherited from me. I can hear Karen in the kitchen and am not sure if she's laughing or crying.

Meg jerks her head towards Giles and edges her way towards Karen's sounds.

At the doorway, he hands me his business card. 'I'll call you tomorrow morning with an exact valuation. A price and marketing plan, should you decide to instruct us.' Giles bites his lower lip. 'Er, I should just let you know that if the house is in two names, we would need both permissions before actively marketing it.'

'That won't be a problem. If we sell the house, it will be because my ex and I both agree to sell it.' I can't believe I've called Adam 'my ex'. 'Well, he's not officially my ex yet, but he will be.' I hear myself stumble over my impossibly stupid explanation.

'It's a tough time.' Giles seems to stare out over my hedges in the front garden. 'Anyway, I must get back. I'll call you in the morning but, in the meantime, if you have any questions, the mobile and email are on the card.'

I watch Giles walk down the garden, past Karen's, mine and Meg's cars. Looking down, I see his surname is not double barrelled, but 'Brousseau', a French name. Hmmm, an Englishman with a possible French father, married to a Frenchwoman?

'Oh, by the way.' He has turned back. 'Email me that CV when you have it done. We have a vacancy for a part-time receptionist. I'm not sure what you're after, but your daughter should probably keep both kidneys?' Both his eyebrows move north and he smiles broadly.

I laugh. 'I will. Thank you.' And then, he's gone.

Chapter Sixteen

'What in hell have you been up to?' Ben's voice seems to echo in the flat. We're in the kitchen and I spot his travel holdalls stacked in the corner, realising he must have dropped them off last night before seeing Beth.

His level of concern for me is slightly worrying. His face, younger and much more handsome than mine, is creasing as he looks me up and down. His eyes, eyes that have had the luxury of being worry-free for the last year, seem uneasy, and his general demeanour is stressed, nervous.

'Why do *you* look so worried? You've just had a year off work, travelling the world.' I take a bite of the warm buttered toast he's handed me and stare back. It smells and tastes divine.

'Don't answer a question with a question.'

'It's difficult to know where to start . . . '

'I see.'

'No, you don't,' I conclude. 'You don't see. Beth has obviously got to you first, and now you think I'm an awful shit who tells lies all the time.'

'Do you tell lies all the time?'

I don't remember the brother who left last year being so persistent. I hesitate a moment. 'No,' I reply. 'Only when it's necessary and only ever to avoid hurting people I love.'

'And how's that working out for you?'

That trace of sarcasm in his voice, that air of judging superiority, makes me want to punch him. I want to pretend we're twelve and ten, shove him to the kitchen floor and knock his stupid lights out. 'Not all of us have had the luxury of chilling in some yoga retreat, with some chanting guru steering our path to perfection.' I chuck the remaining toast in his direction. He ducks and I retreat to the bedroom.

Moments later, he knocks on the door. Inside, I'm packing a bag. 'It's your bedroom!' I yell at him.

He opens the door and his large frame fills the doorway.

'There was very little chanting,' he says, his arms folded defensively, 'and I haven't yet managed to find the path to perfection.'

'Yeah, well, when you do, remember your big brother's had a different journey.'

Suddenly, he's beside me. He is taking the clothes I am throwing into the bag out again and then he holds me tight, a big bear hug. 'Stop,' he whispers. 'Let me be the strong one for a while. I owe you that . . . '

I crumple in his embrace, drop to the bed and cry – deep, heavy, wracking sobs. He doesn't say a word, doesn't leave my side. We sit like that, edged together like bookends, for what seems an age. Eventually, he looks at his wrist.

'C'mon, get dressed. We're going to the pub, you're going to tell me all about it and we're going to get sozzled.'

* * *

129

'How much did Beth tell you?' We're sitting in The Narrow, the closest pub to the flat, which sits at the mouth of the Thames at Limehouse Basin. It's a dull, dank day and the river, as always, is busy, with more traffic on it than the surrounding streets. Ben hasn't replied yet. He seems to be taking his time, watching life on the water go by. 'Ben?'

He shakes his head, as if to bring him back to the moment. 'She told me you'd left, that you have a girlfriend; that "you and she are no more".' He mimics quotation marks in the air with his fingers. 'That's it really; she was a bit sketchy on the detail. Most of the time I spent there was taking that much in, and making sure she was all right.'

'Is she? All right, I mean.'

'She seems to be. She had her friend Karen with her. I think I interrupted a Bridget Jones evening.'

My eyebrows rise.

'You haven't seen *Bridget Jones's Diary*?' He laughs. 'Suffice to say, they had heartbreak music on, they were both dressed in matching pyjamas, and there was spaghetti bolognese followed by chocolate ice cream.'

I find myself nodding, although I have no idea what he means. Beth is not one for matching pyjamas, and she's a 'crisps' girl – she doesn't really like ice cream, unless it's the Ben and Jerry's one with big chunks of caramel in it.

'What did you think of Karen? How long is it since you've seen her?'

Ben sighs. 'Ages, years . . . I don't think our paths crossed at all when I was with Elise.' He shakes his head, a tiny movement, as if to jerk himself from a sad memory. 'Wasn't she married? I seem to remember she was married?'

'She was once, ages ago. It only lasted a couple of years.' My shoulders rise and fall.

'She was married, I was practically married. I guess I never paid much attention but Christ, she's hot. I think I'm a little bit in love with her. Mind you, she's not a fan – of yours I mean. She really has it in for you.'

I swallow half of my pint as I digest what I already know. Karen hates me. This is bad enough, without Ben walking around with a hard-on for her.

'She is a looker,' I agree. 'But watch it. She'd eat you up and spit you out.'

'I look forward to it.' He smiles, raising his first pint of the day to his lips.

'I'm serious, Ben, there's—'

'Adam, we're here to talk about you,' he interrupts, holding a palm up. 'C'mon, let's start at the very beginning.'

I watch my brother, now observing the swell of the muddy Thames again – take in the contours of his face, more obvious after a year in the sun. His eyes seem bluer than they were, a few fret lines around their edges. His hair has been sun-bleached and needs a good cut. He's wearing canvas trousers with more pockets in them than even Bear Grylls would ever need. His T-shirt has a tiny hole at the collar and displays the washed-out logo of some Indian beer; I don't recognize the name of it. He has faded leather flip-flops on his feet and I wonder if his feet are cold. All of this he manages to carry off at forty-one. Rather than look like an ageing surfer dude, he wears the look of a relaxed man, approaching middle age and comfortable in his own skin. I realize that I envy him.

I follow his gaze to the river, full to the brim at high

tide, and wonder where to begin, where exactly is the beginning? Do I start almost a year ago, when he went overseas? That was a time when Beth and I were still making plans, still had a future together. Do I go back to the night I met Emma? That cab journey home? Or my night with Kiera?

'Do you ever think of Mum and Dad?' He interrupts my flow of suitable beginnings.

'Of course. I went to visit them a few days ago.'

'No, I meant, think of the time that . . . ' He doesn't finish the sentence.

'No.' My tone is abrupt. That is not the beginning that I had in mind, and I'm pretty sure I'm not willing to go there.

He doesn't pursue it, just nods. I wave at the waitress to bring me another pint, ignoring the clock on the wall telling me it's only half past eleven in the morning.

'A long time ago, I cheated on Beth for the first time,' is, I decide, my opener.

Ben's blue eyes are steady – he doesn't flinch; not even a flicker of an iris.

'I had a one-night stand.' I see it then, a barely notice-able raising of his left eyebrow. He already doesn't believe me. 'It was just one night,' I continue. 'She was a client.'

'Does Beth know?'

'Yes. I told her. It was a mistake, a stupid fuck-up on my part. But we sorted it, we put it behind us.' Something in the speaking aloud of these words doesn't ring true. I'm surprised that I can hear it and imagine Ben is hearing it with bells on.

'She forgave you?'

'She did,' I reply, 'but she never forgot. I don't think she ever completely trusted me again.'

'Well, she was right not to, wasn't she?'

I sigh. 'Nothing else happened until this year, nearly six months ago.' The waitress arrives with our pints.

'Let's order some food,' Ben says, leaning forward. 'Is it too late for a full English?' He smiles a winning smile at her.

She looks at the clock, then smiles back at him. 'I'll see what I can do.'

I'm unsure how it will go down with Guinness but hear myself say, 'Make that two.' I try my own captivating smile, but she's lost to my younger brother – the fledgling version of myself; the more youthful, honest, trustworthy edition. I sit back in the library-style chair. It is dull, slate grey, mottled leather, with a studded high back and two armrests. I'm holding my pint in my left hand, with my right arm resting on the right armrest. I notice that my skin is pale, veined and almost as mottled as the hide it rests on. I need a sun holiday. Switching my gaze from my arm to the other early drinkers, I try to ignore the full English breakfast flirtations in front of me.

'So, nearly six months ago,' Ben says when the waitress leaves. 'What happened?'

'I met Emma. We were on a works night out.' I shrug. 'What can I say? I fell for her feminine charms. I was flattered that a younger, gorgeous woman fancied me. And the sex is amazing.' I flash a conspiratorial smile at my brother, but he doesn't smile back.

'When did you leave Beth?' he asks.

'A few months after it started. She guessed – tackled me

about it. I couldn't lie. I knew she knew. And, as far as leaving her is concerned, let the record show that I did not willingly leave. She threw me out.'

He seems to ignore this. 'Why didn't you stop the affair, try and persuade Beth to take you back? She did it once before.'

I shake my head. 'She wouldn't even listen to me. There was no coming back from this.'

'Did you try?'

'What do you mean?' I put my drink on the coffee table. The conspiracy theorist in me thinks they've all been talking: Sybil, Meg and Ben.

'Did you try and persuade her? Tell her it was a mistake. Tell her you love her, fight for her?'

'No.' I crack my knuckles. 'I didn't. When she threw me out, I went straight to Emma's and had sex and that's what I've been doing ever since.' I know I sound like a petulant child, but I don't care.

'And how's that working out for you?'

'Not great,' I concede, determined not to rise to his prodding. 'I've made better decisions.'

We sit for a few minutes, silent. I'm trying to convince myself that he is in fact trying to help, but all I can hear is, 'How's that working out for you?' over and over again in my head. It's not, is what I want to tell him. I want to pick up the phone and plead with Beth to take me back, but I know she won't and I know she shouldn't. I'm probably a good man but – even I know – I'm a shit husband.

'Who's Noah?' Ben asks suddenly. 'You never said earlier.'

I swear I can see stars. Little silver speckles of light flicking across my eyeline. On the sparkly horizon, I see our waitress heading in our direction with what look like two lovely breakfasts on a large metallic tray. My stomach curdles, my appetite gone in an instant.

'Adam?' Ben's voice seems muted.

'He's my son,' I tell the riverboats, the captains, the passengers, the seagulls. Somehow, though, Ben hears, and when I turn back to him, his face has aged a decade. Now he looks just like me.

PART TWO

though those that are betray'd
Do feel the treason sharply, yet the traitor
Stands in worse case of woe . . .

William Shakespeare, *Cymbeline*

Chapter Seventeen

I have Ben to thank for the best line in the final version of *the* song, now entitled 'Fall Apart'. It's 'I love you, need you, you're my glue – I fall apart without you'. Josh Skyped me yesterday and literally did a dance of joy at LA's positive response. 'I can taste the Bolli,' he yelled. Me, I'm not so sure. I hope he's right and that it's just my own self-doubt creeping back in. Either way, we'll know soon enough.

This morning, I'm listening to the song over and over again, through my earphones on the walk to work. The High Street office is just over a mile from the house, and I figure if I walk there and back on the days I work, it will counteract the crisps I've eaten over the last few months. I sense, rather than hear, a car draw up beside me and pull the plugs from my ears.

'Want a lift?' Giles has wound down the electric window and is grinning out at me. I hesitate a moment, but my toes are freezing and it *is* a gloomy, slate-grey November morning. I climb into his car, shiver, suddenly grateful for the increase in temperature.

'Excited? Nervous?' he asks, after a couple of minutes. I haven't the heart to tell him I'm crapping myself and that I spent last night driving around Weybridge to make sure I knew the itinerary backwards.

'Are you sure about this, Giles?'

'You're well capable,' he says, looking left and right as he parks the car in his numbered space behind the office. 'Look, you're really helping us out. Stephanie is with us another two months before she goes on maternity leave, and she really doesn't like doing the physical show-overs now. She'll do the research of the rental market, set up the itineraries and take over from you on reception when you're out.'

I nod, determined to show willingness.

'Can I use my own car?' I ask the question that's been playing on my mind. 'Stephanie's is a manual. I don't do gearsticks.'

Giles shakes his head. 'Yours won't be covered for business use. Take this one.' He shrugs. 'I'm in a management meeting most of the afternoon, so don't need it.'

I look around his state-of-the-art Range Rover; chalk-coloured leather seats and a console that looks as though it belongs in an air-traffic-control room. An image of it wrapped around a lamppost pokes itself to the front of my brain.

'Oh no, no, no, no.'

'What? You don't do Range Rovers either?'

'I don't do tanks.'

Giles laughs. 'Here, take it out for a spin. It drives itself.' He hands me the key ring. 'Go on, just take it up the road and back – you'll see.'

Before I know it, he has left and gone in through the back door of the office. I look at the fob in my hand and take a very deep breath. Switching to the driver's seat, I adjust the controls for the legs, move the rear-view mirror and press the start button. Pointing the car out of the car park, I proceed slowly up the High Street, passing by Caroline's office at the end. I wonder how she's doing. Who is occupying her time right now? Is there someone in there now, sitting in the same chair that I sat in for months? Is it a he or a she? Are they struggling with the same problem I had? Do all therapists deal with constant broken marriages, like GPs have to see constant snotty noses?

I turn around the large roundabout and head back. Glancing back up at her window, I realize I needed Caroline then. Now, I need people in LA to *fall apart* when they hear my song. And I need to make this itinerary work this afternoon, so that the staff in J. T. Watkins all think I'm even more wonderful than I've been on reception and maybe offer me Stephanie's job when she goes on maternity leave. I look towards the heavens. One or both will do please, Mrs Universe.

Hours later, I'm relaying the success of my first 'tour' – with a real applicant looking for a real home – to Karen.

'Have I got enough food?' she interrupts me.

'Have you been listening to me?'

'Mrs Scott, weird name because she's Scottish, looking for a huge house to rent. You saw three on St George's Hill and one in Esher. All fantastic. She loves two of them. You drove Giles's tank and loved every minute.' She turns, gives me a pointed look.

'You have loads of food,' I tell her, taking in the array of pots containing chilli, vegetable curry, rice and goulash, all provided by her sister-in-law, Tess. There is also an assortment of tiny canapés, all provided by me via Marks and Spencer's. I pinch one from a stacked plate.

'Come back into the bedroom, your hair is falling down at the back.' I steer Karen past Maeve and Trisha, two of Meg's friends from university who are going to serve the food, and Jack, another friend, who will be on wine and beer duty. In her bedroom, I stand her in front of the full-length mirror, pin the stray bits of hair back into the chignon. 'You look stunning,' I tell her, placing my head on her shoulder and talking to her reflection. She is wearing a clinging red satin dress, one that is totally unforgiving, yet looks so good on her that I have flat-stomach envy. 'What time is Ben coming?'

She casts an anxious eye at her wrist. 'Ten minutes ago.'

'He's a Hall. They're always late.'

She turns around and pulls me to her. 'I'm sorry, you know.'

'What for?'

'For falling in love with him. I know that means awkward times, like tonight, when both you and Adam are here.'

I shrug, smooth my hands over my wraparound dress, rub my not-so-flat stomach. Even having lost a ton of weight, mine still requires enclosure in magic knickers. 'I'm all right seeing Adam, so don't you worry. Tonight is all about you, you forty-year-old, you.' I play-punch her shoulder, just as the doorbell chimes and she heads outside to greet her guests.

I wait in the bedroom, aware that sudden noise outside

means that a large group have arrived together. She deserves a fantastic party with her friends, so what I won't tell her is that I'm actually quite anxious about tonight. It is the first time that I will be in a social situation with Adam and Meg since the break-up. Karen did ask if I was all right with him coming and I knew I couldn't refuse her. If they stay together, he's Ben's brother and I'll have to get used to it. So, at best, tonight's going to be weird. At worst, it's going to be a car crash.

I brace myself for the evening ahead. I think back to that first time when Ben and Karen laid eyes on each other in my house, when I knew straight away that they would be an item. I just hadn't banked on them being such a serious item so quickly. 'You just know when you know,' is what Karen has said when I try to talk to her about it. Ben's as bad, quoting some similar crap to me, when I offered an opinion that they shouldn't be moving in together, after only knowing each other a few weeks. So, tomorrow, Ben is moving into her flat and, conveniently, Adam is staying on in his. And tonight I'm going to keep my trap shut, because I love her and I love Ben and I hope that they will be happy. It's just that I don't believe any more. I don't believe in the whole 'perfect fit' and 'glue' crap. I may have written a beautiful song about it, but it came from a latent, possibly dead part of me.

'What do you think of Jack?' Meg has had a few glasses of wine. I follow her glassy eyes in his direction and see it again. Fucking hell – am I the only one around here not falling in love?

'He seems nice,' I say. 'I haven't really had a chance to talk to him properly. Are you and he—?'

Suddenly, she's nodding furiously. 'I've been dying to tell you. I met him last term. He's a couple of years older than me, sooo bright and we just . . . ' She looks back at me, stops herself and bites her lip. 'Maybe he can come for dinner some Sunday?'

'That'd be great.' I nod less furiously, but lots of nods all the same. 'I'd like to meet him properly, you know, if you and he are . . . '

I can't quite bring myself to say 'having sex' or 'in a relationship' or 'fuck buddies', or any variation on that theme. Aware I haven't seen that look in her eye for a while, I feel a ping on my heartstrings and clench my teeth. Perhaps it's not that I don't believe any more, just that I miss being in love.

I chat to Brian, Karen's brother, and Tess, his wife.

'And what about you?' Brian asks. 'Still thumping that punchbag?'

'Oh, yes.'

'How are you really?'

It's a question I'm used to but still dread – one that invariably results in the use of the 'f' word.

'I'm fine,' I tell them. 'Enjoying the new job . . . the writing's going really well. All in all, things are good.' Though I know the words to be true, I find myself unable to look these people in the eye as I speak. Instead, my eyes are cast over their shoulders towards the front door. Minutes later, I'm vaguely aware of Brian talking about being involved in the new Battersea Power Station development, when Adam walks into the party.

I try and see behind him. He's alone. I let out an audible sigh of relief and immediately relax. Meg has headed in his direction, is taking his coat from him. She kisses him on his cheek and he smiles. He has always loved our girl; loves her fiercely, more than anyone and anything, I think. He looks around, sees me, raises his eyebrows and gives a tiny wave before Meg whisks him over to the drinks table. I watch them, see Adam and Jack shake hands, and feel for her. She has to tell us both about him – tell us separately. Yet again, I'm surprised by how sad this makes me feel. Maeve walks by with a tray of drinks, tells me the food is ready, to please help myself. I do – to two glasses of champagne – and excuse myself from Brian and Tess before heading to Karen's bedroom.

I'm quite happy, perched on a pile of coats, looking like the princess and the pea, when he comes to find me.

'What are you doing in here, in the dark?' he asks from the doorway.

'Nothing, just wanted some quiet time.'

'Can I join you?'

'Help yourself, if you can find the chair.' I nod towards another pile of coats sitting on Karen's bedside chair. He decides to climb on top of them, balancing himself awkwardly – it's as if he wants to be on the same level as me.

'How are you?' he opens with.

'I'm good.'

'How's the job working out?'

'I'm enjoying it.'

'So, Karen and Ben, eh? Who'd have thunk?'

I laugh. It was always one of our silly sayings. 'They

seem happy,' is all I can offer. I see the shadow of his head bob in agreement. 'You're alone?' I can't help myself.

'Yes.'

'No Emma?'

The room is black, but I can feel his eyes sear into me.

'We're not together any more, but I would never have brought Emma,' he says.

The door opens suddenly and a kissing couple hurl themselves into the wall. The kiss is long and hard. They are oblivious to the fact that we are there. Adam and I are still. Silent. The couple pull apart and she speaks.

'We'd better get back,' she says, and I feel myself blush in the shadows at Meg's voice.

The male voice groans. 'You have no idea what you're doing to me out there.'

Meg giggles. 'C'mon, let's go. My parents are both here for Chrissake . . . ' She pulls him from the room.

Adam's voice sounds pained. 'She means "here at the party", doesn't she?'

'She does,' I confirm. There's no way she knew we were in the room.

'That was awkward . . . '

'Yep.'

'Do you know him? Jack? She seems keen on him, talks about him a lot.'

Did he just say he'd split up from the bimbo whore? And how the fuck does he know about Jack when I've only heard about him tonight? Suddenly, the fact that Meg went back to her digs after a couple of days when she normally stays for the whole study break makes sense. I'd felt guilty, thinking that it was because the family, the house dynamic, had changed without her father. Now I know: it must have been to spend more time with a man her father knew about and I didn't. I'm unexpectedly miffed by this.

'Beth? Is she keen on him?'

'Yep.' I reply the only way I can.

'Are you only ever going to speak to me in short, snappy sentences? We used to be that couple, you know.'

'Until your lies killed us.' Yes, my statement is short and snappy, but it's honest. I hear him take a drink.

'Do you think there could ever be a time where we could be friends?'

I don't answer him. I can't. I want to believe that could be possible. I really do. There is a weighted silence before I say. 'Maybe.'

'Anytime soon?'

'Possibly.' I hear him climb down off the coats and approach the bed.

'I miss you,' he says. 'I miss everything about you, but most of all I miss being your friend. I miss you being my friend.'

I swallow hard. Thankfully, the sound is drowned out by raucous laughter from the living room. 'With Karen and Ben together, we'll have to meet more often than we other-wise would have. I know I'll have to see you with other people, but thank you for not doing it tonight.'

He coughs. 'I wouldn't do that.'

I climb down from my pile of coats, am standing right next to him. 'Therein lies the problem, Adam. I didn't know what you'd do. I didn't know you and Miss Shine had finished. I didn't know whether you'd bring her or not. I don't know what you think is appropriate or not, I don't know what makes a lie okay in your head when it's not okay in mine. You say you wouldn't do that, when the truth is you've done a lot worse.'

I can feel his sharp intake of breath next to me.

'Lots of long, un-snappy sentences . . . ' He sighs. 'I'll never stop being sorry for the fool that I've been.'

A tiny part of me feels for him. 'Yeah, well. I'm moving forward, doing something about it.' I walk towards the door. 'Maybe you should try that too?'

Outside, I turn down another glass of wine offered to me by Jack. I smile sweetly, banishing the thought of his tongue plundering my daughter's throat. I search the room for the birthday girl and catch her eye; she beckons me over to where she and Ben are dancing. On the slow walk through the crowd to Karen, I decide three things. *One,* I will try and like my daughter's boyfriend, who for some reason I seem to have taken an unreasonable, instant dislike to. *Two,* I will stay as long as I need to for Karen, but I'm driving home tonight. I look back towards the bedroom door from which Adam has emerged. He looks tired. Broken. *Three.* As Karen pulls me into a dancing hug, I decide that, someday, not anytime too soon, but someday, I will maybe try to be my husband's friend again. Maybe.

Chapter Eighteen

This place looks nothing like it did back when Kiera and I met here ten years ago. Gone are the faded velvet booths, in favour of leather lounging chairs. I shift about, unable to get comfortable in the low-slung seat. Sighing aloud, I lean forward and pick up my glass from the table. Hendrick's and tonic with cucumber peelings – I ordered two in the hope that her choice of drink hasn't changed. Glancing at my wrist, I see she's late.

I go through what I know already in my head. Noah is ill. My son has leukaemia. Acute Myeloid Leukaemia. He has just undergone a second, more aggressive course of chemotherapy. No, I can't meet him. Of course I can't meet him. Don't be stupid. This course of chemo needs to have worked. This course of chemo really needs to have worked, or his only option is a stem cell donation.

I have Googled it. I've spent hours on the laptop and not learnt a whole lot other than what Kiera originally told me on the phone. I've texted her questions and she's answered them as best she can, but I'm confused about what happens next. Or maybe I'm not. Maybe I do know. I do know. I know what happens next. This course of chemo really needs to work . . . My head shakes. It's an involuntary twitch, maybe my brain trying to wrestle the real facts from my skull.

I hear her arrive before I see her. She's hassled, her hair loose and tousled, not like I remember her wearing it. Her coat is undone, despite the cold outside. I tease her, pointing at my watch, but she's not in the mood for jokes as she air-kisses my cheeks.

'I got you a G&T,' I say. 'Hendrick's?'

She takes the glass, frowns at the fact that she has to squeeze in beside me on a sofa, and sips. 'And bree-a-the,' she says slowly.

'You all right?'

'Fine,' she says. 'Sorry I'm late.' She doesn't offer a reason why and I don't ask.

'Gordon know you're here?' I do ask.

'Yes, Adam, Gordon knows I'm here. I'm not the one who lies to their spouse.'

'Ouch.' I'd love to tell her I'm different now, that that's all in the past, but apparently it isn't. The remark surprises me though. It seems bitchy, not like her – but then, I remind myself, I don't really know this woman at all, and she has got a lot on her mind at the moment.

'I've been in hell since you called.' The words are out of my mouth before I can filter them.

She nods. 'I know, it's been a shock to us all.'

Her skin, I notice, is blotchy, probably tear-stained. 'You must be out of your mind with worry.' I whisper the words.

Her eyes fill immediately but she holds it in, reluctant to cry in front of me.

'How is he? Noah?' My hands are clenched together and I've squeezed them between the tops of my thighs.

She shakes her head. 'When we spoke, he was just about to start the second course of chemo. I know we've texted but . . . '

I nod.

'Well, it hasn't worked.' She looks at me, her eyes probing mine. 'There are certain things that shouldn't be said by text.' I know straight away what this means; she told me as much during her original phone call. My eyelids drop. My hands, released from my thighs, knead one another, my right-hand knuckles pressing hard into my left-hand palm.

'So he definitely needs a bone marrow donation?'

She nods. 'Well, stem cell donation, proper name: "peripheral blood stem cell donation". It's an easier proce-dure, just a series of hormone injections to the donor for four days before the extraction itself, and that's then just like giving blood.' Her shoulders move up and down, a gesture meant to reassure me that the donation is easy, something anyone could do.

'Is she the only way?' I will do anything it takes to help him, but I need to know. Now.

'We're all being tested now. I'm not a match, we're waiting on the boys' results . . . '

The boys; the brothers who – since Kiera told them recently who Noah's natural father is – decided to punish me by removing me from their family account. I have, apparently, a 'questionable moral compass'.

'Obviously, there's a chance that some random person on the register could be right, but . . . '

'I'll be tested, immediately.' I'm almost grabbing my coat and running out through the door.

'Adam,' she rests a hand on my knee, 'I'm sorry, but you know. You know we've already been told that a sibling is the most likely match. Meg's only a half-sibling, but they'd really like to test her, if she's willing . . . '

I feel the gin ease its way back up my throat.

'As I said, some things should never be texted . . . In the meantime, I'm moving him tomorrow from Great Ormond Street to a specialist unit in Chertsey. There's an American guy, over on a teaching secondment there, who's agreed to treat him privately. If we can't get a donor soon, he's going to undergo a new treatment from the States. It's pioneering stuff but his oncologists think it's worth a try.'

I'm nodding, but I've gone straight to limbo. Do not pass 'Go'. Do not collect your son en route. A seismic shift has just occurred in my life.

She takes her phone from her bag, checks for messages and puts it on the table in front of us. There's a photo on the screen. He looks so like me.

'I stayed away because you asked me to.' I've picked up her phone and am staring at it. She doesn't stop me. 'I stayed away because you wanted the baby and I didn't want Beth to know. I stayed away because you wanted it that way. You didn't want money from me, nothing. It was easy at first but, since then, there have been so many times when I wanted to drive past the house and just catch a glimpse.' I don't confess to the many times when I have actually done this, as recently as a few weeks ago. I think of every birthday and Christmas Eve where I've just glanced in their windows, the wrapped gift on the passenger seat never delivered.

She squeezes my knee, puts her phone back in her bag.

'You got married.' I turn and look at her. 'I stayed away, knew someone else was bringing him up. I stayed away because you didn't need me. He didn't need me.'

'He needs you now,' she says, 'we really need you now.'

'What does it involve?' Part of me is listening as she explains the procedure and part of me is not. Whatever he needs, is all I can think. She takes my phone, opens up the Notes section, types in instructions and the phone number I need to start the process.

'My moral compass,' I tell her. 'Will you please . . . '

'Leave Tim to me. He's very close to Noah.'

'And Gordon?'

'Gordon's a good father.'

'Are they close?'

She nods, tears finally falling from her beautiful eyes. I pull her to me. Her head rests a few moments on my chest. 'I'm sorry, so sorry that you've had to deal with all of this.'

'Don't be. We'll get through it.' She stands up, already putting her coat on. 'I've got to get back. I've still got calls to make about the move tomorrow, a mountain of paperwork still to sign.' She wraps a scarf around her, slides her bag up her arm. 'Will you tell Beth straight away?' she asks, avoiding my eyes. 'She'll have to know when you ask Meg to help. It might be better coming from you first?' Her leaking eyes now lock on mine.

'You're probably right. I'll be in touch.' I kiss her lightly on the cheek and we leave the bar together, Kiera turning right as we exit and me turning left.

'Adam?' she calls back to me. 'Please, don't take too long.' Outside, the chilled evening air hits and I nod as I pull my jacket tight around me. I wrap my scarf, a Dr Who-style long scarf, a gift from Beth last Christmas, around me three times.

I walk quickly towards Bank station. Nervous anxiety grips my stomach. The thought that I may have to tell Beth everything . . . I can almost hear my head moan as I descend to the Underground.

I'm only just in the flat when my phone pings two messages. I glance at the screen, somehow expecting one to be from Kiera, so I'm surprised to see Emma's name underneath Meg's. I click on Meg first.

'Hey Dad, have some ideas for grand gestures. Call me? x'

Grand gestures to get Beth back . . . Not if I move the Taj Mahal to Beth's back garden will she forgive me when she finds out about Noah. And Meg – I'm not sure I can bear hearing her voice tonight.

Emma . . . We didn't part well and I haven't heard from her in over three weeks. At the time, though her Twitter feed never mentioned me by name, #dickhead appeared regularly in her tweets. I sign in, to see if I've missed something, if there's an explanation for her sudden contact. Nothing. She's been quiet in the Twitter-sphere for more than ten days. I check my phone again, read her message again. I don't want to misunderstand.

'Yours if you want, here tonight. No strings. Consider this a booty call. E. x'

I haven't misunderstood and my dick automatically twitches at the thought of her. I miss fucking her. I miss it so much that, just for a moment, I think if I jump in the car now, I could be there in thirty minutes. It could help me forget . . . Just for a moment . . . Then, I text back an apology – something along the lines of: tempting though her offer is, it wouldn't be a good idea. Still thinking of her, still salivating at the thought of her, I head to the shower. A DIY will have to do.

After lathering my body, washing my hair, I banish all other thoughts and summon an image of Emma naked and . . . nothing. The water's hot. It's too hot, I tell myself. I switch it to a cooler temperature, shiver at the shock, let it run for a moment or two and try again. What the hell? After towelling myself dry, I walk to the bedroom, lie on the bed and close my eyes. There's a jumble of images in my head; only one is Emma naked, her rear end rising up towards me as I take her from behind. My eyes shoot open and I look down. Twitches. My dick is twitching but that's it.

I close my eyes again and my son's image, the one from Kiera's phone, fills my eyelids. He's there and, suddenly, he's not; he's in a hospital bed covered in a web of tubes. My mother's face appears and I ask her to please leave. She is not welcome in my head-space tonight. She is absolutely not welcome. I curl up in a foetal position and pull the duvet over me.

The last step on the stairway creaks but I'm so used to it that I take a little leap to avoid the sound. I walk up the narrow landing to my bedroom at the end, passing my parents' room on the right. The door is shut, yet there are sounds from inside. I stop a moment, listen, my ear rested against one of the orange pine panels. My face creases in disgust. Lunchtime. Parents. Having sex. Not nice.

I let myself into my room quietly and go to draw the heavy curtains. The headache I've come home from college with is one that will only clear in a darkened room. My hand on the first drape, I know immediately. It's like an electric shock to my system. The thoughts process quickly, the reality instant. My father's car is not outside.

'Who's there?' my mother's voice sounds down the corridor. I stand still, unable to move. My door is opened.

'Oh, it's you.' She runs a hand through her bed hair and ties her robe. She stares at me, her probing eyes focused on mine. Neither speaks but we both know. We both know.

I do the drive in twenty-five minutes. It's late so I text her from outside rather than ring the bell. I see her bedroom light go on and she takes another five minutes to come downstairs. Her shadowy silhouette wafts behind the door. She opens it just wide enough to speak through.

'You came,' she says.

'I'm here.'

'I wasn't sure you would, your life being so complicated and all that.'

The dig at my break-up speech does not go unnoticed.

She opens the door fully and I see that, under her robe, she is dressed identically to the image I had conjured up earlier. A tiny bra, matching thong, lacy stockings, heels. Christ . . . I move towards her. She holds a hand up.

'Wait,' she says.

'It's freezing out here, Emma.' I rub my hands together for effect.

'Why did you come?'

I can see her nipples through the thin cotton bra. They're hard, pointing straight at me.

'To fuck you, to see if I *can* fuck you.' My honesty surprises me.

'Harold's asleep upstairs.'

'So I'll fuck you quietly downstairs.'

This brings a smile and she offers me her hand. I take hers in mine and enter the White House for the first time in weeks. Inside, she guides my hand into her tiny pants, parting herself for my freezing fingers.

She gasps. 'You need warming up,' she says.

I feel immediate stirrings and am grateful for small mercies. My life as I knew it may well be broken, but my dick is not.

The Neighbourhood Watch chairman is my old cricket buddy and ex-neighbour, Nigel, so I'll be all right if I'm caught loitering with intent. I'll just drop his name and I'll be fine. The irony is not lost on me – I've already seen both of my ex-mistresses tonight and here I am outside my wife's door. It's two a.m. and I'm due in work at seven. A grand gesture it's not, but I've just dropped a mega-bunch of yellow tulips on Beth's doorstep. Tesco really is open all night.

The card, though, does have a grand message. It says I'm sorry for hurting her, for hurting Meg and other people too. It says I'm sorry for being a crap husband and father. It says I will always love her . . .

Chapter Nineteen

This is just plain weird. I put the bins out last night after midnight, so Adam must have dropped these flowers off after that. I place them in water, snipping the ends on a slant in the hope that their overnight droop may be revived. Just before I head out of the door to work, I remember someone telling me once that soluble aspirin works. So I go back in and drop one in the water.

I haven't time to text him, ask him what he's doing. Something tells me just to accept the flowers and the sentiment because my life is moving on without him. Approaching the High Street, I focus on the morning's work. Today, I have another tour of properties for Stephanie. I'm excited. It's completely different to Mrs Scott's tour, which is one of the things I'm enjoying about this job – no two days are the same. Today I'm showing a woman around three different serviced flats, all top-notch, all très posh.

There's a tiny box on my desk when I reach the office. Intrigued, I remove the top. Inside are two hundred and fifty of my new business cards. I stare at the name, unsure now, seeing it in black and white. Lizzie works, because Ben and my mum use it, but it doesn't really feel like my name . . . It's when I see the maiden name that I've readopted, I'm doubly unsure. I've opened a bank account in her name but who is this Lizzie Moir person? I quite liked being Beth Hall. She's who I've been for so long . . .

I look up to see Stephanie hover over my desk.

'Do you like them?' she beams.

'They're lovely.'

'The applicant will be here at nine fifteen. Would you like a quick coffee? I'm just about to make one.'

I look at her growing frame. 'You sit down. I'll make the coffee.'

'Thanks, Lizzie.' She rubs her back. 'This lady, when she comes in? Try and get her to understand that there's not a huge selection of really good-quality serviced flats. Just let her know these are the best of the best?'

'I will.' I make my way to the tiny kitchenette at the back of the office space. I'd spent last night driving the route in my head, and am now sure that I could do it blindfolded. I make two coffees, since everyone else is out of the office. Outside, I hand Stephanie hers – a decaf, black, no sugar. My latte I try and knock back, just as the door opens.

Stephanie is on her feet, offering her hand, steering the woman towards her desk. I look on, trying my best to remember the woman's name. She's tiny in stature, walking on tall heels. Wearing dark jeans and a short fur jacket, and sunglasses that are too wide for her tiny face.

'Lizzie? Come and meet your lady.'

I put my mug on the desk and try not to laugh. It sounds

159

as if I'm about to offer her a cut and blow-dry. Coat still on, I cross the office and take the stranger's hand.

'Lizzie, this is Mrs Pugh.'

'Hi, good to meet you.' Her gloved hand offers a firm handshake. 'Am I stopping you finishing your coffee?'

'No, not at all, I've finished. Good to meet you too.' I hand her one of my shiny new business cards. 'We've got three to see and I know you're pushed for time, so shall we go?'

Mrs Pugh laughs, pockets the card. 'A woman after my own heart! I do hate tardiness, don't you?'

My first thought is that she has never met Adam, who would be late for his own funeral. As she follows me out through the rear entrance to Stephanie's car, I pray that the gearstick will behave and that I will make it to the end of this property tour looking as if I know what the hell I'm doing.

In the car, I hand her a copy of the itinerary.

She removes a pair of reading glasses from her bag, swaps her sunglasses for them and studies it. 'I don't know any of these streets. Are they all safe, secure?'

I put the car into reverse and, thankfully, it moves without the grinding noise I'd been dreading. 'They're all relatively central, close to Weybridge High Street, and they've all got twenty-four-hour porterage.'

Even if I say so myself, I sound good. I'd rent a flat from me . . . I offer her a winning smile.

'I know serviced blocks are hard to come by so, hopefully, one of these will suit.'

'Is there anything about Weybridge you want to know, Mrs Pugh?'

'No thanks, Lizzie. As long as I can get to the hospital easily, I'll only be using the flat as a sleeping space – and please,' she turns to me and smiles, 'call me Kiera.'

I swear that if Kiera Pugh hadn't liked the third flat, I'd have asked her to come and live with me. I feel that sorry for the poor woman. But she is gushing as we walk around property number three, and I sense this is the one for her. She won't need to come and live with me after all, and I won't need to explain to Meg and Adam why my heart went out to a perfect stranger and I asked her to move in.

'Not quite home, but it's perfect for my needs,' she says as we pull the door behind us and I double-lock it. She grabs my arm with both her hands. 'Thank you, Lizzie,' she says. 'Thanks for finding this place and for listening.' I don't correct her. Stephanie found the place. I'm just the chauffeur. As for listening, I'm trying to swallow the lump that's been crawling up my throat ever since she started telling me her story. I can't help thinking of Simon, and Mum's words, 'Nobody should have to lose a child.' Silently, I pray that Kiera's son makes it. 'Why Chertsey?' I find myself asking her when we're back in the car.

'There's an American paediatric oncologist on a teaching secondment for two months at Chertsey, and he's agreed to private treatment,' she explains. 'I've moved Noah from Great Ormond Street in order to try a new treatment there. It's ground-breaking stuff, but it could help prolong his life. Meantime we're hoping for a suitable bone marrow donor . . . '

I can't help but think at least she's lucky she has money. That's obvious. At least she has enough money to throw everything she has at saving her son. Before we go back into the office and I have to hand her back to Stephanie for the paperwork, I tell her I hope that everything works out. I tell her I'll say a prayer. And I mean it, even though it's a very long time since I've asked any form of higher power for anything.

The next day is not a good day. If I could draw it, it would have drooping eyes and a turned-down smiley face. It is only ten o'clock and, so far, I have made a complete fool of myself and I still haven't heard from Josh. The fool bit bothers me. Giles came around on the way to work, dropped off a bottle of champagne for me from Kiera Pugh, and for some reason I thought it might be the right time to ask if he felt I could do Stephanie's maternity leave cover.

I asked him for a job I am ill-qualified to perform; one I don't even want – which meant he had no choice but to highlight both embarrassing facts to me. He is right, of course. I want to live in my loft and write Grammy-winning songs, but until Josh calls me with any news, that's not even a pipe dream. And though Kiera's gesture is lovely, all it has done on this blue day is to highlight in neon my sad singledom. I have no one to share this champagne with, which just means today reverts to being one big frown.

Unable to work, I play on the Internet. On Pinterest, I make a page of some 'beautiful shoes' I'm going to buy. If Josh doesn't phone me soon, I will just have to sack him and keep his fifteen per cent for Selfridges shoe department. I ignore his voice ringing in my head, reminding me that fifteen per cent of nothing is still nothing. After I fire him and go shoe-shopping, I will lock his bony arse in his shabby, not-so-chic office, where he will starve slowly and his body will be found by Polish builders when they decide to renovate the building in years to come.

I call Ben, who is, after all, my accountant. He picks up on the first ring.

'Whassup, Lizzie?'

'If I fire my agent and spend his commission on shoes, is it still tax deductible?'

'Hmmm. Shoes . . . '

'Yes, shoes. Well, boots to be specific.'

'I thought you were busy writing a song for the movies.'

'It's done, I'm waiting to hear.' I pull a hangnail from my left thumb. 'So, I'm shoe-shopping on the Internet. Selfridges have a particularly sexy pair of boots. They have red soles. I want their babies.'

'Ahhh . . . '

'What do you mean, "Ahh"?'

'Nothing.'

I insist. 'It was a very loaded "Ahh".'

'Call Josh.'

'He won't answer my fucking calls!!! It's driving me crazy . . . '

'Buy the boots anyway.'

'I can't afford the boots unless I get the song thing.'

'They're not tax deductible.'

'No, I thought not.'

'Come up to London tonight, you're obviously bored. I'm meeting Karen at The Waterhole. She'd love to see you. We'll surprise her.'

I hesitate. It's strange to be asked by Ben to meet him and Karen for a drink. I've known Karen since we hooked up at after-school drama club. She was twelve and I was fourteen. I've seen her through one bad marriage and a few bad relationships, so really, deep down, I'm pleased that she's found Ben. But The Waterhole is the place where *we* meet for drinks in town, which means – right up on surface level – my epidermis is trembling with jealousy.

'You could get a train early afternoon,' he continues. 'Meet us at seven. I've booked a booth for nibbles and bubbles. Why don't you come via Selfridges – that way you could actually *touch* the boots.'

Nibbles and bubbles. These are the words that Karen and I use when we go to The Waterhole for a treat. We have lots of tiny titbits to eat and share a bottle of champagne or cava, depending on how flush we are. Despite the fact that I now want to lock Ben in that office with Josh, I push my resentment to one side. 'Deal. Meantime, work out a way to make the boots a necessary expense.'

I finish the call thinking, 'To hell with Josh and Ben. To hell with Giles and his "senior role". I'm going to buy boots.' I ignore the sound of Lucy Fir saying: 'You're a shallow woman! Yesterday you spent time with someone who has a dying child . . . And you're going to buy boots?'

I reason with her – something I've been trying to do, lately, rather than ignore her totally. Calmly, I tell her that – sad as it is – life goes on. I will buy my boots, because I am worthy. And when LA love my song, I will donate some money to the paediatric unit at Oakside in Chertsey. Lucy seems satisfied with this offer. The bitch has finally been silenced . . .

Chapter Twenty

We've agreed to play at St George's Hill since Matt and I have corporate membership there. I have a nine o'clock tee-off booked and Tim Granger has declined lunch afterwards, telling me in his email that he will be visiting Noah before heading back to the city.

This hurts. It's like it's open and out there, but it's not. Tim knows, Kiera knows, Gordon knows, but no one in my life can know – including Matt. I put him off the round of golf, telling him I think it would be good for Tim and me to do it alone, iron out all our creases. Matt was not so sure and pleaded with me to reconsider.

It's eight thirty and, in the car park, I see Tim first. His driver, Cal, has dropped him off, is removing his golf clubs from the boot as Tim waits, head down over his BlackBerry. I remove my own clubs, walk the trolley in his direction, and offer my hand when I arrive.

'Tim,' I say, 'good to see you.'

'I'll text you when we're back on the eighteenth, Cal.' Tim ignores my hand, and my greeting. There's nothing I can do but retract it and walk on up to the clubhouse, hoping he'll follow. Unsure how to behave, I decide there and then to let him take the lead. I'd like to talk about my unfair dismissal from the Granger account. He will no doubt want to concentrate on the fact that Kiera and I created Noah. Either way, this isn't going to be easy.

We play the first hole in silence and are walking towards the second tee. I'm determined to let him have the first verbal shot at me. When it comes, it's a cheap one.

'So, how long were you, a married man, banging my sister?'

I do not rise to the bait.

'Kiera and I were friends. We only ever spent one night together.' In this case, honesty, I decide, is definitely the best policy.

'Once was enough, wasn't it?'

'To what?'

'Fuck up several lives.'

My mouth almost gapes open. *Do not react.*

'With respect, Tim, how have I done that? Kiera told me she was pregnant, told me she wanted to have the baby and that she wanted me to have nothing to do with any of it. I have respected her wishes, especially since she got married when Noah was a baby. Kiera has dictated this whole thing. Whose life have I fucked up?'

He is silent.

'It's not my fault he's sick, Tim.'

'It could be. There could be a genetic link. Maybe your DNA is as fucked up as you.'

I'm suddenly unsure that I should be on a golf course with this man. He's angry. Angry at me, angry at Kiera, angry at the world. His irrational hatred of me has just become crystal clear. Where I thought I could reason with him, I'm no longer convinced. And he's wielding a steel stick beside me.

'You let her go through a difficult pregnancy alone. Just because you were screwing someone behind your wife's back.'

'I never knew she . . . I—'

'You've never given her a penny.'

'She wouldn't let me. I have an account set up for Noah. She—'

'Keep your fucking money, Adam. It's not like he's going to need it anyway . . . '

This floors me. I feel as if he's hit me square on the jaw, when all he actually does is hit one of the best drives I've ever seen. This is a man able to channel his frustration. I should take lessons. Of course, I follow it up with one of the worst shots I've ever hit and end up in the rough in the trees. He laughs.

'Why did you want me off your family account?' There. I've said it. He stares at me, then shakes his head vigorously.

'Because you're a wanker, and you're a wanker who's lost us a shitload of money.'

'The markets lost you a shitload of money. You know very well that money would have been lost no matter who had advised you.'

'Well, let's just stick to you being a wanker then.'

I stop walking. 'You know what, Tim? I have been a wanker to my wife, to my daughter – hell, even the woman I just dumped: guilty as charged. But I have never behaved

167

badly to clients, or to Kiera. We had a one-night stand – both consenting adults. The only person who was hurt from that was Beth, so get down off your fucking high horse.'

'You just dumped someone?' Tim makes a face.

'Yes.' I blush at the memory of the no-strings booty call since then.

'Does Beth know about this one?'

'Yes. Beth dumped me first. She threw me out because of Emma. I've just dumped Emma because I still love Beth. Happy?'

He laughs. 'No. Are you?'

The unspoken implication is one I've wrestled with myself. If I continue to behave the way I do, will I ever be happy again?

'We used to be friends,' I say.

'We did, or so I thought,' he muses.

'What was there to gain, Tim? This is the way Kiera wanted it. She kept the baby and I kept schtum. Everyone was happy, and no one would ever have known any different if Noah hadn't got sick.'

'He's a great kid, you know. Really clever . . . bright.' His eyes widen behind his narrow steel-framed glasses.

My heart falls in my ribcage. I cannot respond.

'Have you been tested yet?' he asks.

'Yes, I'm waiting—'

'How long ago?' he interrupts.

'A few days.'

He shakes his head. 'You'd have heard by now. Good news travels fast. Bad news . . . '

My heart plummets further. Meg. I know I have to do it.

'Your daughter?' Tim reads my mind. 'Exactly how big a wanker does she think you are?' He hits another big shot, right up the fairway. 'Fore!' he bellows to the group of golfers at the pin up ahead.

And all I can think of is how apt his cry is. Warning up ahead! I might as well have it branded on my scalp . . .

While we're not bosom buddies when he leaves, I do feel that I've made headway with Tim. He shakes my hand, thanks me for the round of golf. I ask him to get Kiera to call me.

He nods. 'Are you going to try and see him? Noah?'

'I want to.'

'Gordon won't want you there. Especially—'

'If I'm not a match.' I finish his sentence for him. 'Why upset the balance, right?'

Tim shrugs.

'I want to see him, Tim. He doesn't have to know who I am. I could be a "friend" of the family. I could be a "friend" of yours? I don't want to upset the Kiera and Gordon dynamic, that's not what I want. But I would like to see him.'

'A friend of mine? That may be pushing it.'

I'm silent. There's nothing else to say really.

He climbs into his car. 'Leave it with me,' he says, then pulls the door shut.

I'm left with hope. I hope that I've mended an important bridge and I hope that he may be able to influence Gordon, and that I might get to meet Noah.

Have I the strength and courage to ask Meg? Hope for

Noah may live on through her. Hope for me is fading. She and her mother will never forgive me . . .

Kiera's call comes an hour after the golf and five minutes after the call confirming I'm not a match for our son either. I'm back in the office, still reeling, when Matt enters the room and her number flashes. Instinctively, I pick it up, then realize it's probably not a conversation I should have in front of him. He shows no sign of leaving, so I stick to listening, give her one-syllable replies. 'Have you talked to Meg?' she asks.

I tell her that I will do, to leave it with me, and I hang up the phone.

'Emma?' Matt asks. 'How is she?'

'Hmmm. I guess she's fine, but we're not together any more.'

Matt sits, his eyebrows heading towards the heavens. 'Right,' he says.

I exhale deeply. I am weary, tired of getting everything wrong, tired of so many hidden layers of my life. It's frankly exhausting and, there and then, I decide Matt should know the truth. 'That was Kiera Pugh, née Kiera Granger.'

Matt's eyebrows furrow together in a deep frown. 'Why is Kiera Granger calling you?'

As soon as he asks the question, he pieces together something in his head. I'm sure he has the facts all wrong, because the conclusion he draws makes him spit the next words.

'No – Adam, no – Jesus; please – don't – tell – me – that . . . '

I hold a hand up. 'Kiera's a friend. That's all.'

It's like the oxygen had been sucked out of the room, then comes gushing back in. The relief is tangible.

'Ten years ago, we did have a fling. Now, we share a nine-year-old son. Kiera made it clear she wanted to do it alone, and so I've not been involved in Noah's life.' I'm on a roll. This honesty thing is something I could maybe get used to. I choose not to look at Matt's face, for fear of changing my mind. 'Noah is ill – leukaemia. Kiera got in touch because we need to find a bone marrow match. She had to tell Tim I was the father, hence his reaction to me and my "warped moral compass".'

Matt is making a coughing sound as if he's going to vomit. I still can't look at him. 'Kiera's just calling to remind me that our best hope for a match is Meg. Which means I have to tell her everything, ask her to be tested. Ask her if she's a match to go through a stem cell donation. And, all of this, Beth will have to know . . . ' I stop talking, stand up and turn to look out through my window. My hands are deep in my pockets, my shoulders slumped. I remind myself – looking down at people passing below on the street; traffic on the river – that life, despite everything, just carries on, oblivious.

After a few minutes, Matt appears beside me. 'I can get tested,' he offers. 'I'm sure Jen would too. You never know. Sometimes there are non-familial matches.' He puts an arm around my shoulders. 'Christ, Adam, your life makes me dizzy.'

I smile. 'Thank you. And I know. I've a headache myself thinking about it.'

'What a tangled web?' he continues. 'It's the stuff movies are made of. Maybe you should write it all down, sell it to Hollywood for a fortune.'

I know he's trying to be light-hearted, but his remark makes me think of Beth. Meg said something about her being shortlisted to write a song for a movie. My stomach churns into anxious knots at the thought of how I may be about to really break her heart, this time into tiny, tiny pieces. Tiny, unmendable pieces . . . I pray silently for a miracle, one that will avoid me revealing what a truly spectacular liar I've been for so long.

Chapter Twenty-One

Embankment station. I see the red and white Underground sign flash before my eyes and I leap upwards, just in time, before the door slides shut. Feeling the chill of the Tube station, I pull my coat tight around me and climb the escalator. Outside, I glance across to the swollen river on the opposite side of the street, where a group of students are stacked up against the wall singing loudly. I turn right and head west towards Big Ben. Tucked in a tiny street behind the Houses of Parliament, The Waterhole is packed to the rafters, with all sorts – suited, bespectacled civil servants meet tourists and artists alike.

T-shirted smokers – who must be freezing – hover outside the front door as I push my way through to the rear, oak-lined bar. It stretches for ten metres and each of the many tan-coloured leather barstools is occupied. Opposite these, the worn, tartan-clad booths, where patrons feast on nibbles and bubbles, are equally busy. Ben is standing in the last one, waving in my direction.

When I reach him, it's obvious that he still hasn't told

Karen I'm coming. She seems pleased, hugs me, tells me it's great to see me, but I have an instinctive feeling that tonight, three may be a crowd. I'm trying not to react, hope my upset gets lost in the busy throng of the pub. Ben pours me a long glass of champagne from a half-full bottle. 'Have you heard from Josh? Are we celebrating yet?' he asks. Karen looks up at me, wide-eyed, expectant, like a baby bird in a nest.

'Nothing,' I reply.

She squeezes my hand, pulls me into the booth beside her.

'We will be soon,' Ben says with a confidence I have never felt. 'I'll go and get another bottle.' He heads back in the direction of the bar.

'I'm sorry about this.' Karen's face crumbles. 'I didn't know he'd asked you. I was annoyed enough that he pinched our nibbles and bubbles idea, even before you arrived. I mean, I know he's still trying to impress me, but we have to make our own adventures. I don't want him hijacking yours and mine, just because I told him once what fun it is.'

'I was a little jealous,' I confess. 'Actually, I was a big bit jealous. To be fair, he hasn't been in London for a while. Maybe he just doesn't know where people hang out.'

'Beth, he was gone a year, not a decade. I just don't think he got out much even before he left!'

She's right. Before he left, Ben had been in a six-year relationship with Elise. I wonder how much of the break-up he's shared with Karen.

'He's told me he and Elise didn't go out much. She was a home bird?'

'She was . . . How much has he told you about her?' I choose a black pitted olive from an almost empty plate.

'Not a lot, but then I've not really asked either. I don't particularly want him raking over my past, so I've tried not to with him. I was sort of hoping you'd fill in the blanks?'

I realize I've been dreading this moment since they got together. How do I tell Karen that Ben and Elise split up after years of unsuccessful IVF treatment? Ben wanted to adopt as he has always wanted to be a father, but Elise wanted her own child . . . Since I know Karen wants children too and, at forty, her child-bearing years are limited, I'm hesitant to raise it.

'Not now,' I whisper. 'He's on his way back.'

'More bubbles and some menus for nibbles.' Ben grins, hands us both a menu. We both smile, pretend to look at it, then say together, 'Quesadilla sharing platter, please.'

'Actually, I'll get it.' I stand up. 'I need the loo. I'll order it on the way. You okay with that too, Ben?'

He nods.

I take a note of the table number, place the order at the busy bar and head to the left-hand side of the building, where the Ladies' toilets are. I know it's the best spot in the building for a full phone signal and, sitting on the loo, I remove my phone from my handbag.

Finally, there is one text. Josh. It says: CALL ME. I stare at it. If it was bad news, maybe he'd have just texted the words, 'Sorry, not this time . . . ' Or the same text, 'call me' with lower-case letters. If it was good news, he'd have put an exclamation mark after the capitalized words. I feel queasy as I speed-dial him on #4.

'Where've you been? I've been trying you for an hour.' Josh's voice is soprano.

'What? I've no missed calls, I—'

'Never mind. Are you sitting down?'

The irony of my situation is lost on him. I am, in fact, sitting down on a faded wooden toilet seat, the sort that risks splinters. A caricature picture of Benjamin Disraeli stares down on me from the back of the cubicle door. My knickers are around my ankles. I tell him: 'Yes.'

'You've done it, girl, you've only bloody well gone and done it!' His voice rises a further octave before finishing the sentence.

'What?'

'They want it. They want your song in the movie. "Fall Apart" will be the main movie track. In fact, they're looking at probably changing the movie title to something about glue seams, or something from one of the lines, but they *love* it!'

'They love it,' I repeat, as I feel a wee trickle into the loo. 'They do?'

'Christ, yes, they do. I had the top guy on the phone only minutes ago. I'm talking the head honcho, Beth. They want to meet you. In Los Angeles. Soon as – in the next week or two. You need to come in tomorrow, talk dates, contracts, etc.'

'They want to meet me?'

'Yep.'

'In LA?' I feel another wee trickle out.

'In LA. Soon as—'

I can't see Josh, but I know he's smiling. 'Crikey,' I muster. 'LA. Are you coming?'

'You don't need me! All my hard work will be done by then, but it starts from tomorrow. Beth, we need to talk, so that I can make sure this contract is rock solid, watertight, and that you get paid even if this movie doesn't get made.'

'Right.' I pull my zip up, close my jeans button, one-handed.

'So, come in tomorrow, for elevenses. Coffee and pastries?'

'Eleven, yours tomorrow.' I'm nodding.

'And, Beth?'

'Yes?'

'Well done, you superstar.'

He hangs up before he has a chance to hear me thank him. I tell myself that I'll do it tomorrow. Outside the cubicle, I put my phone down, wash my hands, catch my reflection – I look like something from a home for the bewildered. I don't have to sack Josh. I may even buy those boots. My face looks frozen in time. 'It's shock,' I say aloud, as I make my way back to Karen and Ben.

'So . . . Adam and Emma have split up.' Karen flashes a conspiratorial smile in my direction.

I nod.

'What? You knew already?'

'Yes, he told me at your party.' I take a sip from my glass. 'I'm not sure I care though,' I add, taking my place beside Karen in the booth.

'And apparently he and Ben are about to start training for a mini-marathon.'

Now that does get a reaction. I snort with laughter. 'Adam? Do something to keep fit?'

'I'll be training him.' Ben obviously feels the need to defend him.

'Ben, the only exercise Adam ever gets is either golf, or screwing other women. Good luck with that.'

'He's doing it for charity,' he adds.

'I hope they don't need the money.' I shake my head.

'It's something that's important to him.'

I'm intrigued. 'A charity? That means something to Adam? Which one is it?'

Ben blushes, a fully fledged, cheek-to-cheek, crimson rush of blood. 'I can't remember.' He shrugs it off.

My antennae are twitching, but I choose to ignore that, wanting instead to share my news. The noise at the bar suddenly increases as a birthday group arrive and park themselves just beside us.

'Josh called.'

'What?' Karen raises her voice. 'Did you say Josh called?'

My head bobs up and down.

'And? What? What did he say, Beth?' She is screaming now and Ben is telling her to hush.

'They love the song. They want to meet me – in LA! Soon as . . . !'

Karen pushes me from the booth into a standing position, scoops me into a huge hug, screaming at the top of her voice. 'I knew you could do it, I knew you could do it!'

I can't help smiling. When she lets me go, one of the birthday group grabs both my hands, yanks them up and down and shouts, 'I knew you could do it too!' Then they all start chanting the same thing. I laugh out loud, until one of them actually asks, 'What is it you've done?'

Ben's voice is heard next. 'She's written a song for a movie! She's going to the U S of A!' he yells above the din. They all look at each other and cheer loudly. 'Yay!' 'Wow!' 'That's brilliant' repeats from this crowd of strangers. An unopened bottle of champagne appears from some unknown place and is thrust into my hand.

Step aside, *Pretty Woman*. I'm going to Hollywood.

Chapter Twenty-Two

Roberto is an Italian-born barber who has always wanted to be a chef. He has been cutting my hair for nearly fifteen years and I've yet to pay a visit to him during which he doesn't discuss food with a passion missing from many Michelin-starred successes. It's a busy Saturday morning in the salon, and I'm zoning out as he chats about his brother's bistro in Highgate and how I should visit. The veal milanese is apparently 'magnifico'. I only ever visit Highgate to see my dead parents and, somehow, I don't imagine I'll be stopping off for a meal en route. I smile agreeably as Roberto works his magic with the scissors.

I'm reading a newspaper; when my eyes land on the date, I'm momentarily stunned as I work it out. It is just over three months since I left home. Since I lived in my own house. Which means it's probably over four months since I last made love to my wife. I swallow hard at the thought and am filled with an overwhelming desire to see her, hold her. Aware it's not going to happen, I think back to the night I left and how I felt. I was certain that Beth would need a cooling-off period and then take me back. Even when that looked unlikely, I was certain that we'd someday get back together. Today, nothing is certain in my life. That is the only certain thing.

I walked to Roberto's this morning and Ben agreed to collect me here. I see him pull up outside. We are going straight for a training session at a park nearby. At my feet lies a gym bag – trainers, running kit, all within. Ben has decided to start my training programme with a running schedule. I am apparently going to run three kilometres today. A glance at my watch tells me that is thirty minutes away. I'm terrified. I haven't run in years – I hope I can actually deliver this feat. I've already told Kiera, and though she was thrilled at the intent behind my mini-marathon, she reminded me I still have to speak to Meg. Fundraising is great, but it's stem cells that Noah needs.

I remove my phone from my pocket and text her. She hasn't responded to two texts and one call. I'm beginning to worry.

'Pumpkin, U around L8ter? X'

She replies immediately. 'It's Saturday. I'm twenty, what do you think?'

'OK, wen can I c u next?'

'I'm going home tomorrow to do a clear-out of my bedroom. Mum's nagging, says I have to "clear out my shit as the house may have to be sold". I think it's time for you to start with a GG (grand gesture) or two??? Seriously, Dad, get a grip. Meet me at home in the morning. Mum's working, so she won't be there.'

Shit . . .

'OK', I text, but it's really not. I don't think I can tell Meg what I need to tell her in our family home.

'Can't I just take U out for lunch?'

'No time and Jack cooking dinner for us later on. Have to do it. If you want to see me, that's where I'll be! x'

I agree ten o'clock Sunday and send her back a kiss. I can't believe I got one from her.

Just as I stand up and make my way to Roberto's till, Ben pops his head around the door.

I hold five fingers up. 'I'll be there in five. I just need to change,' I add, heading to Roberto's tiny loo.

When I leave the building, I try everything to postpone my first training session. Ben is having none of it. I feign illness, a headache, a sore leg. I even try being honest and tell him I'm terrified. I ask him whose crazy idea it had been anyway. He reminds me it was mine. I suggest we go and visit Mum and Dad instead, try and shame him into doing it by reminding him it's been years. I even tell him I'll treat him to a veal milanese at a local bistro. He quietly reassures me that, though that's a great idea, we can do it after the three-kilometre run.

Every part of me hurts, but I did it. We stretched for ten minutes before and after, and I ran, without stopping, for three kilometres. I could have continued, but Ben told me to stop, not to overdo things on the first day. I'm pleased. If I can start like this, I can build things up slowly. I'm already looking forward to a run along the river tomorrow morning before I go to meet Meg.

'Lunch before the cemetery or after?' Ben is driving and we are near Highgate.

'After, if you don't mind? Look, we really don't have to go. If you need to get back to Karen . . . I only suggested it to get out of the run.'

'I know, but I should go. You're right. It's been too long.' He runs a hand through his hair and I wonder how often he thinks of Mum and Dad, how often he thought of them while travelling the world.

I say nothing, try and change out of my kit in the back of the car, which is a feat in itself.

'Did you hear Beth's news?' He looks at me in the rear-view mirror.

'How would I?'

'Well, I guess you would if you ever called her. If you kept up an interest in what she does?'

I feel the sting of his words, but bite my tongue. 'What news?'

'She's been chosen to do the movie song.' He checks my reaction in the mirror.

I stop what I'm doing. 'Wow . . . Well, good on her . . . That's fantastic. What—'

'Just call her, Adam. There is no earthly reason why you shouldn't. Use the news as an excuse. It might be good to talk to her about her and not you. Put you both on a new page?'

I tuck my shirt into my jeans and sit back, aware he's still watching me. 'You're right. I'll call her tonight.'

'Good . . . Do it soon. She's off to Los Angeles next week.'

My eyebrows both travel upwards. 'Really?'

'Meeting the producers. Business-class ticket – paid for by the film company.'

'Wow,' I say again. I feel weird. My spirits feel strangely uplifted at the news. She's earned this success and deserves it after years of hard work and rejection. I'm not sure, but I think it's pride and I can't help wondering if I have the right.

'Make sure you call her.' Ben drives up a side street just outside the cemetery. Just past the main gates, he stares upwards. 'I'd forgotten how big these oaks are. They're amazing, aren't they? Remember our one? How big it was?'

The memory is a fond one. We never exactly owned a tree, Ben and I, but there was one that we called ours and it wasn't an oak. It was a sweet chestnut with an enormous gnarled trunk, about a five-minute walk from our house on a local farmer's private land. We'd sneak in there to the small lake with this solitary tree by its side, hook up our swing made from some old rope from Dad's shed. Each summer we'd return, set it up, and swing until exhaustion took over. It seems weird looking back that we were never discovered or asked to leave.

'Mum never wondered why our clothes were wet.'

'Fun times,' I reply, and he nods, smiling wide. 'Up ahead, left. You'll have to park there, then we walk a few minutes.'

'Do you know what Beth's song is called?' I ask Ben. After any nostalgic memory, I automatically end up thinking about her.

'"Fall Apart".'

I nod. 'Sounds like a new one.'

'It is.' He gets out of the car. 'Something she tells me she's had first-hand experience of. So, at least you were useful for raw material.' He smiles again, but I don't think it's funny.

At the graveside, it's him who seems uncomfortable. 'Relax, Ben. Just talk to them. In your head.'

'I have been here before, you know.' He is indignant.

'Have you ever talked to Beth about this?' Ben asks. He is standing, staring into the distance. I am stooped over the vases, trying to avoid kneeling on the damp grass.

'No.'

'Why not?' His question is almost as simple as my monosyllabic reply, but I'm seized by a horrible panic.

'I have never needed to – and for fuck's sake, don't you go telling Karen either . . . In fact, you need to promise me you can keep your mouth shut to Karen. Those two are joined at the hip. If you tell her anything, she won't be able to help herself. I—'

'Whoa! Stop now. I haven't said a word – about anything.'

'Well, don't. Ben, I can rely on you, can't I?' I touch his arm.

'Always,' he says, before looping his through mine. 'We done here?' He doesn't wait to see if I am, just tugs me away, back in the direction of the car.

'That time, I know we don't talk about it . . . It was what Picasso would call "a blue period".'

I nod. My stomach is still gnawing away on itself at the thought of Ben discussing our past with Beth via Karen.

'You were the strong one, held it all together. You found us a home, got me into uni. I owe you.'

'You don't owe me anything. Not a thing. Except maybe to keep your trap shut with Karen.'

He stops walking, tilts his head as if to repeat, 'What did I just say?'

We carry on back to the car park. 'I'm sorry. It's just with you and Karen together, I know the natural thing to do is to share, to be honest.'

'Yeah, well, maybe we've both got faulty DNA there.' He grins.

'I'm serious, Ben. And don't put yourself in the same boat as me. You were always totally honest with Elise, even when it hurt her at the end. I admired that. It's the way you are and that's what worries me.'

'Adam, you've got a lot worse shit coming your way. Noah? You have to tell Meg, and she'll have to be tested and . . . ' He doesn't finish but, if he had, he would have reminded me that Beth was going to find all of that out soon anyway. He would also have added that now might be as good a time as any to tell Beth that my parents had not both died in a car accident. He might have intimated that how they did die has somehow affected me in my adult life and I might have laughed it off, as I always do.

'So, where's this veal milanese then?' He rubs his tummy like a child.

I try not to groan out loud. We did say we'd do it, so I just point him towards Roberto's brother's restaurant.

Pulling into the gravel driveway, my senses seem amplified. The stones crushing beneath the wheels and the voice in my head telling me to turn around are deafening. My fingers, wrapped around the steering wheel, are white and numb. The pungent scent of Beth's potted hyacinths assaults me from the front door. And there's something in my mouth that tastes like pure fear.

I push the doorbell and hear the sound of Meg skipping down the stairs.

'I was up in my room,' she complains. 'Why didn't you just let yourself in?'

'New locks.'

She tilts her head, as if suddenly remembering something important. Her ponytail swishes from side to side. 'Ahh, yes,' she says, as I pass through the door into the hallway. Beth's words still adorn the hallway wall. 'Come on up. Shut your eyes when you get there. I've a pot of coffee, two mugs.'

I'm immediately saddened by the pictures on the stairwell and notice there's a new one, a black and white of Beth and her parents and Simon. I resist the urge to touch them as I climb the steps, wanting to use my fingers to expand the images, like on a phone. Make them bigger. Make those memories feel real.

She's right. Her bedroom looks like a warzone. She points me to a chair, gives me a black sack and explains that anything she hands me must go in the sack. I sit, bag in hand, like an obedient child. Her head jerks towards the coffee. 'Help yourself.'

I nod.

'Are you all right?' she asks. 'You look a little pale. I got your email about the run. You're not overdoing it, are you? It's a long time since you've done anything to keep fit.'

I nod some more.

She hands me some clothes. I pile them in the bag. She pulls a furry toy, a small ragged Eeyore, from the bottom of a wardrobe. 'Dad, look, it's Eeyore.' She giggles.

187

'So it is, love.'

'Do you remember when we got him?'

'I do . . . ' Like it was yesterday. She had been about five or six and was obsessed with Winnie-the-Pooh. We'd spotted the lone Eeyore amongst hundreds of Winnies and she'd begged us to buy him – told us he was lonely and that she was meant to be his mummy.

I lean forward, rest my elbow on my lap, my chin in my hand. 'Meg . . . '

'Hmmm?' She's looking out of the window, lost in the memory of Eeyore.

'We have to talk.'

'I know, you're right.' She jumps up, walks to her desk and pours two mugs of coffee. 'I met Nana yesterday.' She hands me one, smiling broadly. 'Oh, she gave me a letter for you. An old-fashioned letter, eh, Dad? Some people still write them apparently.' She lifts a jacket from the back of her desk chair and rummages through a deep pocket, pulls out a tissue, loose coins and a crumpled envelope. I take it from her, push it deep into my own jacket pocket. It can wait.

'Aren't you going to read it? Never mind.' She waves it away like it's already forgotten. 'The thing is, Nana and I had some great ideas. We had a bit of a Grand Gesture brainstorming session.'

'Meg.'

'Yes?' She seems exasperated that I've interrupted her flow.

'We need to talk. At least, I need to talk and you need to listen?'

She pulls the desk chair away from the desk and plonks

down heavily. 'Go on,' she says, 'I'm listening, but I warn you, I'm not up for excuses. I know you want Mum back. Her, I'm really not so sure of, but that's what we're going to work on and, frankly, I need you both back together. Soon.'

I can't find the voice. There is no way that the words can come out.

'Isn't her news brilliant? She seems so excited about LA.'

I can't do it. I just can't do it.

'She is.' Meg smiles. 'And you know what? The song is fantastic, definitely one of her best. I'm so proud of her.'

'Me too . . . me too . . . Meg, look, there's something I want your help with.'

She eyeballs me, suddenly intrigued. Maybe it's my tone. Desperate . . .

'What?' She sips her coffee, makes a face as it's obviously lukewarm.

'Years ago, you know already, I—'

'Dad, what is wrong with you?' She stares at me as if I'm an interesting lab specimen.

'Years ago, more than ten years ago, I . . . I cheated on your mother. One night. One night only . . . '

She gapes. 'I do not need to know this.' Her head moves side to side.

'You do, Meg. You do.' I'm aware of the distress in my voice. 'The woman, Kiera Granger – she had a child. My child. I knew, but she wanted me to have nothing to do with it. I—'

Meg's head is suddenly still, statue still. Nothing moves, not even her pupils. Her face is ashen, her expression one of total disbelief, total distrust.

'You have another child?' she interrupts. 'Are you telling me you have another child?'

'Yes. A son – I've never known him. That was what we agreed. Kiera wanted it that way and . . . that suited me. I have never told your mother. I have never told anyone until, weeks ago, things changed.'

Meg's eyes have not moved from mine. 'I have a brother,' she says, quietly. 'One my mother knows nothing about. Jeee-sus Christ . . . You really are a piece of shit! Why now? You planning on making us all the fucking Brady Bunch?'

I look away, count the stripes in her carpet. 'He's sick. Leukaemia. We need to test you as a bone marrow match urgently. If you agree, that is. The fact is, siblings are the most likely match and you're his only sibling. Half-sibling.' I correct myself.

She raises both hands to her mouth, then suddenly reaches down to the floor for her wastepaper bin. She breathes deeply, holds her stomach as though she's going to be sick.

'Meg, I . . . ' I stand, move towards her, and she shoves me away.

'Get out,' she whispers. 'Leave now.'

'Please, Meg. Please listen.' I want to scream at her that I get it. That she can be mad as hell at me afterwards, after she's been tested and given Noah a miracle cure.

She stares up at me. 'I don't know who you are. I'm not sure I ever knew who you are.'

'He's just a little boy and he's dying.' I'm determined for her to hear me out.

She bites a trembling lip. 'Leave now. Get out.' Tears

slide down her face, as if a silent tap has been turned on. 'Do not say another word. You and I are finished. FINISHED! And don't think for a second that I'm keeping this from Mum.'

With that, she points to the door. 'Get the fuck out!'

Steadying myself on the back of her chair, I inhale deeply through my nose and exhale through my mouth. I have never known a pain like this. My heart feels as though it has been shredded, minced.

I turn and leave her room. '*You and I are finished*' echoes all around me. It ricochets off the walls on the stairs and the pulsed message seeps into my body repeatedly, penetrates my bones, pierces my brain. I grasp at anything that looks or sounds like hope. The pictures, the memories . . . She doesn't mean it. She's hurting. It's a lot to take in. She's angry and sad. Of course she'll help. We haven't brought her up to do anything else – but she's going to tell Beth. That is as sure and as certain as the fact that Meg has my DNA flowing in her veins, as the fact that Noah has my DNA flowing in his veins. She will tell all, if I don't first.

I'm afraid. I can feel fear in my stomach and limbs – such fear that I have a sense of what my parents felt. It scares me shitless.

Chapter Twenty-Three

It's pissing rain, the sort of relentless rain that bangs against the Velux windows in the loft, making it difficult to concentrate, so I haven't been able to work. Plus, I woke up this morning singing 'Miss You Nights' by Cliff . . . The lyrics made me think of Adam; I can't seem to shake him from my head this morning. I'm staring out through the bi-folds at the back of the house. The garden is in an awful state. We're having a pretty mild winter, but I really need to find a gardener before December sets in and everything just dies. That, or I need to develop gardening skills. An idea forms in my head, and before I have time to dismiss it, I pick up the phone.

'It's me.'

'Hi.' He sounds nervous. Only one word and, somehow, I can tell.

'You all right?' I ask.

'Yes, I'm . . . ' He sighs. 'How're you? All packed?'

I'm not going to LA for another six days, but he knows me so well. All of my 'summer' clothes are washed, ironed and packed already. I have sunscreen, a full make-up bag, hairdryer, straighteners, knickers and bras, all arranged in neat piles in the case. In a separate plastic folder sitting on top of the case are all my travel documents – ticket, passport, insurance. I like to be organized well in advance of travel.

'I'm not going for nearly a week,' I say, 'but yes, most of it's done. Listen, I was wondering. When I'm away, would you be interested in doing some gardening? It's really looking a mess. I could get a gardener, but I thought, maybe you miss it, maybe you'd like . . . You used to love the garden. I mean, it's in both our interests to . . . '

'Er, yes. Okay. If you'd like.'

'I leave on a Sunday, thought maybe you could take the Monday off and stay over?' I decide to leave a note directing him to one of the spare rooms. Our bed is now my bed.

'If you're sure.' He seems a little hesitant. 'Are you sure?'

'Yes, that's sorted then. I suppose I'll have to lend you some keys.' I emphasize the word 'lend' deliberately. I already know he can't get a set cut as they're security locks allocated to me.

'Maybe leave them with Sylvia and I'll pick them up from her?'

'Okay. Have you heard anything from Meg?'

He is silent.

'It's just she's not answering my calls. She was here yesterday. I've been nagging her to sort her room out, but by the time I got back, she was gone.'

'We spoke yesterday.'

'Did she seem okay? She left her room in a worse state than it was when she arrived . . . ' I realize Adam wouldn't know if she was okay or not as he has the emotional antennae of an earthworm, so I don't wait for a reply. 'Don't worry. I'll just keep trying her. I'd better get on . . . Thanks for the gardening. I'll make sure Sylvia has a key.'

'Beth?'

'Yes?' I hear a slight catch in his voice as he seems to hesitate. 'What is it, Adam?'

'You know I love you, don't you.'

I honestly think my mouth has fallen open.

'It's important you know that. I love you. I have always loved you and I always will. I know it's too late, but I want you to know.'

I close my mouth, inhale deeply.

'Say something,' he pleads. 'Anything . . . '

'You're right. Too little, too late,' I say.

'Should I have fought for you?' he asks. 'Ben – other people – keep telling me that I should have fought for you. Made you listen.'

'Other people are wrong. It was never going to happen, Adam. You were too busy reinventing yourself with Emma. You may have loved me, you may still do, but you always loved yourself more. It's beyond you to fight for someone.'

A part of me feels cruel saying this to him, but it's the truth. I'm not saying it to hurt him. I'm even sad, because I know it does hurt him, but I really feel that he needs to grow up, to somehow realize that the world doesn't spin on his axis.

'I'm not quite that selfish,' he says. 'I was vain, stupid and, yes, selfish. But not quite that bad . . . '

'Okay, why didn't you then?'

'Didn't I what?'

'Fight for me? Why did you leave, Adam? Why did you keep on seeing Emma? I thought you'd made a choice and that our marriage was over.' Silence again.

'Let's face it. You left for sex. Lots of it. Lots of different, exciting and new sex with a younger woman. And that's the crux of it. You put your sexual gratification over your love for me and your love for Meg.' I'm on a roll. 'Forget me for a moment. Have you any idea what our break-up has done to her? Have you any real clue how destructive all that brilliant sex has been?'

There is only the sound of his breathing on the phone.

'Have you?' I repeat.

'I'm sorry,' he whispers, and hangs up the phone.

I'm left staring at the receiver. What just happened? I decide against ringing back. There's no point. Instead, I find my mobile in the kitchen and text Meg. I have a worrying niggle and ask her to call me. All the time Cliff Richard is nagging away in my brain. Not for the first time, I lean my hands on the kitchen worktop and work on my breathing. There are times when I do wonder, what if? Like now, after that strange conversation. There are times when I miss him so much, still. It feels like the pain of a phantom limb. Days like this are rare but, when they happen, they're long and lonely. I close my eyes, focus on LA, on Meg and all the blessings in my life. But yes, Cliff. Thinking about tonight, you're right. Those 'miss you' nights are bloody awful.

Giles is coming over. We're having supper and a bottle of wine. It was a spur-of-the-moment decision, made after the phone call with Adam, and I am now officially crapping myself. I did it so quickly that I didn't really think about it. Will he think I'm interested? Am I interested? Will he think.this is like a date? God. What have I done? I've made a lasagne and salad. I have a bottle of white chilled and a bottle of red open. I've had a shower, have worn matching underwear and spritzed scent behind my ears. I'm wearing a favourite dress – one that I know I look good in. Shit, shit, shit. What am I doing? I glance at the oven clock. In an hour he'll be here. I call Karen. After hooting with laughter, she tells me to stop worrying, that it's like riding a bike. She tells me to calm down and have a glass of wine, just one. Then she snorts with laughter again. This is not helping. I hang up on her.

Pouring my one glass of wine, my hand is shaking. Actually shaking, like full proper tremors. It makes me remember a day shortly after Adam left, and I had started to see Dr Caroline Gothenburg. I had such bad shakes that day . . . Caroline would be proud today. I close my eyes, get in touch with my inner Babushka, who is smiling with me, rather than laughing at me. It's going to be okay. Babushka often struggles, living side by side with Lucy Fir, but today she's strong. I am a successful writer. I am a good-looking forty-two-year-old woman, ready to start living again. I am about to have supper with a new friend. That is all. Day by day, hour by hour, moment by moment, Babushka reminds me.

An hour and a half later, I have consumed almost a whole bottle of wine. Giles is on his first glass of red. The lasagne is in the oven. The kitchen smells like Jamie Oliver has been in and I'm still scared witless. Giles has made an effort, looking smart in an open-neck shirt and chinos. He's sitting at the breakfast bar and picks up one of the many congratulatory cards on the side. 'May I?' he asks.

I nod. I suppose now is as good a time as any to confess that I'm only in estate agency for the regular salary. I never dreamt of it as a child. But I did dream of writing songs . . .

He has read a few of the cards. 'So, let me get this right,' he says. 'You have written a song and this song is going to be in a Hollywood movie.'

When I hear it said like that, I sort of want to squeal, but I contain myself and just agree. 'That's right.'

'And the holiday time that you've just booked off. You did say you were going to LA. Is it anything to do with this?' He waves one of the cards.

'I'm meeting the producers.'

'Holy shit! I'm impressed! I mean, you put it in your CV – "Songwriting" – and I thought it was an unusual hobby, but wow! Well done you.'

I bring the lasagne to the dining table. It's already set and the salad is sitting in the centre. When we're seated, I hand him a steaming portion. 'Careful, it's hot,' I say, passing the salad bowl and side plates.

'Did you make this?' He rubs his thighs with both hands. 'I did.'

'A woman of many talents.' He smiles. 'So, your mum's card. Tell me why, in the middle of your mother's obvious excitement at your success, she seems most concerned with giving you a manicure before you leave?'

I laugh. 'My mother is a force of nature. Her latest adult education-acquired skill is all things nails. Gels, nail art, everything. She's now added some sort of holistic healing oil on the hands and, yes, she's desperate to try it out on

197

me before I go.' I shrug. 'She's harmless and she adores me. I find it quite comforting having her spoil me . . . She's coming tomorrow night to paint a personally designed treble clef on my thumbnail.'

'Bring her into the office, I'd love to meet her.'

My face creases. 'I don't think so.'

'Why not?'

'Because she'd probably have us married off.' The words have escaped before I have a chance to filter them.

He laughs out loud at this idea and I'm not sure what's funny, my mother pairing us off, or me telling him that's what she'd be doing. I am of course ignoring the fact that Mum would prefer Adam and me to reconcile above all else.

I notice he's eating a lot of salad and playing with the lasagne. 'Is it okay?' I ask. 'The food?'

He flushes red, puts his knife and fork down. 'I should've said something. I don't eat meat.'

My hand covers my mouth.

'Please,' he says 'it's my fault . . . I normally tell people but, to be honest, I was so shocked when you called and asked me to supper that I just said yes, and then felt I couldn't ring back.'

I go to take his plate away and he catches my hand, covers it with his. 'Please leave it. I'll just have more of this delicious salad.'

I sit down again. 'Sorry.' I've no idea why I'm apologizing. Probably for serving a vegetarian with meat, but it might be because I felt nothing during the hand-touching thing. As it happened, I thought, maybe there'll be sparks, like in the movies. But there were no sparks. And no one knows more than I do what crap they serve up in the movies. I'm disappointed, so help myself to the last of the white. Another glass down. I remove the lasagne to the kitchen and pray he likes apple pie.

Conversation is flowing. He is a lovely, kind, attentive man who seems genuinely interested in me and what I do. I carve two triangles of pastried apple.

'Tell me about you, Giles. I know you were married – do you mind talking about it?'

I need to know if he has cheat DNA in him before I even let him kiss me.

'I don't mind,' he says, 'though there's really not a lot to tell. We married young. We got married because Mireille was pregnant.'

He says the word 'Mireille', pronouncing it with an authentic French accent. As I've learnt tonight that Giles is forty and the twins sixteen, I quickly work out that 'married young' means at the age of twenty-four. Older than I was . . .

'It was tough. We were living in France. I was working there, selling holiday homes to Brits mostly. It didn't bring in a lot of money and Mireille's an artist. Money was tight.'

'When did you come back?'

'Over ten years ago.'

'They stayed?'

'They did.' He sighs, deeply and loudly. 'We just fell out of love. It was friendly; as friendly as two people with two children falling out of love can be. Her parents lived a mile away. They were glad to see the back of me.'

'And the girls. How often did you see them?'

'Not often enough for the first five years. As soon as

199

they were eleven, we both agreed that they should come to school in England. They're boarding over in Walton, so they're with me most weekends and go back to France for all of the holidays. It works quite well now.'

I don't ask how he went from struggling holiday-home seller to privately educating two children. Something tells me the random mention of her parents has something to do with it. I hope not, for his sake. I hope he's made a shitload of money selling houses in Weybridge and Mireille has become a name in the French art world.

It's not long after coffee that Giles suggests he should go, it being a 'school night' – work tomorrow. We are both in the office tomorrow, so I'm anxious that the next few minutes don't make that awkward. At the door, standing under my text-art, he tells me he hates horseradish even more than meat and I laugh.

'You have a lovely laugh,' he says, then he leans in for the kiss. It is tender at first, just a gentle touching of lips, before a full-on kiss. It feels strange, this sensation of another man's tongue in my mouth. His hand is on the back of my head, and that makes me think of Adam, the way his fingers used to lace through my hair. I end the kiss.

'See you tomorrow,' he whispers.

'You will,' I reply, my voice a whisper too.

I close the door behind him, lean my back flat up against it. Immediately, I know I will not be kissing Giles again. I'm cast back to being seventeen again. I felt nothing, absolutely nothing, when he kissed me. Is this normal? Is it because I haven't kissed anyone else in so long? Maybe it's me. Maybe I can say that. 'It's not you, it's me. I've forgotten how to kiss.' I shake my head, grab my phone and head straight up to bed. The clean-up can wait until the morning. My phone registers fourteen missed calls from Karen since I hung up on her. I listen to the last 121 message and smile. She, too, can wait . . .

Lying in bed, I go over it in my head. For the first time in many months, I really miss kissing Adam – the physicality of it. The way he held me, the way he used his tongue, the way I tingled every time he did. I miss making love. I haven't made love to another man in over two decades, so I'm not sure if I miss making love or, again, if I miss making love to Adam. Cliff is back, singing away, and I end up putting my pillow over my head and begging Lucy Fir to deck him.

Chapter Twenty-Four

Tim and Kiera have come through. Together they must have worked on Gordon, who absolutely does not want me near his son. Later today, I'm going to the hospital to meet Noah. They both think it's best if I'm introduced as a friend of Tim's. Before this can happen later today, I have to send another grovelling text to Meg, go for a thirty-minute run and get through a day's work in the office in half the time.

My running gear lies in a squashed ball at the back of the hall cupboard. It whiffs a bit but I pull it apart and add additional layers. It's a month to Christmas and it's cold outside. Water bottle in hand, I leave the flat and, turning left, walk down Narrow Street, past the Italian and Indian restaurants, past the warehouse conversions, towards the pedestrian entrance to Limehouse Marina. Stopping to stretch, I cross the street and start to run. I run around the Isle of Dogs, across the top, past Canary Wharf tower and the shopping mall.

Beth is in my head. With every rhythmic beat of my feet on the pavement, there is another thought of her. It's as though I'm on countdown and I have to savour every image, every memory before she makes that call. Before she tells me that we too are finished, before I give in to the black cloud that has been lying over me since Sunday. Back in Narrow Street, I buy a newspaper and cross the road.

As soon as I hear the sound, I recognize it immediately: brakes on tarmac. Turning swiftly left, I raise an apologetic hand to a taxi driver who swears aloud. I watch his face, his words appearing in amplified slow motion, open hostility tumbling from his mouth. I reach the footpath, balance myself against a wall and rub my temples. My head throbs, as if my brain has loosened from its anchor and is banging off my skull. Sounds ambush me like someone has turned the volume up. Turning around, I move slowly towards the building I now know as home.

In the shower, I stand for ages beneath a scalding flow of water. I am wearing my running clothes. Unsure if this is genius as it means they get washed too, or it's another sign of me losing the plot, I remove them and scrub them with shower gel. I'm not quite ready for the funny farm yet. Hanging them on the side of the bath, I dress for work before shovelling a slice of toast and a tepid coffee down me. Twenty minutes later, I'm sitting at my desk.

In Oakside paediatric unit, my palms are sweaty, my heartbeat loud and irregular. I've been told what to say; I've been told what to do. If I stick to the plan, everything will be fine. I know they don't have to let me see him, so I'm grateful to Kiera and Tim, and Gordon who, though he won't be here today, has agreed reluctantly to my meeting Noah. The story is simple. I'm a friend of Tim's;

I've come to collect him as we're going out for a catch-up with some university friends later. It sounds a little convoluted to me, but I figure they must know what they're doing and, frankly, I'd agree to anything if they let me meet my son, just once.

I make my way to the ward. My phone notes hold all the directions dictated by Kiera and I finally reach the right room. Looking in from a small porthole window in the door, I see Kiera and Tim both laughing inside. On the bed lies a small boy, tubes and wires all over him. He is having an animated conversation with his mother, both his hands in the air, as though he's debating a point. I stand still, very still. He looks just like me, or just like I did at his age. His hair, though patchy, is the same colour and has the same curl running through it. He has Kiera's mouth and my nose and, though I can't see from here, I suspect he has my green eyes. I'm locked in position when I see Tim wave at me and beckon me into the room.

Pushing the door open, I suddenly have second thoughts. What am I doing here? What right have I got to be here? I shouldn't be here . . .

Tim offers me his hand. 'Adam. Good to see you, mate. Noah, this is Adam, the friend I told you about. Thinks he's a scratch golfer but all he does is scratch his head a lot when we play.'

Kiera comes forward, offers me both her cheeks. 'Good to meet you.' Her voice is almost a murmur.

Noah smiles. 'Nice to meet you, Adam.'

'How are you. Feeling?' I know it's lame but it's all I can think of to say. It's impossible to ignore the medical paraphernalia in the room. It's impossible to ignore the tubes and wires attached to the child. It's impossible to come to any conclusion other than this little boy is very sick.

'I've had worse days – how about you?'

'I'm good, thanks.' I was right: his eyes when they meet mine are green. I see it then, immediately – he knows something. His eyes seem to say to mine: 'Hello, Adam. I'm Noah and you look just like me. How about that . . . ' Kiera senses it too. She shifts uncomfortably, starts to fidget in her handbag. I don't know where to look and find myself focusing on the floor tiles. Chequered, black and white, they remind me of a chessboard.

Noah looks over the side of his bed. 'I often think it looks like a chessboard, the floor . . . ' He pulls himself upright against the mound of pillows behind his head. 'Sometimes, at night, if I have to lie on my side, I look down and move pretend pieces around the floor. Do you play?'

I'm left wondering if the child is a mind-reader, but I nod. 'It's been a while but I used to – a lot.'

'We should have a game,' he says. 'I get bored playing with myself on the DS. And these two are rubbish.' He smiles at his mother and uncle. 'Dad's not so bad, but he's easy to beat if I concentrate.' Suddenly, his breathing seems a little laboured, as if talking has exhausted him.

Kiera approaches the bed, leans into him, where he automatically loops her arm for her to pull him upright. She gently massages his back. 'You need to take it easy,' she whispers. 'Enough chatting for today, time to get some rest.'

'I'm fine, Mum, really.'

'Rest,' she says firmly, 'now.'

Noah's eyes roll upwards. 'You're fussing.'

'Someone has to.' She kisses his forehead.

I find myself moved by the scene. I've only ever known Kiera as a friend, someone I had an illicit, fun night with. Now, she's here – an anxious, loving mother to her child, the child I helped create. It's surreal and I feel as if I'm watching a film reel.

'We should go, Adam.' Tim gathers up his coat and briefcase, leans into the boy and high-fives him.

I want to say, 'No. Please, just another few minutes. Please, just let me look at him?'

I say nothing, but offer him my hand.

'Come back for that game of chess?' he says.

I nod and turn to leave with Tim.

'Adam?'

I look back over my shoulder.

'What university did you go to?' he asks.

My eyes dart to Tim's. I went to King's College, but I've no idea where Tim went.

'We went to Brunel,' Tim replies, then glances at his watch. 'C'mon, we should go. The boys will start without us.'

I paste a frozen smile to my lips, mutter a goodbye, and exit ahead of Tim.

'That was close,' he whispers when he catches me up. 'I'd swear sometimes, that kid can see through walls.'

'Do you think he suspects something?'

Tim shakes his head. 'Nah, he's just fishing. I've got to get back to London for a meeting, Adam. You okay from here?'

I nod, wave him off. Tim heads out to the west entrance car park and I head back, through a warren of corridors, towards the east one.

Quickening my pace, I feel an urgent need to get out of here. Convinced Noah asked the question for a reason, I have a vision of Kiera appearing with tears in her eyes or, worse, Gordon appearing with murder in his. I wanted to meet my son, but I do not want to upset his family dynamic.

Without warning, my gut begins to heave and I know I'm going to be sick. I scan the hallway and see a male toilet up ahead. Running, I push the swing door open and barely make it to the cubicle before my stomach empties. Gripping the sides of the bowl, I vomit continuously for what must be a few minutes. Finally, I try to stand. My legs unsteady, I balance myself against the stall wall. I wipe my mouth with some toilet paper and open the door. Thankfully, the room is empty. I wash my mouth out, spray in some mint freshener. My reflection shows a man who looks much older than my forty-three years. My skin is pale, veined, my eyes heavy and dark. Though I keep my hair cut very short, a few of the tiny curls at the edge of my hairline are stuck in a line of sweat. Noah has curly hair . . . Noah has very little curly hair left, presumably from chemotherapy.

I straighten out my clothes, take the opportunity to sit in a chair, just by the inside of the door. I wonder why it's here. For the elderly? Infirm? Selfish middle-aged men who find their shoulders unable to carry their load? The chair is hard plastic, not designed for comfort or to encourage sitting for long.

A man enters the room, looks at me, and asks me if I'm okay. I nod, mutter a thanks and stand up. I need to get home and it'll take ages at this time in traffic. Outside the men's loo there is a vending machine; I search my pockets for coins to feed it for a bottle of water. Just drink the water, I tell myself as I unscrew the cap. Drink the water, get in your car and drive home slowly. Do not drive to

Weybridge, which is no longer your home. I'm tempted. Just drive the ten-minute drive there, ask Beth if I can stay over and crash for the night. I am deciding it's a very bad idea when I hear my name being called.

'Adam?'

I turn around to see Kiera.

'You still here?' she asks.

'I, er—'

'You okay? You look a bit green around the gills.'

I shrug. 'I'm okay, just been sick,' I find myself confessing and nodding towards the men's toilets.

'You shouldn't drive. I'm heading home for an hour. Come back, have a hot drink?'

I'm confused. Kiera lives in London too.

'I've rented a flat nearby.' She reads my face. 'Just while Noah's here. You really shouldn't drive, you know. I'm meeting Gordon back here in an hour, so I could drop you back to your car then.'

I feel my head bob up and down before I realize I've actually agreed to this.

'It would be good to have a chat anyway. Let me know what you think of Noah,' she smiles. 'I just need to pop in here quickly – won't last until home.' Her head nods towards the Ladies.

I watch her tiny frame push through the swing door, have no time to wonder if a drink, hot or cold, in Kiera's local flat is a good or a bad idea, before I hear my name being called again. This time, I recognize the voice. As I turn towards it, I hope I'm dreaming and soon discover I'm not. God, I decide, is fucking with me. Oh yes, fucking me large.

Chapter Twenty-Five

Typed on my iPhone, my 'To Do' list looks more organized than a paper version, but it's still too long. I only have a few days before LA and this list makes me feel dizzy. My morning, so far, has been spent in the offices of a man called 'Bear'. I have no idea how Bear got his name: whether his parents had a sick sense of humour, or whether he was given the nickname when his stature was greater than it is now. But I do know the Gospel according to Josh says that Bear is the best in the business for funky, 'with it', 'songwriterly' websites.

Josh is right – the man knows his stuff; after spending a few hours at his office in Chiswick, I have the bones of what looks like a really exciting website. Josh has insisted that the whole thing be up and running with songs I've written but are as yet unsigned – all up there before Friday. Great. Bear (who is in fact a small, geeky-looking guy with scant hair and John Lennon glasses) and I have our work cut out . . .

Right now, though, sitting in my car parked outside Bear's office, number eight on the 'To Do' list is glaring up at me. I have been putting it off for too long and can no longer ignore it. Closing my eyes, I count to a hundred. Then I start up the car and point it in the direction of home.

Five minutes from the house, I take a turn off the A3 and head towards my three o'clock appointment. When I get there, I walk through to reception. I'm nervous. Having Googled what to do, I am here, because I know I have to be. Every cell in my body is screaming 'No.' At reception, I'm handed a clipboard, asked to take a seat, fill in my details, then someone will be with me shortly.

I stare at the page. Having spent all morning building the www.beth-hall.co.uk website, I'm not too keen on using my real name, so fill it in as Lucy Babushkowizc. As a combination of my inner saboteur and my fabulous inner core, I think it does reflect some parts of me. The rest of the questions I answer as honestly as possible, apart from my date of birth – for some reason, I make myself two years younger.

About fifteen minutes later, I hear the name being called and look up. A young girl, not much older than Meg and very similar in looks to her, beckons me through to a smaller room. There we are met by an older, more matronly looking woman. She is seated, while the Meg lookalike stands. 'Matron' asks the questions. In a kind voice, she explains what sort of questions are on the way and what else may happen. I try not to gulp.

I'm asked if I have had any medical problems, any outward physical signs of trouble. I shake my head, but tell them I'd like them to check anyway. I'm asked if I've had sex with anyone from outside the UK recently. I try not to laugh. They are not to know I haven't had sex with anyone since Adam. There's every chance when they get down there to have a look, they may need a can opener.

I'm asked when I last had sex. I tell them, then explain a little about the circumstances, about why I'm here at the Genito-Urinary Medicine clinic, a fancy name for the place I have to come to, to check if I've acquired any sexual diseases from my philandering husband.

I see a glance pass between them, realize it's probably quite common, this situation. A woman, or indeed a man, having to check out they're okay after years of being with the same person, years of being with the same unfaithful person. I can tell from that glance that I'm not alone. Unsure if I feel better or worse, they ask if I'm able to give a urine sample; they prepare one of those kidney-shaped cardboard bowls with a needle to take a blood sample. Inside, I'm starting to seethe. That fucker. That shitbag. Christ, there's times I hate him . . .

I fill the tiny sample bottle and hand 'Matron' my bottle of warm pee. I make a fist to let her take some blood. I open my legs and let her part the folds of my undercarriage with her gloved hands. During this last part, my eyes are closed. I say some sort of prayer – a muttered gobbledegook cluster of words that pray to some God somewhere that I have nothing nasty, that she doesn't spot some foul rash. She raises her head, unsnaps her gloves, smiles and tells me everything looks fine and I heave a very deep sigh of relief.

I'm asked how I'd like to receive my test results. As quickly as possible, please, is what I'm thinking, but we agree that they will call my mobile. I thank them and exit, stage left.

I am trembling as I come out to the car park. Hoping no one sees me, I skirt the edge of the clinic and enter the main ground floor of the adjoining building. My shakes need a coffee before I drive home. I snake my way through the

crowds and I'm almost at the Costa concession when I see
a familiar figure up ahead of me. Confused, I call his name.

'Adam?'

He turns to face me, his expression one of pure horror.
'Beth,' he says. 'What are you doing here?' As he speaks,
he walks, steering me by the elbow, back towards the
exit.

I stop moving. 'I've been to the GUM clinic to have
myself tested. Why are *you* here?'

He looks as if he is about to die on the spot. 'I'm . . . '

'You're what?' I'm aware that he's looking back over
my shoulder to where we just came from. 'Who are you
here with?'

He doesn't reply.

'Did you hear what I just said, Adam? I've just had a
woman checking my bits for nasty rashes. Now what the
fuck are *you* doing here?'

He's steering me again.

'I've been visiting a friend. I was just leaving . . . '

I grind myself to a halt again. 'Who? Who were you
visiting?' I notice how pale he is, how much weight he's
lost. It would look good on him if he wasn't such a ghastly
shade of wan. A thought that he might be ill flits through
my mind – maybe he's been having tests?

'Just a friend of a friend. I said I'd pop in and visit if I
was out this way.'

I am at the Costa bar and, though I don't believe a word
he's saying, I need a coffee more than I need a row in the
middle of the hospital. 'I need a coffee. My visit to the
clinic has traumatized me.'

'Right,' he says, his eyes darting up and down the

corridor. 'I'm sorry. I mean, of course I'm sorry that, you know, you feel you had to go there.'

I snort out loud. 'Are you having one? Tea? Coffee?'

'No, no, I don't want anything.' He glances at his wrist. 'I've got to go, Beth. Sorry to be so short, but I've got to go.' Within seconds, he's vanished, and I'm left standing there, a fiver in my hand, my mouth wide open.

I order a double latte and sit on one of the armchairs near a large pillar, wondering what just happened. From the throng of people around me, I see Kiera Pugh walk towards the exit next to me and remember her son is in hospital here. Shame flushes my face as I look down, place myself behind the pillar, trying to avoid her eyes and the inevitable small talk. Though I feel for her right now, I'm more concerned about Adam. He was behaving like a madman. A madman with something else to hide . . .

In my driveway, I'm greeted by my very irate mother.

'For Christ's sake, Elizabeth. Five o'clock means five o'clock. I've been sitting here for over an hour and it's bloody cold.'

'I'm sorry, Mum, really sorry.' I unlock the front door and turn the lights on. I cannot tell her the truth and say she didn't make my 'To Do' list and so I forgot she was coming. 'I got horribly delayed on the A3,' I lie.

'I'll keep my coat on for a while,' she grumbles as I turn the thermostat up. The temperature outside has really dropped this week and the house is cold.

'I've put you in the green room,' I tell her, trying to cheer her up. It's the warmest room in the house and, because it looks over the garden, it's also my mother's favourite bedroom. 'And I thought we'd get a takeaway, a nice treat.'

'What you mean is you have no food in.'

I make a face. 'There's no point. I'm away soon for a few days. Chinese or Indian?' I put my arm around her.

'Chinese,' she smiles. 'Are you excited? Los Angeles, eh? Your dad would be so proud. Will you play me the song?'

'I will. Let me just grab a shower, Mum. I'll take your bags upstairs. Put the telly on?'

I'm heading upstairs when she yells at me to leave the nail bag downstairs. I leave the smaller, patent, orange one that rattles. A Chinese, a manicure, my mum telling me that my song is worthy of a Grammy, some Sky Plus recordings of good television drama and a glass of wine. All in all a good evening, if only I can stop thinking about Adam Hall, the madman.

Upstairs, my mobile flashes, just as I get naked. I grab it, seeing it's Meg. 'Long time no speak, stranger. Are you okay?'

'I'm fine, Mum, just busy.'

I throw a towel around me to keep warm. 'I've tried to call you a few times, left a few messages.' I'm trying hard not to sound accusing. 'You never did finish your room.'

'I know. I'm sorry.'

'How's Jack?' There's a downbeat tone in her voice and I'm wondering if he might be responsible.

'He's fine. He's been great actually . . .' She stops herself. 'Listen, are you in tomorrow night? I need to see you before you go to LA.'

I am supposed to be seeing Giles tomorrow night. A night out at the cinema. I couldn't tell him that I don't like the cinema, because he knows from the first time being at the house that I do. I couldn't tell him that I don't want to go for fear he'll kiss me again, because I'm too nice to say something that awful. And I've decided I really didn't like the kiss. So, I agreed to go, and now hopefully Meg is going to offer me an excuse to get out of it. I may, however, have to ham up her urgent need to see me.

'Well, it'll have to be tomorrow night then,' I tell her. Suddenly, I'm worried. My mummy antennae twitch. 'Are you all right, really?'

'Don't be silly, Mum, I'm fine. I'll be there about seven?'

'Okay, see you then, love you.'

'Love you too.' She hangs up.

I drop the towel and wait for the water to heat up. Shivering, I go through the call in my head again. Leaning against the tiles, I say another gobbledegook prayer, my second of the day. Counting my prayer for Kiera Pugh's child, it's my third of the month – of the year – in a decade. I step under the steaming spray and ask all the gods who are listening to please not let Meg tell me she's pregnant. And, just for a moment, an ever-so-brief smidgeon of a second, I think of LA and how I'll like it. And whether I could stay there forever . . .

Mum is sitting in her favourite chair, eyes shut, head back, and her leg moving gently in time with the slow ballad music. She takes a sip from her glass of wine, eyes still closed. I can tell she's listening to the lyrics. When it's finished she looks across at me. 'Brilliant, darling, really, it's brilliant. The best you've ever written.'

I can't help but beam.

'Do you believe it?' she asks. 'The words of your song?'

My smile turns itself upside down. 'It's not about Adam

and me,' I say, a tad too defensively. I start to clear the plates in front of us. It had been a lovely laptop supper until now.

'Why not? Don't you think it could be?'

I sigh. 'It's for the movies, Mum, not real life. In real life people can't always reconcile.'

'I know that. But what if it's what he wants and what you want deep down? I know it's what Meg wants.'

There are times when Sybil Moir frustrates the hell out of me, and this is one of them. I know she and Meg are close, but I don't want her filling Meg's head with false hopes.

'Meg knows it's not what I want, deep down or otherwise. Nor is it what I need. She'll get used to the idea soon and she'll always have both Adam and me in her life.'

Mum stands, walks across to the kitchen and loads the plates in the dishwasher. We pass by each other as she heads back and I'm trying to squash the Chinese foil containers into the recycling bin. She puts her arms around my neck. 'I just want you to be happy.'

'I will be, but not with Adam.'

She sighs into my hair. 'Maybe he just has to show you he still loves you.'

'It wouldn't make any difference, Mum. It's just too late.'

'I see,' she says, then moves away, fills her glass with more pinot grigio and retires to her favourite chair. 'It's nine o'clock,' she calls back. '*Game of Thrones* is on. I'll do your nails in the morning.'

Later I fall asleep dreaming of Tyrion and Adam duelling for my love. And I wake, wondering, what if . . . What if he really fought for me?

Chapter Twenty-Six

On the way home, my head hurts, my heartbeat is irregular, I have a nagging pain in my arm and I'm driving a car. Not a good combination and, since having a heart attack at the wheel is not something I want, I pull over and try to breathe deeply.

Kiera rings and I press the Bluetooth. 'What happened to you?' she asks.

'I had to go, sorry.'

'Are you all right, Adam?' She sounds concerned.

'I'm fine, it's just been a long day.'

'Look, there's no easy way of saying this without nagging, but I need to know if you've asked Meg.'

Kiera's concern for me is now making sense.

'Meg hasn't spoken to me since I asked her, Kiera. She told me we're finished – never to speak to her again.'

Kiera makes a gasping sound.

'I've texted her, emailed her. Told her what she has to do. She knows the urgency and I know she'll do the right thing.'

'Thank you. I'm sorry.'

There is nothing else to say. I mutter a goodbye, start the engine and flick the radio on. Not in the mood for music, I turn to LBC, where there's a debate in full flow. The voice of a woman, identified by the host as Rabbi Rebekah Morley, speaks in clear tones.

'It's because of the absence of God in most people's lives!' She seems outraged. 'It seems like most people now-adays are happy to sin as long as they're not discovered. For too many people, it's not the "doing something bad" that bothers them, it's the fear of being found out. It seems to be okay as long as that doesn't happen.'

A softly spoken man interrupts.

'Hold on, let's be clear here. What's a sin? Do we go by the Ten Commandments?'

I switch channels and unscrew the cap from my bottled water. The soft harmonies of the Eagles do not distract me from the earlier mention of the Ten Commandments.

Honour thy father and thy mother.

Thou shalt not kill.

Thou shalt not covet thy neighbour's goods.

Thou shalt not commit adultery.

I've never envied Sylvia or any other 'neighbour' a thing and I've never thought of killing someone – not really. I have committed adultery and I did honour my mother and father – to a point. That is, until their last double act – but that's something I don't want to think about right now. I simply haven't got the head-room left.

At home I pour a large Jim Beam, no ice. I swallow it in three gulps and pour another. I pull a seat out at the tiny table. Opening the letter I'd found in my pocket earlier, I see it is two pages long. Sybil's flowery handwriting stares up from the pages, which smell of her home in the Cotswolds – something like lavender and rosemary mixed together. I haven't had a handwritten letter in over twenty years; if it wasn't from Sybil, I'd be quite excited. I straighten out the many creases on the page, take another gulp of whiskey and begin to read.

Dear Adam,

Yes, you are and have been dear to me, despite the fact that you've been a total idiot. I've been wondering how to contact you, since you didn't respond to the message I left on your phone. You cheated on her, Adam. It's unforgivable. You should never have done that, not to my beautiful, sensitive, loving daughter. That said, I know without even talking to you that you'll want her back. I know from talking to Meg you want her back. Meg just wants you both to get back together, to have her family whole again. I also know Elizabeth will come around. If you give her time, show her that you still love her, don't give up on her, she will find a way.

I swallow hard, stand up suddenly, knock the whiskey tumbler over. In the bathroom, I pull my clothes from me, change into my running gear. My head, I'd swear, is making whirring sounds I feel so fucking dizzy with it all. Grabbing keys, I slam the front door, leave the building and start to run. I run for miles, sticking to the pavement as I've forgotten my reflective gear. I run for miles with only my thoughts. I run for miles, telling myself that Forrest Gump has nothing on me. By the time I return home, I'm greeted by the scents of my neighbours' dinners wafting through the communal hall.

Inside, I ignore the broken glass and the mess. Still sweating, I pour another drink and sit on the sofa with Sybil's pages.

When I was a little girl, I dreamed of getting married to a man I loved and who loved me back. All grown up, I realized the man I did marry was a complex bastard. But I loved him, and he loved me back. I loved him enough to forgive the fact that he loved alcohol more than me. He never drank a drop until our son died, and after that he never stopped until it killed him. Other people told me I was stupid for staying, but I know what worked for me and Elizabeth. The life in between was still worth living.

I digress. You probably know all of this through Elizabeth anyway. The point I'm trying to make is that LOVE, real love, can truly overcome adversity. So, Adam. Do you REALLY LOVE her? Your Beth? Above all else? Like she deserves to be loved? If so, now would be a good time to let her know.

Yours,

Sybil x

Crunching the broken glass into the wooden floor, I cross the room to the table and drag the laptop towards me. My wife deserves the very best love that the world can show her, but she also deserves the truth, and it should come from me.

'My dearest Beth . . . '

I type the document in Word, two fingers only, but at speed. The need to write this letter came over me so strongly while reading Sybil's that I need to get it out there before I change my mind.

Tonight, I'm hurting because I lied to you again when I bumped into you at the hospital. I want to stop doing that, telling you lies, so I've decided to write to you.

Right at this moment, I hate myself.

A long time ago, you asked me to go to counselling, and I think we lasted two sessions before I convinced you it was a waste of time and that we were fine and that you were fine and that I was fine. I lied again. The full truth is that I had a one-night stand with a woman who was then a client. It was, I swear, just once but we have a child.

I have never been involved in this child's life. That was the way the woman involved wanted it and I was never more relieved to hear those words. I do need you to know that I have been unfaithful to you only twice – recently with Emma, and years ago that once with Kiera, who is mother to Noah.

The fact that there's a child will have you reeling. Don't imagine that I don't know how this will hurt. Don't imagine that I don't remember how hard you and I tried for that second child. I remember the disappointment in your eyes every month; it was mine too . . . I know the existence of Noah is the thing that you'll never be able to forgive.

I'd love to be able to say that the weight of my lies is the sudden reason for my honesty. That's not true. I'm telling you this now because, if I don't, Meg will tell you anyway – and I wanted this to come from me. You deserve that, at least.

Noah is ill. Kiera, his mother, contacted me recently to let me know that he has leukaemia. Without a stem cell donation, his future is bleak. They have tried to find a match from the donor register and all known family, without success. I have been tested and I am not a match. I have told Meg the truth and asked her to be tested. She is a sibling and Noah's best hope. I knew, when I asked her, all of this would come out. I knew, but I had to do it. He's only a little boy, an innocent child who asked for none of this.

Despite all of this shit, please know that I'm so proud of you and thrilled that you have finally been recognized for the amazing songwriter that you are. You deserve everything that's coming your way, Beth. It's just the beginning of a journey that will be everything you ever dreamed of, when you were squirrelled away in the attic with your keyboard, guitar and your words.

I will always regret what I've done, the hurt I've caused, and I will always love you.

Adam x

I read it back only once. Then I call it 'Letter to Beth'. Then, without thinking about it, I attach it in an email to her with the words, PLEASE READ THIS in the header. Then, I press send. Then, I feel my eyes fill. I will myself not to cry, instead allowing my body to rock forward and back. I wonder how I'm ever going to be able to go on without her. I want to call out her name. I want to pick up the phone and plead. But all I can do is wait, wait for the fallout . . .

Chapter Twenty-Seven

'Don't worry, I understand. Really, it's not a problem.'

While I have not exactly lied to Giles, I haven't exactly been honest either. I made Meg's visit to me sound like it's a matter of life or death. Now, listening to him, I feel guilty.

'Will I see you before you go?' he asks.

I'm confused. Does one kiss mean we're 'seeing' each other? I hope not. I hope that it's just what people say when they mean they might bump into me in Waitrose.

'No,' I tell him, just for the avoidance of doubt. That way, prospective kisses and Waitrose have both been ruled out. 'I've got such a lot to do,' I add, to soften the blow.

'Good luck then – text me when you're there?'

Fuck, he does mean the non-Waitrose seeing me thing. I say I will, and hang up. And I no longer feel guilty. Nah, one dodgy kiss does not a 'seeing-me-thing' make.

I check my emails, deal with the one from Josh attached to a long list of bullet points. He is, at this stage, making me much more nervous than I need be, but I can't be cross with him. The film company have paid for a hotel for two nights, but he's suggesting I should stay for a third. He has a list as long as my arm of appointments of people to see, places to go. Hollywood . . . Even the word makes my flesh goose-bump with excitement.

I close the laptop, staring at my nails. My mother has painted them a garish pink and I don't have time to get them redone. One of my thumbs has a treble clef, sort of turned into a heart. It's bloody awful, but I couldn't tell her. I did manage to stop her doing it on both and now I'm wondering if I have time to remove it all. Have I got enough acetone? Mentally, I put it on my 'To Do' list as I gather together the ingredients for supper. I'm making another lasagne, this time for someone who will eat it – Meg. When I think of her, my stomach lurches. She's okay. Nails aside, everything's going to be okay.

The lasagne is bubbling away in the oven. Meg's last text says she's running an hour late, but I'm not panicking. She will be here soon. Sitting at the breakfast bar in the kitchen, I focus on what's happening over the next few days. I am going to LA! I'm a happy girl. Pouring a glass of wine, I open the email that has just pinged through on the laptop. It's from Adam and contains an attachment that says PLEASE READ THIS. It feels a bit like Alice in Wonderland and I giggle aloud.

My instinct is screaming not to open it. I open it anyway. Immediately, the words jumble up in front of me. He's a liar who wants to be honest – good. What? A child? What child? What the fuck?

I can't swallow. I have no spit. There is none, my mouth is dry. I lick my lips. Leukaemia. Kiera.

I stand up, push the laptop away from me, like I've been scalded. Kiera, Noah, sickness. Oh my God . . .

My hand is clutching my upper left side. It's as though, if I don't keep it there, my heart will actually leap out of my chest. It will find a way. It will spring through my ribs and land on the kitchen floor, pulsate a little in front of me before it withers and dies. Right there on the oak planks. My heart will fucking die and I will just stop breathing.

Adam has another child. With someone called Kiera. He was at the hospital. So was Kiera. She has a sick child.

I rush to the sink. Only liquid comes up. I've been so busy, I haven't eaten since breakfast. I spit, turn the tap on, rinse my mouth out with cold, limey water and try to stand up. My head feels like it doesn't belong on my neck. My brain feels like it doesn't belong in my head. My life has just taken a turn that surely belongs in someone else's life.

The pull of the laptop is magnetic and I'm back at the stool, yanking it towards me. My eyes fill with a torrent of tears I had never believed possible. I had so wanted another child . . . We – we had so wanted another child. And all the time, he . . . I read on and get to the part about Meg.

It all makes sense now. Her recent distance, her need to see me before I go to LA. Fucking hell, the poor girl. She . . . The poor girl.

I hear her car pull up outside. I'll kill him. I swear. That fucking bastard. And Kiera Pugh . . . To think I felt sorry for her: that fucking, husband-fucking whore. Meg's key turns in the hallway door. I try to stand up and go to her, but my legs won't move. They feel as though they've been weighted with cement. I'm telling myself to walk on out to the hall, grab my daughter in a bear hug and never let her go, but moving is out of the question.

She comes into the kitchen, takes one look at me and bursts into tears.

'You know?'

I nod. Continuously. Tiny nods, like my head has developed a relentless tremor.

She comes to me instead, wraps her arms around me, then eventually stands back. 'How?' she asks.

My head jerks to the laptop. 'Read that.'

I refill my glass, pour one for her. 'Are you staying? Driving back?'

She doesn't look at me, continues reading. 'I'll stay,' she whispers.

I fill it to the brim.

'Right,' she says after a couple of minutes, pushing the laptop away and lifting the glass to her lips. She hasn't even taken off her coat yet.

'Have you had the test?' I manage to get the words out. 'Today . . . '

'When will you know if you're a match?'

'A few days, next week?'

'What happens if you are?'

'I'll go through a stem cell donation. Let's not talk about that.' She makes a squeamish face and starts to take her coat off.

'Leave it on,' I tell her. 'Can you drive me somewhere?' I switch the oven off, glance around the kitchen for my keys. My legs suddenly have motion and I move to the coat rack in the hall, throw the first coat to hand over my clothes.

'Where are we going?' She follows me.

'Just drive,' I tell her, as I close the door behind me. 'I'll show you the way.'

When we're there, I ask her to wait in the car, saying that I'll only be a few minutes.

'Mum?' she calls to me and I bend back into the passenger seat. 'You're scaring me,' she says.

I reach across, cup her face with my hand. 'Don't be scared. I'll be straight back.'

I am buzzed in by the porter. He knows me, after all. I am one of those trusty estate-agent girls from down the road. He looks up from his paper and smiles as I pass his desk. At Kiera's front door, I hesitate just a second, then I ring the bell.

She answers moments later. 'Lizzie! What a surprise. Come in.' I can see her face compute the fact that it's late evening and wonder what the hell I'm doing here. And what the hell am I wearing? She can't help herself. She's staring at my coat, which is, in fact, Adam's old Barbour. He uses it for gardening. I find myself questioning why it's still on the coat rack in the hall.

'My name is Beth,' I tell her.

Her face wrinkles in confusion. Well, it wrinkles around the eyes. Her Botoxed forehead doesn't move.

'I was christened Elizabeth. My mother calls me Elizabeth or Liz. My brother-in-law, Ben, always calls me Lizzie. My friends, though, my husband, they all call me Beth.'

It's instant. An immediate flash reaction. A look of absolute dread.

I have come here to slap her face. That was what I imagined doing back in front of my oven, with its by now

227

burnt lasagne. I have come to feel the back of my hand on her cheek. To leave my mark on her. To let her know who I am. To let her see the wife's face. I have come to hurl insults. To let her neighbours know what they are living beside.

Now that I'm here, all I see is a woman who looks almost as bad as me. Her face is drawn, her eyes shaded from weary tears. It strikes me that it's only women, women who have such a capacity to cry.

'Will you please come in?' Her voice is little above a whisper.

I shake my head. 'My name is Beth Hall. My husband is Adam Hall. Our daughter is Meg.'

'Lizzie, Beth, I don't know what to say. I'm sorry.'

'You have a son.' My mouth is dry again.

'Noah . . . '

I stare at her.

'Meg,' she says to me, and I can't tell if it's a question, a statement, a word, or what.

At that point, I turn around. Meg is waiting for me in the car. I have nothing to say to this woman. Yes, she's a husband-stealing bitch. But she's a husband-stealing bitch whose son is dying.

She calls after me. 'Beth, please. Do you know if Meg . . . ?'

The lift is waiting for me. All I have to do is press the bell and I'm in its inner sanctum. Minutes later, I exit to the bitter chill of a November evening. Meg has the car running to keep warm and I jump in the front.

'Do I want to know?' she asks, as she turns towards home.

'The mother.' I pull Adam's Barbour up around my neck, shivering. 'She lives in there. Temporarily. While the kid's in hospital.'

I can tell she's wondering how the hell I know this.

'Is she still alive?' Her forehead rises to produce line after line after line.

'Yes, she's alive. I never touched her. And don't frown. It's bad for you.'

Meg giggles. 'Frowning? Frowning is bad for me?' Mum, my father is an arsehole. He's bad for me. I have a brother I've never known. Let a girl frown?'

'You're right. Frown away, my love. Frown away. Let's go home and get completely sloshed.'

She agrees with me. It's a good idea, she tells me, but I already know her heart's not in it. Probably because it's bruised and battered and maybe even broken, like mine.

I huddle deeper into the coat, reach out and turn the heater up. 'It's getting colder,' I say.

'No shit, Sherlock,' is her reply. 'And you're on your way to LA.'

The sooner the better, I think, feeling cold to the core.

'I should warn you Karen's at home.'

'Karen? Why?'

'We can get sloshed, all three of us.'

'Why is Karen there?' I am immediately suspicious. 'Oh God, no . . . Please tell me Karen doesn't know about this.'

'I called her. I was terrified how you might react, so I called in the troops.'

I'm really miffed but try not to show her. Of course I would have told Karen, but Ben has only just moved in with her.

'And she has a bag with her,' Meg continues talking. 'Probably an overnight one, or it could be quite a big bag.'

'What the fuck, Meg . . . '

She takes her eyes off the road a second and turns to glance at me. 'I just spoke to her. On the phone when you were in with the mother. Karen was coming down for support anyway, but has since learned that Uncle Ben has known about this, this "situation", for a while. She's furious and has walked out.'

I am completely confused. Karen has left Ben in Karen's flat. I guess she couldn't throw him out, because Adam's in Ben's flat. Which means I get Karen. Her car is in the driveway when we pull in. The security light beams down on her and she turns to face me as we get out of Meg's car. She gives me a big shrug that says something like, 'The whole world has gone mad.'

'Can I stay here while you're in LA?' she asks as we embrace. I bury my head in her shoulder, remembering that Adam is due to spend some time here in the garden then. He wouldn't dare now. He really wouldn't dare.

'Of course you can,' I say. 'Although I hate to point out the obvious: that Ben is in your flat and he should be packing the bag?' I nudge my head towards the holdall which is, thankfully, not too big.

'He will be, when I've had time to think and clear my head.'

I unlock the door to the smell of burnt cheese and decide immediately that I am never, ever again cooking a lasagne. Having failed to smack the hell out of my husband's ex-mistress, it's the only decision I make this evening that I think I'll stick to.

Chapter Twenty-Eight

This much I know. Meg has had her test and we are awaiting the results. Beth has read my letter and has not replied. Verbally, screamingly, by email, post or by carrier pigeon. No reply. Nada, nothing . . . I don't know what I expect, but this nothingness is a killer. I only know she has read the letter because Ben told me. Apparently, Karen is now in Weybridge. Ben is in Karen's. I am in Ben's. It is one big head-fuck.

Today is Sunday and Kiera has agreed to let me see Noah since he's been asking if I can play chess with him. She is telling me off as we walk up to the ward together – telling me that I seem to swear a lot more than I used to and please, can I not do it in front of Noah. Fair enough . . . I want to laugh, because she's right. Ever since I placed my life down the toilet, it appears that my mouth thinks it lives there. Potty-mouth Beth is tame in comparison to me.

At the door of the ward, she places a hand on my arm. 'I should tell you. Beth came to see me.'

My stomach plunges into my groin. 'What? How?'

'It doesn't matter. I just wanted you to know. She was very upset.'

'She has a right to be.' I shrug.

'I hate the fact that she's had to find out. I hate the fact that I've hurt her. She seems like such a nice, a good,' she corrects herself, 'woman.'

'She is.'

'I'm sorry,' she says, yet again.

'You know what, Kiera. You and I can say sorry until the end of time and it still doesn't change a thing we've already done. Let's try and make something good out of the mess?' I nod my head in Noah's direction.

'You're right. One other thing. I haven't told Gordon you're here. I will do, but I haven't yet.'

'Bloody hell, Kiera. The last thing I need is Gordon in here on the warpath.'

She glares at me, presumably for my language. 'I'll tell him,' she says. 'I just have to find a way to tell him the truth – that Noah asked for you. That he's asked to play chess with you.'

'Do you think he knows something?' I watch our son, head down in a book, through the porthole in the door.

'He can't, can he?' she says. 'But then again, Noah's a bright boy. Before you showed up, he'd already noticed that there were no pictures of him as a baby with Gordon. We were going to tell him and then he got sick . . . '

I squeeze her hand. 'Please. I don't want to lie to Gordon. There have been too many lies. I'm weary.'

'I'll tell him,' she whispers as she opens the door.

'Yo.' Noah looks over the rim of his book and greets us.

'Hello, darling.' Kiera's kiss lingers on the child's forehead.

'Adam. You came back,' he says.

'Your mother tells me you want to play chess.' I open my rucksack and pull out a board game. It's Ben's, actually, but when I found it in the flat, I thought it would be a good idea. 'If you're going to play chess with me, we have to play properly, and that means feeling the pieces, not moving them around as a two-dimensional image.'

He already has the box open and is placing the pieces in their correct squares.

'Is this yours?' he asks. 'Did you play with this when you were little?'

I hesitate. 'It's my brother's, but yes, I did play with it.'

'You have a brother?' The child is looking squarely at me.

'Yes, his name's Ben.'

'Older or younger?'

'Younger.'

'By how much?'

I catch Kiera's smile.

'Do you always ask this many questions?' Her smile is matched with one from me.

'Always,' he says. 'How much younger?'

'Almost two years.'

'You're lucky.' He sighs. 'I'm an only child.'

Kiera is now biting her lower lip. 'Would you like a drink, love? I'm going to go and get a coffee for Adam and me.'

'An OJ please,' he says without looking up.

'Latte with two?' she asks me, and I nod my response.

'So,' Noah says after his mother has left and he is moving his first pawn. 'How come Mum knows how you like your coffee?'

'I've known her a while,' I reply, carefully. 'Your family are clients of mine, so although Tim and I go back a long way, I've known your mum for years too.'

There is a constant whirring in the room, which I realize is coming from all of the machines around the bed. I look at a few of them, trying to figure out what their function is.

'I could have sworn Mum acted as if she'd just met you the first time you were here.'

I'm unsure how to react. Maybe if I pretend I didn't hear . . .

'Does my dad know you've come?'

Another question I have to ignore. Maybe I can tell him I'm a little deaf. He has already taken a few of my pawns and a knight. This kid knows his chess.

'Adam? Does Dad know you're here?'

'I'm not sure.' I cough. 'It's awfully noisy in here, isn't it? And hot? My mouth's really dry.'

Noah rests his head back on the bulk of pillows behind his neck. 'It's the machines,' he says. 'And coffee is on its way.'

By the time Kiera returns, he has taken most of my pieces and I know I'm moments away from being beaten by a ten-year-old. She hands me a steaming coffee and I take a cautious sip from the tiny hole in the plastic lid.

'I need more practice.' I look up from the board, letting him know I can smell my defeat.

'You'll just have to come more often,' he says.

I don't reply. Kiera has leapt from her chair and is walking through the door.

Noah strains his head to try and see around the corner. 'It's Dad,' he whispers. 'And boy, does he look pissed off.'

Though I'm quite sure Kiera will not like his choice of vocabulary, I'm too scared to turn around and see what's going on. I gather up the chess pieces and place them in the box.

'I was three moves off checkmate,' he tells me.

'I believe you.'

'Why is it, Adam, that grown-ups aren't just honest with each other? It's so frustrating. What's the big deal here? I want to play chess with a friend of Uncle Tim's.'

I swallow hard, my back to whatever is going on out in the hallway. 'Sometimes, grown-ups . . . ' I stop myself. Shut the fuck up, Adam.

'What,' he says, 'sometimes they what?'

I raise my shoulders up and down.

'Sometimes grown-ups are arseholes. I'm the one who's dying here.'

Gordon, ignoring my presence completely, just passes me by on his way in to see his son, leaving Kiera and me outside in the corridor.

'You didn't have to come out,' Kiera says. She looks exhausted.

'He'd already thrashed me.'

'Gordon and I were due to meet here later but, to be honest, I think he knew I was sneaking you in.'

'If Gordon doesn't want me here, I won't come. Please, the last thing I want to do is to cause more trouble.'

'Adam, Noah wanted to see you again and that's all I'm concerned about.' She sips her coffee, makes a face, and tosses it in a nearby bin. 'I've just spoken to the consultant. We're waiting on Meg's results. If she's not a match, we can start the programme immediately. If she is, he'll get the stem cells instead, as that's more likely to be successful.'

I nod, but am already lost. Though Kiera has explained the new treatment from America that Noah would be a UK pioneer for, I'm not sure I understand it. It involves many different comprehensive treatments of the blood. What I do understand is that it's last-chance-saloon stuff, and I find myself praying that Meg is a match. Apart from Noah's plight, all of the turmoil in my fractured family will have been for nothing . . .

'Will they do the donation here if . . . ' I don't finish the sentence.

'Probably not. I think he should go back to Great Ormond Street. I don't want to move him again but, with a donation, I'd prefer him to be back under his original oncologists.'

'I'm going to take off,' I tell her.

'Leave Gordon to me, Adam. If you want to see Noah and he wants to see you, Gordon's going to have to find a way to man-up.'

I'm surprised at the anger in her voice but say nothing. Instead I hug her, briefly. She feels tiny in my arms, bird-like. 'Go and get yourself a cheese bloomer, you're fading away.'

She laughs, 'Look who's talking. How's the training going, by the way?'

'Good. I'm running every night now.' I don't tell her

that it's the only way I can ever get any sleep. She looks as though she has problems of her own in that department. 'Sponsor me. I have a page on "Just Giving".'

'I will.' She kisses my cheek and pushes the swing door. 'See you next time.'

I head out of the hospital. The day is bitterly cold, with the remnants of last night's frost still crunching underfoot. I glance at my watch. Unsure of what time she's flying, I head quickly to the car, turn the heat up high and Google flights to LA from Heathrow today on my iPhone. Sunday 30 November 2014, there are two flights – both later this afternoon. I head straight to Weybridge.

Her car is in the driveway. So is Karen's. I steel myself and ring the doorbell.

Karen answers. Without speaking, she simply glares at me.

'Is Beth here?' I pull my coat tightly around me.

'I'm just about to drive her to the airport.'

'Can I see her?'

'Doubtful . . . '

'Karen, it's freezing out here. If you're going to yell at me, or just scowl at me, can we please do it in the hall?'

'No. You can freeze your fucking rocks off out there. Maybe if they fall off, it'll stop you using them.'

'I need to see Beth before she goes.'

'She does not want to see you.'

'How do you know?'

'Beth?' Karen yells into the house at the top of her voice. 'Do you want to see Adam?'

There is silence.

I tilt my head, raise my eyebrows.

'She doesn't want to see you.'

'Oh, for God's sake. Let me in my own bloody house.' I push past her into the hallway.

'That's assault,' she hisses. 'You stay the fuck here!' She wiggles a talon-tipped finger at me and heads inside, presumably upstairs to where Beth is.

Within minutes, she is back. 'She does *not* want to see you. She wants you to leave now.'

'I'm not leaving.' I make a point of staring at Beth's words on the wall.

'I'll call the police.'

'This is still half my house, Karen. Call whoever the fuck you like. You want to get snotty? Beth had no right at all to change the locks on a house we both own. Now, go and tell her I want two minutes of her time. Please. Just two minutes.'

'Leave it, Karen.'

I hear Beth's voice from the living room.

'Come inside,' she tells her. 'I'll be fine.'

Karen gives me a withering look and vanishes. Beth appears in front of me, half in, half out of the hallway.

'What do you want?' she says.

I can't help scanning her up and down. She's stunning, in a black polo neck and jeans and heeled ankle boots. Her hair, now long enough to wear up, is pinned up by a diamanté barrette. I'm momentarily speechless.

'I never meant—'

She puts a palm in the air. 'Adam, if you've come to say sorry. If you've come to say you never meant any of it to happen. If you've come to tell me that – somehow – your lying to me for ten years about another child can be made right, stop now. It can't. It can never be made right.'

'I know that.' Christ, I can feel a lump in my throat. 'But that doesn't mean I shouldn't try.'

'Don't. Don't try. Don't bother.'

'I have to.'

'Please leave. I've a plane to catch.'

From inside the living room, music begins to play. Karen is trying to drown me out and I'm getting pissed off.

She pokes her head around the corner. 'Did you hear her? She has a plane to catch.'

I can feel a red mist descend. I just want to talk to Beth for two minutes. Two minutes of uninterrupted explanation before she goes.

'Karen, please just fuck off. This has got nothing to do with you. I need to talk to my wife.'

'Your *wife* does not need to talk to you.' She has come back into the hall now, is squaring up to me, and that mist is becoming a deeper shade of scarlet.

'Move out of the way, Karen.'

'Make me.'

'Are you jealous, is that it?' I push my face towards hers. 'Would it just kill you if Beth actually talked to me? And who the fuck are you? What's your advice? You telling her to dump me? Like all the men in your life who dumped you . . . When they realize what a bitter, toxic bitch you are.'

'Stop it, Adam. Stop it, both of you.' I hear Beth's voice, but the bull has been released.

'Remind me to talk to Ben, tell him what you're really like. That you've never been able to have a proper relationship.' I go for the jugular.

Karen backs away like she's been scalded.

'Leave now, Adam.' Beth approaches me.

'I've only just started.'

'You've said enough,' Beth screams; she points at the door and orders me out of the house.

I oblige, slamming the door behind me in a manner that nearly takes it off the hinges. In the car, I try and steady myself. Shit. I don't even mean that crap about Karen, she just got in my face.

I lower my head, tap it rhythmically on the steering wheel. There is nothing I can do. No sorry, no text, no letter, no flowers, nothing – *nothing* will fix this. Rather than give Beth food for thought in LA, all I've done is make her hate me more. Well done, mate, I tell myself. Just keep pushing the self-destruct button. One day, it'll be sure to work.

Chapter Twenty-Nine

I really want to scream at Karen. Since this is not a familiar emotion, I try and work my way through my annoyance without raising my voice. On my bed is a pile of clothes – several piles of clothes, in fact – equalling one big mess. There are forty minutes left before we have to leave for the airport.

'Why don't you just pack it for me?' I suggest. She has, after all, unpacked my beautifully tidy, well-organized case, where I knew exactly what I had and exactly where it was. She has no understanding that any inkling of OCD that I have only kicks in while cleaning toilets, making my bed and packing a suitcase. Proving this, she separates my original choices into a 'TAKE' pile and a 'LEAVE' pile, and a third pile of her suggestions – a 'TAKE AS WELL' pile. I'm trying hard not to retire to the corner of the bedroom and put my thumb in my mouth.

'You don't want to look like a frigging nun.' She is referring to my two pairs of black Capri pants and white tops.

'Nuns do not wear Capri pants,' I tell her, replacing

them and the piles in the suitcase. 'Nor do they wear them with Converse trainers.' I push my white pair with a red stripe back, into the top-right corner of the case.

'Please take this.' Her voice is almost pleading as she holds up a long silky dress.

'Where am I going to wear that?' I'm beginning to lose it and start pointing frantically to my watch.

'To a nice dinner in LA. With a nice movie producer or record producer or some sort of producer guy.'

She places it neatly on top of the folded clothes. 'It'll need an iron when you get there.'

'Fine, fine. Have I got everything? You've confused me now. Did the make-up and toiletries go back in?'

She closes the lid. 'Everything's in there, Beth. Now go and get a coat and scarf. It's brass monkeys outside.'

I brush my teeth first. Gripping the sink, I'm trying to pull myself together, but my nerves are shredded. The last thing I needed today was Adam pitching up at the door. I spit and practise my smile in the mirror. Count, Beth, count. Just stop thinking about the shit in your life and start thinking songs. Songs. Songs . . . I grab my coat and scarf and head down to the car where Karen has already put my case in the boot.

'Are you sure?'

'Relax.' She slams the boot shut. 'Everything's in there that should be. I've locked it. Here's the key. Here's your wallet with your documents. Check them and put them in your handbag. Let's go.'

I check everything as instructed.

'You nervous?'

I nod. 'I just can't help feeling I shouldn't leave Meg,

not right now. Not when she's going through what she is. Maybe I shouldn't go.'

'Get in the car, Beth. I swear if I have to hit you over the head to get you in the car, I will. This is your moment. Meg will be fine, what the hell else could you do if you were here? Wait by her side to see if she's a match or not?' Her voice is rising. 'It's for a few days. I promise I'll keep an eye out for Meg. Get in the bloody car.'

I do as I'm told and slide into the passenger seat.

Karen tuts loudly. 'You had better get on that plane, Beth Hall. I mean it. If you don't, I'll never speak to you again. And I won't be responsible for what I'll do to Adam.'

We haven't spoken at all about Adam's appearance at the house. About what he said. Not a word. We both just turned the music off, went upstairs and continued with the unpacking and repacking.

'Enjoy your moment. You'll be great.' She taps my arm reassuringly. 'And don't think about him. He's so not worth it.'

'I'm sorry about what he said to you.'

'Forget it. He was fired up. I goaded him.'

'He doesn't mean it.'

'Don't stick up for him, Beth. He has to be responsible for the things he says and does.' She blows out a deep sigh through O-shaped lips.

'I know, but he never loses his temper and what he said—'

'Fuck him. Did you notice how thin he's got? I was a bit shocked.'

I know then that the subject is closed, so I reply. 'All that running . . .'

243

'Around after women,' she adds.

I don't smile. He's an absolute bastard of the first order, but something in me feels bereft. It's like a part of me has died.

'He cried,' I tell her. 'I could see he was crying as I threw him out.'

'Boo, bloody, hoo.'

I try and concentrate on where I'm going to, rather than what just happened at the house. 'It is, I guess, time to move on.' I smooth out imaginary wrinkles in my black jeans.

'Have you shaved?' Karen asks, her eyes not moving from the road.

'What?'

'Have you shaved?' she repeats.

'Enlighten me.'

'Your bits. Down below.'

I roll my eyes. 'Jesus Christ, Karen. No, I frigging well have not shaved my bits.'

'You'll have to. And when you do, you'll know it's really time to move on.'

I try not to laugh. She's right. My lady garden right now looks like something wild – unpruned and unloved.

'LA will have waxing salons. Treat yourself, go and have it all off.'

I shake my head. 'Can we talk about something else other than my dishevelled pubes?'

'I'm just saying. It's a long time since you've been on the market. You'll need to go bare, or nearly bare. It's what men expect nowadays.'

I'm almost insulted. Does she really think I don't know

what's current? I may not have been with another man for two decades, but I read magazines, watch television, know all about those vajazzle things.

'Adam liked it almost nude,' I tell her. 'But I just might get it all off and have a vajazzle in LA.'

'Attagirl,' she grins as she pulls onto the motorway.

I am, finally, settled in my seat. It's a window one, where obviously I will be able to see if the engine's on fire, or if the pilot ejects. There is only one empty seat beside me and I hope it stays that way. I'm really not in the mood to make small talk to a total stranger over the Atlantic.

No sooner is the thought formed than a man appears, throws a large holdall in the overhead locker and places another smaller bag on the seat. I try not to look up. If I don't engage him, then I won't have to tell him that I have never flown without my husband before. I can't actually believe it myself, but it's true – I have never flown without Adam . . . The knots in my stomach have multiplied like gremlins since boarding. At this moment in time, I'm afraid if I speak it would come out like a squeak.

I try and relax, check my iPad is charged and on aircraft mode, turn off my mobile phone and sit back. I close my eyes and stretch my neck muscles before looking down again.

'Would you like a glass of champagne?'

I raise my head slightly, nod to the hostess, who hands me a fizzing glass from a tray.

'Nuts?'

Of course I am, I want to say. I can't even make eye contact with my neighbour. I'm as fucking nutty as they come.

'Would you care for some nuts?'

I shake my head. The gremlins would vomit on top of Mr Man next to me. I'm not eating anything for a while.

He is, at last, sitting down – seems to be comfortable. He has removed from his smaller bag an iPad, a newspaper and a pair of reading glasses. I can tell all of this by straining my left eye to the edge of its socket, while it seems that I'm still looking ahead. Right ahead of me is the tiny screen that shows the aircraft is still in London. I wonder how to switch this thing off. Adam always dealt with aircraft paraphernalia. I'm frustrated because I don't want to watch the aircraft's progress in flight. The only way I'm going to get through this alone is to pretend I'm in a simulator. We aren't really going to leave the ground at all. It's just a day-long simulation of a transatlantic flight.

'Just pretend you're in a car.'

Shit. Mr Man is speaking and I think he's addressing me. I peer to my left. He is tall. I can tell this even from his seated figure. He's wearing a striped, open-neck shirt and a pair of faded denims. His shirtsleeves are rolled up and both arms are tattooed. On his right I can make out parts of a dragon. He looks as though he has a full head of sandy hair, but it's difficult to see because he's wearing some kind of bandana thing on his head. He holds his hand out to me.

'Nice to meet you. You seem a bit nervous.' His accent is East Coast American – not quite Boston, but not as clipped as New York.

I force my hand in his direction. 'Beth Hall, good to meet you too.' I'm not sure it is – good to meet him – but for now, I'll give him the benefit of the doubt. I take a second look at the headgear thing and hold my counsel.

'My ex-wife used to be a terrible flier. She'd just pretend she was in a car. It seemed to work.'

Christ. Thirty seconds and he's letting me know he has an ex-wife. Do I need to know this?

'What brings you to LA?' he asks.

'Work,' I tell him. I debate fibbing and telling him I'm a movie producer. 'I'm a songwriter.'

'Really?' He seems to straighten even more in his seat. 'I'm a musician – a drummer in the band called The Brothers.'

It's my turn to sit up, and boy has he passed my 'awe' test. The Brothers are one of my favourite bands, a modern-day version of the Eagles, with a really fresh fusion of rock, pop and country. I'm impressed, wonder why I didn't recognize him, and come to the conclusion it's the bandana. The drummer guy has a head of wild hair that obscures his face most of the time. And while I don't expect to be booking a vajazzle as soon as I disembark, at least the next eleven hours don't seem quite so terrifying. I listen carefully to Mr Brother above the noise of the engines and wave at the stewardess for some nuts.

I am a little drunk. Mr Brother, whose real name is Jeff, but is known by friends as 'Pink', because of his avid gay following, looks like he's a little drunk too. His eyes, which two hours ago were a deep shade of ocean blue, have a sort of glazed, slightly bloodshot look. I have just got to the interesting part of my life, as I now know it.

'So, you see, I don't just have another woman to deal with, I have another child too,' I tell Pink.

He nods, says nothing, like it's the most normal situation in the world. Maybe it is in LA or whatever part of the US he comes from.

'He's been lying to me for ten years. *Ten* years!'

Pink takes another sip of his whisky.

I'm still wondering why my plight hasn't elicited a response.

'Are you a cheat, Jeff, I mean Pink? I mean, don't tell me if you don't want to, but you did mention you had an ex-wife. You are in a band. You obviously travel a lot, probably have women throw themselves at you.'

For some inexplicable reason, I feel the need to mime the word 'throw' and toss some of my drink all over Pink's faded jeans.

'Ooops, sorry.'

'It's okay. And yes, I cheated on my wife. Learned my lesson when she left me though. Never did it again.'

'D'ya think it's just in men's DNA?'

He laughs. 'Women cheat too, you know.'

I shake my head. 'No, no they don't. I know lots of women and I don't know any who have cheated.'

'Then you're lucky, because they do. Really.'

I am unconvinced. 'I would have gone to dinner with you, you know.' I raise my glass to him and down the rest of my champagne. 'I can't now, obviously, now that I know you have the gene.'

'I might have asked you.' Pink smiles.

The hostess is standing in the aisle beside our seats with the meals we had ordered from a menu when we boarded. Pink pulls his tray down and leans across to pull mine down for me.

'We should eat,' he says.

'You're a wise man, Jeff Pink.'

He hands me my tray. The starter is a fishcake that smells a little fishy. When I tell him this he laughs again, offers me his green salad as a swap. We switch plates and I concentrate on eating some leaves. I munch through two bread rolls, hoping it will soak up the alcohol.

I drink lots of water during dinner, try and regain some focus, apologize to Pink if I've talked a load of shit since we took off.

'I've loved your company,' he says.

Really? I can't help but think he's full of it. I've done nothing but bad-mouth the general male population.

'If I did ask you to dinner in LA, would you overlook my defective gene?'

I blush. The feeling of a red flush crawling over my skin is how I know I've sobered up. 'I might. Dinner is dinner, right?'

'That's right. Dinner is dinner.'

'Just checking.' The last thing I need is any transatlantic lingo confusion. I need to know upfront if agreeing to dinner is code for dinner and a shag. Christ, I have been out of the game too long. 'Dinner would be lovely,' I hear myself reply.

'No fishy fish, I promise.'

His bandana has loosened and I can see a head full of straw-coloured curls underneath. It looks like it's all being held up by a band and is probably quite long. Adam keeps his hair clipped very short and I find myself wondering what it would be like to run my hands through a man's hair. I wonder what it would be like to touch him. I have to look away as my blush deepens and I feel a warming in my groin that has been absent for too long.

Catching my breath, I stare out of the window.

'You okay, Beth?'

'Yes, fine,' I tell him, willing the high-rise colour away. I swear I've actually wet my knickers. I stare at the wing of the plane, the tiny little light flashing underneath it. Maybe I've drunk too much and it's just leaked straight through. Or maybe, I've got my period. Fuck, what if it's my period? Mentally, I calculate that I'm not due for a while. I try and place my hand between my legs under the tray table. I close my eyes. No, just Pink then.

I don't know whether to be pleased or horrified. For the last eight months, I've only ever been wet with the help of my trusty vibrator. Dear God in heaven, only me. Only I could find my mojo fantasizing about a man named Pink.

'Beth?'

I turn around to see the stewardess standing next to him.

'More champagne?' he asks.

I put my hand over the top of my glass and shake my head. I need to keep my wits about me. I need to be absolutely certain that the words mile and high and club are not said aloud, or even whispered. I need to be absolutely certain that I do not lose my senses and offer up my weedy lady garden to this man at thirty thousand feet.

Chapter Thirty

For the last ten days, I've been running to the office, changing when I get there and running home again. Ben can't believe my times and tells me not to push myself too hard. All I need is to finish, he reminds me, not to finish in Olympic time.

This Monday morning, I meet Jen just outside the lift when I get there. She has a young girl with her, about Meg's age, and introduces her to me as Matt's niece Becky, the new intern. I nod, apologize for my sweaty hands and head to the Gents. After a quick shower, I knock on Matt's door.

'Becky?' I ask him, my head craned around to see him.

'My niece. We spoke about her?'

'We did?'

'She's finished her History of Art degree; I thought she could help Will out with procurement.'

Wilhelm 'Will' Trask runs our small but elite Art department – so small, in fact, that it only has two people, him and now Becky. His role is to source art, ideally sought-after pieces that will likely increase in value, on behalf of mainly Russian and American clients.

'She's going to have to travel. With Will?' I raise my eyebrows. Will, though single, has a reputation of being a ladies' man.

'Kettle and pot?' Adam replies. 'And hands off.'

I raise both my hands in protest. The thought of looking at a woman my daughter's age is beyond even *my* wildest dreams.

'Have you heard from New York?' I ask Matt. 'I've been in touch with Mark – he's found the right office. We need to move quickly.'

'He mailed me too. I'm just trying to sort out the final funds.'

I can't help but think he looks worried rather than excited. Though we've both been involved, it's really Matt's dream being fulfilled with the setting up of a small New York office of Hall and Fry. 'You going to go over and see it?'

'Flight booked for Thursday. Don't you ever look at our office diary?' He shakes his head, holds a hand up to excuse the fact that he has to answer whatever call is coming through. I wave a goodbye and pass by Jen and Becky, which makes me think of Meg.

I try calling her again, walking back to my office. The results are due and I've left messages to let her know that – despite her hating me – I'm there for her, especially since Beth is away.

Surprisingly, she answers.

'You're there,' I say.

'What do you want?'

'Just to know you're all right.'

'You can't even be honest about that, can you? What you really want to know is if I'm a match for your bastard sprog.'

I've known what to expect, but still, her words make me wince.

'Well, I am,' she continues. 'There you have it. He must be your son, eh? I must be his sister after all.'

I am stunned into silence. While I hoped and even prayed that a match would be found and while I knew Meg was probably the best hope, I was afraid to believe it might be possible.

'I found out this morning. I've only answered the phone to tell you,' she says curtly.

I can't help but notice she hasn't called me 'Dad' yet. I hang my suit jacket on the back of the chair at my desk, stare at the pale, twist-pile carpet under my feet.

'What are you going to do?' I ask her.

'The right thing. I've got more blood tests tomorrow, to double, triple make sure, but they expect them to confirm everything. Then, I have hormone jabs four days before the procedure. That itself is apparently just like giving blood.'

'Can I be there?'

'I don't need you there, nor do I want you there. Mum will be back.'

'I'd like to.'

She interrupts me, laughing. 'But this isn't about what you'd like, is it, Dad?' She ends the call.

I blink at the phone. The good news is that she called me Dad. The bad news is that, yet again, I sound like an uncaring bastard.

There is a knock on my door.

'Come in.'

Becky comes through with a cardboard tray of coffees. 'White latte with two?' She hands me a large takeaway cup with a black 'x' across its plastic lid.

'Thank you.' I offer her my hand. 'Sorry I couldn't shake this morning. I'd run in from home.'

'Yes, Jen told me you're running a mini-marathon next week.'

The reality of someone telling me that it's actually next week I'm running thirteen miles for the Anthony Nolan Bone Marrow Charity makes me feel the need to sit down.

'Allegedly,' I say.

'I couldn't run for a bus, me.'

I know she's just trying to be friendly to the other partner in the business. I know she's just being polite but, right now, I'm not in the mood for small talk with Becky or anyone else.

'Thanks for the coffee.' I raise the cup in acknowledgement and, at least – as she turns to leave – she has the grace to know she's been dismissed.

I try to work. I have two meetings with clients this morning. One a family representative who is unhappy with the financial wrapper we're offering his pension fund. I have agreed with Matt that he can do all the talking for this one and I can just sit. The second is a new client – a referral, ironically from the Grangers. Matt thinks that this is hilarious. But as the morning crawls by, I realize there's very little that I find funny in the world nowadays.

I have triple layers on leaving the office. It's dark outside and I make sure the last layer I wear is the reflective one. My rucksack on my back, I exit the revolving doors at seven thirty-six p.m. I push a button on the stopwatch on my wrist and turn left up Embankment. When I reach the underpass, I head up the slip road alongside Blackfriars Bridge, then snake a route through narrow streets, back onto Upper Embankment Road. The incline, which only a week ago would have brought me to my knees, is not a problem. I run rhythmically, my heartbeat the louder background sound competing with the traffic.

At Tower Bridge, I stop, navigate the crossings at walking pace, then start to run up the Highway. At the Shell garage, I stop again, a sudden piercing pain in my chest almost felling me. I bend over, try to catch my breath. The pain radiates from my chest down my left arm. I grab it, squeeze it, to try and ease the discomfort. Fear grips me. Trying not to think about it, I walk into the garage, towards the double sliding doors. I see a man there, seated on a rug at the entrance, a cup between his knees. I remember thinking, 'Poor bastard – it's too bloody cold to have to be outside begging.' And that is the last thing I remember . . .

I'm in my parents' bedroom. It's morning and I've only come upstairs to tell them I'm off to work. It's August and I have a job at McDonald's before heading back to university next month. They're both normally up way before me, so I feel a little odd, knocking on their bedroom door, and even more strange when I enter without being told to. There is something off immediately. The air is stiflingly hot, the room is a sauna and needs the window opened.

'Mum? Dad? I'm off to work.'

Nothing. I cross the room to the window, pull back one of the curtains. When I turn around, I know immediately.

I'm shocked, I realize that. But somehow, I'm not remotely surprised.

'Mr Hall?'

I open my eyes. There's a tiny flashlight being moved up and down in a vertical line. I make a face.

'Please,' I say. 'It hurts.'

'Glad you're back with us.' The male voice with the torch speaks. 'Can you hear me okay?'

I nod, barely, but he sees it.

'Good. You passed out, had a minor heart attack, Mr Hall. Nothing to worry about. We got you here in time. You're on the mend and you'll make a full recovery – just a shot across the bows, eh?'

I'm trying to fathom the fact that I'm forty-three years old, fighting fit, and have had a heart attack, minor or otherwise.

'Stress is often a factor. We'll have to sit down in a day or two and work out the "why". Maybe overdid the running, eh? But for now, you rest up. Let us take care of you. Is there anyone you'd like us to call? We've tried the ICE number on your mobile, but I'm not sure if we got anyone. Did we get anyone?'

I can make out his profile turning towards someone else to ask the question, but I have no idea what he's talking about.

'Ben.' I manage to speak, my voice a weak whisper. 'Call my brother Ben.'

Time passes. I awake to a gentle prodding on my hand and open my eyes, less painfully this time.

'I told you not to try and beat Mo Farah.' It's Ben's voice and I feel an overwhelming sense of relief.

'Get me out of here,' I whisper.

'You're not going anywhere.' I hear a chair scrape along the floor and feel him sit beside me. 'You're in here for at least a few days and then you're coming back with us.'

It is only then I notice Karen lurking behind him.

'Hi,' she says. 'You okay?'

'Peachy,' I tell her.

'Good, I'm glad.'

A small laugh tries to escape me but ends up as a strangled cough. I am quite sure that, given our last meeting, Karen probably wished a heart attack on me. Ben pulls me up, bangs my back. 'You're all right', he says. 'You're all right.'

'What have they said?' I ask him when I catch my breath. 'The doctors.'

'Minor heart attack. So small it barely registered. Nothing to worry about. Bed rest. You have raised cholesterol, but apparently that's not uncommon in middle age.'

'Watch it,' I tell him.

'They're suggesting you cut back on the running for a while.'

This makes me feel sad. I have loved running, both the physical training and the working towards something where I might make a difference.

'You won't be taking part in the mini.' He states the obvious and I nod.

'Meg?'

'I've told her. I'm sure she'll be here . . . '

I want to tell him not to bet his flat on it, but I feel incredibly tired.

He seems to sense it. 'We won't stay. I've brought you some pyjamas.' He points to a Marks and Spencer's bag at the end of the bed as he stands. 'When you come out you'll come back to Karen's for a few days, until you've got your strength back.'

'No.' It comes out more strongly than any other word today. 'You haven't got the room – you both work from that second bedroom. No . . . I'll be fine. I'll take the pills, watch crap telly, eat some soup and I'll be fine. No, Ben. That's final.' I struggle to get the words out but they see I won't be moved on it.

'We'll see,' he says. 'Maybe I'll—'

'You're not coming back either. Karen, take him home, please.'

Karen nods to me. There was a time when a kiss would not have been awkward and would have been a given. 'Take care,' she says and, to be fair, it sounds like she means it.

Chapter Thirty-One

After exchanging details and a kiss on the cheek with Pink, I collect my bag from the carousel. There is an enormous – I mean huge – grin on my face . . . I can't actually believe I'm here. I take my bag to a nearby chair, open it up and put my coat and scarf in, removing a lighter denim jacket. My body clock is already skew-ways, having managed only five hours' sleep on the plane. A glance at my wrist tells me it's 10 p.m. locally, which means that as soon as I get to the hotel, I should really go to bed, try and get some more sleep. I hang my jacket over my arm, try to look 'casual' like I'm used to being in LA, and walk through customs.

There's a driver outside in the arrivals hall with a sign that has BETH HALL on it and underneath it says the word PARAMOUNT. I remind myself to ask him for it – a keepsake, to tell myself in two weeks' time that I didn't dream this. The car he directs me to is in fact a white limousine. In America, I'm quite sure it's a smallish one. In the UK, it would be known as stretched. In the back of the limo, big enough to carry eight people comfortably, there is more champagne. I debate, just for one moment, having a glass. I'm out of harm's way. Pink has gone in another direction and I'm just here with Boyd, who is apparently 'my driver' while I'm in LA. I resist temptation, as I pass the huge LAX letters on the opposite side of the road, and instead jot some notes in my iPhone as I chat with Boyd about the real places to see in Hollywood. I immediately text it to Meg, attached to the simple words: 'Arrived safely. Love you x'.

The time passes so quickly that it seems only minutes before we are on Rodeo Drive. I've only ever seen Rodeo Drive in the movies and am trying not to gasp. Despite the contract terms Josh has negotiated for me on this deal, I'm not so sure I'll be spending too much time in *these* shops. Real money, potentially life-changing money, will only be made when the film is released and it's been a success. Boyd turns a few corners and, within seconds, we're parking outside the most gorgeous hotel I've ever seen. Its sandy stucco frontage is lit up by tiny nocturnal spotlights and, unlike some of the larger high-rise hotels, it looks just like someone's house. I look back over my shoulder in the direction we came from and realize it's so close to Rodeo that a talented spit would reach it. Maybe I'll have to have a splurge or two after all . . .

Boyd takes my bag from the 'trunk' and walks up the six steps of the hotel, where a young man takes the bag and greets me by name.

'I'll pick you up at ten thirty tomorrow, ma'am,' Boyd says.

'You will?'

'To take you to the studios for your appointment, ma'am.'

'Lovely,' I tell Boyd, in a new-found tone that indicates I'm used to addressing chauffeurs. 'You have yourself a good night, Boyd.'

'Thank you, ma'am.'

No sooner has Boyd left than Carl takes over. Carl takes my bag through to reception where they confirm my 'Brighton Street-facing room'. Apparently, it catches the sun for most of the day.

I'm asked if I'd like a complimentary drink at the bar before going to my room and I think: why the hell not?

It's a Sunday night in LA and, though the bar is busy, it's not heaving, which suits me fine. I'm steered towards a barstool where a man by the name of Toots asks me what my poison is.

'A gin and tonic, please.' I hoist myself up onto the barstool, hopeful that the G&T might make me sleepy.

'Hendrick's, Tanqueray?'

'You choose. Make me one that I'll want every evening.'

Toots smiles. 'I'll make you one that you'll want at least two of every evening.'

I watch him use Tanqueray gin, Fever-Tree tonic and garnish the tall glass with lemon and lime wheels and a few juniper berries. As I take a sip, I try not to wonder why I asked for a G&T. It's Adam's favourite tipple, not mine. I immediately banish him from my brain, telling myself he doesn't deserve head-space. Apart from the fact he's a two-timing sleaze with another family, his name I decide is far too ordinary. In the last twelve hours, I have met men called Pink, Boyd, Carl and Toots. I raise my glass to Toots the bartender and, after the first taste, nod at him.

I suspect he's right. I'll be ordering at least two of these when I'm back.

I people-watch for about half an hour. The buzz of the bar and the lure of another Tanqueray make me want to stay, but my eyes are beginning to close. From the reception area, I'm shown up the wide staircase to my first-floor room. It's small but perfectly formed with a huge bed. As soon as Carl has shown me the ropes and left, I jump on the bed, face down. Turning over on my back, I give a little squeal. I'm in LA. I'm really here, and tomorrow morning, after my meeting with the producers, hopefully I'll have some time to kill before I see some musicians the producers want me to meet. Then, Rodeo Drive, here I come.

It's six a.m. and I've been awake since four when Meg texted. She is, it seems, a suitable donor for stem cells to her half-brother. They want to do the procedure as soon as possible and it's scheduled for next week, just after I get back. Part of me feels sick, anxious for my only child being embroiled in her father's mess. But, strangely, a bigger part of me is relieved for another, innocent, sick child. I text her back: 'You're a star. I'll be there with you. Thank you for being a young woman I'm so proud of . . . xx'.

By seven, I'm showered and dressed in what Karen refers to as my nun's clothes – white shirt, black Capri pants and my Converse trainers. Mya, the hotel receptionist this morning, has given me a map, marked out a diner for breakfast and a nail salon that opens at eight. I put my denim jacket on. It's warm, certainly warmer than a UK December, but I still need a jacket in the shade. I check the map, cross over to the sunnier side of the street and walk for about five minutes.

The diner is quiet, but open. I sit myself down in a red pleather booth and, as soon as I scan the menu, it's clear I'm in LA.

'I'll have a skinny latte and an egg-white omelette with mushrooms.'

No wonder everyone I've met looks like they need a good cheese sandwich.

I take a deep breath and blow it out slowly. I'm really here. I take a photo of the diner, and text it to Meg and Karen, knowing by the time I get a reply, I'll be sitting in an office somewhere on the Paramount lot.

Having had my fat-free breakfast, I head around the corner to the nail salon. True to Mya's word, they open early and it looks busy. Their receptionist fits me in and I feel relief that I'll see the back of the disastrous treble clef on my thumb.

'Oh my,' the technician allocated to me says.

'My mother,' I tell her. 'Not me . . . Even I couldn't make that bad a job of it.'

'You're English,' she practically sings. 'I just love the English accent, it's so cute.'

For the next hour, I listen to Ava tell me about her life. Anything I ask her about LA, she either ignores or doesn't really give me an answer. I get details about her boyfriend, about the fact that his mother is living with them, about the fact that she works twelve-hour days to support all three of them. I guess she's not really the person to ask about the best points of interest for an English songwriter with a few days to fill. To Ava, LA is the place she happens to live: nothing more, nothing less.

She does, however, after giving me the best French mani-cure I've ever had, refer me to her colleague Maria, who is apparently the greatest 'waxer' around. It was when I was talking to Ava, I thought, why the hell not? I have the time. It would be silly not to. When in Hollywood, have a Hollywood . . .

Boyd is at the hotel just before ten thirty. He hands me a lanyard, which somehow already has my photo on a VIP pass. I am now a very important person, I tell myself. Lucy, who has been very quiet since I got to LA, giggles out loud. I silence her immediately with an imaginary scarf covered in skulls, the sort they only sell in Rodeo Drive.

The sun is now scorching and I'm glad of the air condi-tioning on the way to the meeting. It's a five-minute car ride and, when Boyd flashes his pass, he glances at me in the rear-view mirror, indicates that I should do the same. I wave my lanyard at the security guards and, before long, having passed by what appears to be the more touristy part of Paramount, we arrive at what looks like a small business park of various offices. Boyd opens the door of the car for me outside an impressive revolving door. 'I'll wait here for you, ma'am,' he says. It sounds like a promise, but I just nod.

Having had to wait in reception for ten minutes, counting to one hundred in Spanish, German and French, I am ushered into an office, where two men sit opposite a coffee table. Part of me zones out and I struggle to bring myself back to the moment, to convince myself that this is really real and that I need to listen, to be present.

Jonas, the main man is, in fact, the movie's director. His handshake is vigorous and double-handed, one hand shaking mine with the other covering it. I am again fascinated by the names of people in Hollywood when Jackson, the movie's head honcho producer, introduces himself. I smile what I hope is an engaging smile. His is the only name I've heard of via Josh and he is apparently the man I need to impress.

Coffee is brought through and they get right down to business. While Jonas is busy sizing me up, Jackson is busy talking facts. I think they're both wondering what I'm like. Am I funny, reliable, talented – is their risk a risk worth taking, gambling on a relative unknown for a big-dollar movie?

Jonas is telling me they love the song. It will take pride of place in the story's timeline. While I'm here, he'd like me to meet with some musicians to discuss a slight change musically. Lyrics are all the same, just this small hike in the crescendo of the middle eight. Would I be happy with that? I don't say what I'm thinking. I don't tell them that a small or large hike in the middle eight is fine. I want this song in the movie – whatever . . . I do tell them that I'll be happy to meet with the musicians later on and see what they have in mind. This I say with a smile mainly directed at Jackson.

Two hours later, after more posturing by the big boys, I have left Paramount, fairly certain that they're also looking at another song of mine called 'Echoes' for a different project. It's a song I wrote years ago, but I keep this to myself. Hell, it's about heartache – a timeless theme. Their parting words to me indicated they would be talking to Josh later today.

My head is reeling with such extreme excitement that I have to use some of the breathing techniques Caroline taught me to calm down. I fill my lungs as quietly as possible and exhale slowly. Right now, I'm sitting in a music studio in downtown LA. It is so 'state of the art' that I can't help touching it, stroking the sound keys, staring at the screens. It makes the double Apple Mac screens in my attic look Jurassic. Peter, who appears in front of me, explains that they're ready. Within seconds, the session musicians they've booked start to play from behind a glass screen. They're good, very good and I'm captivated, lost in the music – *my* music. I pinch myself, not once, or twice but three times. I only stop for fear of bruising.

They run through it a few times until we all agree it's pitch perfect. Having said my goodbyes, I'm on my way out to meet Boyd thinking life can't get much better when my phone vibrates and I open a text from Pink. 'Dinner tonight? I know an amazing steakhouse in Santa Monica . . . ' And in that moment I'm introduced to a whole new world. I can nearly hear Aladdin in the background. Except this has nothing to do with romance. This is lust. Pure and simple. I reply immediately telling him I'd love dinner, hoping that despite my insistence when we met that dinner would mean dinner, that it might in fact mean sex. Not really caring how lovely or not this man might be, I now know it's possible to just want to shag someone. I smile at Boyd as he opens the car door for me. Who knew?

Boyd drops me outside Manolo Blahnik's. Although I feel the lure of his shoes like a magnetic pull, I resist and head towards a lingerie store I spotted from the car. The area is busy and I suddenly feel very self-conscious, as though everyone's staring at me. Surely they know I'm about to buy shagging underwear? Surely they know that under my black Capri pants I've been defuzzed. The people, mostly women, chatter as they walk along and I try, head held high, to blend in, ignoring their yappy, rat-like dogs on bling-ridden dog leads.

Stopping to take the street in, I look right and left. I tell myself to take a moment. Breathe – to savour the fact that I'm in Rodeo Drive. It's much narrower than I'd thought it would be. There are two lanes of traffic on each side of a central reservation, but somehow it still feels smaller than I'd expected. Flowers are planted the full length of the central part of the street. Tall palm trees are spaced about three metres apart. Surroundings duly noted, like any good tourist, I enter the shop hating myself for not really caring. I just want some gorgeous underwear. And I want Pink to take his time removing it from me sometime soon.

I'm at a steakhouse facing Santa Monica Beach. The setting is too beautiful. The man opposite me is too beautiful. Any moment now, someone will tap my shoulder and tell me to read the small print but, until then . . . I'm wearing the dress that Karen insisted I pack. Thank you, Karen. Thank you, hotel, for ironing it.

We order steaks and salad and a bottle of red. He doesn't say a lot, but what he does say is almost all complimentary. How beautiful I am, how sexy I look in my dress . . . It's then I realize that he wants to bed me as much as I do him. After teasing my beef with a steak knife for a while and double checking that any wives in his life are definitely exes, I find myself suggesting that we go back to my hotel room. Adam crosses my mind, a tiny flash, too small to notice. I think about Meg and remind myself that Karen is right. There's nothing I can do until I'm back. I miss her; she'd love it over here and, someday soon, I'll take her back with me and we'll take Rodeo Drive by storm. In the meantime, I'm in LA about to do something I've never done. Just relax, I tell myself. Try and relax.

Pink calls for the 'check', and before I know it we're in a cab heading back to the hotel. He is holding my hand, rubbing the top of my thumb with his and, fuck me, I can't bear it. It has been a long time and this man is likely to be the beneficiary of many months of frustration.

Never before. Never before have I felt like this . . . The man is an orgasm machine. He should be patented. His fingers and tongue linger over every inch of my body. His gasp of pleasure at my nude undercarriage makes me grateful I got up early. He turns me over, every which way but loose, and insists on my leaving my underwear on. I'm strangely grateful for this and find his teasing aside of my $200 knickers with his tongue one of the most erotic things . . . Having played with me for ages, he finally removes them and fucks me slowly. He is gentle for such a big man and, when he enters me, he seems to hold his breath. I realize I've almost closed up and must feel like a frigging virgin. When I come, he comes quickly after. He leaves me spent but wanting more.

While he sleeps, I reach across to my phone in the charger. I'm about to switch it on and check for messages when a hand stretches across and he whispers, 'Leave it.' I laugh, my hand dropping over the side of the bed onto Pink's trousers on the floor. Condoms spill from his trouser pocket, and though part of me is horrified that he knew I'd be this easy, the bigger part of me turns around wanting more.

This time, I sit astride him and, feeling him fill me the way he can, I'm sorry that it's taken me this long to discover wanton sex. And, as I move above him, building to another climax, I'm aware of exactly what this is. Sex. Brilliant, uncomplicated sex. A real first for me.

When sunlight spills through a crack in the curtains from the Brighton Street, sunlit side of the hotel, I get up and shower. I order some breakfast for both of us through room service – some fruit, muesli, tea and coffee. He must be hungry – neither of us ate much dinner last night.

I'm right. He eats everything on the plate and drinks two cups of black coffee. He takes a long shower and joins me on the edge of the bed, just as I'm about to dry my hair. For a man who says so little, he is very persuasive. All he has to do is stroke my face with the back of his hand. I'm momentarily torn. I have a full itinerary of touristy things to do. Then again, I could delay them and just enjoy the only attraction I'm interested in in Hollywood. If Pink featured in my Hollywood tour guide, he would be a five-star ticket. So I do what any woman would – I get back into bed with him.

With Boyd's help, who is thankfully on call to me today, I have an itinerary waiting for me at reception. Since the studio people don't need to see me and I have the day free, they have obviously told him to take me sightseeing in LA. As I take a seat in the back of the car, I glance down at the sheet of paper and switch my phone on. It immediately goes crazy.

There are several missed calls and lots of texts from Josh, the final one reading 'CALL ME OR I SHALL COME OVER THERE AND HUNT YOU DOWN!'

I listen to several voicemails before I hear a voice I don't recognize.

'This is a message from Newham General Hospital in London. We have a Mr Adam Hall here and I understand you're his emergency contact number. Please could you call us as soon as possible? My name is Lisa and the number here is . . .'

I clutch my chest, check the time of the message – 09.30 LA time, this morning. Fuck, fuck, fuck. I ask Boyd for a pen, listen to the message again and write the number on the back of the itinerary before dialling it. The neon clock on his dashboard tells me it's after half past five in the afternoon over there.

I manage to speak to someone who tells me what's happened. Relief seeps over me when I realize he's okay. The thought had crossed my mind that Adam would be capable of dying, just because I was over here forgetting him. The next voicemail is from Meg; as soon as I hear her troubled voice, guilt for my beautiful night last night overwhelms me.

'Mum, where are you? I've been trying to call all day! I *need* to talk to you. Call me – *soon as* you get this message. It's important, Mum.'

My fingers jab her number on my mobile. I nod apologetically at Boyd in his rear-view mirror, lean forward to increase the air con in the back of the car as a powerful flush rises on my cheeks. Relief blasts through my veins, overwhelms any guilt, dampens the tint of self-reproach on my face as soon as I hear the click of her phone being answered. For a few seconds' wait, in just a short space in time, I hold my breath, hope that everything at home is not really falling apart just because I've managed to forget them for a few hours.

'I'm sorry, I'm sorry,' I blurt. 'My phone was charging and I . . . Are you all right? Have you spoken to your dad?'

'No. Where were you? I've been trying you for ages?' She sounds relieved, not angry. 'Do you know already, know about Dad?'

I tell her about my call to the hospital, reassure her that I've been told he's okay – just a scare.

'I've spoken to them too,' she says. 'They've said the same to me. Typical, eh? Dad has a heart attack just when we're both mad as hell at him.'

'It's just a scare,' I repeat. 'He'll be fine.'

She's silent.

'You'd love it out here. Correction, you will love it out here when we come back together. The shopping is brilliant and there's so much to do and see.' I eyeball the itinerary, wonder quickly if I could still do it. I'm flying back later tonight anyway, and I'm damned if I'm getting an earlier flight just because Adam has decided to take centre stage again. 'Plus it's warm at this time of year, just lovely,' I add to Meg.

She tells me she'll look forward to it. Then we talk briefly about the elephant in the room that is a stem cell donation to her brother next week. By the time we hang up, she has talked it through calmly and seems in control. I am again in awe of my own daughter.

'Boyd,' I catch his eye in the mirror. 'This programme, can we really do it all today?'

'Yes, ma'am.'

'Let's go then!'

We manage to squeeze most of it in. He drives me to the Hollywood Bowl and the Hollywood Hills, where I take pictures of the famous white letters. They seem from a distance to be etched into the mountain, though I see now they hang from large white lattices. We go to Santa Monica Beach and Pier. I don't tell him I've already been, albeit briefly. I take some sightseeing snaps of the ocean, before heading to the Hollywood Walk of Fame. I cover only about three of the fifteen blocks of Hollywood Boulevard, before Boyd picks me up and drives me to the Griffith Observatory. All the while my mind is reeling with confusion. Adam lying in a hospital, Meg wired up to tubes and Pink, yes, Pink and his expert hands.

Back in the hotel bar I'm exhausted, sated, wondering when I can come back again. My packed bag resting against my leg, I'm sipping on the G&T that Toots has made for me while I wait for Boyd to return and take me to the airport. I dial Adam's phone and he answers after one ring.

'Hey you, what time is it in LA?'

I smile, relieved at the sound of his voice. 'Never mind that, are you okay?'

'I wasn't sure you'd call.'

'Neither was I.' I raise the gin to my lips. 'I guess I had to check you're alive.'

'And kicking,' he says.

He's okay, I'm relieved, and suddenly I also feel all sad to be leaving somewhere I've instinctively loved. The rest of our conversation is quick and I've tuned out by the time we hang up.

Adam is alive and kicking and my break from reality is, it seems, very much over.

Chapter Thirty-Two

Five days in here and they're letting me out. I'm mid-lecture.
I'm being told that had it been any worse, they would have
put a stent in me. I'm being told to take some blood-
thinners, take my cholesterol-lowering medication and not
to do anything too physical for at least three weeks.

Right. No running then.

'No running,' the doctor says, reading my mind, 'and
no sex either. You'll know when the time is right, but take
a break for a while.'

I try not to laugh out loud. I try not to wish that I'd
had the 'shot across the bows mini-heart attack' last year.
That way, Beth would be by my side; driving me home to
the house we share in Weybridge. She'd mind me, nurse
me, feed me . . . I'd do some gentle gardening to help build
me up again. Instead, Beth is probably already home from
her LA trip, jet-lagged in Weybridge. I'm not sure where
she is. I only know she's not here.

I shake the doctor's hand, agree that I'll be back in a
week for a check-up and put my rucksack on my back. It

has my keys, the running clothes they cut from me, a pair of pyjamas, my trainers and a bottle of water inside. I'm wearing clothes Ben brought in for me, denims that are swimming on me and which I have to hoist up at the waist, a sweatshirt that has seen better days – all of it hidden under an overcoat and my long scarf.

Outside the main entrance of Newham General Hospital, the air is bracing. I'm wrapped like an onion, but I still feel the cold. Anxious to get back, I hail a cab, and within five minutes I'm home. Home . . . It's not really home and never will be. In the flat I toss the keys on the tiny hall table. There's a note there, which I strain to read without my glasses.

Adam, hope you're feeling okay. I've done a food shop for you, put it all away in the fridge and cupboards and I changed the bed. The other linen is in the drier. Get better soon. Karen x

PS I feel bad about the time we argued. You're not my favourite person because of what you've done to Beth, but you are Ben's brother and you and I have been friends for a long time. I hope, in time, we can regroup?

I walk into the kitchen and open the fridge door. It's full of healthy fruit and yogurts and all the things that are, no doubt, on the diet sheet I've been given. Not a piece of bacon in sight. The cupboards are the same. The naughtiest thing I can find is some sugar-free muesli.

I walk to the window, look out onto the busy street below. The café opposite beckons and, without even taking my coat off, I leave the flat and head straight across the road to the riverside greasy spoon. I promise myself that it will be the last full English I will ever have but, right now, I'm starving, and muesli just won't cut it. While I wait, I text Karen, tell her I'm home, thank her for the thoughtful food shop and tell her that whatever 'regrouping' means, I'm up for it.

'Just recover our friendship', she texts back.

'Sounds good', is my thumbed reply.

I let Kiera know what's happened by text, assure her I'm fine, tell her that as soon as I can I'd like to see Noah. I resist the urge to text or call Meg. I'm still reeling from the fact that she never came to see me. It hurts far more than the vice-like squeeze I felt on my heart last Monday and I still don't get it. I know she's winded from my deceit; I know she told me we were finished, but . . . this is my little girl. I didn't believe her then. I didn't think she really meant it. Now, I do, and the pain is something no fucking statin or blood-thinner will cure.

I drink two strong coffees, eat a plateful of food. The eggs are fried, sunny side up, and the bread, my only concession to improving my health today, is brown with seeds in it. I clear the plate and ask for another helping of toast – with butter.

With the prospect of the weekend stretching beyond me, nowhere to go, no one to see, I already feel restless. A quiet angst fills my lungs, making it hard to breathe. I swallow the pills I need with the last of my coffee and pay the bill. Not being able to run, I decide to, at least, walk up along the river. I make it as far as the riverboat stop, just by the steps up to Canary Wharf, before the tiredness kicks in.

It feels overwhelming, as if I have no choice but to stop. I look up. I know there are twenty-three stone steps because last week I was running up and down them, Rocky-like. Today, I turn around and slowly walk back to the flat. Maybe next month . . .

I download the fourth series of *Breaking Bad*, make myself a cup of tea and settle in for the day. Wrapped in a blanket, I stare at the television and lose myself in the lives of a fictional teacher-cum-drug overlord. Somehow, his life seems more real than my own.

At six o'clock there's a knock on the door, not a ring on the bell from the main door downstairs, but a knock on the actual flat door. I press pause, gather my blanket around me and peer through the spyhole.

I open it quickly, almost tripping myself up.

'Dad,' she says, walking past me.

'You came.' I'm reminded of the last time I saw her and she screamed that we were finished.

She looks back over her shoulder. 'I did.'

I shut the front door and follow her through to the one room that combines the kitchen and living space. She has automatically walked through to the kitchen. I return to the sofa.

'I've been immersed in a book about the psychology of serial killers,' she says, 'and I've come to the conclusion there are worse people in the world than you. So, here I am.'

I'm not quite sure what to say. I'm thrilled she's here. I'm not so thrilled she's here because, in comparison to a habitual murderer, I'm not so bad. I say nothing.

'I've brought some food. Soup and a cooked chicken with salad. I Googled what you should be eating.'

I try not to shiver at the mention of a salad. Outside, the slate-grey sky is threatening snow. Salad in December. Thank you, Heart, thank you very much.

'It was only a shot across the bows,' I repeat the medic's words. 'More a warning.'

'The thing about warnings.' She peers over the breakfast bar between the kitchen and the living room. 'Is that you have to decide to listen to them?'

I nod, the guilt over my only meal today already setting in.

'You watching *Breaking Bad*?'

'Yes, just catching up.' I don't tell her that I've already watched seven episodes today. 'Meg, thank you for coming.' I'm not sure how else to say it.

'I can't stay long. Jack is expecting me. I'm here to make sure you have a meal and fill you in on the procedure – that's all.'

There's a finality at the end of her sentence that confirms she's still pissed off at me.

'Jack is wondering what sort of family I have,' she continues. 'This year I'm dealing with the break-up of my parents' marriage and the discovery of a secret – and, oh, dying – brother.'

She's counting out my sins on her fingers.

'Oh, and some stem cell donation thrown in for good measure.'

She has only reached her third finger, but looks as though she's not finished and, yes, put like that, my guilt is multiplying as she speaks. It feels as if it's in the fibres of the shabby tartan cloth wrapped around me.

'Not to mention the fact that all of this means that you're a liar. When you left us first . . . '

I inhale deeply, wait for the sucker punch.

'When you left us,' she repeats, then bites her lip, 'Mum was the one who told me to keep communication lines open with you. She was the one who told me that you'd lied to her but never to me, but that's not true, Dad, is it? You've been lying to me all along too.' She stares at me, but I have no response. Nothing. 'Talk about something else,' she demands as she stabs a cooked chicken with a large carving fork. 'Just do, before I decide this was a bad idea.'

'Are you getting the hormone injections?' Probably not the best change of tack, but it's all I have.

She nods. 'Yes, a nurse comes in each day for the four days beforehand, gives me a quick shot . . . '

'Will your mum definitely be with you for the extraction?'

'She will.'

'Okay.' No invite for me then. 'Are you staying to eat?' I try and keep the hope from my voice. I'm desperate for her company for a few more hours.

She hesitates. 'I'll have some soup with you, but then I've got to go.'

Outside, a small sprinkling of snow is beginning to fall. It leaves a dusting on the narrow wooden slats of the balcony. Part of me hopes it becomes a flurry and that it settles and that we get snowed in and that she can't leave for a while. Maybe if I could get her to listen, she might look me in the eye again . . .

Just minutes later, we are both sitting at the tiny breakfast bar supping soup. It tastes delicious.

'Have you heard how your mum got on in LA?'

'She had a fantastic time. They love her out there.' Meg swirls her soup around with a spoon then takes a sip. 'Of course, she was floored when she got the call from the hospital. *That* upset her.'

'I know. I feel bad. She must have got a fright. I hate having disturbed her time over there.'

'It was obvious, talking to the medical people, that you were fine. Both Mum and I talked to your doctors separately.'

I eat the last of my soup. 'They must have wondered. Wondered why neither of you turned up.' I try not to sound resentful.

She shrugs, half smiling. 'I asked if your life was in danger and they said no. She did the same. If I wasn't going to come to see you from Clapham, there was no chance she was coming from LA.'

'Of course not . . . '

Meg clears the soup dishes away and plates up my dinner. 'Right, I'll head off and leave you to it.' She slips her coat over her shoulders, puts a floppy, woolly hat on her head. 'Why did you never tell us about your son, Dad?' And there it is, the eyeball look. Probably the real reason she's here. The Meg I know will always want to know why . . . Why are there leaves on the trees, Daddy? Why are boys different to girls, Daddy? Where do colours come from, Daddy? Why do numbers happen the way they do, Daddy? Why are you such a lying bastard, Daddy? Her penetrating eyes fix on mine with such intent that I avert my own. I can't bear that accusatory stare.

I've known it's coming, this exact question, but it still floors me. I sit back down, on the edge of the sofa.

'It was like if I didn't say it out loud, it wasn't real.' It's a crap explanation, I know.

'But Mum knew about this Kiera woman anyway. Pregnancies happen, although honestly, the lectures I've had from you over the years on safe sex?'

She's right. I've been a hypocrite as well as a liar.

'I might have liked to know my brother.'

'It would have killed your mother. It would have killed us, me and her. And it would have killed me and you.'

She shakes her head. 'I disagree. It's done all of that now, but only after years of lying.'

'We'll never know how things might have worked out. I did what I did because I thought it was best for everyone.'

'You know you did what you did because it was best for you.'

My shoulders slump and I stand up. Her final, caustic line stings. She will probably never understand how lies beget lies. One leads to two, then three, then thirty.

'Maybe,' I concede, as she walks away, and I know that, despite her being here, forgiveness is a long way off.

'Enjoy your meal,' she says, pulling open the front door and then, without a hug or a kiss, she's gone. I stare at the plate of chicken and know I'll never eat it.

Chapter Thirty-Three

'Are you sure?' Giles asks me, his frown ageing him immediately.

I nod my reply. I'm on the rota to work today and, though lingering jet lag tells me I should have stayed in bed, I'm determined to get through it.

'We'll need Adam's consent before we market it.'

'You'll get it.'

He smiles, excited no doubt at having my beautiful home to sell. I've made sure I'm sitting behind my desk when I tell him. I don't want a hug or a kiss or anything that could be misconstrued. I have no idea how to let this man down gently, but let him down I must.

What I do know is that since my experience with Pink in LA – since the sheer beauty of it, I'm now ruined. I will never again accept mediocre sex. And, though I know that level of wonder I felt at being with a man who isn't Adam will never happen again, still – any further liaison with Giles would be unfair to him and to me.

'Supper tonight?' he asks.

'I can't, Karen's coming around.' She is. It's not a lie. I wish it was. I wish I could go home to my bed and sleep, but Karen is insistent.

'Tomorrow then?'

'Oh Giles, I'm sorry, but I haven't even properly unpacked yet. Plus Meg's in hospital tomorrow.' I have not told him or anyone the full details, just that Meg is having a procedure. No one knows it's in an attempt to save her brother's life – the brother she has never known, because her father chose to hide him from us.

Giles looks disappointed, no doubt wondering how my unpacking stops me eating, but he nods and walks away. I'll have to talk to him, to try and explain, just not today.

Glancing at the electronic diary, I see I have a full day. My first appointment, in ten minutes' time, is to meet an inventory clerk at Kiera Pugh's flat. I grab my bag and head off.

I try not to think about her. The woman who slept with my husband all those years ago. The woman who, while I was trying to persuade Adam to seek help about our marriage, was having his baby. But still, as I pass the concierge in Kiera Pugh's building again, my stomach is turning and twisting with angst and my heart is pumping wildly. At the front door, I knock first, then let myself in with the keys.

'I delayed the inventory guy.' Kiera Pugh is standing in the middle of the living room. 'I asked for you to be here, so we might have the chance to—'

My feet have taken root in the walnut flooring. I stare down and wonder when and where these narrow planks were once a tree. 'I have nothing to say to you.'

She nods. 'I'm quite sure there's lots you want to say to me, but you're too civilized.'

'You don't know me.'

'No, I don't. All I want to say to you is thank you. Thank you for letting your daughter do what she's doing. Noah,' she coughs, 'despite how he was conceived, has a family too. We all love him very much and Meg, she's giving him a real chance.'

I'm being pulled by the floor. I'm frightened that I may never move again, that somehow, the tree's glue-like sap is alive again. It's wilfully determined to have me stuck here with this woman forever. 'Meg is a grown-up. She makes her own decisions.' I do not want her thinking I influenced Meg in any way.

'I'm sure she does, but she has made it clear that she doesn't want any contact with Noah or me or any of his family, so I wanted to be sure the message got to her. Thank you, from the bottom of my heart.'

I say nothing.

'I've got to go, Beth. Noah's been on a course of chemotherapy prior to the donation. It's pretty toxic and very hard on him. I just left for an hour in the hope that I'd catch you.'

Some splinter in my heart snaps away. However angry I am at Adam, this boy does not deserve this. No child should have to go through it. Kiera Pugh has already walked towards the front door.

'Kiera, I'm not sure I'll ever forgive you and Adam, but I wish Noah every good luck. I hope he can get better.'

Her eyes brim with tears. 'Thank you,' she says. 'We need all the luck we can get.'

After she's gone, I need to wait until the floor relinquishes its hold on me, until the blood from my heart can pump through my body, until my toes can feel its nourishing supply. Minutes later, I'm still there, motionless, when a man lets himself in. He's waving an inventory, telling me how we've upset his day's appointments having delayed the first one. For a moment, I debate launching myself at him, screaming that he has no idea what being upset means. But I don't. I smile and tell him to get started. I'll be right behind him. Soon as I can move . . .

'Tell me *everything* and do not lie. I know you were with someone, I knew the moment I saw you! You might as well have "I've shagged someone!" tattooed on your forehead.' Karen sips a cup of tea. I'm having my own version of a Los Angeles G&T. She points to her forehead as if to emphasize where my shameful tattoo should be, but all it does is remind me of tattoos, namely Pink's. On cue, I blush.

'So, start with what's his name?'

'Pink.'

'Like your face. What kind of name is that?'

'Jeff's his real name,' I say. 'But he's known as "Pink". He's a musician with The Brothers, the drummer, has a huge gay following, hence, you know, "Pink".'

'I know them!' She surprises me, since her music tastes are stuck in the eighties. I grin. 'The drummer, eh? Was he good with his hands?'

'Very.' My blush deepens.

'You little minx.' Karen seems to be studying me in a new light. 'Was it very different?'

I snort with laughter. 'To what?'

'Adam.'

'Adam is forty-three and saves his exploratory nature,

sex-wise, for other women. Pink is a thirty-six-year-old musician and yeah, I know . . . ' Karen is miming sticking two fingers down her throat. 'I know it's a cliché, but the man is both talented and sculpted.'

'Fuck . . . ' Karen sighs.

'Yes, we did. A few times actually.' Both of us laugh out loud. 'And yes, it was different, it was special, but it was what it was. Sex. It was only sex.'

'You didn't have any feelings for him?' She feigns horror.

'None, other than lust. Pure, unadulterated sexual desire.'

'You're sounding like Adam now.'

'Maybe I sort of get where he comes from.'

'Oh, no. No, no, no . . . ' Karen shakes her head. 'You are not going to excuse his behaviour, just because you were randy. There's a difference. You hadn't had sex in so long. That makes your needs just that, a primal *need*. Him, on the other hand, he was already having sex with you and he wanted more different sex with someone else. That's just greedy.'

As usual, she puts perspective on it and reins me back in.

'Have you seen him?' I can't help it. A trace of concern sneaks into my voice. 'Meg says he's fine but—'

'He *is* fine. He has to take it easy for a few weeks, but other than that, he's good. Some statins for his cholesterol, that's it.'

She doesn't ask me why I haven't gone to see for myself.

'I've had enough of his drama, Karen,' I offer by way of explanation. 'It was only when I was away and thought about it. He's the worst drama queen I know. Affairs, hidden children, and now a heart attack – or a mini-one – just when . . . Whatever . . . I'll go and see him – just not today.'

That's both Giles and Adam I have managed to put off until another day.

'Are you and he okay?' I'm concerned about Adam and Karen, ongoing. The last time they had seen each other at the house had been awful.

'We've moved on. We both have to. Whatever about you and him, or you and me, I'm in love with Ben and Ben's his brother.'

'In love, eh?' I play-punch her elbow.

'I do love him . . . He's the first man I've ever imagined being with for the rest of my life. The first man I ever thought I might want children with.'

Oh shit, sticky-wicket stuff. On cue, she comes up with the words I've been dreading since they got together.

'So tell me, why exactly did he and Elise split up?'

Just for a second, I wonder if I'll get away with, 'Gosh, is that the time? Must dash', and beat a hasty retreat, but no, it'll never work.

'Haven't you asked *him*?'

'I have. He's vague. My sense is that it's something to do with children, but I'm not sure what. I'm right, aren't I?'

'Have I told you about Pink's tattoos?'

'I knew it.' She sips her drink, pensive.

'He has one on his thigh. It's Chinese symbols, and when I asked him what they meant, he told me it said *Beth*.' I wait for a response. 'I thought it was funny. I mean, he obviously just swaps the name for whoever he's with, right?'

'Right. They did try, didn't they, to have kids, I mean?'

Oh yes, they tried. Yes, they tried. I don't want to talk about this. I think it was five or six IVF attempts. Elise is a backing singer for a lot of celebrity acts, and every penny she earned during their years together went towards yet another unsuccessful effort to be a mother. It was hard on them both. Her, because the fault lay with her damaged tubes, and him, because he knew he could father a child, just not with her . . .

'You need to ask Ben about this,' I tell her.

'I'm asking you.'

I give in. 'They tried for years to have a child. When they couldn't, Ben was willing to adopt but Elise wouldn't. It broke them in the end.' I keep the facts deliberately minimal. 'Anything else you'll have to ask him.'

She is nodding, but I can tell the exchange has upset her.

'Listen.' I put my arm around her. 'You should go home and talk to Ben. I'm still jet-lagged and need an early night. Tomorrow, Meg's at the hospital.'

'Shit.' She makes a face and glances at her wrist. 'I'm sorry. I'll get off now. How is Meg?' she asks as she gathers her things.

I fill her in on how Meg is. Healthy, happy, in love, unforgiving as far as her father is concerned, but willing to donate some of her essence to a sibling she has never known.

'You should be proud of her.' Karen hugs me. 'She's a special girl.'

'I am and she is.'

'You'll have to add "Pink" to your artwork.' Her head angles to the hallway wall. 'You know, to your list of likes. Just add "rolling orgasms in LA". You won't even have to name him.'

I laugh out loud. It's not a bad idea.

Chapter Thirty-Four

'It's one of the advantages of working for myself.' Ben is explaining his ability to control his working hours to me like I'm a two-year-old.

'They just tweaked my heart with a few meds, Ben. They didn't give me a frontal lobotomy.'

He looks confused, turns his head to glance at me from behind the steering wheel. He's insisted on coming to the flat and driving me to Great Ormond Street in my car, telling me that I shouldn't be in charge of one yet, and explaining to me that none of it is any bother – he can catch up on his work the next day. I know I should be grateful, but I wish I hadn't told him I was going. I wish I hadn't said a word and just got a taxi because now two of us will arrive in an already crowded situation.

I press the CD player into action and am both surprised and suddenly tense when I hear Elise's voice singing back to me.

'Is that . . . ?' Ben looks at the dashboard as if it has just spontaneously combusted.

'I'll turn it off.'

'No, leave it. I always love listening to her sing. I've not heard her voice in ages. Is this one of Beth's?'

'It must be.' I have no idea how it's in the car and it shows just how long it is since I've played a CD.

We listen to the song, both immersed in the story of a woman who misses her lover, despite being involved with someone else.

Echoes of your heartbeat,
Echoes of your sounds,
Day and night shades of you follow me around.
An imitation lover is lying here with me;
He's a real beauty, so why can I not feel?

'Do you think Elise ever misses you?' I ask him, grateful to be potentially discussing him rather than me.

'Who knows?' he says. 'It's been over a long time and we haven't kept in touch.'

'Seems a shame. You were together for so long.'

'It was just too raw,' he replies, as Elise builds to Beth's chorus.

He looks like you, he talks like you,
Knows just what to do.
But he ain't you,
He ain't you, babe, he ain't you . . .

I make the decision and reach forward to switch it off. The conversation, it seems, is doomed to be about me. 'So, my second hospital in less than a week . . .'

'No more heart scares, please.'

'No. I just want to see Meg, visit Noah quickly, and then we'll head straight back.'

'I still think you should have told Meg you're coming.'

'She'd tell me not to.'

'And you're okay seeing Beth?'

Am I okay seeing Beth? It's a tough one. I'm hurt beyond hurt that she hasn't called me since her return. Although I've been telling everyone how uncomplicated and normal my heart complaint is, Beth is the only one I want to ham it up to. All I've had is that initial call from LA – one where she definitely wasn't even listening to me by the end of it.

I guess I know why. But, despite everything, Beth is still the kindest person I know living. Even after everything I've done to her, she would call. She'd call just to check I'm all right, hear my voice. And she hasn't.

'Adam?'

'Yes,' I say. 'I'm fine seeing Beth.'

Beth asks me to leave as soon as she lays eyes on me. I'm not ready for this.

She nods at Ben before she repeats her request.

'Adam, Meg told me she doesn't want you here. And what she wants is what she gets. Now please, have some respect and go.'

'This is the second time you've asked me to leave your company lately.' I'm trying not to lose my temper.

'Yes. Last time you manhandled Karen, and this time you're ignoring our daughter's wishes.'

Ben turns to me. 'You manhandled Karen?'

'An exaggeration,' I tell him, before facing Beth again. 'In between I've had a heart attack and I've come to see Meg.' It's a cheap sympathy attempt, I know.

'It was more a shot across the bows,' Ben tells her, his head shaking in a way that says he can't believe what I just said. 'Just a warning.'

'I know that. I spoke to both Adam and his doctors when I was in LA.'

I sigh, lean my back against the nearest wall and decide that pleading is my only option. 'Please. Please don't make a scene. I want to see Meg when she comes out. At least, when she does, let her know I'm here and give her the choice?'

Beth relaxes, seems to consider this and then sits. 'Fine. Just promise me that you'll leave if she doesn't want to see you.'

I nod, take a plastic seat next to hers as Ben mouths the words 'Coffee' to us both. I turn the offer down. Coffee is a 'no-no' on my diet sheet, but Beth asks for a latte. We both watch his back walk away.

'How was LA really? Tell me all,' I say.

She blushes, an immediate scarlet flush from her neck to her hairline.

'Great, it was great,' she says. Both her hands are resting on her thighs; suddenly they start to move up and down, as though she's ironing out creases. 'It was great,' she repeats.

'They took the song?'

'Yes, but that was all confirmed before I went, really. They wanted to meet me and also discuss another song for a different project.'

She falls quiet, twitches in her seat, her eyes darting around the corridor as she avoids mine.

The behaviour is familiar, though not coming from Beth. To my knowledge, she has never been dishonest with me, but I certainly know how I behave around her when I'm hiding something.

'Did you meet someone?' The words are no more than a whisper.

Rather than look away, she angles her face towards mine.

'I didn't *meet* someone so much as have sex with someone.'

'Right . . . '

Her green eyes remain on mine as her eyebrows arch. It's as if she can't believe that's all I have to say. Nor can I, but my mind is trying hard to process what she's just said.

The idea of Beth with another man is one that I've always been afraid to think about. I never want to see the image. Now it's like a film moving slowly, unfurling in my brain, frame by frame.

'I don't know what to say.' I shrug. 'You're free to do whatever you please . . . '

'That's right.' Her eyes fire up. 'It was sex. Fantastic sex, but only sex.'

I feel a strange, cramp-like pain in my chest, one that almost renders me speechless. 'The idea still hurts,' is what comes out of my mouth when I do speak.

'Welcome to my world,' she says, and stands to meet Ben, who's heading in our direction, cups in hand.

'How much longer do you think she'll be?'

Beth turns around, blows the steam off her latte. 'Not

long. What's the hurry? You have somewhere else to go?'

I do actually, but sneaking off to see Noah right now is probably not the best idea. But then again, she's just had sex with another man. Fantastic sex with another man.

'I wanted to pop in and see how Noah's doing.' Brave, Adam. Very brave.

Beth touches her hair with her hands, then tilts her head left and right, as though she's stretching out her neck muscles. 'I thought that you'd never had any contact with him. I mean, that's what you told me.'

I sigh. 'I never have – at least, not until a couple of weeks ago, when yes, I asked Kiera if I could meet him. He doesn't know who I am.' I'm not sure why I feel the need to reiterate this, but I do.

'He doesn't know who you are?' Beth turns towards Ben, rolls her eyes. 'Who are you, Adam? What does that remark mean? Do you mean he doesn't know you're his father? Well, you're not, are you? You were a sperm donor, that's all. It takes a lot more to be a father. But then, being a father also means not letting down the child you *have* raised, and you have a big fat fail there too.' She stops to draw breath.

'I'll be back in fifteen minutes.' I can't stand it any more. Nothing I do or say is ever going to be good enough. Fuck her and her fantastic sex. I leave her and Ben to have the default conversation about what a bastard I am and walk the two flights up to Noah's room.

Kiera and Gordon are both standing outside. He has his back to me but I can tell he's staring through the window in the door.

'Adam.' Kiera comes forward and hugs me. Gordon nods,

the briefest movement of his head, but it's a nod all the same. 'If you want to see him, please be quick. He's asleep now, but the chemo is really taking it out of him.'

'Maybe just a minute?' My eyes address Gordon, who nods again.

I enter the room and cross to the bed. Noah looks a ghostly shade of white, with huge black shadows under both his eyes. He seems to have shrunk since I saw him last, and I'm not ready for the lump that this scene is leaving in my throat. 'Hello, mate,' I whisper. 'Looks like you've been through the wringer, eh?'

His eyes flutter, then open.

Shit, I didn't mean to wake him. Quickly, I move in front of him, so that his parents can't see him through the window.

'Adam,' he says, 'you came back.' His voice is croaky. 'Not up for chess today.'

'No problem. You just get well. I've been told not to stay long.'

I see his hand move as if to stop me going, but he doesn't have the strength. He tries to catch my eye instead.

'Are you my father?' he asks. Blatant, simple, just like that.

Beth's earlier comments echo in my head and I look away. 'Of course not,' I tell him. 'Your father's just outside the door here with your mum, willing you to get better.'

'Yes, yes he is,' my little boy replies.

'You get well, Noah.' I touch his nearest hand briefly and turn to leave.

'Adam?'

I look back.

'You're a nice man,' he whispers.

'Thank you,' is all I can muster. I leave without saying goodbye to Gordon and Kiera. My pulse is clunking in both ears.

'*You're a nice man. You're a nice man. You're a nice man.*' The words echo in my head over and over again.

My dying son is the only person in the world who thinks I'm a nice man.

'You knew when we were going that Meg didn't want to see you.'

Ben is so matter-of-fact that I want to thump him. His daughter did not just refuse to see him. This is the same daughter who I was the first to hold when she was born. The same girl who squealed to be fed and squealed when she'd been fed. The same girl who cried, red-faced and tight-fisted, when she was tired, and did the same when she woke up. The child who loved to take comfort from her daddy holding her. The little girl who seemed to recognize a father's calming embrace. I can't believe she can't remember that . . .

'Women are funny,' Ben continues. 'Maybe it was just that she wanted her mother there. You know – when kids aren't feeling their best.'

He's trying, but I do wish he'd shut up and just drive.

'How was Noah?'

'Not good. He looks grey, dreadful.' I keep our exchange to myself. Nobody else needs to know that, despite him being only ten, he's clever enough to have worked things out.

'When are you going back to work?' Ben asks.

'Tomorrow.'

'Is that wise?'

I give a small snort-like sound. 'Probably not. But then again, I'm not known for my wisdom . . . I'll cab it in and home every day. I'll do shorter days this week. You have to understand, Ben. I'll go crazy if I'm not busy.'

He doesn't reply. I wonder – if I could look inside his head – whether he's thinking I'm crazy anyway. Probably . . .

'I wish you'd come and stay with Karen and me, just for this week. I hate the thought of you being alone at the moment.'

I tap his left arm. 'Thank you, but I'm fine. I have to get used to being alone and, let's face it, I've got no one to blame for that but myself.'

He flinches, moves his arm. 'Sometimes, Adam . . . sometimes you should focus on the good things, rather than feeling sorry for yourself.'

'I'm not feeling sorry for myself.'

'Yes, you are. You have a beautiful family. You have a beautiful wife, a fabulous daughter and now a little boy too. I'm not even going to go there about why you never told me about him, promised myself I wouldn't do it, you've not been well.'

I rub both of my eyes, wish I could stop him talking. 'I'm sorry. I should have told you.'

'Yes.' He's nodding slowly. 'Yes, you should. You have two children. I haven't managed to father one yet, Adam.'

I stare at the road ahead, bite my tongue, but I can't help myself. 'Ever wonder if that's why I *didn't* tell you?'

He makes a face and we sit in silence for a few minutes. 'I don't want to fall out,' he says, eventually. 'I shouldn't have said anything. Not now, not with what you're going through.'

'We're not going to fall out, mate. I love you and I'm sorry.' I can see his head debate a reply but he says nothing. I'm aware it's the first time I've told Ben out loud that I love him. He reaches his hand across, places it on mine and squeezes. His way of saying 'Me too', I guess.

The rest of the journey is quiet. Just before I get out of the car, he turns to me.

'Look . . . ' He hesitates. 'There's no easy way to say this, but I think you should consider seeing someone.' He keeps his eyes on mine as he delivers this line.

'See someone? What? Like someone professional?'

'Yes. Nearly everyone talks to a shrink sometime in their lives nowadays. Your marriage has broken down, your relationship with your daughter is fractured, and your son, someone you've never known, is dying before you get a chance to know him. Not to mention Mum and Dad?'

Put like that, show me the number, I'll dial it right now. I feel a powerful shaking threaten but, before it takes me, I bite down hard, my bottom teeth almost grinding my top.

'It's okay, Adam.' Ben squeezes my hand again. 'I'm sorry if I was hard earlier. You'll get through this. You will.'

I can't help feeling that I'm still the big brother who's expected to cope and that his words are more an order than a statement . . .

Chapter Thirty-Five

It's a week since the procedure and Meg has insisted on going back to her housemates and to Jack, back to the student house in Clapham she calls 'home'. I'm not sure if that's because I'm adamant that this one is going on the market and she feels as though she no longer has a home. Hashtag Guilty Mum, as she would say . . . I'm wandering around the rooms in the house. The cleaners I pay once a month to come in for a few hours and blitz the place have been in this morning and it all looks shiny and new and . . . homely. I have a sudden doubt. Why? I never wanted to sell the house. Why, when I was in LA, did it seem like the right thing to do?

Sighing deeply, I sit on the edge of my bed. This is why the house should be sold. The bed's not mine. It's Adam's and my bed. It's Adam's and my bedroom, and the house is a permanent reminder of the breakdown of our marriage. The simple fact is he's not here and, even though I don't want him to be, the whole thing feels wrong, like something that's been untethered from its secure holding. This house is off kilter with just me in it.

So, I'm meeting him for a drink in an hour to tell him my decision. I don't expect him to object. He knows he's never coming back here, and splitting the equity in the house seems a fairer way of moving forward. Giles already has some buyers lined up – just awaiting the go-ahead from Adam.

Giles . . . He so wants to share this bed – or any bed – with me. It's never going to happen and I've told him as much. In as kind a manner as I could. I lied – told him that I'm just not ready and can't imagine being ready for a very long time. He's such a nice man that I can't tell him I simply don't fancy him. Karen says I need my head examined, that Giles is local and loving and to give him a chance. But in my head Giles is a local, loving man whom I never want to kiss again, so sex is out of the question. And, following my Pink experience, I now know I need sex . . .

Pink . . . The man is in my head. In every crease and fold of my skin. In my bodily fluids, in my mouth. I think of him all the time. Not in an 'I wish he was here' way, nor in a 'Shall I call him?' way, just in a more wondrous way. Like, I can't really believe any of it happened. Did I really have this encounter? Is it really that simple to have uncomplicated, no-strings, fabulous sex? Am I really booty-call material? Perhaps I'll ask Adam later. If anyone knows, he would.

An hour later, I'm sitting in a bistro two minutes outside Clapham Junction train station. Adam is driving, since Meg has agreed to see him and he's going over to hers for supper afterwards. She did ask me but I declined. Now is not the time to play Happy Families with Adam.

The bar area is decorated for the season, with tiny white lights weaving through the rafters, and potted, scarlet poinsettias scattered around. The windows have snow-sprayed images – stars, angels, parcels and lanterns – and the tables are adorned with festive cloths and napkins.

While I wait, I make notes in my daybook. I've taken to keeping a record of all the things I need to do and things I've already done. It's not a diary, but it does help keep me organized. Today's last entry, made this morning, consisted of notes taken during my telephone conversation with Josh. He has the final recording of 'Fall Apart', and wants me to come in to hear it in his office rather than just send me the link. I have scribbled down, 'Why?' A niggling worry crosses my mind and I wonder if they've changed the middle eight dramatically?

I look up and see Adam approach and close my daybook. I'll worry about it later. Seeing him, I hope we can put our last meeting at the hospital behind us. I just want to move forward. He leans down to me, kisses me on the cheek, and I think of Giles and Pink together. Adam is a good kisser. In fact, he's a very good kisser – probably the best kisser I've known, if we're just talking kissing.

'What are you drinking?' He beckons a waiter over.

'I'll have a G&T, please.'

His eyebrows arch and his mouth curves. 'Really?'

The waiter arrives, pen and notepad in hand.

'I'll have a Tanqueray gin with Fever-Tree tonic, lemon and lime twists and a couple of juniper berries, please.' The waiter writes it all down, nods, then looks at Adam.

'I'll have a Diet Coke.' He smiles. 'When did you start drinking gin?'

'Oh, it doesn't matter when. What matters is that I like it now. I guess times move on, I'm different.'

'Yeah, well, don't change too much. You were pretty good as you were.'

I'm not sure how to take this. I've never been very good at accepting compliments, especially from Adam. Maybe because, as soon as he ever started to compliment me, I knew he was up to something. He's playing with his red and gold napkin, making an origami something out of it.

'What was it you wanted to talk about?' he asks, head down, his brow furrowed in concentration over an emerging mouse or goat or whatever shape he's going for.

'I think we should sell the house.' I let the initial shock remark sit mid-air for a moment before continuing. 'It's a good time to sell, the market has risen in the last year. We could both buy something decent when we halve the proceeds. Giles, the manager where I work, says it will sell easily and that we should get top dollar at the moment.'

Adam is now looking up and focusing directly on me. His origami attempt discarded, I stare back and notice how he's aged. Just a few more lines around his eyes. Dark under-shadows, which used to be a sign of him being temporarily overtired, are now permanent residents.

'Well? What do you think?' I press him for a response.

'I think you seem to have it all worked out.'

'Adam, I asked you here to talk about it. Let's face it, months ago when you left to shag Miss Restaurant Owner, you'd have bitten my arm off to get me to sell the house.' I can't help myself. Even when I try and rein it in, he brings this out in me. 'Look, I'm aware that you're still paying for most of its running costs and, honestly, I don't want that to continue. I don't see why you should have the worry, especially at the moment. I also want my independence.'

Our drinks have arrived. I stir mine and take a large gulp.

'Why "especially at the moment"?'

'You've just had a heart scare. Stress is a factor. Bad as you are, I really don't want you keeling over on us.'

He shrugs. 'Why not? Seems to me you'd get all of the house then.'

My teeth bite into my lower lip. 'Only if we're still married.'

He stares at me over the rim of his soft drink. 'Are you saying what I think you're saying?'

I shake my head. 'I'm not sure. There's really no going back, is there? I mean really? Our marriage is over, Adam. We're both still young and we should both be free to move on.'

I can see my words wound him and I take no pleasure in this.

'Ben thinks I need help. That I should see someone professional.'

It's such a complete one-eighty change of subject that I sit back in my chair, unsure how to respond.

'He's probably right. I can't remember how he put it, but when he paraphrased my life for me, I sounded like a nut job in the making. And he doesn't know the half of it.'

I reach across for his hand, an unconscious move. 'You will know if and when the time is right; you will know if you need help. I did. And it did help, really.'

He stares down at the table, at his hand under mine. 'Feels nice,' he says.

I take my hand back. 'Can we put the house on the

market? We don't have to talk about anything else right now.' I can't do it. I cannot push the divorce point at this moment. Besides, I may be ninety per cent sure it's what I want, but I need to be one hundred, and when it comes to the complete dissolution of a marriage – it's still early days. 'It makes sense – we could both buy again and it takes a lot of pressure off you.'

He nods, lifts my glass and tastes. 'Good version of the G&T,' he says. 'Did you discover it in LA?'

Alarm bells start to ring in my head. Now is probably not the time to discuss my LA discoveries, so I do a one-eighty back on him. The words surprise me as I hear myself speak them. 'How is Noah?'

He seems startled, probably remembering the way I spoke to him at the hospital, but he seems grateful that I asked. 'I saw him last night. Kiera and Gordon let me play chess with him.'

'At their home? Do you think that's a good idea?' I blurt. 'I mean, is it fair on Noah? It's not as though his parents are going to tell him anything.'

'Not at home – he's still in Great Ormond Street. He's such a bright kid. I think he's worked it out for himself.'

I sit back in my chair and think about this. 'Be careful. There are a lot of people who could get hurt, Adam. Please be careful.'

'I am being. He's the only person in the world who doesn't judge me, Beth. The only person in the world who has a chat with me about my day. Beats the hell out of me every time we play chess.'

I want to say that he's only a child. That he doesn't know Adam the way I do. That's why he doesn't judge.

'Has it worked? The donation?' is what I do say.

'Who knows? We've just got to hope . . . I should go soon, get to Meg's. She's cooking supper.'

I nod. 'Have you plans for Christmas?' It's only ten days away and I haven't really allowed myself to think about it yet, but Meg has asked if Jack can come. It seems he'd rather spend it with her than go to the Lake District with his family. Since it's probably my last Christmas in the house, of course I've agreed. My mother will, as usual, attend. The only missing person will be Adam.

He runs a hand through his hair. 'I haven't thought about it. Ben mentioned something about him, Karen and me all going to a restaurant.'

I can tell he's thinking about our home – the house and the memories of Christmases past that it holds.

'Just wait until the new year, will you?' he asks. 'Before putting it on the market? You don't want people traipsing in and out over Christmas, and another few weeks won't matter. You're right. We need to sell it, but I just need some time to get used to the idea.'

'That's fine. It can wait until then.' I drain my glass and stand up, wrap myself up in my bubble coat. It's freezing outside. 'Be careful on the roads. There's going to be a heavy frost tonight.'

'I didn't know you cared.' He smiles a closed-mouth smile. It's the same smile that I fell for decades ago.

'I care.' I lean up to him and kiss his cheek. 'Some part of me will always care.'

He holds the back of my head, just for a moment. I know he wants to linger but I pull away.

'Just one word of advice?' I say. 'When you get to Meg's,

please make the evening about her. She's been through a lot. Don't mention that you've been playing chess with Noah. It won't go down well.' I don't bother mentioning that it hasn't really gone down well with me either.

His face wrinkles. 'I don't want to lie any more.'

'She's not going to ask. Just don't bring it up?'

He nods, but I can tell he doesn't get it. In his head, Meg knows of Noah's existence. She's given him potentially life-saving stem cells. She wants him to live, possibly some-time have a relationship with him. She should know that Adam is trying for the same. This is how Adam sees it.

It is not how Meg sees it. Meg is horrified that her father has deceived us both for a decade. She is appalled to find another sibling that she has never had the chance to know. She feels she *had* to do the right thing, because she would never forgive herself had she not. But none of it is all right with her. Tonight is just the beginning of healing her frac-tured relationship with her 'motherfucking father', as she calls him.

I tap Adam's arm. 'Trust me on this, Adam. Just make it about her. She needs to believe she's the centre of your universe.'

'She is. You are.'

He looks sad when he says those words; looks as though he really believes them and, hearing them, it's easy to forget what a selfish shit he can be.

'But, she'd be okay with the chess thing, surely?' he asks again.

I shake my head and am left wondering, yet again – selfish or stupid or both?

Chapter Thirty-Six

Today is the twelfth day since my son received stem cells from my daughter. During this time, a small amount of time really, my life has changed irrevocably. I move through the offices in work, doing what I do. I talk to people who expect me to talk to them, in the same way I always have. I call my daughter every day and let her know that I love her. She is melting a little towards me, slowly but surely. I see my son every second day. We play chess together and, each time I visit, I'm hoping and praying for an improvement in him. During this time, we both pretend that I'm a friend of Uncle Tim's from university. Hell, pretence is second nature to me, but I'm not pretending when I admit I love him. I have grown to love this little boy . . .

Today is also five days to Christmas, and Noah is being allowed home for a fortnight. The hospital room and outside corridors are a hive of activity. I'm trying to stay out of the way while he's being prepared for transportation in the ambulance and while drugs coming from the pharmacy are being waited on. Kiera and Gordon have stepped

307

away for a break and Noah and I are alone. I have asked him what he would like to be when he grows up.

'A pilot,' he says with all the confidence of someone who already is.

'That's brilliant,' I tell him, as he leans forward. I automatically move to fluff up his pillows. 'You can have flying lessons from about the age of sixteen, I think.' I decide to check this out on Google later.

'Just five and a half more years,' he says brightly. 'I can do that.'

I squeeze his hand. 'Of course you can.'

'What did you want to be when you were my age?'

'Not what I am.' I muse, thinking more about my character than my career choice. 'I think I remember wanting to be a policeman.'

Noah is nodding. 'If I can't be a pilot, I'd like that instead. Where are your mum and dad?' he asks suddenly.

I'm surprised by the change of subject and I'm not quite sure how to answer.

'Dad's mum is alive,' Noah goes on, 'and Mum's dad is alive, so between them I have one set of grandparents. They're both really old.'

I laugh. I know nothing about Gordon's mother, but I do know that old man Granger is only about seventy and he's as sharp as a tack.

'So where do your parents live, Adam?'

My mouth is dry. My eyes linger on his for just a moment, but it's a moment too long. He knows who I am. And he knows that I know he knows.

'I'd like to meet them someday,' he says.

'I—'

'There's no hurry,' he adds quickly, a pink flush appearing on his cheeks. 'Tell me about when you and your dad played chess when you were little?'

He is so adept at changing the subject that my son puts even me to shame and his question jolts a memory.

Dad has let me win again. I tell him I know what he's doing and he just laughs. He tells me he wants to talk to me about Mum and, as I pack the chess pieces away, I'm immediately on my guard. He tells me that I'm an adult now that I'm eighteen. He tells me that I need to try to understand Mum more, cut her a little slack, and asks me if I ever wonder what it must be like to be her. I listen as my father tells me all about my mother's manic highs and depressive lows and her in-betweens. I listen, nod a lot, and do not take him on. My father will not have a word said against my mother and it upsets me. She might be ill but she's also an accomplished goddamned liar.

'Adam?' Noah's voice brings me back. 'Did you play often?'

'Yes.' I smile at him. 'Not as often as you and I are going to though.'

At that moment, the moment when I perhaps have said something I shouldn't have, something that could be construed as a confirmation of his suspicions, he rewards me with the biggest smile I have ever seen. A lump catches in the back of my throat.

A nurse comes by to check his blood pressure.

'I'm just going to grab a coffee,' I say. 'Be back in a minute. Do you want anything?'

He shakes his head.

Outside the room, around the corner, I find Gordon and

Kiera sitting in a soft-chair 'family' area. They're seated together on a sofa and, opposite them, holding Kiera's hand, is a woman. It's only when I get near that I recognize her voice. I stop, taking the scene in, as Kiera looks up.

'Adam,' she says.

Meg turns her head and stands, her hands immediately smoothing out her jeans. 'Dad, I've come to visit Noah. Though obviously not on the best day, what with him being moved home . . . '

I'm speechless, and aware that Gordon looks distinctly uncomfortable.

'Kiera and Gordon have agreed that I just meet him as an anonymous donor,' Meg explains. 'We don't want to confuse him.'

'I'll stay out here, I was just off for a coffee.'

Kiera looks grateful. She doesn't want Noah seeing Meg and me in the same room together and I don't want to tell her that she's too late. I don't want to be the one to tell her that Noah has definitely pieced some of this together. He has worked out who I am, but thinks I'm the donor. Introduce Meg and he'll go off deducing more facts. I say nothing, reach across for Meg and give her a hug. 'Thank you,' I whisper in her ear. She doesn't pull away.

Ten minutes later, Meg exits Noah's room. The fingers on my left hand are laced through my right ones, clasped together, making them numb and white. She approaches, sits beside me. 'I guess I was curious.' She shrugs. 'He's a nice kid.'

'He is.' I stare at my wan knuckles.

'Had loads of questions for me . . . Who I am? What my family is like, where I live? I just kept it all vague. Told him that the register had contacted me because I'm a match . . . ' She turns to face me. Her coat, lying across her lap, falls to the floor, and I pick it up, pass it back to her.

'I'm sorry.'

'He looks like you.' Her head is bobbing, as if to reassure herself it's really a fact.

'I know . . . '

'He told me he's had a friend playing chess with him this morning. Is that you?'

'Yes.'

'That's good. He's a sweet kid.' Meg's voice cracks. Tears threaten to fill her eyes. 'He looks so sick . . . ' She stands, seems embarrassed by her emotions, leans down and air-brushes my cheek with her lips. 'Don't tell Mum I've been here, okay?' With that, she puts her coat on and walks away.

And, for once, I have no words. None at all . . .

Today is Christmas Eve. Kiera called me earlier and asked me not to come for what had been a scheduled visit. Noah has a worsening cold and visitors aren't allowed. I stare at the hand-carved chess set that I stopped wrapping when I got the call. It's only the latest in a long line of presents bought for Noah. Every year, just before Christmas, I buy him a present, his birthday too. I choose it, wrap it, do a drive-by past the house in Hampstead. I think about knocking on the door and asking Kiera to give it to him, but I never have. I've always bottled out, thinking of the wounds I would open. This was going to be the first one I could actually give him.

So I give to those I can. Last night, I drove to what I now call Beth's house and dropped off presents for her and Meg and Sybil. Karen and Ben's lie wrapped on the sofa, ready for when I head over there later.

Kiera's words roll around in my brain. Fear sets in and I wonder if she's lying just to keep me away over Christmas. I will never be part of their family. It doesn't matter how I feel about Noah, or even how he might feel about me. I suspect this is Gordon's doing. He has tolerated me being around, because he's had to. Yes, it's bloody Gordon's doing.

I don't want to go to Karen and Ben's. Paranoia about Gordon's plan to get rid of me has set in. I am not in a mood for paper hats and a plastic turkey dinner in their local restaurant, perched on grimy chairs. I'm not in the mood for drinking enough to merit the fact that the restaurant has been chosen, not for the fantastic Christmas fare, but because of its stumbling distance from Karen's flat.

My phone vibrates and falls from the coffee table to the floor. I pick it up and connect the call. Meg.

'Hi Dad.'

'Hi love, how're you?'

'Good. We're all here—'

She just stops short of saying 'except you . . . ' 'I have something for you. Will I see you over the next few days?'

'That's up to your mum, love. I don't want to intrude.'

'She says come over for a drink on Boxing Day. Later on.'

Not for lunch then. I suppose a cheating bastard should be grateful for small mercies.

'I'll pop in for a quick one Boxing Day evening. Have

a lovely day tomorrow, darling. I hope Santa's good to you, that you get everything you want.'

It's an expression from her childhood, but her silence tells me it's unlikely.

'Have fun with Ben and Karen, Dad.' She hesitates. 'Love you,' she adds.

Meg loves me. I'm sure Ben loves me, but would never tell me. I think Noah is fond of me. It's enough, I tell myself. Keep it together. Push on, keep going. It's Christmas . . .

I wrap up warmly, take the bag carrying Ben and Karen's presents, some booze, chocolates and some overnight clothes. I leave the chess set, my fingers lingering on the beautifully carved king. In a parallel universe, I know that Noah would have loved me. I convince myself that it still might be possible. Maybe if I love him enough, even from afar, maybe love will ripple across the airwaves back to me.

I lock the flat and head downstairs to the garage. Outside, there is a frost and a light dusting of snow. It doesn't look as though it will settle, so the bookies will have a bright, rather than white, Christmas.

Karen has obviously been warned to be nice to me. I can almost hear the conversation that would have happened. Ben would have reminded her about everything I've been through, everything I'm now going through, as I wait for someone to tell me that Noah is going to be allowed to grow up. Karen would at that point probably have reminded him that most of my problems are of my own creation. But, for now, she's being so nice to me – I'll take it.

They have cleared the spare bedroom, where they both

work from. All of their office equipment has been moved to one tight corner. In the centre of the room, they've made up the sofa bed and provided a bedside light. Not quite home, but I give them a grateful smile.

We're drinking champagne. I try and join in the celebratory spirit of Christmas, but I feel empty. It's an emptiness I don't recognize and struggle with. My life, as I knew it, has gone. Where there was once a home, there is a blank space. Where there was once a family, there is a gaping void. I'm looking at Ben and Karen gazing lovingly at each other. She doesn't know it yet, but he's going to ask her to marry him tomorrow. The irony of this is lost completely on my brother. I try and be happy for them. I am. I'm not jealous of their happiness. I just find it hard to watch, when my own seems a distant memory.

I break away early, give them some time together. Sitting on the edge of the sofa bed, my head in my hands, I try and imagine a bright future. What does it look like? Beth and I in cottages in Weybridge – maybe next door to each other? Meg, working in her dream job – something that allows her to study mad minds; Noah playing football or rugby, with me and Gordon next to each other on the sidelines.

None of it fits. Nothing fits into the shape that my life is any more. My phone pings with a text and I look at the screen. Kiera.

The words seem to flash in neon at me. 'Noah's got bad chest infection, heading back to the hospital. Def no visitors. Will keep in touch. Kiera.'

I sit very still for a while. I can't go there. I can't drive because I've been drinking and, even if I could, even I know

I shouldn't. My next instinct is to pray, but I have no idea where to start. The last time I prayed properly was when Mum and Dad died. Shivering, I rub my arms warm, try and summon some words from my childhood. Words that will plead with the Higher Powers. I ask whoever is listening to please help him. I ask whoever is listening to help Kiera and Gordon. I ask whoever is listening to please help me. Help me get through Christmas without allowing the black hole inside of me to consume me. Please . . .

It's two o'clock on Christmas Day. There is radio silence from Kiera, despite my texts, and I'm antsy. Karen, Ben and I are seated at a table for three in the corner of her local bistro. The white wine is warmer than the food, but food, at this point, is only fuel to keep me breathing. My phone is on the table, though I've already been asked by Karen to put it away. In the end, like a resentful teenager, I told her why I needed it out and asked sarcastically for her permission. She doesn't deserve this, yet here I am, doling it out.

There are children running around our table and I'm trying not to lose it. Why do parents not keep their children in check in public?

I turn to the couple two tables away and ask them politely to stop their children darting around us. Harrison and Georgia are both called by their parents. For now, they return, with their noisy toys in tow, to the folds of their family.

'You all right?' Ben puts a hand over mine.

Yes, is the appropriate answer, but I can't say it. I'm not. I feel an overpowering sense of negativity engulf me. I nod in his direction and take a sip of tepid wine. Trying to think of anything other than where I am and why – I wonder why the ring hasn't appeared yet. I would have thought it would be a 'first thing in the morning' gesture, but I say nothing, just in case I ruin that too.

'Anything yet?' Karen jerks her head towards my phone, nesting neatly next to my cutlery.

'No, not yet.'

'He'll be fine,' she says chirpily, and I want to smack her. He has cancer. He's just had a stem cell donation. An infection is not good news. I say nothing as Harrison and Georgia run by my chair once more. One of their toys, a remote control car, has got its antenna stuck under my chair.

'I have to get out of here.' I stand suddenly, take my coat from the back of my chair. 'I'm sorry but I need some air.'

Outside, I sit on a freezing breeze-block wall. The icy cold seeps through my jeans and infiltrates my bones. Ealing high street, just opposite me, is busy. This astounds me. Why are all these people driving on Christmas afternoon? Why are they all not nestled in the bosoms of their families? Most families, I remind myself, are not like the one I had. Most are probably like the one I have. Broken, split, fractured . . .

Just for a second, I think about it. I could just walk ten feet and fall in front of one of these cars. It feels so simple a solution. I won't have to deal with the awful anxiety I can feel invading me. I won't ever have to feel like this on Christmas Day again. I can really make it look like an accident, just a little stagger. It's as though my mum and dad are summoning me.

From the corner of my eyeline, I see Ben standing at the

window. He has me in his crosshairs and I feel his osmotic thoughts penetrate. 'Don't you dare,' he's saying. 'Think of me; think of the poor driver whose life will never be the same.' My shoulders slump forward and I hate myself for even contemplating it. I stand up, breathe deeply, blow circles out of my mouth and make my way back to the heavy oak door – to Ben and Karen, to Harrison and his remote control car and to mediocre Christmas pudding that tastes nothing at all like Beth's.

Back in the flat, I corner Ben.

'So, Romeo, where's the ring?'

He shushes me, tells me he's going to wait until the next day, until they're alone.

'Not having second thoughts?'

He shakes his head.

'Will you still want children?' I whisper. I've had just enough shitty wine to make me brave. 'Because she's forty, you know. You might be out of the frying pan and all that . . .'

'I love her. If we can have kids, great. If not—'

'They turn into Harrisons anyway. Little shits with noisy cars.'

Ben smiles. 'Or Georgias?'

'Little she-devils with a noisy Nintendo thingy.'

'I remember Meg as a child,' he begins.

'Meg,' I point a finger at him, 'was a *noisy* baby. She cried a lot.'

'I remember her as a thoughtful child.'

'She was. Thoughtful, chatty, funny. After about two, she was great fun.'

'Not all Georgias and Harrisons then . . . '

I shake my head. 'No, I hope it works out for you both.' I put my arms around him and pull him into a bear hug.

'What's this love-in about?' Karen's head cranes around the doorway from the living room to the hall, where Ben and I are standing. 'Can anyone join in?'

I open an arm and she merges into the clasp. We all hear my phone ring in my pocket and, moving apart, I pull it out. 'Kiera, everything all right?'

I listen to her broken sobs and am immediately aware that it's this moment in time that I'll recall in the future. This split second where my life is ripped into two halves. The before and the after. I can feel my legs fold under me, feel both Karen and Ben reach out to grab me. The phone drops to the floor and Kiera's desperate keening sounds from four feet away. It battles with a sloshing, gurgling sound in my head which must be my brain melting.

'He's gone,' I whisper. 'My lovely little boy is gone . . . '

PART THREE

I love you, need you, you're my glue,
I fall apart without you

Chapter Thirty-Seven

Love, could you taste it, was it real?
This love you made me feel.
Love, did you get its heady scent?
This love was heaven sent.
Now that you're gone, who will I love?
Now that you're gone to a world up above.
Now that you're gone, my life's no longer whole,
I'm empty, alone, no heart and no soul.

I've got my writing mojo back. Up early, I've been in the loft for hours when the smell of burning toast makes me take the stairs down, two at a time. Meg is on the phone and oblivious. I point to the smoking toaster. Too late, the fire alarm sounds and she goes outside to continue the call. My eyes rise to the heavens – it's pissing rain and she has no coat on. What can be so important? I wave a tea towel at the alarm, waft the smell out of the window and make myself a strong coffee.

The neon clock on the oven blinks. Mum will be up in

ten minutes. Jack is obviously sleeping in. It's New Year's Eve. We're all still here; no one has quite made it back to their own bed since Christmas. Thankfully, Sylvia is having some sort of soirée tonight that will take our minds off the fact that Noah is being buried the day after tomorrow.

Meg is ashen when she returns.

My stomach plunges. 'What's wrong?'

'That was Ben. Dad's gone AWOL . . . '

There's some Scottish guy dancing to 'Mull of Kintyre' in Sylvia's hallway. Meg, Mum, Jack and I are standing on the edge of the kitchen, each of us nursing a glass of champagne, none of us feeling like celebrating. I check my phone. Nothing. This is ridiculous. I swear I will finally kill him this time. I'll make it painful and slow, so he feels every moment. My murderous thoughts are interrupted by the phone actually ringing. I dart out of the back door, away from the music, plugging my free ear with my finger.

'Ben?'

'I've found him.'

'Is he okay?'

'Not really. He's cold, soaking wet, delirious.'

My head shakes involuntarily. 'What's he playing at? Where was he?' The rest of my body shivers in the December chill.

'At the cemetery . . . He was in Highgate. With Mum and Dad . . . '

I'm completely confused. Adam never visits his parents' grave. In all the time I've known him, even when I've asked him about it, he waves it away, tells me that it's only a resting place for their bones. 'I don't . . . Why? Has he been out all night in this weather?'

'Just all day, he must have spent the night in the car. I don't know. Look, Beth, he's not making sense. What he needs now is a warm bed and some rest. Can I bring him home?'

My senses prickle. 'This isn't his home any more, Ben.'

'Beth, he's in a bad way.'

'Mull of Kintyre' has been replaced by The Proclaimers walking 'Five Hundred Miles'. I stare through Sylvia's window at the revelry, rub the cold from my arms. 'Just bring him back,' I tell Ben before hanging up.

In Sylvia's hallway, I learn that the strange man in the kilt is a true Scot as he waves his tartan skirt suggestively at my thighs. I have no energy to laugh. I gather what's left of my family and we leave as quietly as possible, knowing Sylvia won't need an explanation.

Mum and I change the linen in her room. She can sleep with me tonight.

'Would you not . . . ?' she begins.

'No, I would not.' Adam is not coming back to my bed tonight.

'It just seems an awful lot of work to—'

'Mum!' My voice is louder, sterner than I want it to be. 'Please?' I plead with her. 'Not tonight. He needs our help, but this is still *Adam*?'

She looks at me, eyes narrowed, reluctantly nods, and together we change the sheets in the green room.

Ben brings him straight upstairs. No small talk. Adam sits on the edge of the bed. He's filthy and silent.

'Should you try and shower him?' I ask Ben. I wring my hands together, unsure if I should help or leave.

'Let him sleep,' is his reply.

Meg comes into the room with a large whisky. 'Dad? You okay?' She sits beside him and guides the glass to his mouth. He swallows it in three gulps, whispers a thank you to her.

'Do you want something to eat?' I ask as he lies down fully clothed.

He shakes his head. I glance at Meg, envious of how she's just got this moment so right and I . . . I have no idea what to do, how to react.

Practical, I tell myself. Just be practical. 'You should get him out of those wet clothes.' I direct this at Ben and leave the room to find something. Outside, on the landing, I take several deep breaths as I walk to my bedroom. In the closet, where I've put most of Adam's clothes, my hands root through the piles until they land on something suitable, an old pair of pyjamas – that will do.

They seem to rise of their own accord to my nose, but the scent I inhale is only of fresh laundry. They no longer smell of him. I walk back to the spare bedroom, open the door and hand the pyjamas to Ben. Adam is sitting on the edge of the bed, trousers already removed, staring out through the window into the black night. He looks small, curled and vulnerable, and a lump catches in my throat.

As I leave, Ben looks at me and shrugs.

Shortly after, Ben joins the rest of us in the kitchen. My heart goes out to Jack who is almost as silent as Adam in this whole exchange. An innocent bystander in the fragmented family of the girl he loves. I was so wrong about him, my initial instincts unfair – he really seems to care for Meg. Ben looks at his wrist and I can tell he's worried. He only has an hour to the countdown.

'Go,' I tell him. 'Get back to Karen. He'll be fine. We'll look after him.'

'I'm sorry . . . ' he starts.

'Don't be.' I practically usher him out through the front door.

He turns. 'I'll come back for him first thing Friday morning.'

Meg is suddenly beside us. She reaches up and hugs Ben tightly around the neck. 'Don't,' she whispers. 'I'll get him there.'

'Are you sure? You said you didn't want to go. It's no problem.'

'I've changed my mind. I want to be there and I'll take Dad,' she says.

This is news to me and I'm unsure how I feel. Somehow, Meg's refusal to acknowledge Noah – other than what she felt she had to do for him; was obliged to do for him as a fellow human being – has somehow meant she's been on my side. I instantly hate myself. Since his death, all bets are off.

We do the countdown together. It's a rather muted affair, champagne-free, all of us clutching a warm cup of hot chocolate instead. My mother and I head up to bed, leaving Meg and Jack with some time alone.

'I'll just check in on him,' I tell Mum as I pass the green room. She nods, already through my bedroom door. The room is quiet, completely still, dark apart from the crease of light from the landing. Approaching the bed I see his body, a foetal curl under the duvet. He's dressed in the pyjamas

I'd found earlier and his clothes lie on the back of the bedside chair. I catch a whiff of cigarettes from them as I pick them up with my left hand. My right hand I place under his nose, feel the breath exhaled, and for now I'm relieved he's alive. Just so I can strangle his stupid neck tomorrow.

'My parents took me camping once.' His voice is weak.

'Adam,' is all I say.

'We went to Scotland, up near Loch Ness. It was freezing.'

I wait.

'Ben was on a school trip so it was just the three of us. They had a big fight. Took it outside our tent, like the difference of a canvas sheet meant I couldn't hear. I could hear. They always argued about Ben. Yet he was still the blue-eyed boy . . . '

He moves his head, seems to frame me in the dark.

'She used to take pills.'

I say nothing.

'Ben thinks I need pills but I did it to protect him, you know. And other shit. I did it to protect you . . . '

'Get some sleep, Adam.' I sigh as quietly as possible. 'You—'

'I don't need pills, Beth. '

I give him a reassuring tap on the leg through the duvet, say nothing, and leave him to sleep.

I don't want to be seen here so, at first, I stay in the car. Sorry as I feel for this poor child, this is another family's pain. This is Adam's pain. I have had enough to deal with. I cannot and will not be a part of seeing this child buried. Not when I resented his very existence, and grieving by his graveside feels a little like I'm lying. My mother looked right through me when I tried to explain this to her over breakfast. She's gone back to the Cotswolds and I'm sure her disapproving head is still shaking.

I walk to the far end of the graveyard, the area where Ben told me his parents are buried. Finding the plot quite quickly, I'm not sure what to do when I get there. Do I pray? Since I met Adam about a year after his parents' death, I never knew them. And he has never seemed to feel the loss of them, so I assumed they weren't close.

The grave is a surprise – well tended with fresh, potted, flowers. The inscription gives no clues: 'Myriam and Ian Hall – they lived and died together.'

I read it a few times and wonder what it is I wanted to learn here. What the hell is wrong with Adam? Has the loss of a child he didn't even know really tipped him over some edge? I walk away, button my coat and am none the wiser.

Back in the car, parked well away from the funeral cortège, I see Ben and Meg walk towards me, Adam propped up between them. Part of me wants to go and smack him. For fuck's sake, pull yourself together, I want to say. Then, as he nears the car, I see his face. There is pain etched in the lines around his eyes that used to be laughter lines. The frown lines that run from each side of his nose down to the edges of his mouth look deepened, furrowed. His eyes are sad. The words of my latest song echo in my head:

Now that you're gone, my life's no longer whole,
I'm empty, alone, no heart and no soul.

And, despite myself, my heart aches for him – my sad, flawed, altered husband.

Chapter Thirty-Eight

I have mentally counted the days of the week since New Year's Eve, now remembered as Black Wednesday. The countdown appears in my head as a picture – six vertical black lines on a wall and a seventh forward slash mark diagonally placed through the other six. Robinson Crusoe-style. Noah's funeral, line number three. Two days spent in bed, lines four and five. Life decisions, line number six. Talk to Beth, forward slash, day seven . . .

When she calls this morning, the conversation is brief. Josh is taking her to a black-tie do at the Royal Albert Hall tonight, can I check and see if her long black dress is here at Ben's flat, the one with the thin gold belt? I know the one she means immediately, remember her wearing it to a client dinner we had when she was living here with me. I look on her side of the wardrobe and tell her yes. Yes, it is. She swears quietly, then tells me she's on her way to get it. She'll come by train – it'll be quicker. When she hangs up, my lungs feel tight. Beth has unwittingly made face-to-face conversation with me – today, day seven – unavoidable by coming here.

I pace the flat like an expectant father. Talking to myself, I open the balcony door to allow some air in, then close it again because it's bloody freezing. I go over and over my reasons for doing this at all; talk myself out of it, and then tell myself I have no choice. I try and imagine the questions she'll ask.

When she arrives, her cheeks are pinched pink by the outside temperature, her hair rolled up under a brown trilby. At first, she looks as if she's just going to grab the dress and run. I persuade her to stay for a coffee, the scent of the Arabic brew already permeating the space.

'What's up?' she says, blowing into her mug. 'You look particularly tightly coiled.' We are seated less than eighteen inches from each other at the small breakfast bar.

'Well.' I clear my throat. 'I wanted to let you know I'm going to The Rookery for a few weeks. It appears I've got some shit to work out.'

Her head tilts. I watch her compute what this means. Her husband going somewhere to talk his shit through. Her cup is placed slowly on the worktop. Her lower lip protrudes ever so slightly as she nods. 'Okay . . . '

'I'm leaving later today.'

'Right . . . When did you decide this?'

'Yesterday. Apparently my health insurance in work covers me for losing the plot.' I attempt a weak smile in her direction.

She doesn't speak, just removes her hat and shakes her hair loose. It's long, so much longer than when I last ran my fingers through it. She's had a fringe cut in. It suits her; rests just above her cat-green eyes. The eyes that I fell in love with. When I first met her, they told me that behind

329

them was a good soul; they told me that they laughed regularly, and they told me that she would make me happy. I look away. 'But there's things I need to say to you first.'

'Adam, seriously?'

I feel the eyes stare.

'I'm not sure I want to know. I'm not sure I can take any more. I think this, this stay at this place, is probably a good idea. You should probably—'

'Beth, please . . . Just listen? I'm trying to be honest here.'

She laughs, and what comes out is a small, sad, unfunny, sound . . .

'I know, I know . . . ' I hold my palms up in surrender. 'There's things, so many things that . . . Look, I wanted to tell you the truth about my parents. No doubt it'll come up and I wanted to tell you first.'

She frowns. Whatever she had been expecting me to say, it didn't involve my parents. 'I'm listening.'

I can tell she's steeling herself against whatever it is I'm going to say, so I spit it out. 'My parents didn't die in a car crash. I lied to you when we met. They killed themselves. My mother, she took enough pills to fell an elephant and my father . . . ' I lean forward, place my forehead in my hands, my elbows on the worktop. 'My father felt he couldn't live without her and so did the same. I found them.'

She's so quiet, I turn my head in her direction. Her frown has multiplied ten-fold. She goes to speak, then decides against it, looks away so I can only see her profile. The eyes close.

A helicopter hovers overhead. Next door, someone runs

a shower. Above all of this, I can only hear the sound of Beth's breathing.

I want to touch her, but don't. It would be so easy. Just reach out; she's only an arm's length away. Fold her up in my grasp and never let her go.

'I couldn't tell you. I couldn't tell anyone.' I try and answer the question I think is rolling around her head, my voice no more than a whisper. 'I couldn't admit it to myself. They left us. They left Ben and me, Beth. They left us all alone.'

Her barstool scrapes the oak flooring as she stands. She walks across to the balcony door, opens it, inhales the air outside deeply several times, then closes it again. Staying there, she stares south in the direction of the river, arms folded across her chest, her back to me.

'Why did you never tell me? I don't understand.'

'It never happened.' My lips tremble. 'I just pretended it never happened. I don't know. I had no words. I just invented an easier reality . . . '

'Any more secrets, Adam?'

I'm silent, trying to figure out my reply, when she turns abruptly. She comes back towards me, grabs the evening dress, her handbag. 'Whatever else you need to say, however you're going to answer that question, just hold it for five minutes.' Glancing at the clock on the wall, she says without looking at me. 'I need something stronger than coffee. You coming?'

It is ten thirty a.m., the morning after my arrival here. Outside the tall windows of this man's oak-panelled office, there's a huge expanse of grounds that I didn't see in the dark last night. Tapered lawns, still covered in January's frost, stretch into the distance until they lose themselves in a forest of pines. I glance up at the man behind the desk who has asked that I call him Tom. He's a bit of an oddball, looks more like a dull accountant than a supposedly educated psychiatrist who deals with nut jobs for a living.

He's taking notes, writing down what I say and I'm not sure I like this idea. I've just told him about my parents, and Ben, and I want to cross the room, rip the pages out and tell him they're mine. I didn't want to tell him at all. This morning I convinced myself that telling Beth yesterday, telling her everything I possibly could about anything, would be enough. I convinced myself I'd have a look around, maybe just talk to this guy for this first booked session, then turn around and go home. Apparently not. I've only been here half an hour and I'm already thigh-deep in buried truths.

'How did you sleep?' he asks.

'Like a baby, because I took whatever they gave me to help me sleep. Tonight I'm not sure I will.'

'Why not?' Tom peers over tortoiseshell spectacles.

'Because I want to sleep without pills . . . I do not need to start taking pills. I want my life back. That's why I'm here. It's why I signed up for this. It's why you experts are being paid a shedload of money.'

He raises his eyebrows. 'Tell me more about that life. The one you want back. What does it look like? What do you miss most?'

Beth. I miss Beth the most.

I'm a man beleaguered by guilt. I blame myself for my marriage break-up. I blame myself for Meg's pain when Noah died and – sometimes, some days – I even blame myself for his death. Maybe it was my germs. Maybe it was something off those old chess pieces that found its way into his delicate bloodstream . . .

'I don't know,' I say. 'I just want my life back.'

He nods.

'Talk to me about your brother. How did he take your parents' death?'

'Very badly.' I still remember the sound of his body-wracking sobs.

'And you?' He raises his eyes from his notes this time.

'I didn't have time to dwell on it. I had to take care of Ben.' I'm aware my answers are blunt, but so was the time. The stark, frank, blunt truth is that my reluctant memories are of fearful times spent filling out forms, working two jobs, applying for grants for Ben to study Accountancy and reassuring him that of course our parents had loved us, when it felt like they never had and they'd abandoned us. Already, I'd started lying. Already, it just seemed the right thing to do.

He waits for a minute before speaking. 'So, if I asked you for the first word you think of when you think about the death of your parents, what would it be?'

I crick my neck left to right. 'Selfish.' I glance at my watch, willing this time with Tom to be over.

'Selfish?' He writes it down.

'Well, it's the worst, isn't it? I mean, I've been called selfish in my life and God knows I have been, but that? Neither of them thought about Ben and me.' I think back to Christmas Day, that brief moment outside the restaurant when I thought how easy it would be to fall from the pavement under a lorry.

'It was cowardly.' I nod my head as if it's the only

conclusion I could ever come to. I have never spoken about my parents' death, and I'm immediately afraid. My life has always existed in safe compartments, my mother filed away safely in the one labelled 'Mum', never to be intentionally opened. I close my eyes and she's there. The memory of her scent is vivid. I feel if I raised my nose in the air, sniffed gently, I could smell the intoxicating aroma of jasmine.

'She used to smell so good, my mother . . . '

'Can you tell me your earliest memory of her?'

'She's singing . . . it's Christmas because it's some sort of carol. Ben and I are in the same bed together and she's kneeling on the floor beside us.'

'Were you happy?'

'Yes, very . . . I was probably only three – aren't most children happy at three? Anyway, that was then. She stopped singing.' I am only realizing this. I scrabble around in my head trying to remember when. Was I three, six, eight, fifteen? I can't remember. I look across at Tom. 'Will this take much longer?'

'That's up to you, Adam.'

'I think I've had enough for today. I'm rather tired.'

He stands, waits for me to do the same and, with an open arm and hand, leads me to the door. 'I'll see you in the morning. Ten o'clock.'

I nod and pass through into the hallway. The place reminds me of a hunting lodge. Though there are no stuffed animals or trophy heads of stalked deer hanging on the walls, the copious wood panelling and dated tartan décor gives it the feel of somewhere the gentry would have visited during hunting season. For now, it's a building that houses people on the edge. People who are struggling for whatever reason and, looking around, there seem to be quite a few of us.

I head outside. My hands, stuffed low in my pockets to keep warm, are trembling slightly. I tell myself it's the cold. Get a good walk in, then back to my room for a bit. Minutes later, at the end of the gardens just before the copse of pine begins, I find a low-lying wall of uneven stone. I balance myself on it a moment. All around me, the ground is frozen. Tree roots burst forth, rupturing the soil and its icy cap, determined to break through. I stare at them, realize that – now I'm here – my memories will do the same. They will demand to be seen and heard, bursting through whatever fragile wall I've built around them. Things I've buried for years. Things I've never felt the need to acknowledge. Things I've kept from the people I love.

I look back at the building where this will all happen, hear the loud gong that must mean lunch. I think briefly of home, of the home I once had. Beth will soon be moving. She told me yesterday – on only the third day that the house had been on the market – that we'd had an asking-price offer, with a short-term, same-day exchange and completion. I told her to take it and move on with her life. Of course I hadn't really expected her to agree. Some part of me still believes that Beth will walk in here, past Tom's panelled office, and declare her undying love for me. She will tell me that, despite my flaws, maybe even because of them, she truly loves me.

I walk towards the gong, hope that I will sit, have lunch, then go to my room afterwards. I hope that I can ignore the temptation to walk straight through the building to my car waiting on the other side.

Chapter Thirty-Nine

There is so much to do that I feel quite nauseous thinking about it. I've asked Josh not to contemplate calling me for a fortnight and anyone who's around has been roped in to help in some way. The packers are booked for this day next week; before that, I have to clear the house of things that are not coming with me, or going into store for Adam. I have made sets of labels. 'Rubbish' will go straight into one of two skips already on the driveway; 'Adam' will get boxed up and put into store for him; 'Donate' will be boxed for charity and 'Tawny' will be moved to my new home.

Tawny Avenue, though only four streets away, could not be more different to where I live now. It's a short, narrow street of Victorian semi-detached houses, all originally built as workers' cottages. When I first saw it, just before Christmas, I fell in love with it, and luckily it's empty, the owners wanting a quick sale. It has two double bedrooms, a small third, which will be fine as a studio room, plus it's only one of two (being at one end) of the thirteen cottages that has a garage to one side.

I'm excited about the move. I'm nervous about the move. I'm terrified, because I'm packing the house and Adam's not involved. His email told me just to take whatever I want, to put aside enough furniture and things for him in a two-bedroom flat and to do whatever I want with the rest. I hate it. I'd almost prefer him to fight. To argue with me.

Though visitors are discouraged, I'm going to see him. I need to see he's strong in this process, because the one thing that I've always been able to rely on is his strength. Even when he's being a prick, I swear he's a strong one.

In the midst of all this, I've been commissioned by the LA film producers to give them a third song, which I have yet to write. And Karen has thrown a blind date into the mix. Months of research by her on some 'Date a Friend' website has resulted in Glenn, her choice for me, and the man I'm meeting blind at eight o'clock. I've tried desperately to get out of it, but Karen is on a mission, so I try not to think of it all and head upstairs with my roll of parcel tape and labels.

I'm in my working space in the loft making up more of the flat brown boxes. Ten of them face me, their bottoms taped, making them as secure as possible. Around me there are stacks of boxes already full. Knowing it has to be done, I head into the storage corner of the loft that I've not entered since we moved in. Adam keeps all the Christmas stuff from bygone years in there, but for the Christmas just gone, I rebelled and bought new decorations and tree lights rather than enter the unknown. God only knows what I'm going to find.

Thankfully, the light works in there. Little more than a

crawl space, I get in on my hands and knees, leave the door open for more light, then sit with my back against the inside wall. I shudder at a spider's web next to me then pull things towards me, make piles, and quickly come to the conclusion that most of it is junk. I save the old Christmas decorations, boxing them up for Adam. I save all of the old photo albums, boxing them for storage in my garage. Someday, we will both have to go through them . . . I pull an old wicker basket towards me and behind it sits a trunk I don't recognize. The basket contains more photo albums. Rather than repack them, I seal the basket with lots of gaffer tape, stick a storage label on it and push it through the door back into the loft.

Pulling the trunk towards me, I'm tempted not to even open it, but just to label it storage. Already, the task of packing this house up is so daunting that I cannot contemplate going out tonight. Karen will kill me. She has both warned and begged me not to bow out. My blind date and my twenty years' worth of crap to pack – these are the thoughts in my head when I open the lid of the trunk.

There are packages inside. Presents, lots of them, all wrapped up, some with Christmas paper, some with birthday paper. There's an old, round cake tin I recognize from years ago. Inside that are lots of what look like greeting cards, all addressed to Noah. My mouth drops open as I realize what this is. I count them out. There are nineteen, almost two for each year of his life. Birthday and Christmas. I pull open the paper on a newer-looking one. Two DVDs – *Madagascar 3* and *Brave* . . . I'm tempted to rip every gift open, but something stops me.

Next to the cards in the tin is a bunch of photos, all held

together with an elastic band. They're all taken from a distance. They are in date order. The first says on the back, '2007 – Noah on the Heath'. It shows a shot of Kiera sitting on a park bench, a small boy sitting beside her. She is feeding him pieces from a peeled banana. The last, dated almost a year ago, a shot of Noah getting into a car outside an impressive-looking house, would have been taken just before Adam left me. Now I know he was doing a Lord Lichfield on his son as well as having an affair. These things aside, what I can't get over is how like Adam the child was.

I'm suddenly cold. I tell myself it's because sitting in a cupboard in an attic *is* cold, but it's more than that. It's shock. Seeing his face, his smile. It makes him more real; and even I, who would have resented him alive, can't quite believe that he's dead. That lovely face, just like Adam's, his hair, just like Adam's . . . And he's just not here any more. No more gifts, no more photographs, no more memories. I can't cry any more, so I pack everything back into the trunk, label it 'Adam' on the side and sit there until my fingers are numb.

I should be angry. It's confirmation of his 'other life'. Though I believe him when he says he didn't actually 'live' this other life, there must have been a part of him that wanted to. A part of him that wished he had a parallel universe where Noah and he lived side by side. All those photos. Here in our house, less than twenty feet from where I work every day. He knew I'd never go in there – I haven't since we moved in. I should be angry. I wonder if the child had lived . . . Then I stop myself. We were over before I learned about Noah. I cup my hands and blow into them, rub my hands together.

I'm just about to close it, seal it all up, when I spot another envelope stuck in the lid. It's been Sellotaped in. It's different to the others; I can tell straight away that it's older, and curiosity gets the better of me. I remove it. The envelope is practically falling apart and pulling it from its secure holding hasn't helped.

I take a breath, pat my chest, sense immediately what this is. Signed by Adam's father, this is the actual letter he left for Adam. I read it twice, then twice more; even though it confirms everything Adam recently told me, seeing it scribed in his father's hand makes it more real, more tragic. A sound escapes me, a baying cry . . . No words come. Just pure emotion. And then, as if I'm in fear of being watched or discovered, I carefully fold it back in its ageing cover and tape it back into place.

I push the trunk out into the loft, drag myself out after it and tape everywhere that it's possible to tape. Heaving myself back against the wall, I'm exhausted. I stare at it, feel the essence of the little boy that was. I pull my phone from my pocket, punch some numbers and speak to my mother. I tell her I love her. I tell her that – because of recent events – I feel her loss of Simon more. I understand how it must have hurt her and how much she still misses him. I talk about Dad and I talk about Adam. She listens, tells me she loves me, then tells me no one should have to lose a child – not even Adam.

After hanging up, I head to the shower. I need to wash all the dust off me. I need to wash this overwhelming feeling of sorrow down the plughole. No one has come out of this feeling anything other than sad. Kiera, whom I think of sometimes, must be devastated. I know Adam is, Meg too. Though she went to the funeral, she has avoided speaking about it since. For her, it seems to be an episode she'd rather forget. For me, I know discovering the truth sealed the fate of our marriage.

So I'm sad, and a trunkful of Adam only makes me feel worse. It can't have been easy for my cheating bastard of a husband to want to see a child and not be able to; to buy him gifts and never give them, and instead to fill a box and hide it in an attic. Nor can it have been easy for him to find, read, dissect and decide how to act on that letter all those years ago.

In the shower, the tears come. Why could he just not have told me the truth? He did try and explain, but the question just loiters in my mind. When we met, why not just tell me? And Ben, what about Ben and . . . ? I hold my face up to the almost scalding water, wash away the tears. I'm surprised that I am never quite spent and there are always more. I'm also surprised that I have a new understanding of how complex my errant husband is. I am not surprised when the first thing I do after the shower is text Karen to say that I'm sorry but I'm no way near ready for a blind date.

Chapter Forty

If there's a staffroom here, I'm sure that Tom goes in there after our sessions, heaves a sigh of relief and makes himself a stiff drink. I myself am always beat afterwards. Ten days in, ten sessions at an hour each, group therapy in the afternoon; quite frankly I'm bored hearing my own voice. I'm bored talking about me. I'm not interesting enough to fill all those hours, all those pages that Tom has crammed with facts. There are surely more injured people in this place, other people that really need this level of discussion.

I've just explained this to Tom, or tried to, at least. Now I can hear him defend, in his gentle tone, my story, tell me that it is in fact a very interesting one. I'm underselling it, apparently. Young man discovers both his parents dead, realizes his mother first committed suicide and his father followed. Perhaps, Tom wonders, I've been harbouring feelings about my mother's role in their demise.

I exhale loudly. I really am not going to get out of this place until I say it. I'm not going to be able to leave until Tom has a blockbuster notebook.

'Yes, I suppose I do.'

He nods. Tell me something new; his eyes speak without flinching.

'I loved my mother, I really did, but I didn't like her much. She was hard on us and she didn't treat my dad very well. He did his best.'

'How was that, your dad doing his best?'

'Anything she wanted, she got. He dealt with all of her mood swings.' I shrug. 'As well as anyone could have. He worked like a Trojan, tried to encourage her, but it was never enough. She just wasn't a very happy person . . . ' I've discovered that thinking, talking about my mother makes me want to close up and shrivel, rather than open up like I'm trying to. 'Do you mind if we talk about something else?'

He thinks a moment. 'Tell me, after they died – was there anyone else, anyone to help?'

I scratch my head. This guy is like a Rottweiler – sinks his teeth in and doesn't let go. I'm sure we've been over this . . . I glance around the room for any means of escape, guess that those French doors to the grounds are probably locked, so I submit.

'There was a lot of stuff to deal with. The police and the insurance company, just immediately afterwards, but it was clear that we were alone, that I was alone with Ben.'

'No relatives?'

'No. Both my parents were only children. My mother's parents had died when she was young, I never knew how, and my father's father had died the previous year. His mother was in a local old people's home and died the year after him. Then I had to try and finish my degree, get Ben into uni, run two jobs to pay the rent, all the while—'

'Looking out for him.' Tom supplies the end of my sentence.

'Yes. I did what I had to do, but I wanted to do it too. Ben and I were close, are close. We only had each other back then. Thankfully, I met Beth the following year and things got easier for me. She just made everything better, always has.'

'Yet you betrayed her.'

Ouch, goddamned ouch. Just call me 'Judas' now. I take a deep breath. 'Yes.' I have a sudden, awful, anxious feeling that maybe I'll never get out of here. If I open the Pandora's box that is my parents; if I dwell on why I did what I did to Beth, it could just mean endless talking and no answers . . .

'Have we nearly finished? My wife is coming in to see me at eleven.' I need to get out of this office, just to know that I can.

Tom is giving me a very strange look and I'm choosing not to analyse it. That's his job, after all.

Beth is sipping tea from a proper teacup, which for some reason I find comical.

'What's so funny?' she asks. We are sitting in one of the communal living room areas.

'You. And your pinkie finger.'

She laughs. 'Well, it's quite a posh place, isn't it?'

'Should be fucking posh with what it's costing.'

'Adam Hall. Language.' She mocks me in the same tone, using the same words, as I have for years with her. 'You've developed quite the trashy mouth.'

'I'd never before realized the liberating feeling of a good swear.'

She nods, smiling. 'On a serious note, how's it been?'

I shrug. 'It's okay. I sit every morning and talk to Tom about my feelings. Some of the time, I imagine dressing him in more trendy clothes. He really has the most appalling dress sense. He is one big beige vision.'

'You're re-dressing your therapist?' She smiles.

'Yes. He needs the help. Then, in the afternoon, there's group therapy, which I don't always go to. In between I eat and read.'

'So, what have you learned about yourself?'

'That I'm a selfish bastard, though not quite as selfish as my mother, who chose to take her own life, probably knowing that my father would follow, leaving me and Ben on our own . . . '

'Big stuff.' She stares at the carpet under her feet, something with a fleur-de-lis pattern and a plush pile. 'But you're talking, really talking?'

I laugh out loud. 'There's not a lot else to do in here, Beth.'

'I know but, well . . . sometimes, it's easier to hide.'

'No hiding places here – believe me, I've looked.'

She shifts from cheek to cheek in her chair and I can tell she's not exactly comfortable in my current surroundings. 'I'm still struggling with why you never told me.'

My head twitches, left to right. It's almost a shudder. 'I couldn't. I thought about it many times, but once I'd started the lie, it was just easier to keep it up.'

'But why lie in the beginning?'

'You'd have left.' My voice is louder than I intend, my tone matter-of-fact.

She's shaking her head.

'It's what I believed, Beth. Right or wrong, I thought you'd hear what weird stock I came from and take off . . . Besides, I was in survival mode.'

'I'd never have judged you OR your parents. And Ben? Don't you think that—?'

'Please . . . Not now, Beth.'

She hesitates, looks as if she's about to say something, then changes her mind. I'm relieved. Frankly, this is sounding too much like what goes on in Tom's office.

'Enough about that.' I clap my hands together lightly. 'How's Meg? I've been worried about her.'

'She seems better now.' She hesitates again. 'Time heals. She's back amongst her friends now, got to concentrate on her final year. She'll be okay.'

'And you?'

'The movie is being shot at the moment. I was going to go over and see the scene where the song will be used being filmed but, to be honest, with everything that's happened . . . And the house move.'

I don't argue.

Beth looks over my shoulder. 'Don't look now, but I think that must be your beige therapist heading in our direction?'

I turn my head to see Tom a few feet away.

'Adam, sorry, don't want to interrupt, but I've left that book in reception for you.'

'Thanks, Tom.'

He nods, glances at Beth and walks away. I don't want to introduce her. Somehow I'd prefer anyone I talk about to remain faceless.

'You're right,' Beth says in his wake. 'Bloody awful dress sense.'

We sit for a while, people-watching, as Beth calls it, before she announces she should go.

'Stay a while longer?' My voice reveals a tiny plea.

'Adam, I've got a whole house to pack.'

'I know, I'm sorry . . . Just fifteen minutes, please. Tell me something funny. Something I can laugh about later, when you've gone and I'm in the group, listening to other people's strange lives.'

She looks hesitant, reminds me that I too have a strange life, and launches into the tale of Karen's attempts to get her dating again. I try not to react. The knowledge of her being on a dating website is not funny. I try and laugh at the bits I know she'd expect me to. I try not to show how I really feel and then catch Tom walking by again. My conscience prickles. What the hell am I doing here if I can't submit to being honest?

'Actually, I'm not really sure how I feel about this.'

'What do you mean?'

'You on a website. Dating.'

She's quiet for a moment, lifts her bag from the floor to her lap, then faces me. 'It's not up to you though, is it, Adam? We're separated; we will be divorced at some point. I'm here for you, to help you through whatever crap you've got going on since Noah died. Many women wouldn't be . . . But do not presume you have any influence on my life any more. You don't.'

I swallow hard. 'You're right.' I attempt a rescue, but she has already stood up, her bag placed firmly between us as I stand too. 'I'm sorry.'

'You're always sorry afterwards, Adam. Maybe that's something you should talk to Tom about.'

She leans to my cheek, but if there is a kiss I don't feel its touch. 'Bye Adam. Stay well,' she says, then turns on her heel, and walks away. It's a sight I should be used to but it never fails to make me shiver. One day, I'm afraid she will walk away for good.

I mention this in group this afternoon. There are six of us here, quite a small gathering, with a therapist I've not met before, Fiona, in charge of proceedings. It doesn't take the group very long to suggest that maybe I'm not afraid of losing Beth, that maybe my greater fear is being alone, that maybe I suffer from abandonment issues. I rebel at first. I quite enjoy my own company. Despite what everyone's been telling me for the last year, I'm a good guy and I'm quite comfortable when I'm on my own. Someone argues back. Apparently, that's not the same thing. Being on my own is not the same thing as being alone. Or being left alone . . .

I don't like the sound of this. It's something that Tom was trying to get me to see earlier, something he said about my parents leaving me? Beth leaving me, divorcing me, puts me in the same place. On my own, and alone as well.

I thank people for the insight and let others speak. I'm only half listening to Rosie talking. She's a young girl, about Meg's age, and normally shy to speak, but she's in full flow today. 'Fuck other people!' is what gets my attention. 'We're not in here to keep other people happy. We're here to fucking sort ourselves out.'

'Hear, hear!' I want to say, but instead I just smile as Rosie clears her smoker's throat.

'We've gone off-piste.' Fiona is obviously trying to pull

the group back to whatever track she'd been on when I zoned out.

'Ask Adam,' Rosie says. 'How's he doing with the whole forgiveness thing?'

I can't speak. I've done enough talking today, so I just shrug.

'I know I have to,' she says, 'but I *can't*, don't you people get that?' She shakes her head.

I look at Rosie – so young, so destroyed and so bitter. With a father who abused her and a mother who ignored it, she has a right to be all of those things, but her determined stance looks tiring.

'If it's any help,' I say as I stand to leave, 'I wish I'd had the ability to forgive my parents all those years ago, when I was your age.' I tap her shoulder as I pass. 'Would have saved a lot of angst on my way here . . . '

I leave them to it, head back to my room via reception and collect the book Tom left for me. I shut the door behind me. 'Alone at last,' I say aloud to the empty room and toss the book on my bed. All I can see in the title is the word 'suicide'. I'm never going to read it. I don't need a book to know that my parents loved themselves and each other more than they loved me. More than they loved Ben. I don't need a book to know that I found this rejection unbearable, that I've never really dealt with it. I don't need a book to know that no matter how I square it off, trying to understand my mother's instability, I still feel like they betrayed me, betrayed us. I don't need a book to know that I have never grieved for them, or forgiven them. And I don't need a book to tell me that I probably need to do both . . .

I slide my back down the door and sit on the floor. I stare at my scuffed shoes, remind myself to polish them when I get home, remember I have no home and wish that I could just cry. If I could howl, maybe it would feel better.

Closing my eyes, I complete a mental 'grief list'. My life with Beth, my home in Weybridge, my perfect relationship with my daughter, my dead son, my dead parents. Quite a list – quite a lot of grieving yet to do . . .

Chapter Forty-One

'My husband's a selfish man.' I am sitting opposite Desmond from Tooting, as Glenn from Woking decided after I cancelled him that I was unworthy of a second chance. Desmond and I are in a pizzeria and I'm eating bruschetta with a strong flavour of garlic. I ordered it within three minutes of meeting Desmond as I knew immediately we would not be playing tonsil hockey together. Not tonight, not ever.

It appears the main thing Desmond and I have in common are selfish spouses to whom we are still attached by law. He assures me that he's getting a divorce. I want to assure him that I don't care about his assurances, but don't because it would be rude. All I can think of is how I'm only here because Adam's reaction to me dating pissed me off. Because of him, I allowed Karen to persuade me to go out with Desmond from Tooting.

To be fair, even I thought Desmond had it all on paper. His photo, a fairly genuine representation of the man, shows a tall, athletic guy with a gorgeous smile. His hobbies list music and dancing. He has no children, so no potential stepchildren to worry about. He runs his own PR business, so he's solvent and intelligent and responsible.

In real life, he still has all of these qualities, especially the Hollywood smile, which I reckon meant spending several months in a dentist's chair. He does, alas, also have a voice that makes Joe Pasquale sound like a tenor. If my nerves are grating after the first three minutes, I know there's no point.

Unable to blame Karen, unable to blame poor Desmond, I smile through the rest of the meal, but life is just too short . . .

'I'm not doing it.'

Ben looks over the roof of his car to me. 'Please?'

'No. I've been in already. I've done my bit.'

'He's asking for you. Please?'

'No! Look around you?' I gesture to the boxes still waiting in the hall, to both his and my car already packed to the brim. 'I'm grateful you're helping me today, but if going to see Adam again is a condition, I'm not doing it, so go home now.'

I climb into my car. 'You can either follow me or not. If not, put those boxes back in the hall and pull the door behind you.'

I drive away, my heart racing in my ribcage. Ever since reading that letter in the loft, I feel uneasy around Ben and I'm suddenly angry at Adam. It's his brother he should be talking to, not me.

Since Tawny is vacant, the current owners have allowed me access before completion in order to help me out, and

I have to use any time I have off work to move my belongings into my new home. Within minutes, I pull up on the driveway and am relieved to see Ben follow close behind.

I push open the door and pick up the pile of junk mail gathered by my feet. Turning off the hallway to the right, I carry the first box into the main living room. It's a big room, designed to be both living and dining; thankfully, the walls are painted a neutral taupe shade and the cream carpet is almost new. It's a blank canvas that is about to be filled with boxes.

'Looks good, Beth.' Ben places another box next to the one I've brought in and looks around him. 'It's in really good nick, isn't it?'

'Have a look back here.' I lead him to the rear of the house, through a door into what is an extension to the original Victorian building.

'You'll have to learn to cook,' he says, his jealous eyes hovering on the new range.

'I can cook.' I'm indignant. 'I've cooked you many a fine meal.'

'You,' he says over his shoulder, 'have only ever cooked me lasagne, or maybe something else mince-based.'

I stop to think, rub the edge of the range with the sleeve of my jumper. I'm quite sure that Ben has attended at least one of my more experimental dinner parties over the years.

'No, I haven't.' He reads my mind as he carries in two stacked boxes. 'Elise and I never joined you when you were doing your posh girl stuff. "Confeeeeeee duck" was one I vividly remember turning down.'

I smile at the memory. Confit duck was one of my specialities a few years ago, when Adam and I used to compete with our neighbours, Nigel and Sylvia, to create the finest dinner parties. There was a period of a few years where we'd rivalled Michelin chefs, until we all decided it was too much like hard work and we should just enjoy each other's company with simpler, less stressful, food. I see my reflection in the stainless-steel range and wonder if I'll ever again be that person, or even if I want to be. I'm sure I'll feed Nigel and Sylvia in this space, but will I ever go to that bother again? It will, more than likely, be a bottle of wine and a takeaway.

In the meantime, I'm going to their house later tonight for a 'good luck with the move' supper, and I find myself wondering who'll be there and what Sylvia will cook. I tap my new range lovingly. 'Don't worry. I'll use you,' I reassure it. 'Really, I will.'

'You're talking to the appliances?' Ben is standing in the doorway with his feet apart and both hands on his hips. All he needs is an orange T-shirt and he's a Mr Muscle lookalike.

'I am,' I say. 'Talking to appliances is perfectly normal. Have you seen the back garden?' I lead him to the narrow French doors that overlook an orderly, perfectly formed green space, with just one slightly wild, untended area behind the garage.

'It's not like the garden at The Lodge, is it?' he says, wistfully.

'Adam was always the gardener there. This is fine for me.'

'Will you mind, once all your stuff is in?'

'Mind what?'

'Don't get me wrong.' He holds a conciliatory palm up

and I can already tell I won't like what's coming. 'This place is amazing. Karen and I would love a place like this, but when you bring all your things in, it's going to be a bit crowded. You're used to so much space.'

'I've been used to being married and I'm getting used to not being.'

He winces.

'I'm used to space and I'll get used to less,' I add.

Ben leans against the back wall, looking outside. 'Are you guys really finished, Beth? Really?' He faces me on the last word. 'I saw a big difference in him yesterday when I saw him, a big difference. He seems to be back on his feet, seems really together; is looking forward to being back at work. He looks a bit thin still, but hey . . . '

'I'm not going, Ben. I've had enough. I'm spent. The Adam show has been switched off. No more drama, no more telling me he doesn't like the idea of me seeing other men. I mean, really? Where does he get off?'

'He still loves you.'

I shake my head. 'In his head, yes, he still loves me, but that's because he can't have me. When he had me, he wanted Kiera and then Emma.'

'I know two is two too many, but it is only two. Two in twenty years.' The man is desperate.

I stare at him, gaze at his irises until he has the grace to look away. 'Does your new fiancée know you feel this way? That two affairs is acceptable as long as it's spread out over two decades?'

He blushes at the mention of Karen. Ever since they got engaged, they have been nauseatingly sweet with each other. 'I'm not saying that. I—'

I interrupt him. 'How did Adam take the news, by the way? That you two are engaged?'

'He knew it was coming. He knew I was going to ask her on Christmas Day, then Noah died and there was just so much going on with Adam . . . He was pleased. I think he's really pleased for us.'

I know he will be. Despite his dick wanderings, Adam is a real romantic.

'Can't you forgive him? Make a new start, here?'

'It's too late. This is my house and, besides, I don't love him any more.'

Ben raises both his hands to his mouth and presses hard on his lips. He moves forward and back in an almost rocking motion. It's a reality check he wasn't expecting.

'I'm sorry,' I add. And I am. I wasn't expecting to hear those words myself. I'm not even fully sure I mean them.

'Well, I guess Adam needs to hear that.'

'I'm not going to visit him in The Rookery and tell him I don't love him any more, Ben, especially if he's doing well. I'm not going back there.'

'Even though he's asked for you?'

My eyes blink, slowly, rhythmically. 'Can't do it . . . Can't see him . . . '

'Beth, please?'

'Christ, Ben. *No!* Don't you get it? Why does he want to see me anyway? I'll tell you why. It'll be another apology. There'll be something else he's sorry for.' I storm out through the hallway, the front door, to my car. 'Have you no clue what "*can't*" means?' I yell back. 'It's a different word to "*won't*"!' I take another box from the boot and march back indoors, stacking it in the living room.

Six boxes more and I've finished. Hands on my hips, I call from the door. 'Are you staying here?'

'I have never asked you to do anything. Never,' he says from the same position in the kitchen. 'I'm asking you to do this one thing. If not for Adam, then for me.'

I walk to the kitchen door. Seeing him there, I'm torn. Everything Adam has been through with his parents, Ben has too and though he doesn't know it yet, there's more to come. He hasn't looked up, doesn't want to meet my eye. I shake my head; a 'Grrr'-like noise escapes my lips and I run my hands through the roots of my hair. 'If it means that much to you,' I tell him, 'I'll do it. Ten minutes with him – no more.'

He approaches me, arms open, sweeps me up into a bear hug, lifting me off the floor. 'Thank you,' he says. 'Skinny Minnie. You need to eat more,' he calls back to me as he heads out to empty his car.

My feet plant themselves back on the ground and I watch his back. Shit. . . I'm not sure what I've just agreed to by going to see Adam again, but I already wish I hadn't.

It's not a confit-duck night, but nor is it a lasagne or a takeaway. Home-made beef wellington is the main course and I am salivating thinking of it. I've just finished telling the gathered table about the time I tried to feed poor vegetarian Giles some beef lasagne. On my right, Ginny, the neighbour who lives on the other side of Sylvia, is still laughing. On my left, a man I've never met before is grinning politely.

'You're not a vegetarian, are you?' I ask, a little worried.

'I most certainly am not,' he says. 'I'm a carnivore looking forward to his beef.' He holds his right hand out. 'We haven't really met properly yet, have we? I'm Jon, by the way. No "h", Jon Roper.'

'Hello, Jon no "h" Roper, I'm Beth, Beth with an "H" Hall. Otherwise, I'd be Beth All and that's just not true.'

He smiles, a broad smile that changes his face completely. I find myself mirroring it, immediately offering my own best smile. 'How do you know Nigel and Sylvia?'

'I work with Nigel.'

This makes sense. Nigel is a dentist. He has a thriving practice nearby in Woking. A sudden memory of Desmond and his dentistry brings a slight frown.

'Are you okay?' Jon no 'h' Roper asks.

'I'm fine, sorry, just thinking of . . . Never mind.'

'Well, Beth-all, I've decided that is what I'll call you. Put him or her out of your mind. You'll get wrinkles.'

'And I have enough of them . . . '

'Not really. You have a lovely face.'

Shit. I'm fishing. That is exactly what I wanted him to say. I'm fishing and I'm flirting. I feel a red heat spread right across the top of my chest. I take my napkin and fan myself as discreetly as fanning myself with a white napkin allows.

'Here comes the beef wellington.' Jon leads the applause as Sylvia brings the already carved work of art to the table.

'So, Beth,' Nigel calls past Amy and Pete, Sylvia's sister and brother-in-law. 'What are our new neighbours-to-be like?'

'A young couple, the Elliots, two children, both girls, aged about ten and twelve. She works from home, something in sales, and he's in the City.'

Nigel nods. 'We'll miss you. We'll miss you both . . . '
He realizes what he's said immediately. The daggers look
from Sylvia brings a swift apology. 'You know what I
mean . . . '

'I'm only around the corner, Nigel. As for Adam, I don't
know where he'll end up, but I do know he'd love to hear
from you.'

'Veg?' Jon leans towards me and whispers.

'Yes, please, everything,' I say. 'You guys,' I address the
table. 'You really don't have to "not see him", you know.
We've all known each other a long time.'

'He behaved like a shit,' Ginny says. 'I don't want to
see him again.'

Jon has piled my plate high with veg, looks at me for
confirmation as he wields the gravy jug.

I nod, then shrug in Ginny's direction.

'I want to see him,' Nigel confirms, 'if you have no
objection, Beth. In fact, I wish I'd contacted him before
now. I feel bad about that.'

'Before now would have meant taking sides,' Sylvia says.
'It's probably better to have let some time pass.'

I pick up my knife and fork. 'Sorry, Jon. We're discussing
my errant husband, almost ex-husband. We all used to be
friends together.'

'Until he did the dirty on Beth,' Amy says, without
looking up.

I chew the beef slowly. It's delicious. While I want Jon to
know I'm single and available, I'm not sure I want him
to know why, so I silently glare at Amy.

'Silly man,' Jon says, turning towards me.

And that's when it happens. Nothing to do with his

smile, or his firm, friendly handshake – it's all in the eyes. His lock onto mine and I swear some sort of electric current flashes between us. I'm not sure I recognize this charged event. It's different to with Pink. That was pure lust. This is lusty but not lust. It's flirty but not flippant. This is something else and I immediately want more.

'Are *you* married?' I find myself asking him.

'No. I'm a widower.'

I put my cutlery down. 'I'm so sorry. How long ago did she die, your wife?'

'Actually, we never married, but we were together for twenty years. Lisa died four years ago.'

I feel like I've been felled. Death and sorrow seem irre-sistibly drawn to me at the moment. I can't even ask how she died. I can't express my sympathy. I really should just chomp down on this gorgeous meal and forget the electric Jon no 'h' Roper who has lost his wife, partner, whatever. Forget I ever met him. Be rude. Turn to your right and just talk to Ginny for the rest of the evening.

'People never know what to say.' He turns to me and shrugs.

'They never know what to say when they find out my husband was a cheat either.'

'Silly man,' Jon repeats and smiles. 'I knew what to say.'

'You did,' I agree. 'You did.'

'Beth-all, would you like to have dinner with me some-time?'

'Alone, without the neighbours?' I hope he understands sarcasm.

'Bring them if you like, but I'd rather you didn't.'

I think again about Desmond from Tooting. Desmond,

with whom I have no spark, from Tooting. I think about Adam, sitting in The Rookery, pontificating about whether I should date or not. And here I am, sitting at a friend's dinner table, with a gorgeous man, who's so sparky, I may just spontaneously combust. Why am I hesitating?

'I'd love to.' I smile, a shy smile, because that's the way he makes me feel. He makes me smile like Princess Diana, all eyes down and coy. He makes me curl my hair around my ears. He has never touched me except for a brief hand-shake, yet he makes me feel beautiful. And I like it . . .

Chapter Forty-Two

I cannot wait to get out of this shithole. For all its expensive wallpaper and considered pieces of furniture, no doubt chosen by some designer in Chelsea, and all its smiley, happy faces and helpful people, the place has the underlying scent of a hospital. On cue, one of the girls from my therapy group walks by, her antiseptic spray in hand. I move aside quickly in case I'm caught in her disinfecting mist. I am so done with the frigging sickbay . . .

In the weeks since my arrival, I've had to learn to talk about how I *feel*, something that Tom has been at pains to point out is very different from me telling him what I *think*. Today I'm doing both. We're discussing Noah. I'm sharing that the depth of feeling I had at his death took me by complete surprise. I still feel completely gutted and totally cheated out of the relationship that would have grown. I think it's unfair and I think if I allow myself to grieve for him, I will fall apart into tiny little pieces.

'You know already,' Tom says, 'that if you harbour your grief, don't express it, that it will only be stored and eventually it will eat away at you. You know this because we've spoken about the same thing with your parents.'

I blink rapidly. 'I'm angry,' I blurt out. 'I let the truth of Noah unravel to my family because I had to try and save him. It was all for nothing. He died anyway. Beth and I are broken, probably beyond repair, and Meg doesn't fully trust me any more. All of that – for nothing. If I could at least have watched him grow afterwards . . . Some of it would have made sense.'

He's nodding, the top of his pen resting on, sometimes tapping, his lower lip. I watch this habit regularly. He never quite chews the pen, just threatens to.

'And since talking the other day,' I continue, 'it's like I've unleashed this . . . giant. I'm angry with my parents. They just threw their lives away, decided they weren't worth living when Noah . . . ' I swallow hard. 'Noah wanted to live so badly, a little boy who wanted to fly planes.'

I stare out of the window towards the grounds. Outside, the air is heavy with a morning frost; the iced soil crunches underfoot as people walk by, behind the long voile that screens us from passing eyes.

'I'm sure it doesn't seem fair,' Tom concedes.

'He was ill, he fought death all the way; my parents, on the other hand . . . '

'Do you ever consider that maybe your mother couldn't help it either? You tell me she had crazy highs and desperate lows. Nowadays she'd probably be diagnosed as bipolar.'

My face displays how unimpressed I am by any new labels for Mum's behaviour.

'It seems you're quick to judge, when maybe, just maybe, she couldn't help herself.'

'She was always quick to judge me,' I snap back.

Tom shrugs. 'It's a cruel illness, manic depression, so difficult to manage, and just as undiscerning as any cancer.'

I bite my tongue, let his remark sink in. This idea that my mother couldn't help her illness any more than Noah could help his . . . *She stopped singing* . . . I've railed against my mother's actions for so long that it's second nature. Trying to think of her in a kinder, more forgiving light is difficult. Rosie pops into my head and then Beth, and I'm grateful, lean forward, hands palmed together between my legs. 'I've been hoping that Beth will forgive me. To do that I know she has to accept me for the flawed bastard I am. I guess I need to try a little of that too.'

He's quiet a moment, lets my own words sink in with me, then asks, 'Do you think that your relationship with Beth is beyond repair?'

'She seems to want to move on. To put me and all my lies behind her.' My shoulders slump. 'I hope I can convince her. I want to try and convince her to give me another chance. I've asked her to come and see me again before I leave here.'

'To say what?'

'A lot of what we've talked about here has shown me why things went wrong. When I think back to Kiera, it was when Matt and I had grown the business too quickly in the beginning. We had real money stresses – I mean stresses where we could have lost everything – and I never told her. I never talked to Beth about how I felt nauseous going into work every day. I kept it all in. It's what I do. And eventually I find a release that doesn't involve her. In a way I keep her, us, away from it all – keep it safe.'

Tom has the pen in his mouth.

'What's wrong?' I ask him.

'I get what you're saying, but are you excusing your behaviour because you've found reasons for it?'

'I can never excuse it. All I can do is understand it and apologize for it. Hell . . . ' I make a face. 'Maybe even forgive myself for it?'

'Good plan.' He smiles. 'Are you writing everything down? Is it helping?'

I nod.

'You've certainly got more clarity than you had last week.'

'Last night, I tried to write down what had been going on in my life when I met Emma.' I look across the desk. 'To see if I could see a pattern. Not making excuses, just looking . . . Beth and I hadn't been physically close for a few months. There wasn't a reason – it just happens that way sometimes when you've been married a long time.' I stop and pick a hangnail from my left thumb. 'Work was fine, so it wasn't that.' I look up. 'But Ben was in a bad way . . . '

Tom has a face that does not show emotion. I don't think he's meant to show feeling in this job, but some sentiment has just sneaked through to create a straight frown line just above his eyes.

'I've looked after him his entire life. He had just come out of a long-term relationship where there were fertility problems. It had put a lot of strain on them as a couple and I—'

'You couldn't fix it.'

'Exactly. It's my job to look after him and I couldn't. I

365

threw money at the problem, tried to help that way. I tried to help prop him up but the stress was endless. Eventually, they broke up and Ben took off abroad for a year.'

Tom is either writing or doodling in his book. I want him to look up, to look at me and tell me I'm onto something, that there may have been reasons, other than me being a complete bastard, for destroying the family I loved so much.

'I met Emma just after Ben's life had gone to rat-shit.' I shake my head. 'Maybe I am just looking for excuses. It's sort of academic why it started. I could have and should have finished it way before I did.'

'When is Beth coming in?'

'Tomorrow evening.'

'Have you ever tried writing to her? Sometimes, if you write a letter—'

'I've tried that before.' I don't want to remember how big a Pandora's box my last letter opened. 'Beth's a "look me in the eye" sort of girl. She prefers me within swearing distance.'

He grins. 'Are you going to the group later?'

'No.' I feel shattered. This talking, healing stuff is exhausting. 'I think I'll curl up with a movie in my room. I can't believe how tired I am, how wearing this whole process is.'

'You still running every day?'

I nod. The grounds are so beautiful, I'm running a couple of miles a day. I don't push myself – it's easy and keeps my head clear.

Tom stands and I look at the clock. We're five minutes over, a first. Normally, I leave skid marks at the exit, five minutes early.

'Enjoy your film, Adam.' He smiles as he gathers up his notebook and books. 'Have an afternoon off. You deserve it.'

During a walk in the grounds later, I find Rosie sitting on the bench where I always stretch when I go for a run. Today, I've chosen just to walk, wanting to feel the bracing cold on my face and enjoying being able to wrap up against it.

'Do you mind?' I ask if I can take a seat beside her.

'Help yourself,' she says, 'just don't snitch on me.' She wiggles the cigarette held in her fingers.

'I'm lots of things, but I don't think I've ever been called a snitch.' I sit beside her, pull my coat tightly around me. 'It's freezing today.'

She nods.

I glimpse her troubled profile. 'Are you all right? You're not often out here.'

'I'm fine. Bored out of my fucking tree.'

'I know, the tedium, it's knackering. There's really only so much internal gazing I can do, but there's no escape.'

'There is.' She nods towards the nine-foot-high wall beyond the trees in the copse.

'Rosie, we're all here voluntarily. You'd be more comfortable walking through reception!'

She gives a throaty laugh and hesitates a moment before replying. 'I know. Tom spent an hour with me earlier trying to get me to understand why I always take the hard road. If there's an easy route from A to B, apparently I would circumnavigate C and D to get there.'

'Tom, eh? Mr Beige . . . He's good though.'

'Mr Beige.' She purses her lips around the filter of her cigarette. 'I like that.'

I don't ask how she's managed to find them in here, but shift around in my jacket. 'Why aren't you freezing?' I say.

'Don't feel the cold much,' she replies, before turning to face me. 'Don't feel, full stop.' She laughs at her own apparent joke. 'You still love your wife, don't you, Adam? Beth, isn't it?'

I'm surprised she's suddenly brought Beth up, but I nod, tell her that I do.

'Unrequited though?'

This makes me think. 'Not exactly,' I say finally. 'I think if you asked her if she still loves me, she'd say "yes", but she doesn't trust me and I'm not sure she can ever put what I've done behind her.'

'So, you have to let her go.'

I shiver again and stare at this tiny, birdlike woman, half my age, giving me advice.

'Maybe—'

'No "maybe" about it.' She stubs the end of her cigarette with her boot and I notice that it's a timeless Doc Marten type. 'If you love someone, that might mean letting them go, especially if you're not what they need . . . ' As she looks straight at me, she raises both arms over her head and stretches them out. She then removes the packet of cigarettes from her denim jacket and shakes it at me.

'No. No thanks.' I stand up, her words echoing in my ears like tinnitus. 'You coming in?' I ask as she finally shivers with the cold. 'It's bitter out here.'

'I'm all right a while longer.'

'If you're sure . . . ' I unravel the narrow Dr Who scarf

I have wrapped around my neck several times and give it to her. 'Here, take this at least. Help keep your head warm.'

She smiles, surprised, rubs the scarf as if to feel its softness. 'Thanks.'

As I walk away, my heart goes out to her – a child in a woman's body who's dazed by a tiny act of kindness.

In my room, I watch *Die Hard 4*. I want to lose myself in a testosterone-fuelled film with nothing about feelings or emotions, just car chases, explosions and macho men strutting about with guns. I only leave when I hear the dinner gong. Two more nights of this food, I think as I shut my door behind me. The first thing I'll do when I get out of here will be to go to McDonald's . . .

It's late and I'm in bed. I don't remember how I got here. I'm lying perfectly straight, perfectly still, both hands by my sides, the duvet tucked under my chin. There's a strange silence about the place tonight. The normal clatter of reception staff, nurses, doctors, chefs and cleaners doing their jobs seems muted.

I jump up and start dressing. The bag I'd come in with is small and is packed within minutes. At reception, they try and stop me, ask me to at least wait until morning. I don't.

It's worked. It's done its magic. It's helped me understand me, but now I have to get away. I cannot and will not take this on. If I stay here, if I have to analyse this too, it will set me back. This I know like I know I need air to breathe. And, right now, I need to taste the air in the outside world. I need to savour it, breathe it deep, inhale it in my lungs and be grateful that I can. I need not to ask any more questions. I need not to wonder how death attracts itself to me. I need to move on with my life, because life is precious and painfully short.

They found Rosie at about six o'clock, probably just as Bruce Willis was being declared a hero. She used my scarf. Perhaps she hadn't been pointing to the wall as a means of escape. Perhaps she'd meant the trees all along. I won't ever be able to ask her and I'll never know. The police kept my scarf as evidence, told me she'd left a note. I have no idea what it says, but I hope it helps whoever may have loved her during her short life.

Chapter Forty-Three

I am standing in my own house. The movers have just gone and I'm surrounded by boxes and chaos, but they're my boxes and my chaos. Adam called me earlier to congratulate me, which feels very strange but nice. I never did go and see him again in The Rookery since he called to say he'd left a few days early and sounded as if he was in a much more positive space.

I run my hands along the railway sleeper on top of my fireplace. There were cleaners in yesterday and, apart from the dirt I've brought in, the place is spotless. My fireplace . . . I hear a dull thud coming from the room above. Meg is upstairs sorting her room out. She has been a dream, wonderful. Despite her missing The Lodge, she's determined not to pine and seems genuinely to love this house. Closing my eyes, I think of my old house, the home I never thought I'd leave. Adam is there now with Giles, probably walking through each room, touching the walls, tapping into the memories. He said he wanted a last look around the place before the keys are handed over. I've asked him to pop in for a drink, though Lord knows where I'll find a glass.

I run up the stairs to Meg's room, push open the door. 'How's it going?'

She has already put her bed together and made it up with the new set of linen she bought this morning. She winds tiny fairy lights through the bars on her headboard, plugs them in and, hey presto, Christmas in February. Smiling, she claps her hands like a child and I know everything's going to be okay.

'Cute.' I give her a hug. 'Your dad's coming over for a drink later. You up for him staying for a sandwich, or do you think it's a bad idea on day one?'

She shrugs, sits herself on the floor next to the bed. 'The man's got to eat.'

'Right, you keep going here.' I nod towards the boxes of clothes she has yet to unpack. 'I'll start unpacking some kitchen stuff. Maybe find some plates and glasses. You do have enough storage, don't you?' I wring my hands, glance at her two-door built-in wardrobe. It's a far cry from the wall of storage she's used to.

'Mum! Kitchen! Now! Stop worrying.' She looks up from her perch. 'I love it, Mum. We'll make it home . . . '

I head downstairs, trip over a box in the hallway and swear aloud. The first swearword in my new house and it comes from me. Lucy Fir is delighted. Having been dormant for a while, she has now reappeared, telling me the house is too small, that I am quite mad, that Jon no 'h' Roper will break my heart, that Ben and Karen will never work out and that Adam is not as healed as he's pretending to me.

I hope I'm doing the right thing having him over. He seems fine. Ben tells me he's fine. Matt says he's thrown himself into work and Meg, the person whose opinion I respect most when it comes to Adam, assures me he's ready to move on with his life. What harm can a sandwich and glass of champagne do? I tear open one of the many kitchen boxes.

The first one reveals a set of champagne glasses, a birthday present from Karen last year. Having asked her and Ben to stay away until tomorrow, they're coming then and have promised that, before they leave, everything will be in its place and there will not be a cardboard box in sight. I jump as the front doorbell peals through the house. I have to stop for a moment before I realize what it is. It's a trilling version of a children's nursery rhyme. I grimace – that will have to go. Opening the door, I'm greeted by a hamper-bearing man in an apron.

'Happy New Home!' he almost sings to me, and thrusts the huge wicker hamper into my arms. 'Can you sign here, please?'

I try not to laugh, place the basket at the foot of the stairs and turn back to the guy holding a digital signature machine.

'Enjoy!' he croons and I pull the card from a red ribbon.

TO MY FAVOURITE CLIENT WHO IS GOING
TO MAKE ME VERY RICH, WHICH WILL OF
COURSE MEAN THAT SHE WILL BE
RICHER . . . RELEASE DATE FOR MOVIE IN
THE US IS 16 MAY. TWO WEEKS LATER FOR
UK RELEASE – NOT LONG NOW. 'I'M A
CELEB' WILL BE BEATING ON YOUR DOOR
AND YOU'LL HAVE TO EAT CRITTERS AND

SLEEP WITH RATS. BEFORE THEN, ENJOY THE
HAMPER IN YOUR NEW HOME. LOTS OF
LOVE, JOSH XXXX

I do a little skip dance in the hallway.

'Who is it from?' Meg yells.

'Josh, who else?' I look at the Fortnum and Mason offering, carry it through and put it on the kitchen floor next to the boxes. The table is already stacked high. From the table, I move the ready-made sandwiches I'd bought earlier into the fridge, next to the wine. I promise myself looking at it that the next time I shop, it will be for healthier options. Next, I hand-wash the few glasses I'd found, leaving them to drain on the oak worktop. It's not granite, but it's mine.

Giles phones to say everything has been sorted. The Elliot family, the new residents of The Lodge, have arrived, and he's given them the keys. Adam has, he tells me, also just left and he's on the way over. I thank Giles. He has been one of my luckier finds in life. I love working with him and – since we established there will be nothing romantic happening between us – he has become a real friend.

Within minutes, the front doorbell tolls again. I walk through the hallway, rub my hands on my thighs and open the door. 'Adam, welcome.'

He's standing there; a bottle of champagne and a card are thrust at me.

I take the bottle, invite him in, receive a kiss on the cheek and hear the rumble of Meg moving in our direction.

'Dad!' She runs down the stairs and throws her arms

around him. I'm surprised, yet he doesn't seem to be, and holds her so tight her face actually reddens. 'It's good to see you here.' She pulls back. 'You look really well.'

'Thanks, Pumpkin . . . So this is it, eh? His eyes skim the narrow hallway, up towards the landing.

'Let's go through to the back.' I lead them along to the kitchen.

'Wow, Beth. It's lovely, really.'

I'm trying not to react, to control my facial muscles. His comments are such stock statements that I'm tempted to laugh, to ask if he's being sarcastic, but I can tell he's not. So I smile, nod my thanks, hand him and Meg a glass and ask him to do the honours with the bottle he's brought. It's cold – we might as well drink it. He asks if he can see the rest of the house and Meg offers to give him a guided tour.

'I'll wait here,' I tell them, moving some boxes so we can sit at the kitchen table. I spotted it in the window of the High Street charity shop – it's identical to the wood of the worktop. I move my fingers along its edge. It's not really my style but it will serve its purpose. When I get my royalties from the song, I'll replace it all. I shake my head with frustration. It's because Adam is here. Somehow, with him in my new space, I'm doubting the whole move.

He and Meg are suddenly opposite me, pulling out chairs. Meg fills her glass again and I notice Adam's is still almost full. The way they're talking, it's obvious that, unlike me, Meg has in fact seen him recently.

'It's great, Beth.' He taps my hand, which is resting next to my glass on the table. 'And it really is only around the corner. No time at all and you'll have it looking shipshape.'

Really? I know he's feeling well. He looks great too, but what has this man done with Adam. No sarcastic comments like: 'Where did you get the table?' or 'Nice kitchen, shame about the worktop.' I smile a tight smile, come quickly to the conclusion that Adam is simply being nice and my inner saboteur is alive and kicking.

'I'm glad you like it. Means a lot,' I hear myself telling him, without even knowing it was true. 'Did you get a look at the garden?'

He nods. 'Saw it from upstairs. Small but perfectly formed and you should be able to manage it.'

'Mum's threatening to grow vegetables.' Meg grins. Then we all laugh, knowing it would take a nuclear holocaust for my fingers to turn green.

'What do you think of Uncle Ben and Karen, Dad?'

'They seem besotted. Good luck to them.' He raises his still-full glass and we all automatically follow suit.

'Any date yet?' Meg offers to refill mine but I cover the top with my hand. I have too much to do. I can't fall asleep on the job. At least not until I screw my new bed together.

'I haven't been told yet, but I think it'll be soon. Why wait?' he shrugs. 'That said, I guess it'll be when they find a new place, and he's got to sell the flat first for that to happen.'

My forehead creases. 'Ben's selling the flat?'

'Yes. Put it on the market last week. It'll go quickly too; in fact he may even have an offer already. Crossrail is due to open soon and property around there is shit-hot.'

'What will you do, Dad?' Meg asks the obvious question.

He sits back and laughs. 'I'm not sure, but one thing

I'm not going to do is worry about it. Something will come up. I have money ready to move whenever that happens.'

I scratch my hair above my ear. 'Will you want something around here? I can help look if you want?'

'I haven't thought about it. I guess today had to happen first, eh? Seeing The Lodge really go . . . ' He laughs out loud. 'You know, I was almost going to get Giles to offer them money to back out. It was just for a moment. Then I realized how stupid it would be, me living there on my own.'

Meg is choked up and trying to hide it.

'Right, enough of that . . . ' He stands up. 'You've got some beds that need making up upstairs, Beth. Would you like me to help Meg do that while you get on down here? I've got about an hour before I have to head back.'

I nod, speechless, not really sure how I feel about Adam putting my new bed together. I've sent our old one to storage for him. 'Thanks,' I mutter, and watch their backs move down the hallway.

I remove my phone from my back pocket and make a call.

'Hi,' he answers. 'How's it going over there?'

I sigh, so glad to hear his voice, keeping my own low. 'It's good, we're getting there.'

'You asked me to stay away, so I have, but are you sure? I'm happy to come over and help.'

The idea of Adam and Meg upstairs making my new bed, while Jon and I are downstairs unpacking kitchen boxes, does not appeal. 'No. Really, Meg's here.'

We've both discussed that we should take things slowly. That means not advertising the fact that we're seeing each other to our children yet. I don't think Meg's ready and, though he only has older stepchildren, none living with him, he wants to be careful too.

'No problem,' he says. 'You're still okay for lunch tomorrow?'

I haven't quite worked out how I'll get away from the house with Karen and Ben here, but I'll figure out a way.

'Looking forward to it, see you then.'

I hang up the phone and see him then, leaning with his back against the wall in the hallway.

'I didn't want to interrupt,' he says, his eyes examining my hall carpet. 'Toolbox? I need a screwdriver. Meg has one but it's a Phillips. I need . . . '

My head is bobbing up and down. Of course he needs a screwdriver. Toolbox . . . I point to it under a box in the corner of the kitchen.

'It's okay, Beth. Really . . . ' He approaches me, holds his arms out to hug me, and tilts his head as if to ask if it's all right. I move into him. Unable to remember the last time Adam held me, I can feel my eyes fill. It's still so fucking familiar and natural that it hurts. I fit under his arm perfectly and his fit around me like a clasp. 'It's okay. I want you to be happy. We all have to move on. Life's too short.'

I nod into his chest, swallow hard so I don't cry. He smells lovely, bergamot, like Adam of old. Memories of that goddamn letter in the loft fill my head. I want to talk about it, tell him he should talk to Ben, but he seems so, well, so *stable*. 'I never asked you about The Rookery . . . '

I can feel his chest rise and fall.

'It was hard but it was necessary,' is all he says. 'I won't ask you who he is.' He changes the subject. 'But make sure he's good to you.'

Before I know what he's doing, he has placed a hand under my chin and tilts my head upwards. I'm frozen in time. His lips touch mine and then they don't. It is so quick that I wonder if it happened at all. 'Make sure he's good to you,' he repeats, then lets me go. I watch him lift the toolbox and leave the room and all thoughts of Ben and letters and anything other than that kiss vanish.

When he leaves some time later, my mood has changed from one of extreme excitement to one of extreme confusion.

Meg is helping me in the kitchen and soon notices. 'You've been quiet since Dad left, you okay?'

'Just tired . . . I guess it's all a bit overwhelming.'

'It's funny, isn't it? When he's being a prick, we're pissed off at him but worried. When he's being like he used to be, we're still worried. To be fair, he can't win.'

'Has he talked to you about The Rookery?' I'm trying to gauge when she saw him last.

'Not much. I haven't wanted to pry. I'm just grateful to have my dad back.' She looks around the room and says, 'You've done the right thing, Mum. We can all move on now and it's thanks to you. You've always been the strong one.'

I burst into tears and the second member of the Hall family is hugging me today in my new kitchen.

'Let's eat,' she says after a long cuddle. 'We forgot to feed Dad and I'm famished.'

I take a seat and watch her put a load of sandwiches on a plate. She makes a cup of tea, seems to know I don't want to drink more alcohol. 'One green tea,' she says, handing me a mug. 'Don't know how you drink that shit.'

'It's good for you.'

'Nope, it's good for *you*,' she replies, making a face. 'It's for middle-aged people dealing with midlife crises who need extra antioxidant thingies to help them cope.'

Middle-aged. Midlife crises. Fuck a duck, really? I can't help smiling at the description.

'Maybe that was Dad's problem.' She catches my eye. 'Not enough green tea.'

I laugh. 'I'm glad you're here, darling.'

'Where else would I be?'

I know she could be lots of other places, but chose to be with me here tonight. Whatever else Adam and I may have screwed up, Meg has turned out to be one wonderful young woman.

But I find myself pondering how wonderful she'll be when she meets Jon, her strong mother's new boyfriend.

Chapter Forty-Four

If Ben apologizes one more time, I may do him some damage. We're at Highgate, on a bright Saturday morning, tidying the grave and planting spring flowers in colourful pots. The daffodils and forsythia scream yellow, their scent heady and pungent.

'I just feel bad,' he says yet again, as he presses hard on the overflowing compost. In the background, people pass us by, some heads bent, thoughtful, their losses seeming more recent. Others nod and smile as they walk by, their grief spent long ago.

'Don't,' I tell him for what will be the last time before I wrestle him to the earthy ground. 'It's your flat, yours to sell, and you'd be crazy not to take this offer.'

I mean what I say. He has an asking price offer, requiring exchange and completion in two weeks. He should grab it and run for the hills.

'What will you do?' he asks.

'I'll find somewhere else! There's a flat I'm having a second look at tomorrow. It's on the river near Fulham.'

'Really?' Ben has a wide grin on his face. His relief that I am house-hunting is palpable. 'To buy or rent?'

'To buy. The market's on fire. I don't want to lose out by renting.' What I don't tell him is I'm not sure I'm ready. The flat I saw is wonderful – more river views, having been spoilt by living in Ben's – and I can afford it, but am I ready? Am I ready to buy myself what will be a middle-aged bachelor pad?

'Can I see it?'

'You can see it if I decide to buy it. The last thing I need is you telling me to buy it just because you feel bad.' I tilt my head at an angle, widen my eyes and give him a cross-eyed look, let him know I'm joking.

'We never did talk about The Rookery,' he says, cramming too much soil into the last pot.

'There's not much to talk about.'

'Did you speak about this?' He eyeballs the grave. 'Their suicide? Hiding the facts for so long from Beth? I think hiding things from her almost became second nature to you.'

I laugh, a small, low laugh. 'You're wasted as an accountant, Ben. The Rookery needs your skills.' I bend down to help with the pots. 'Do you remember Mum singing?' I blurt out.

He puts his head back, raises his face towards the sky as if he's trying to pick at a memory. 'I do,' he says. 'She was always singing when I was little. Everywhere, any time, any place . . . '

'Then she stopped.'

His face, now lowered again, frowns. 'I'd never really thought about it.' He plays with some of the potted soil with a hand trowel.

'It came up, when I was talking about her.' I hesitate, not wanting to say too much. 'I spoke about her a lot.'

'Take me with you next time. I could fill a few sessions talking about Dad, then your therapist could realize how fucked they both were. You bitching about Mum and me about Dad.'

I'm surprised and wary of the angry undertone in his voice. 'So how does that make you feel?' I try a joke to diffuse it.

He stands, stretches his long limbs. 'Why do you think I never used to come here, Adam? Still don't if I'm honest, not unless it's with you.'

I shrug. 'I guess I've always put it down to you being pissed off at the way they left us.'

'Yes that. Of course that. But I'm angrier at Dad. Something always told me that Mum was mentally ill. I sort of knew even back then that she was going to self-destruct. But Dad . . . Why would a man with two children who still needed him do that?'

I hold my breath.

'You never showed me the actual letter.' His words puncture the chilled February air, slicing through it like an ice pick.

'At the time you were—'

'I think I'd like to see it.'

'Sure,' I shrug, hoping he'll forget he asked, wondering if I'll get away with losing it in the house move.

'I don't know.' He gathers the gardening tools together. 'Maybe it's better left alone.'

'Maybe,' I say, leaving the word lingering between us.

'He never liked me.'

My head shakes. 'That's just not true, Ben. I don't know where you're getting that from.'

'Adam, I'm not eighteen now! You don't need to protect me from my bloody awful parents any more!'

I do. I do. I do. I do.

'The truth is Mum gave you a shit time. Everything was always your fault. And Dad, Dad gave me a shit time in a much more subtle way. He'd look at me funny, make me feel left out, send me off on school trips so you three could go to fucking Loch Ness together.' He throws the trowel he has in his left hand on the ground, pulls the lone gardening glove from his right and tosses it on top, stands up. 'I'm sorry. You've had enough to deal with. This is why I don't come here. I'll wait for you in the car.'

I watch his back as he walks away, his stride long and determined. My eyes close. 'He has a way to go,' I whisper to my parents. 'And I suppose I still do too.' I tap their headstone a couple of times with my fingers, put the tools and compost in a plastic bag and walk away, desperately telling myself off on the way back to the car. I scrabble to find some more forgiveness, knowing they had trouble coping, knowing they were flawed and that absolution is the only way forward. But when I see Ben's troubled face in the passenger seat, I find it hard, and I'm not sure I'll ever come back here myself . . .

Meg is walking beside me. It's the day after the cemetery and we're strolling through Kingston Park. The place is awash with cyclists and families walking with children and dogs. In the distance, a herd of deer gathers under a copse for shelter. Dark rain clouds have gathered above.

'It looks like rain, we should head back to the car.' I steer her around and walk in the direction we came from.

We're both quiet as the drizzle starts. 'Kiera contacted me,' she says, breaking the silence. 'She sent a letter to me, care of Mum at the estate agency.'

I say nothing. It takes her until she's putting her seat belt around her before she continues. 'She just wanted to thank me again for trying . . . '

Through the loss of my marriage, a stay in the funny farm, and facing up to my parents' suicide, it is always Noah, the mere mention of him, that will bring a lump to my throat. I swallow it; will it to disappear.

'It was a nice letter.' She shrugs, then reaches across and hugs me. 'So,' she raises her voice to a more upbeat tone, 'how far is this flat then?'

'Fifteen minutes if the traffic's good.'

'You'd be nearer me,' she states.

'Only for a few months. When you finish your degree this year, the sky is the limit. Have you thought about what you want to do?' I start the engine and point the car towards Fulham.

She buries herself in her wide polo neck. 'I don't want to think about it! I don't want to be a grown-up!'

I laugh. 'You're right. It's really not all it's cracked up to be.'

Late Sunday evening and I'm sifting through work papers. I never seem to have enough time to read everything I should for work. The paper streams are endless. The television, *News at Ten*, is on mute in the background. The email printout on top of the pile is a request from Matt for my part in approving final hire costs in New York. While my life has been spectacularly unravelling, Matt has been building our empire and making our long-standing joint dream of an overseas office something close to reality. The list of expenses is endless. Beneath them is a bullet-point list of Matt's fee-making and cost-saving ways of covering it all, every penny. He is a diamond. I open my BlackBerry and send him a four-word email. 'You are a diamond', I tell him. Then I put a smiley face.

I lean back in the chair and rub the bridge of my nose, papers sliding from my lap to the sofa. Today has been a good day. I've spent time with Meg. I've put an offer on a flat, a two-bedroom brand-new unit overlooking the river at Fulham. It's charmless and as yet unfinished, but Meg has assured me she will help make it look like a home. It's a good option, the only problem being that I have to leave here next week and the flat won't be ready for at least six. Unless I can find a short-term rental, it may not work out.

Beth crosses my mind. I'm due to meet her at the storage unit she's renting in order to go through all the stuff from The Lodge. As I think of her, an idea takes shape in my mind. I stand up, flick the kettle on for a cup of tea. I remove my glasses, rub my eyes. It could work. I could win her back. I know I could. If I were living there with her, in her house, just for a few weeks, I could do it. I could show her how I've changed. I could be the most unselfish person she has ever come across. She would ask me what I'd done with the old Adam Hall. She might even tell me that she misses parts of him – just a few – and she just might fall in love with me again.

Chapter Forty-Five

I asked Karen to come. Meg can't make it and I think I may need someone with me. Josh is beside himself, pacing in and out of his office, calling to his receptionist, Melanie, asking her to get Karen a tea. Karen's on a health kick, off coffee and grumpy with it, complaining all the way about the crowds on the Tube.

On the low-lying table in front of us, there is an array of cakes like never seen before in Josh's office.

'Everybody okay?' He finally sits opposite us, his iPad propped open on the table beside the pastries. I have a strong Arabica in front of me. Karen has a peppermint tea. 'Can I get anyone anything else?'

Karen kicks my ankle. She has always been a sucker for American accents.

'Josh, sit down and show us the link.' I'm now more nervous than him. 'Promise me you haven't looked at it?'

He gives me a daggers look as if to say: 'Puh-lease. Would I be behaving in this manner if I'd already seen it?' Then he leans forward and presses open the link sent from

LA. Any second now, I will see a scene from the movie's rushes. The music starts, the soft voice of Marilee Garcia fills the room. I hear my melody, its matching lyrics play over the scene. It features the female lead, sitting in the Museum of Modern Art in New York, waiting for the lover she knows isn't coming. She's seated on a bench staring at Monet's *Water Lilies*. She has tears in her eyes. There are flashback scenes of him, memories of their time together. I hold my breath, wait for the end, then glance at Josh, who has a hand over his mouth and is looking at me. Karen squeezes my arm; when I turn to look at her, she's crying. Karen never cries. Never . . .

'It's real,' she says quietly. 'It's really real.'

'Fucking right,' Josh says, and we all laugh, me knowing and Karen sensing that my well-brought-up Midwest American agent never swears. 'It sounds great, doesn't it?' he adds, anxious for my approval.

'It does, it does . . . ' I'm rubbing my tummy, feeling both apprehensive and excited, aware that this moment is probably as good as it gets, as good as it will ever get. 'Marilee's voice is perfect for it. I'm glad she agreed to do it.'

'Ten days to the single download, with the soundtrack album to follow on movie release date in June,' Josh says.

I go to speak and he holds a palm up in the air. 'Don't worry, your super-agent already has it all covered.'

'Right . . . '

'You are going to be rich, girl,' he adds, rubbing his hands together in a Fagin-like gesture.

'I'll buy some granite worktops . . . '

'You can buy a quarry,' he says.

'I'll convert the garage to a studio.' I'm on a roll.

'Just move,' he says, 'buy your old house back. One in the face for Adam. Though, in a strange way, we have him to thank.'

My face must register how I feel about this.

'If he hadn't been unfaithful, you might never have written this song,' Josh explains.

Karen is quiet. I look to her for help, but instead see her lean forward before projectile vomiting across the cakes.

'Oh God.' Josh turns a ghastly shade and yells for Melanie.

I pull Karen to her feet. She is both green and apologetic.

'No coffee, dislike of crowds, vomiting on the pastries.' I count the offences out on my fingers. 'When were you going to tell me?' I hold her by the shoulders.

'Whenever you suggested lunch or a drink,' she sobs. 'Christ, I feel awful. I'm so sorry.'

'Does Ben know?'

'Yes, we only found out on Friday.'

'How far are you gone?'

'About six weeks.'

Josh makes an 'oh' sound in the background. Melanie has arrived with reams of kitchen roll and a plastic bag. I take it from her and start clearing the mess. It's obvious from her face she is one of those people who can't stand puke. Josh too. He stands in the background, his hands on his hips, his mouth a straight line of distaste.

'Air freshener, Melanie? And open the windows, Josh.'

They do as I ask and I scoop the mess up into the bag. I hand it to Melanie who holds it out in front of her as if it's going to explode. Karen looks on, her face frozen.

'I'm so sorry,' she repeats.

I laugh. 'Get used to saying that, hon. You're getting married and about to become a mum. C'mon, let's get you home. In a taxi – no buts, you're going home by taxi.' I steer her out of the room. 'Send me that link, Josh? Sorry about the cakes.' I stop and kiss his cheeks. 'Well done. You are "the bestest" agent in the whole wide world.'

Josh flushes. 'I am, aren't I? You're not so bad yourself.' He kisses me back. 'I'll send you the link. Look after Mama here.'

Outside, it's raining and I have no umbrella. I manage to hail a taxi and place Karen in the back. 'Go home. Get some rest, give in to it. No work and – ' I hold both of her hands in mine – 'congratulations. It's fantastic news. I'm thrilled for both of you.'

Karen gives a vacant nod, calls her address out to the driver and is gone. I'm left standing on the corner of a Soho street in the rain. I look up to the heavens and smile. Karen is having a baby. Ben is having a baby. My song is in a movie, a real movie. I want to celebrate, to do a Gene Kelly dance on the pavement. Instead, rather than tackle the Underground again, I hail another taxi. Hell, I can afford it. I ask him to take me to The Big Purple Box storage centre in Wandsworth, where I have an appointment with my ex-ish husband.

'Jesus . . .'.

Adam is a little overwhelmed at the sheer amount of stuff we still have.

'Christ . . . ' he adds, running a hand through his hair. 'Seeing it here like this. It's weird.'

I nod. It is. Weird and painful. We're standing here like lost souls, just staring at the rows of furniture, piles of boxes, scattered paintings. The detritus of a broken marriage. I have the sudden and uncontrollable urge to cry, managing instead to keep it to a soft sniffle. He grabs my hand. 'It'll be fine,' he whispers, though I have no idea what that means.

'I guess you have to take what you want and then the rest will go to charity.' I'm appalled at my own words, unable to believe that so many memories have to be discarded for lack of space. For the first time, I regret selling The Lodge.

It's as though he reads my mind. 'We did what we did,' he shrugs, letting go of my hand and heading towards a chest.

Immediately, I know it's the one from the loft, the one I found with all of Noah's things and . . . He stands over it, stares down, unable to touch it. 'I suppose you looked inside.'

'Yes.'

'Do you hate me?' He has turned around to face me. 'For hiding it all from you?'

'I don't hate you, Adam.' I shake my head and take a seat on a stray garden chair. 'I've had moments where I thought I did. I hate what you did. I hate the fact that you cheated, that you were weak, that you hid all of that from me and weren't brave enough to be honest, but I don't hate *you*.'

He takes a seat on Noah's chest. 'You must have had a better therapist than Tom.' He shrugs. 'Because I think I still hate me.'

'Well, don't. It won't help you move forward.'

He breathes a deep sigh. 'I wanted to tell you. Right at the beginning when Kiera told me. When we went to see that counsellor?'

I nod.

'But I just couldn't. You were so forgiving of the fact that I'd been with her. You still loved me so much and I just couldn't, *wouldn't* ruin that. For you or for me.'

To my horror, he begins to cry. He strokes the chest as if it contains something he can't bear.

I'm stuck, unable to move, just looking at him. Something tells me to stay exactly where I am.

'How come you loved me, Beth? Why did you love me?' When he looks at me, my heart shreds. I see the man I have always loved sitting opposite me. He's crying, in need of comfort, solace and loving, and I'm stuck to a weathered, verdigrised garden chair.

'Believe it or not, you were always easy to love.' I pick at a tiny area where the surface is peeling from the arm of the chair.

He shakes his head. 'They didn't love me enough and, ultimately, neither did you.'

I know immediately that he knows.

'You're human. You read the letter, anyone would. My mum and dad,' he says. 'They loved each other more than they loved me or Ben. According to Tom, I harbour resentful feelings about that.' He gives a low sarcastic laugh. 'No shit, Sherlock. No fucking shit.' Adam locks eyes with mine.

'They left me and now you've left me.'

I take a moment to respond and, when I do, I move over to him, get down on the floor beside him. I take his

hand. 'I loved you with all of my heart. I loved our family
unit, our home, the life we built together.' My jaw hurts.
'I loved the way you moved, the colour of your hair, the
feel of your skin, the way you laughed, everything about
you. You left me, Adam. The problem was never how much,
or if, I loved you. It was the way you loved me back. You
put yourself first, not me.'

He lowers his head, sniffs some more, stares at the ribbed
concrete floor of the storage unit.

'I get it.' I squeeze his hand. 'Knowing what I know now,
I get it. They left you on your own. It would feel like they
never loved you, but I'm sure they did, in the way that
they knew how. And I loved you very much. Know that,
will you? I want you to know that.'

I have no idea why I feel the need for Adam to know
how much I loved him. It's more than the fact that I feel
sorry for him.

'Secrets and lies,' he whispers. 'It was secrets and lies
that killed you and me. I love you more than I'll ever love
another soul.' His lips tremble as he speaks. 'I'm not making
excuses but they taught me well. Secrets and lies,' he repeats.

'Adam, does Ben know?'

He shakes his head so rapidly from side to side that I
think he'll be sick.

'Don't you think he should?'

'Christ, no.'

'You should tell him. He's a big boy.'

'If Dad wanted him to know, he'd have asked me to tell
him.' Adam looks at me wide-eyed. 'And there has never
been the right time.'

'Your father should never have given you that burden.

You need to tell him. Karen's pregnant. They're having a child together. '

I hesitate, suddenly unsure. 'What if they ever have a problem like Kiera had to face?'

He nods slowly, the realization hitting him. It's time for Adam to share his father's letter with his brother. I place an arm around his shoulders and rub him, like I would do if he were cold. I tell him it's all going to be all right.

'No, it's not,' he says. 'We're sitting in a tin can with our life's worth around us. I've been a selfish prick and all I want is to pick up the pieces, grab hold of you and beg you to give me another chance. Please. Just one more chance. I'll show you I can be different.'

'Adam—'

'Don't tell me you don't love me any more, please, just don't say it out loud.'

I turn his face around to look at mine. 'You're bad for me, Adam. I've had to work that out. You do your best, but your best isn't what I need. I need someone to love me completely, totally.'

'I do. I did. I've changed. The time in The Rookery, did I tell you about Rosie? Rosie, the poor thing . . . '

He begins to shake. Not a trembling shake, but a cold all over, shaking shake. I can't stop him. He's shaking and weeping and it's all I can do to put my arms around him and hold him. I look to the heavens. So much for him being better. And who in God's name is Rosie?

Chapter Forty-Six

'I'm really not sure about this.' Beth has insisted on driving and now addresses the windscreen.

'Look, I don't need or expect you to come in, but I have to talk to him.' I hear the words but don't mean them. I need her in there with me. The shakes have gone but I'm not sure I trust myself to do this properly. 'You were right. He, they, need to know.'

'I'll come in with you.' She doesn't realize it, but she's nodding, as if to convince herself. 'I mean, if you'd like, I'll come in with you.'

'I'd like . . . please.'

Ben has the letter in his hand. He has read it once and is now reading it again. His free hand scratches his hairline just above his right ear.

'Right,' he says, finally putting it down on the coffee table in between him and Karen and Beth and me. Karen is quiet. She has, I've noticed, a waxen look about her. Her eyes, normally bright and wide awake, have dark circles hovering beneath them. Her skin is blemished and her spiky hair looks lifeless. She has lost weight, something – with her height and build – she can't afford.

'May I?' she asks.

Ben nods. 'Why don't you read it out loud?' He sits back on the sofa, closes his eyes.

Karen starts to read. '*Adam*,' she begins, '*I know you'll find this, find us and for that I'm sorry. I came to bed tonight and found your mother cold, stone cold. She had taken a whole bottle of her tablets. I got in beside her and cuddled her, but no one's coming back from that. So I've spent half the night wondering what to do and to be honest there's no choice. I can't live life without her. I simply can't. You and Ben are grown-up now. You'll both be all right. She found out for certain this week that Ben is not my son.*'

Karen stops reading, raises her right hand to her heart and pats it, gently. Then she reaches for Ben's hand before continuing.

'*After his recent bout of pneumonia in hospital, I made her have Ben's blood group checked against mine. I made her do it so I could know, but I suppose I've always known and me making her do it has pushed her over the edge. I can't really live with that.*

'*I'm sorry. I hope you're strong enough for this, Adam. Do what you will with the information about Ben. Tell him or don't, but please look after him and look after yourself.*

'*Dad.*'

'So,' Ben says. 'No real surprise there. What I don't get is why you never told me?' He is staring across the room at me.

'You were so cut up when they died, felt they should never have left us. I did want to tell you but there was never, *ever* a good time.'

'Jesus, Adam, it's been over twenty years—'

I interrupt him. 'When would have been right, Ben? When you were about to start uni? Or maybe when you failed your first-year exams? What about your finals – remember that year? Or afterwards during your working life, when you were made redundant twice? Or maybe during one of the six years you were with Elise, when you both tried so hard to have a child?'

Ben sighs, a slight flush rising in his cheeks. Karen grips his hand tighter.

'Dear God, Ben! I know I'm often accused of doing things or not doing things for my own selfish reasons. But this? I had nothing to gain by keeping it from you. I did it to avoid hurting you.'

'Do you know who my father is?'

'No. I do not.' I am aware of a sweat developing under my arms during this Darth Vader moment.

Karen shoots a look at Beth and suggests making coffee; Beth follows her to the kitchen. Ben and I are left, absorbed by our own thoughts, the silence in the room palpable. Minutes later, Beth and Karen return with the drinks.

'Why now?' My brother is first to speak.

I glance across at Beth.

'I asked him to tell you,' she says. 'I asked him to tell you this afternoon and he knew if he didn't do it straight away, he'd talk himself out of it.'

Karen frowns.

'Ben, you did your grieving over all those years.' I almost

choke at the mention of grief. 'I've realized lately that I have yet to do mine. Maybe telling you is part of that.'

'Plus . . . Karen is having a baby.' Beth addresses Ben. 'When you have your baby, God forbid, what if you had to face what Kiera Pugh did? What if you needed to know?'

'I don't know who your father is, Ben.' It's my turn to slouch back in a chair. 'But if you ever need to try and find out, I do know someone it might have been.'

'Tell me everything.' Ben hunches forward, his head in his hands. 'Everything you know. Now.' He closes his eyes again. Karen cuddles up against him, slides an arm around him.

I tell them about the time I found Mum with a guy when I was at college. I tell them about the time many years earlier that I'd seen Mum in town having lunch with that same man. I remind Ben of the times the man had been present in our home over the years. He was an old school friend, someone we knew only as 'Dave'.

'Right,' he says again when I've finished talking.

'You know what? It's late.' I stand and Beth stands up right after me. 'We should go.' I catch Ben's eye. 'I'm sorry. You guys have a lot to talk about.'

Ben gets to his feet, crosses the room, opens his arms and envelops me. 'No, I'm sorry for what they did – to you, to me, to us.'

I pull back. 'They were flawed, very fucking flawed, but they probably did their best.'

I look at Karen, who is unconsciously rubbing her tummy. 'Beth says you're not feeling great. It passes. In a few weeks' time, you'll be glowing.'

'And a few weeks after that,' she too stands up, 'I'll be

fat.' Ben pulls her to him. I can see he's already in protection mode.

It's as if he's read my mind. 'I know you were only trying to protect me, but you are hereby officially released from that.'

We say goodbye quickly; enough has been said. Back in the car, Beth asks me what I want to do. I shrug, unsure of what she means.

'Do you want me to drop you back to the storage depot to get your car? Or you could just come back to mine, the spare room is made up. I can drop you to your car early in the morning.'

No contest.

It's ten thirty. I'm in Beth's kitchen sipping hot chocolate.

'Are you hungry?'

I shake my head.

'Well, we should eat something. All I've had all day is half a Danish. While you were in the loo, I took some shepherd's pie out of the freezer. It's in the oven.'

A freezer full of food. It's one of Beth's things. There was always cooked home-made food ready to come out of the freezer at The Lodge, usually the end of a lasagne. 'Not lasagne?' I ask.

She grimaces. 'I never make it any more,' she says, reading a text that has just pinged on her phone.

'I'm not stopping any plans you had, am I?'

She shakes her head and I can see she's lying.

'You're lying,' I say. 'I've always been a better liar than you.'

'You have. Okay, I did have plans, but they can wait.'

'The guy you're seeing?'

She hesitates, then nods.

'I'm sorry. I've messed up your night.'

'It's fine.' She pats my arm as she makes her way to the oven. 'We've rearranged.'

'Is it serious? This thing with this guy?' I'm half hoping she'll lie again if it is.

'I'm not sure. He's a lovely man, seems kind, sincere. We get along.'

My chest feels like there is a tightening vice around it. 'Tell me about him.'

'No . . . ' She comes to the table and sits beside me. 'Tonight, we talk about you. Anything you want to talk about. Anything that didn't get said at The Rookery. I can take it if you can.'

I say nothing.

'Look, it's not obligatory either. It's just you seem to want to talk now whenever we're together. And I don't want you to feel that you can't. If you're up to it, I don't want you to hold back.'

'What if all I have to say is that I want *you* back.'

She has her elbow on the table, her hand over her mouth, thumb placed on one cheek and her fingers stroking her lips side to side. I want to reach across and kiss her, taste her again, but I wait for her to speak. 'It's not going to happen, Adam.'

'Because of this other guy?'

She sighs aloud. 'No. He has nothing to do with you and me. You and me are like Humpty Dumpty. Not even the king's horses and—'

'I made mistakes, Beth.'

'Who's Rosie?'

'She was a girl at The Rookery. Just a young girl I met there.'

Beth makes a face. 'Were you and she . . . ?'

'God, no. She's no older than Meg. She was a girl in group therapy. Had been abused by her father.'

'Shit.'

'She was great, a really wise old soul in a young person's body, you know?'

Beth nods.

'She killed herself. Hanged herself with my Dr Who scarf, the one you got me a few Christmases ago. I'd lent it to her to keep warm.'

Beth's mouth drops open.

'I know. It's like flies to shit: trouble and death – all drawn to me. It's why I left early.'

She goes to the fridge, pours two glasses of wine and hands me one. 'What did the police say?'

'She left a note. There was no doubt that she . . . They still have my scarf.'

Beth takes a sip of wine. 'You seemed so together when you left The Rookery. Even when you left early, I was so sure that it had worked for you.'

'It helped. I left the morning after they found Rosie. I couldn't bear more navel-gazing over the whole thing. Tom would have had me talking about my parents and her for another year. I just had to get out of there.'

She walks to her oven. It's a small range, not like the one she had at The Lodge. She pulls down the door and, with gloved hands, removes the pie, placing it in the centre of the table. 'Leave it for a while,' she says. 'It's hot.'

There is a silence sitting between us right next to the pie. I break it first. 'I guess I'm a work in progress.'

'I'm sorry.'

'Not your fault, any of it.'

'I know that, but it's still shitty.'

'That, it is.'

'Are you going to be okay?'

I reach across, touch her face with my fingertips and stroke her cheek. A memory flashes in my head. Me bringing her coffee in the loft at The Lodge. Her, perched in her wheelie office chair, both screens lit up in front of her, her headphones on. She's singing, quite loudly but doesn't realize it. Her eyes are closed. Both her palms are up and she's pushing the air rhythmically, shoo-bopping to some track. Beth . . . 'Did you mean what you said? That there's no chance for us?'

She chews her bottom lip, nods her head. 'I meant it,' she whispers. Tears cloud her eyes as she places her own hand over mine.

'I'll be okay.' I sit back in my chair. 'Not as okay as I'd be with you, but I'll be okay without you.' I can't help staring at my wife's beautiful face. I can't bear the fact that someone else will look on her beautiful face and touch her like I just have. In my head, I wish I could summon all the king's horses and prove her wrong. But she's probably right, and there is nothing else to be said.

The next morning it is strange to wake up in a single bed in Beth's house. It is strange to have her dropping me off at a storage depot in Wandsworth. It's strange to feel the way I feel, like something has lifted from my shoulders –

but what, I don't know. I can't make sense of it. In the office I bury myself in work. I glance at, but don't read, the ten CVs Matt has asked me to study. 'We really have to appoint someone soon!' is what he's scrawled on a Post-it attached to the pile.

At midday, it's also strange to bump into my brother in the corridor. For a moment, I wonder if I'm dreaming, then I remember he's doing some forensic accounting for us, some due diligence stuff on the US expansion.

'Hi,' he says. 'You okay?' He looks drawn, charcoal shading under his eyes.

'I'm okay.' I give him a hug. 'You? Did you get any sleep?'

He tells me he did, chats for a while about work stuff. It's a bit like last night didn't happen, but I know Ben, and he's just taking time to absorb everything. I listen patiently, aware I'm now running late. Glancing at my wrist, I tell him I've got to run. Sorry.

'You all set for next week?' he calls back to me.

I smile and nod, don't tell him that I haven't started to pack my stuff from his flat. I don't tell him that I haven't got any further on the flat in Fulham. Having accepted my offer, they're pressuring me for solicitor's details and I've not called them back. I tell him none of this and head down the corridor towards the boardroom. The Granger brothers will be sitting in there with Matt, plus two people they're introducing us to with huge family office needs in New York.

All of this seems and smells like chaos, but I'm strangely calm. Since early this morning, lying in Beth's spare room, I've known how all these jigsaw pieces will fall. I've seen how the new picture will look. It's not ideal. It's far from my ideal, which saw Beth and me finding a new way of being – slowly but surely getting back together. Since this morning, I've seen that the new world order means that loving Beth means letting her go. Thank you, Rosie Bloomfield, for your wisdom. As I place my hand on the door to the boardroom, I do it in the knowledge that I'm going to suggest dumping the CVs, ceasing the search for a new hire. I'll kill a few birds with one stone. I'll go to New York.

Chapter Forty-Seven

I'm fine. Meg is fine. Jon is fine. Karen is pukey but fine. Ben is fine. Adam is . . . okay. 'Fall Apart' has trended on Twitter. My website has, according to Bear, had so many hits that it almost crashed. Production is in place for Marilee Garcia to release 'Fine' as a follow-up single. Money that I could only dream about has hit my bank account this morning. Everything is fine.

Only it's not really. I have a bad feeling I can't shake off. Ever since the night Adam stayed over. I'm terrified that because I let him back in my space, somehow he's infiltrated it, somehow he's just here. And he wasn't here before I let him stay. I flick the kettle on to boil.

My hands shuffle through the brochures on the table. Jon brought them around last night – various options for garden rooms. We've measured it out and I can have a pimped-up shed as a proper music studio in the back of the garden without it impacting on the space too much. That way I keep the garage. Giles says it's a great idea, that I should always do that for resale purposes. So, I decide this morning, I'm going to have me a garden studio. I hover my forefinger above one of the brochures, let it land on it. This one – I'll have this one.

I pour the water into two cups from the kettle and head back upstairs. In my bedroom, he's still lying down, his face turned towards the window. Slices of light slip through a crack in the curtains, which I hate but he loves. I place a cup of tea beside him, bend over to kiss him. 'Jon, some tea.' He takes my hand and kisses it.

Without opening his eyes, he says, 'Thanks.' I know he'll take a few minutes to wake up. I know he won't mind if his tea is cold. He'll still drink it. He'll still have a smile on his face. And I know all of this after only a few weeks of him waking in my bed or me waking in his.

I sit up, on my side, plumping the pillows behind me, and sip my tea. In a few minutes, I'll have a shower and I'll try to wash it off – this feeling that I can't shake. Last night, when Jon and I made love, I imagined he was Adam. I feel so bad about this, I can barely admit it to myself. I don't think I could ever say it aloud. If I was still seeing Dr Caroline Gothenburg, would I admit it? Would I say, 'Last night I was making love to the man in my life. I imagined he was Adam. Not Johnny Depp. Not Liam Neeson. Adam.'

I drink my cooling tea, listen to Jon's gentle snore, reach out and stroke his back softly. He stirs a little. If I could see his face, he'd have a tiny smile on it, just a faint curve on one side of his mouth. He has a lovely mouth – full plump lips and a Cupid's bow that many women would kill for. I love how he kisses me. They're not melting kisses, or Pink-type 'I am going to die right here and now' kisses, but they're tender and loving and . . .

In the shower, I soap my body all over. I have a chat with Lucy Fir and Babushka. Lucy is, for once, trying to reason with me rather than shouting in my ear. She asks me if I want tender and loving in my life. Babushka interrupts. She tells me what I don't need in my life is Adam. She is firm. She is adamant. She asks me to remember how the man makes me feel when he hurts me and he will hurt me again if I let him. That, Babushka says, is certain. I rinse the soap, stand under the scalding spray for ages, let the water run over my neck muscles. I stretch my legs, my arms, my fingers. Singing softly, I acknowledge the voices in my head. Round one to Babushka.

Towel around my head, dressing gown on, I head back downstairs. It's Saturday. Jon has obviously decided to sleep in. I look out over my garden, think back to the days in The Lodge. The reality is I feel for Adam. He's in my head because I feel for him since the scene with Ben last week. It's tragic stuff, but his tragic stuff, I remind myself. I cannot own it because I feel sorry for him and I cannot let him commandeer head-space that currently belongs to Jon. Or Johnny Depp. Or Liam Neeson.

Closing my eyes, I rub them with my thumb and forefinger. Though I need him to be gone from my head, I accept he probably never will be. He'll always be there lurking in the background, looking on. And I'll probably let him, because I loved him so very much for such a long time. I still do. I acknowledge I love the man, not in the same way I did, but I can't turn it off completely. I can't close it off and tighten it like a tap. It's different. I still call it love but it's not the same. I smile, tell Babushka and Lucy to move over and let him in. I reassure them that he won't be there often, but ask them that, when he is, to please play nicely.

While I make my second cup of tea of the morning, I start to plan how my studio will look. I take a few sips then run up the stairs. I pull the towel from my head and lean over Jon, tickling his face with my wet hair.

'You'll catch cold,' he mutters, his hand reaching out and opening my dressing gown. I let it slide off me and he pulls me in beside him. 'Good morning, Beth-all,' he says. 'How are we feeling this morning?'

I giggle. I told him once about Lucy and Babushka and now he refers to me as 'we'. If only he knew, Adam has been offered some space as well. It may not be a long-term thing, probably just a short-term lease, but I'll see. For now, I ignore my busy head and enjoy being cuddled by this man. No one else. This man. Jon no 'h' Roper.

It's only two hours later that my rationale is challenged. I have metaphorically put my husband to bed. I have filed him appropriately, kindly allowed him into my head under controlled supervision.

So why, when I listen to his voice on the phone, does my stomach plummet and my heart hurt? He talks for a while. There are lots of good reasons, all of which I agree with. I know this because I'm nodding, but he can't know it because I'm speechless.

'Beth, are you there?'

'I'm here . . . '

'You're not saying much.'

'I'm not sure what to say. Two weeks ago you were buying a flat in Fulham. Today, you're moving to New York.'

Jon looks up from reading his newspaper at the table. 'Adam', he mouths to me. I nod.

'It's really the best thing, for all the reasons I've just said. Besides, it's not forever. I could have it all set up in six months or it could take a lot longer. Who knows?'

'Who knows?' I repeat.

'How do you feel about it?'

I want to burst out laughing, but stop myself. Now? Now, he thinks to ask me how I feel. 'You have to do what you have to do,' I say. 'Meg will miss you. We'll both miss you.'

He sighs. 'You know I'll miss you both more. Anyway, I'm off in five days.'

'So soon?'

'There's no point in waiting. I have to move out of Ben's. We need someone in New York urgently. No reason it can't be me.'

'What will you do? Get a flat there?'

'A hotel for a few weeks until I find my feet. The office is sorted, more minor hires in place. I'll find a flat in a few weeks. Listen, I'm trying to arrange a meal. A kind of Last Supper. You, me, Meg, Jack, Ben and Karen. Sybil if she'll come. Are you free tomorrow night?'

I look across at Jon, who's pretending that he's not listening. 'I will be. Let me know where and when.'

'I'll text you later. Just need to talk to Ben.'

'Have you talked to Meg?'

'I called you first.'

I don't reply.

'Hey, I heard your song on the radio this morning. Surreal . . . That lyric, the one about falling apart and the glue?'

'Yeah?'

'It's good. Great lyric. Great song. You bloody deserve all the success, Beth, you really do.'

'Thank you.'

'Of course, you wouldn't have been able to tap into heartbreak with such feeling unless I'd been a shit. So I like to think in some way I've helped.'

I can almost see him grinning.

'That's what Josh says.'

'He's right.' Adam laughs.

'Probably . . .'

Jon stands, gathers up the brochures and moves to the living room. We're going out in a minute to the showroom, to choose the size and model and order it.

'I've got to go,' I say. 'We're heading out in a minute.'

I know all he hears in that sentence is the 'we', but that's okay.

'See you tomorrow,' he says. 'I'll text you the details when I've spoken to everyone.'

'Okay, bye.' I hang up the phone and stare at it. Adam is going to New York. To live. In New York.

'We should go soon if you have to be in work by one?' Jon speaks without looking up from the chair he has moved to. He's right. I have to cover for Steph at the office this afternoon and I'd really rather not. And, although I've made the decision to leave the agency to devote all my time to songwriting, I'm torn. I will really miss Giles and the crew. I pull my open laptop towards me and open my mailbox. In the 'drafts', the email that I've written resigning from the company is sitting waiting to be sent. My forefinger hovers for just a few moments before I lower it and press send . . . Adam. Is going. To New York.

'Right,' I tell Jon. 'Just let me get my jacket.' I run up the stairs, stop at the top, rub the left-hand side of my chest. Adam is going to New York. Not Fulham. New York. It's a little bit further away. I exhale slowly. And it's the right thing. It's the right thing for him. I look down to the hall over the banisters. Jon smiles up at me. It's the right thing for everyone.

Guido's, an Italian restaurant in Weybridge, is where we have had many a happy family meal. For this reason, I'd rather be somewhere else. I'd rather Adam had chosen another restaurant, one where maybe we could create new memories. The last time I was here was months ago with Meg, just after Adam left, and I feel the past wrap itself around me like an old cardigan as soon as I enter.

I'm last to arrive. I kiss everyone on the cheek and take my seat between Meg and Mum at the circular table. Opposite us, Karen and Ben sit almost clamped to each other. They have the look of love and fear combined that is present in all pregnant couples. Adam is sitting beside Meg, who has Jack on her other side. He's talking to Ben as Meg and Adam chat animatedly about shopping trips and having somewhere to stay in New York. She has even mentioned she may take a master's degree there.

My mother rests a hand on my leg, squeezes it. 'Keep it together,' she whispers, and I give a silent nod, trying not to think of losing Meg to the Big Apple.

There is a lot of conversation around the table tonight, not much of it coming from me. Mum tells us she is starting

a new course in September, a foundation degree in counselling. Adam catches my eye and we both start to laugh.

'Now, Sybil?' He has never called my mum 'Mum',
despite her requests over the years for him to do so. 'Now,
you do the counselling?'

The joke is almost lost on her, but not quite. 'Like
you'd have listened to me, either of you, as a mother or
a counsellor . . . You may laugh, but I'd like to make a
difference.'

'You make a difference to me, Mum.' I smile at her.

'And me, Nan.'

'And me, Sybil,' Adam admits. 'To be fair, even when I
deserved shooting, you never did. So thank you.' Adam
raises his glass in her direction. Mum smiles, a little embarrassed, then changes the subject and asks Karen if she has
stopped throwing up yet, just as my spaghetti alla putta-
nesca arrives.

Garlic bread, bruschetta, three flavours of spaghetti fill
the centre of the table, yet Karen picks at a small wheat
cracker from a box in her bag.

'I'm sorry,' she whispers. 'I don't trust myself to eat.'

'It'll pass,' I tell her. 'Like most things in life, the discomfort is temporary.'

'That's ironic, you saying that, sitting here,' she says.

'I know.'

Adam is filling my glass and looking at me. It's sweet,
a loving glance; one that says he'd do anything for me. In
a strange way he is, he's moving away . . . I smile back,
excuse myself for a moment to visit the loo.

The Ladies at Guido's is tiny. It has two loo cubicles
and one shared sink area. When I enter, I see another

woman at the sink and automatically stand back to let her leave the room. As she turns, her face breaks into a wide grin. 'Beth! I thought it was you but wasn't sure. Haven't got my glasses on.'

Caroline looks gorgeous, dressed in a slinky black jersey all-in-one outfit.

'Don't worry,' she says. 'I wouldn't have greeted you outside, but in here?' She gestures to the loo's surroundings. 'How are you? How are things?'

'Good.' I nod. 'It's nice to see you.'

'I have to confess I've been following you on Twitter. Your song . . .. I'm thrilled for you. You finally gagged that saboteur, eh?'

'Oh, she tosses the gag off every now and then, but I think I have her measure.'

I can't help thinking about the first time Caroline and I met. I was betrayed, panicked and afraid.

'And you?' she asks, tentatively.

'I'm better, much better,' I tell her. 'I think I've found Beth again.'

'I'm glad,' she smiles. 'And—'

'Adam's outside, with the rest of the family.'

She's nodding, her eyes careful not to judge what that may or may not mean. I think about what I've just said. He is the father of my only child and my first love. He is family, always will be.

'We're not together,' I tell her. 'A lot has happened, too much to come back from really. But we're okay with it, both of us moving on. I've met a new man.'

'You have?' Caroline looks as if she's about to do a happy dance. 'I'm pleased for you.'

'And Adam, Adam is moving to the States this week. New York.'

Her eyebrows go north but she says nothing. We swap a few more facts, a few more niceties. She tells me her door is always open and she leaves. I follow her out, back to the table. Taking my seat, I realize that I have forgotten to have a pee. But I also realize that I feel good, weightless. I have a new man in my life. I have a lovely family that, some day, he may be a part of. Jon may join this round table group along with Karen and Ben's baby sometime soon. In the meantime, I'm happy for Adam to go. The reality is that Jon and I have a chance to grow if he's not around. We have a chance to see if there is something real without him looking on.

And Adam. He will miss us, but he'll survive and he won't be alone for long. Survival is in every strand of his DNA, but being on his own is not. I'm guessing it won't be very long before I'm told from the States, 'There's this woman and . . .'

Epilogue

The walk from the apartment on East 77th Street to Midtown West 53rd only takes about twenty-five minutes, but I hail a cab. The humid heat of mid-July is stifling and a cab ride means I arrive without my shirt stuck to me. Five minutes of midtown traffic later, I enter through the glass doors of the Museum of Modern Art and make my way up to the Monet exhibition, with the three-panelled oil-on-canvas displays. I sit on the middle bench. It's the one I feel affords the best view of all three canvases at once. The bench can seat three or four people, and there have been times when I've had to share it, when someone else comes into the room and decides that yes, the best view really is from here. They sit next to me and I try not to resent them being here. Here in my space that, despite it being memorialized in film, I call my own.

Today, I'm alone. I'm happy to drink in the quiet. I remove my mobile from my jacket pocket, thumb her number and wait. I've taken to calling her from here at the same time every third Saturday, 11.30 New York time,

16.30 GMT. She doesn't, of course, know where I call her from.

She answers with a happy, 'Hi.' She's out of breath, like she's been running. We chat, about Meg, about work, about her upcoming trip to LA. I joke that since we'll be on the same landmass, maybe we should try and meet up. She laughs it off, tells me it would be easier for me to come back to London for a visit. I don't push it, since I already know she's taking Jon to LA with her. The gospel according to Meg . . .

She asks me if I've seen the movie yet. I tell her yes, of course. I don't tell her I've seen it twice. As I'm talking, my eyes are glued to the lily pads. I swear they're moving in the gentle sway of Monet's pond. I swear that in the colours of the picture, the greens, the blues, the lilac hues, I somehow see her face.

She's laughing at something, brings me back to the moment, and I realize she's talking about Sybil, who has finally started her counselling course. Beth tells me she's driving her mad with her own brand of analysis. I can't help smiling – I love the sound of Beth's laugh. It's something I miss terribly.

Someone comes to sit beside me, almost hovers on the edge of the bench, like he's sensitive to personal space. An older man, he removes a small notebook and pen from a linen jacket. My cue to look at my watch and leave. We have been talking for over fifteen minutes and now I'm late. I make my way to Terrace 5, hoping there'll be an air-conditioned table free inside, rather than outside, where I would probably shrivel in today's heat. Beth is still in full flow telling me Karen, now six months pregnant, is 'as big as a house' and Ben is walking around like the cat that got the cream.

I enter the restaurant and immediately she waves at me. I stop walking, wave back, and hold five fingers up so she knows I'll still be a few minutes.

'How are you anyway?' Beth asks. 'Come on, you've been months over there and I've never pried before. What's happening?'

I know she's asking if I'm alone, if there's anyone in my life.

'Funny you should ask,' I say to Beth. 'There is this woman . . . '

Acknowledgements

This book is now a real thing; something that I can hold in my hand, with pages and a spine I can run my finger along and my name on the front and . . . It is only real because I've been helped along the way by so many people and a lot of good fortune.

I have to thank my family, which firstly means my six mad siblings, and all my in-laws. You are, probably without exception, a little bit bonkers and I love you all. A special thanks to Annie, who has listened while I doubted and read more than a few versions of YM&OP. To my mother, thank you for sending me a book in the post years ago with a note attached saying, 'You could do this, you know.' You were right, Mum, and thank you for always having faith. To my Dad, alas no longer here with us, thank you for the writer's DNA. I hold your handwritten 'scribbles' dear to me and am sorry that you were always a frustrated writer in a corporate world. I promise to try and live the dream for you.

To my friends – where would I be without you? I've

been blessed over the years with many true, original, loyal and funny friends. Too many to mention here individually, but you know who you are, whether I've shared food and wine or tears or all three with you. A big thank you to you all, especially Mary and Steph, always there . . .

My world now has a wealth of writer friends that years ago I would never have dreamed possible. A big hello and thank you to all my friends on Twitter and Facebook. God, how I love procrastinating with you all! Long live the internet! When I first started writing, years ago, I joined an online forum (www.writewords.org.uk) filled with lots of other hopeful novices like me, which provides an environment where writers of all levels could share their work for critique. There, I met so many lovely people who, despite my husband's initial concerns, did not turn out to be 'dribbling weirdos' but lovely, lovely people who to this day are firm friends. Thank you to anyone I met along the way there, like Jacqui C Ward (brilliant beta reader, and so on the button with her critique and ideas), Clodagh Murphy, Essie Fox and Caroline Green. A big "Yay", as she would say, is sent to Keris Stainton who took a group of us to our own forum, 'We Should Be Writing'. I'm grateful to you all, girls.

Huge cries of emotional, heartfelt thanks go to writer pals Claire Allan and Anstey Spraggan. Claire, you have been a mentor and friend. You were the first one to say, "You can write, girl", and you've been the one to kick my sorry ass when I was ready to give up SO many times. You have always encouraged and believed and for that I'm just so enormously grateful. An accomplished writer, working journalist and Mammy to two – I don't know how you do it and am in awe . . . Anstey, what fun-filled, fear-filled and nerve-wracking times we've shared! Racing each other to finish novels, critiquing and encouraging each other along the way. Thank you, friend, for being there every step of the way and for introducing me to the mad Moniack Mhor writers. Time with you and the 'Maniacks' has helped me learn so much and not just how to drink wine . . . Thank you guys and gals.

Anyone who has struggled to have a novel published will know it's almost impossible to tread the traditional route without an agent. And mine is one in a million. Maddy, you're more than an agent. You've become a friend and someone I hope to always have in my life. Your championing of my writing and hard work on my behalf has fuelled my confidence and together we can make great things happen. Thank you so much to you, and Cara too, for everything you do.

To the editorial team and everyone else behind the scenes who made this book happen at HarperCollins, a huge thank you. A special thanks to Kim Young – since that first meeting we had, I've known that you're in my corner – and to Claire Bord, Penny Isaac and Charlotte Brabbin who, between them all, helped YM&OP become the book it is today. Thank you for guiding this sometimes confused author through the process.

And finally, to my own family. Kate and Jane, you are my inspiration. Both now wonderful young women, there's not a day that goes by where I'm not grateful for the fact that, somehow, you chose me to be your Mummy. I love you both all the way to the moon and back and beyond and back again. Thanks to Chris and to our darling Esme, who makes me laugh and want to squidge her tight every single day.

And Aidan. My man. My soul-mate. This book could never have happened without your incredible, never-ending faith, love and support. Thank you, I love you forever.

You, Me and Fionnuala Kearney

What was your inspiration for writing *You, Me & Other People*?

My mum once told me that there is no such thing as 'falling in love', that you have to 'climb in love', and life has shown me that most loving relationships are complex things. I wanted to look under the skin of a 'good' marriage in trouble – which really meant looking at what went wrong and how and why. Examining both points of view felt important to me as although the wrongdoer is often simply that, sometimes in reality things aren't quite as simple as the word 'betrayal' implies . . .

Did you always have ambitions of becoming a writer?

Yes! Ever since I could hold a pencil and realised that if I thought about it, words would spill out and I could make up stories. I went to my first creative writing class thirty years ago! Work and family meant any early efforts were just that, efforts, until a few years ago when I got serious and gave up my job to pursue writing.

What has been the most challenging part of the writing process?

I love what I do and every day I feel privileged to walk across the landing to my office to go to work. Writing a novel does require planning and structure but sometimes I think it's easy to get bogged down by this. For me, it's really important to give the characters I'm writing about the freedom to take me where they want to go. This, though, can be challenging too as it's important to know when to yank back on their reins.

Would you say that you identify with any of the characters in the book? Which ones and why?

Definitely Beth. I'm also a 'creative', a wife and mother and what Beth discovers is one of my worst nightmares.

Many of them are laden with impossible choices – was it a challenge to tap into the characters' mindsets and make those decisions for them?

Not really. When I'm writing a novel and a situation arises I always ask myself, 'What would/will "X" do here?' They genuinely tell me what needs to happen, and at the times when I've answered that question more as myself than my character, it never works – it just feels clunky and wrong. During the first draft process I become so immersed in their lives that I begin to think more like them than me!

Did you always know how the narrative would end?

I guess this answer is a perfect example of my reply above. Through writing the book, I always *wanted* Adam and Beth to reconcile. Beth, however, decided en route that it really would not be the best thing for her and, ultimately, I agreed . . .

What would you like readers to take away from the novel?

That we're all constantly evolving and capable of learning more about ourselves and others, and that it's our flaws as well as our strengths that make us human.

And can you tell us a little bit about your next book?

Whereas *You, Me & Other People* examines a marriage, my next book peels away the layers in the lives of friends: married man Theo and older, single woman Jess. At only forty-eight she's living in the 'sandwich years' where she has both a grand-child and an elderly parent who need her, not to mention her adult children . . . Theo's forty, fed-up and frustrated with a seemingly perfect life. It's still a work in progress but I'm enjoying living in Theo and Jess's heads!

Reading Group Questions

At the very beginning of the novel, we learn that Adam has been unfaithful – and more than once. Does this immediately box him in as a stereotypical cheater? Does your opinion of him change over the course of the book?

Meg's relationship with Adam is very strained for most of the novel. Does Adam try hard enough to rebuild the bond? Does he ask too much of Meg?

Adam obviously has his flaws as a character – can you forgive him these flaws once his troubled past comes to light? Do you think that we're all products of our past to a certain degree?

Beth initially can't bear the idea of selling the family house, and you could say that she gains real self-awareness in writing about herself on the hall wall with her Tiffany Blue paint. What do you think this means? Is identity often tied up with a sense of place?

One of the presiding themes in the book is the suppression of secrets, and the way in which the truth eventually rears its ugly head. Can lies and happy endings ever coexist? Is there such a thing as a selfless lie?

Meg undergoes a stem cell donation for a half-brother she's only just learnt about. Adam spends a good part of his life carrying around the burden of his parents' death in order to protect his brother. What do you think the author is trying to say about family? Do we have an innate responsibility towards them no matter what?

Beth and Adam are married for a long time, and yet we're made to question all that shared history. Is it ever possible to truly 'know' someone?

At one point Adam says about Noah: 'He's the only person in the world who doesn't judge me, Beth. The only person in the world who has a chat with me about my day. Beats the hell out of me every time we play chess.'
What does this tell us about Noah's role in the narrative and the depth of Adam's feelings towards him?

Beth and Adam's relationship is amicable at the end and they both have new love interests. Were you satisfied with how things panned out for them? Do you think they ever could have worked things out between them?